P9-CRN-307

A
Prodigal Slice of the Heart's Pie, an Introduction

The stories in this collection are about companionship: companionship between human and dog. While these stories take place in a world occupied by every sort of human accompaniment besides the dog—cars, bars, daughters, dollars, disasters—the bond between human and canine outshines or outlasts the other incidental presences—a lone luminescence charged by the light of attention. Generated by the very differences—polarities—between the two species, the interspecies bond casts its illuminating glow over the rest of the story, offering its power—however brief or dim—to the plot's entanglements, the characters' enlightenments.

For all their personal details and specific dramas, each fiction in *The Company of Dogs* is a story about your dog and my dog. Although an astonishing variety of stories continues to be written about dogs, each one that I have selected has invited its dogs as companions; no other work or motive determines this alliance. But it is more than the nature of companionship—its dailiness, responsibilities, repercussions, pains—that has prompted these authors, and so many other contemporary writers I couldn't include, to hazard a passionate, urgent look at this singular partnership.

Think of a friend as someone who provides you with resonance, with perfect acoustics—an ear to return whatever you have expressed. [*] Then isn't the dog a perfect friend? Just as the dog's hearing far exceeds our own, what the dog returns to us through its delimited friendship is just as exceptional. Deprived of our language, the dog can still retrieve our words like bones we've hidden so long and so well we have forgotten their whereabouts, have all but forgotten their importance. Over and over in these stories, dogs return to their humans what has been buried or banished from everyday view: something more treasured than obedience, fealty, exuberance, or affection.

GUARDIAN

Though travel keeps Penn from ownership, he dog-sits
a golden retriever named—or misnamed—"Angel"
the weekends her owners sail at their summer home.
They furnish Penn with toys, her rations, a leash,
the six commands that govern Angel's world,
and a lengthy list of, well, recommendations.

His neighbors' gratitude matches his own.
Penn's missed the dogs—not one, but the continuing
presence of Dog that ran through their lives,
out an unlocked gate, and on to somewhere
misnamed "a good home." The dogs were guests;
they stole the family's hearts like a set of towels.

[*] Roland Barthes, *A Lover's Discourse.*

These days, Penn is the visitor at his home,
a man whose comings and goings he greets himself.
People who think they know, prescribe a pet
for Penn, threaten to surprise him with a dog.
Once, on his own, Penn parked outside the pound,
between trash cans a third-grade class had painted
with the bright, mournful faces of kittens and pups,
and two crowds of letters that Penn mistook
at first, PREVENT LITTERS, then understood.
(He mistook the tears, too, as he backed out,
and how they came surprised from him, from kennels
of grief abandoned by the breeze of getting on.)

Angel adopts her temporary master
so heartily it still embarrasses Penn
to take it personally. Nudging his hand,
delivering toys, the dog has taught this man
which ones to throw and which to pull, where
to scratch and to walk, and how a bed is shared.

"On Sunday, Angel turns nine," the neighbors tell Penn
as they leave. "That's sixty-three in human years,"
the woman explains, bestowing on the dog a kiss
that's clearly human enough. "We've never missed
a birthday before. So Angel's counting on you
to celebrate a little. Just you two."

Penn's been suspicious of equivalents:
One's weight on the moon. Miles of matchsticks
laid end to end. Centigrade. Metrics.
Or multiplying a canine's age by seven,
demonstrating some human factor to redress
the pet's prodigal slice of the heart's pie.

Arithmetic can't make something what it's not,
but then, it did make Penn a businessman.
It won't make Angel a man—no, a woman—
nor an angel, however sweetly guardian-
like she is hovering over, watching Penn
with needle, iron, paring knife, and pills.

Penn himself turns sixty-three on Friday.
Coincidence, on the other hand, he trusts:
it's the unfair happening alongside the fair.
Though man and dog begin this weekend like others,
within a leash's length, exploring a street
that Penn had only known from stories above

and his assigned parking space beneath,
Penn does attempt to find something special
for the dog's day, a treat befitting her years.
In the driver's seat, Angel waits while Penn
surveys the costly ham- or chocolate-flavoured,
indestructible English rubber chews.

She promptly halved the ring on the ride home,
intently consumed it all before bed,
and woke Penn heaving it up on the quilt at dawn.
The rest of their time, Penn dreams of his own presents—
birthday, retirement, the chance for a dog of his own.
His first, really. Not the children's or the neighbor's . . .

a companion to grow old—at least, older—
beside. 63 + 12 years
with a devoted . . . 84-year-old dog,
(Isn't a mutt's lifespan even longer?)

would make Penn 75. Another dog?
A dozen years? Penn at 87?

Such health, such luck, such foolish accounting aside,
could Penn survive the whole housebreaking,
heartbreaking shebang again? "Ask me
in a year," Penn says to Angel, stroking her thick,
thickening coat, celebrating this weekend
that love so happened to litter his way.

THE DAWN OF COMPANIONSHIP

The dog has been a part of human culture since the end of the Ice
Age. From that moment until the moment of this writing constitutes
a humbling one percent of human time on earth. A mere 12,000 years
ago people ceased wandering, constructed villages, and began the domestication of plants and animals. *Canis lupus*, the wolf, was the first
species to make the transition from the wild, the first and perhaps only
true ally humans would ever find. The passage from Maurice Maeterlinck that begins this book accounts for why the cat, cow, horse, and
other creatures have not accommodated our lives to the extent of the
dog. And Amy Hempel explains it with a folk tale: In the garden of
Eden, all creatures lived in perfect harmony until man discovered sin.
And then "a chasm opened up that divided man on one side, from all
of the animals, on the other side." And the chasm continued to widen,
"until at the last possible moment, it was only the dog that leaped
across the abyss to spend eternity with man."†

Clarence Day attributes this unique complicity to the dog's nature.
From the evolutionary point of view, he asks, what if dog, and not

---

†Amy Hempel, "The Center."

primate, had evolved into human? Considering the various untaken roads of evolution, Day finds that dog would have offered "more spirit. But they have lost their chance of kingship through worshipping us. The dog's finer qualities can't be praised too warmly; there is a purity about his devotion which makes mere men feel speechless." But, he concludes, dogs are "vassals, not rulers. They are too parasitic—the one willing servant class of the world. And we have betrayed them by making under-simians of them." *Behave like us not like your kind*, we have taught all dogs, and so "they let us stop their developing in tune with their natures. . . . Dogs have more love than integrity. They've been true to us, yes, but they haven't been true to themselves."‡

By the time man and woman could write, their lives had become inextricably involved with and even dependent upon dogs. The story of the dog is the story of a relationship with humans. The inspiration for this collection issues from this interdependence: Couldn't stories with dogs provide us exceptional occasions to learn about ourselves, particularly compared to any other nonhuman presence in a story? Isn't this the pervasive and ultimately ethical question posed in Blake's much-quoted lines, "A dog starv'd at his master's gate/ Predicts the ruin of the State"?*

This is explicitly what Milan Kundera writes in *The Unbearable Lightness of Being*, a novel that offers several superior insights into this relationship. "True human goodness," he writes, "in all its purity and freedom, can come to the fore only when its recipient has no power. Mankind's true moral test, its fundamental test (which lies deeply buried from view), consists of its attitude toward those who are at its mercy:

‡Clarence Day, *This Simian World*.

*William Blake, "Auguries of Innocence," a litany of humane interdependence that also includes these couplets: "The Beggar's Dog and Widow's Cat, / Feed them and thou wilt grow fat" and "The Bleat, the Bark, Bellow, and Roar / Are Waves that Beat on Heaven's Shore."

animals." Mankind, Kundera rules, has therefore suffered "a fundamental debacle, a debacle so fundamental that all others stem from it."

A recent archaeological discovery urges us to linger another moment over this historical, primal view of the human/canine bond. In
northern Israel, a team of archaeologists discovered a late Paleolithic
grave. Its contents held a pair of skeletons—an elderly human of un-
determinable sex, and beside it, the bones of a five-month-old domestic
dog. The remarkable aspect, according to the discoverers, was that
"whoever presided over the original burial had carefully arranged the
dead person's left hand so that it rested in a timeless and eloquent
gesture of attachment, on the puppy's shoulder." The tomb not only
supplied "the earliest solid evidence of animal domestication," but in
addition, the archaeologists argue, it implied "that man's primordial
relationship with this particular species was a deeply affectionate one.
In other words, prehistoric man may have loved his dogs and his other
domestic animals as pets before he made use of them for any other
purpose."

The stories of this anthology are about this original—*first* and
unique—relationship to dogs in which company is the abiding provi-
sion. The popular and political introduction of the term "companion
animal," as opposed to "pet," intimates something of our current reevaluation. In each selected story, the relationship between human
and dog exists for its own sake: No duty, engagement, work, politics,
social action, or assignment determines its significance. The dogs are
not guiding a hunter or a physically impaired individual, trotting around
the ring of a circus tent or a best-of-breed competition, accompanying
a fashion model or an airport narcotics agent, submitting to a veterinary
student or a dog groomer, chasing criminals or racetrack rabbits, protecting merchandise or sleeping children, winning an illegal fight or
the incredulous heart of a parent whose child the dog has rescued from
searing flames or sweeping currents.

And just as the dogs' dealings with humans are not prescribed by any imposed duty, so the record of human companionship is not charted through philosophical or political endorsements. In practical terms, this means that I have not stipulated that the included authors adhere to an agreed-upon set of moral judgments and ethical choices. My selection, nonetheless, does reflect my own adjusting level of comfort as I projected it into this anthology. These ethics will be made more explicit in the Afterword. Still, the authors of these stories might choose to wear leather or fur, eat meat, hunt, or use products tested on animals. The fates of animals in their care may, in fact, be interpreted as unconscionable or inexcusable in the eyes of one or another faction. Although these practices do not provide the subject or the significance of their stories, this is still nothing to take lightly. I have only my own dawning clarity on the complicated matters of human stewardship to shore my own work-in-progress authority, to embolden me on what is ultimately a philanthropic endeavor. The ethics that determine human attitudes toward the nonhuman are under serious reevaluation, vociferous condemnation. Though late and long in coming (at least for a general public), this education has accelerated momentously in the last decade. Now, fed by an urgent reeducation of our legal, philosophical, commercial, medical, and ecological systems, we are being presented with critical and incriminating information, and, more optimistically, with a chance to make personal choices that can better the fate of the world's many populations.

THE NEWS CONFIRMS WHAT WE'VE ALWAYS SUSPECTED

And so it is the perplexingly rich nature of companionship that distinguishes these stories from any other kind of fiction involving dogs. There are no dogs that you might find in a good children's book or fable, a tale of sporting adventures or heroism, a veterinary or scientific observation, or a personal anecdote about an exceptionally devoted or distinguished creature. Nor is there a dog that merely features, as in the vast majority of fiction, as yet another confirming aspect of reality. Notably, these are stories with dogs, not dog stories. There isn't a single story here *about* a dog. True, all stories are about people, since people write the stories. But in *The Company of Dogs*, the relationships with dogs reveal something about our lives that stories *about* people cannot. Why this is so, and how this occurs, is the subject of the remaining Introduction.

As our perceptions of dogs in our lives evolve, so our stories work toward that reassessment, translating and naturalizing each new awakening. Psychologists have recognized—formalized—the palliative, stabilizing influence of a dog on coronary health, blood pressure, and even something as basic as one's sense of well-being. Sociologists have documented the productive responsiveness a dog elicits in the rehabilitation of abused or delinquent children and the sustaining fulfillment a dog can provide the elderly or emotionally disturbed. And our stories are taking this affirmation seriously, turning the news back into what we have, all along, believed in our suspecting hearts.

Advances in computer science and medical technology, the growing complexity of bioethical and ecological crises—these, too, have challenged our hapless understanding of the role of dogs in the world. As mentioned, these fictions are not filled with indignations or political actions, yet an awareness of puppy mills, vivisection laboratories, canine abuses and pet overpopulation does inform these stories with a social conscience; it does add a pressure to these stories. There is, at least, an available and sad contrast between the lucky lives of our own animals and those we hear or read about.

HOW STORIES TRANSLATE THE NEWS

I can't infer each author's agreement, but I suspect that the desire to write a story containing a dog comes from everyday and not exceptional encounters with dogs. Our experience of living with dogs is so long-

standing and widespread that one might think it should be second nature for any of us to define, decode, or even dismiss the drama of our time with dogs. But this isn't the case. We are still trying to understand the "openhearted and inscrutable, the simple and complicated, animal" that James Thurber reported on nearly fifty years ago.†
And we've yet to understand much of the other side of the story, the dog's. "It is unfortunate," Thurber wrote in an earlier anthology, "that there can be no companion piece, set down by the dog, to complete the picture. He has not yet learned to communicate his thoughts to paper. But give him time. The planet has, after all, barely cooled off."

If only the dog could! What dogs must know about us! As veterinarian and ethologist Dr. Michael Fox insists, dogs are constantly watching us. They are such superb observers of our behaviors. Are we not, in essence, their pack, their wards, their protectors, their work? People are always saying how their dog detects an event before it happens, how dogs seem to sense our slightest emotions, just as their auditory and olfactory senses bring earlier, keener information to their brains. They are so tuned to the nuances of human behavior that, Fox suggests, "they are perhaps much closer to their owners, in many ways, then their owners are to them."

Alas, *The Company of Dogs* is another one-sided collection—the human side of the relationship. But I do want to insist that even this human side is an exceptionally available and engaging fictional resource.

My own life is hardly more abundant in the number of dogs that intersect it. (I'll admit my un-innocent eye does pick out a dog's presence.) But it doesn't require an ethologist, humanitarian, or even dog lover to notice the prevalence and potency of a dog's presence in our lives. The world needn't undergo a lyrical or magical transformation in order to display the dog's radiance in our small worlds, although

†James Thurber, preface to Jack Goodman's *The Fireside Book of Dog Stories.*

Robert Fox describes one imaginable scene in which the sunset turned "into the soft, wrinkled belly of a female dog. Then the various lawns assumed the colors and textures of dog coats—long- and short-haired, one-color and dappled. All the foliage . . . was likewise adorned with a plumage of tails." Perhaps if we could hear or smell like a dog, we could witness, as Fox describes, our human world so invested with canine presence.

In the next few sections, I have offered brief narrations of a few encounters with dogs. My hope is to demonstrate how readily the imagination is seized by even a few details in such outlines. Seized, I say, because even though the dog has been a part of our culture for millennia, we are yet startled by the dog's importance and shocked by our own affection—and this troubles us into storytelling. Juveniles, essentially, in our assessment of this human/canine relationship, we require a story to help clarify the thinking about our wealth of mixed feelings.

SEE ME, SEE MY DOG

A middle-aged Canadian man is flying to Columbus, Ohio, with a seeing-eye dog whose own eyes are milky blue and nearly sightless. The dog's broken-toothed, white muzzle with its panting tongue protrudes into the aisle of the plane; the flight attendants step carefully around it. To the woman across the aisle, asking all the obvious questions about the dog, the man announces, "After ten years, today is our last day together." His voice is as loud as the flight attendant's advising us of the unlikely loss of cabin pressure. It embarrasses me to hear his answers, to be implicated in the woman's inquiries. In Columbus, he will obtain a new companion, his third. "My old friend here," he says, "she has been like a wife to me, always there no matter what— no, more like God." The dog, we learn ("we," meaning nearly every-one for several rows back), is to live out her last years with someone who doesn't require the dog's work. His interviewer has several more questions about the dog—"Is this her first flight? Does she like children? . . ." Finally the man replies, "I wonder if maybe you have problems with your eyes, too; you don't see me, only my dog."

What he doesn't tell the woman, what a storyteller might continue to elaborate, I have begun to imagine as I stare at the page I have pretended to read since lift-off, pretended will distract my irrational tears from flowing. The cabin is pressurized not only with its air mixture, but with the conspicuous presence of this dog. I wonder about the new home where this aging animal will live beyond the single relationship that provided her lifelong rewards and love. I think about this man exchanging dogs roughly once each decade—two behind him already, one imminent, two or maybe three others ahead—a Canine constant. I can't dismiss the irony of the dog's own blindness. I can't keep my heart from silently volunteering our home for such a retired animal. And because this isn't a story that I am actually writing—it's all a rush of questions and images that weather an entire flight—I risk a pathetic figure for this man: links in a lengthening chain, each a dog's decade, each to be broken before a new one can be added.

ROUNDS

There is possibly a story (there is certainly an unusual setting where an event is about to occur) in the ward of the hospital where a golden retriever, antiseptically bathed and sporting a white neckerchief—a token uniform like the nurse's crimped hat—climbs gingerly onto the bed of a terminally ill patient, and lies carefully among the life-support devices as if it were another hope-filled treatment. For half an hour (after which the dog is conducted into another room, another bed, and so on throughout the ward, throughout the morning), the retriever happily submits to this affectionate contact. I watch an excerpt of this pilot project on a televised news program. The patient informs the reporter that her family has stopped coming to visit. "They're too scared," she offers quite matter-of-factly. "They're too uncomfortable, too sad. But the dog isn't. The dog comes every day and is glad to see me."

When the news special concludes, I wonder what it would be like to be the caretaker who readies the dog—dogs, rather, since there is, in fact, a small troupe of retrievers—for daily rounds. How quickly the flood of narrative begins: I can see one of those dogs visiting someone I have recently lost to a terminal illness . . . my own retriever in that comforting position . . . a fictional character in such a bed, in such a ward, and a dog coming to visit who is, coincidentally, so much like one that had shared his life. I haven't stumbled on the story I might tell, but just this much note-taking exposes the matrix of feelings that underlies and precipitates a story. And that narrative instinct is simultaneous with the desire to *read* such a story about this complicated, emotional relationship, a desire we may all share whether or not we possess the talent to commit such a story to prose.

CHAIN OF FOOLS

There may or may not be a story that could include the dog who has come into my yard while I have been writing this Introduction. She has a tether of broken chain padlocked so tightly around her throat that the fur has abraded beneath it. I think I recognize the dog as a distant neighbor's (on our walks, my own dogs have introduced me to most of the canine homes): an overweight shepherd who recently gave birth to a mixed litter. I return the dog to the yard—the chain link matches—where it spends all of its time. Aside from the fact that it has no collar, license, identification tags, food, or water, I see that the muddy yard is littered with—embedded with—shards of shattered bottles. In this regard, the yard offers little contrast to the house and to what I suspect the interior offers its human residents.

If there isn't a story here, there was a letter to my neighbor that was nearly as difficult to compose.

Each of five subsequent mornings, the dog and her chain return. The last time, I manage to find someone at home. The dog and the man opening the door acknowledge one another with little appreciation. My expressed concerns are even less appreciated. When the door closes, I'm left considering the genuine options available to me: Report the man to the local humane society? Offer to adopt the dog myself? Try to provide clandestine care for the dog? Assume that I have made the smallest difference?

I add myself to the chain of fools. If I am only now concentrating, concerting my efforts in this area of human neglect, what can I expect or demand of a family whose own circumstances seem to provide none of the basic advantages I have enjoyed most of my life? True, the privilege of caring for a dog demands basic care. True, the cleaning of a yard or filling of a water bowl hardly require a privileged lifestyle. And what is also true is that the self-righteousness that seems to come with the territory slinks from my hands like the returned shepherd, dragging its chain into the house.

ANOTHER CHAIN

Unpacking a box of miscellaneous items in the garage, I come across Carey's collar, twenty-four inches of light chain with a cluster of charms—heart, fire hydrant, state of Ohio (ID, rabies, and registration tags). Carey was *my* first dog, a dog that lived with me and not my entire family. Carey was the puppy who chewed the spines of my college textbooks, the corners of my record albums, the letters dropped through the mail slot. Carey was the dog who taught me how many ways a twenty-year-old can fail a dog, despite whatever training love can muster. Carey was the aging dog my parents adopted when I went to graduate school, the dog who wouldn't leave my father's side while my father recuperated from each of his heart's damages. And when Carey's own body began its rapid deterioration, my father reminded us that Carey was the dog we owed a similar vigilance; and so we learned to administer the daily injection that kept him continent, helped the dog up and down the steps, in and out of the house, and offered Carey (ourselves?) a few more unanguished months together.

Automatically, as I do every day when I walk my present dogs, I slid the links of Carey's old collar through one of its end rings and formed a circle of chain. A straight line turned to a circle. And there it was: Carey's neck, restored in the perfunctory gesture.

A TAIL WE COULD WAG

It is difficult to admit the daily joy and daunting love we feel for these creatures to a friend or to a reader. The fiction selected here responds to that strain. There is a reluctance, but by no means a refusal, to acknowledge how a dog can be the perfect therapist, the one who can elicit, from even the most reluctant, a monologue that goes unchallenged and unmocked; how the dog can afford us the irrepressible chance for tenderness and physical contact; how the dog can, somehow, "humanize" the most alien or impersonal situation; how the dog can prompt occasions when adults allow themselves abandon, unselfconsciousness, unqualified play. W. H. Auden expressed this aptly: "In moments of joy / all of us wished we possessed / a tail we could wag."

Perhaps it is humor that provides the most comfortable mode for acknowledging this intimate, intimidating side of human/canine relations. Surely we have come to revel and even revere the quirky, fascinating, and bizarre humor in a life with dogs. Why else the appeal of David Letterman's "stupid pet tricks," if not to provide a public forum for the accidental behaviors and stumbled-upon stunts we have secretly and overtly encouraged in our own dogs? And if those routines are televised instead of written, they still allude to an inventive level of characterization that we have welcomed. Humor, stunts, routines, all help to create the *story* of one dog in one family, and that is, in miniature, where these stories are focused.

While fictions continue to be published that center on a dog's pranks and antics, silly and mock-heroic exploits, the stories gathered here do not compose their narratives of such behaviors; rather, the humor provides a textural element, more specific details from this *ad hoc* relationship. For instance, they divulge, collectively, that we all have private voices for our animals, vocabularies, shticks, quirky privileges.

Charles Barsotti has created, over a period of years, a series of cartoons that toys with the expressible and inexpressible communication between people and dogs. Engaged in brief or allusive interactions, they produce a shorthand record, a midpoint between a written story and a shown or told story. The wit and aptness of his observations, demonstrated in the suite of cartoons on pages 137–44, capture such quickened and insightful instances that a story—that of our own dogs—seems to be implied in each.

As one example, consider this Barsotti drawing. Rather than belabor like explanatory prose, the drawing quickly releases the humor bound up in the scenario's implied emotions: there is the puppy, Rex, eternally puppyish, eternally faithful to his human companion; there is Little Bobbie, now an elderly man whose life continued for fifty years beyond his dog's years; and there, at St. Peter's gates, the two reconvene their earth-made companionship. While issues of longing, mortality, the soul of one or another species, and the nature of the afterlife are all at stake and at risk, the cartoon works like a vaccine, introducing a small, nonthreatening dose to help combat such dear and debilitating thoughts.

"SO YOU'RE LITTLE BOBBIE; WELL, REX HERE HAS BEEN GOING ON AND ON ABOUT YOU FOR THE LAST 50 YEARS."

PICTURE YOURSELF

An excursion into another medium—the photographs of William Wegman—can best initiate our investigation of the attractive and multiple role of canine companionship. Like the cartoons of Charles Barsotti, they, too, are companion pieces, works that chart the affective qualities of this rare alliance.

Just as these selected stories are not "dog stories," William Wegman's photographs are not "dog photographs." In both instances it is what the dog elicits from the human creator that is, finally, the subject. And while the "subject" of Wegman's work is often a Weimaraner—the late Man Ray, Fay Ray, and now Fay's offspring, Batina—his pictures depart from the amateur's typical pictures of the family dog by the same magnitude of difference that distinguishes Wegman's 20″ × 24″ Polaroids from the amateur's 4″ × 5″ Polaroids. When his

Weimaraner puts on the garments of leisure, poses among office furniture, dons unwieldy costumes of copper screening, net, roller skates,
paper bags and so on, it is Wegman who describes this excerpted scene
from human civilization. It is Wegman who decides when to shoot the
pictures—through his commands, through his observations of the dog's
spontaneous actions. It is Wegman, ultimately, who has defined, or
rather *discovered*, through the dog, a way to show us ourselves in a more
risible guise, in a sleeker form, in an amateur's unthreatening genre,
in a whimsical "creation" that is unsettling because of its cross-species
misplacements, serene frivolity, elegant hybridization. We recognize
Fay as a dog in her quintessential and classical role as the nude of the
dog world. Wegman clearly understands the Weimaraners' unique capacity for this sensuality, neutrality, purity. And we recognize Fay as
a human in her role as this dressed, decorated, and dramatized object.
She is both utterly ridiculous and utterly adorable, as we ourselves
are—that is, when we bother to look.

And, most critical, Wegman's dogs are not "dogs" but *the* dogs
with whom he has shared his house, family, and friends, *the* dogs whose
lives have been involved in an ongoing, hardworking relationship with
the camera. Wegman understands that his dogs, posing in the studio,
are pitched at the same level of excitement that comes from hearing
keys in the door, a leash removed from its hook in the closet. Between
Wegman and his dogs, between photographer and subject, there is a
fixity of attention we might call love.

An intimist photographer—that is, someone who records the domestic, rather than the outside, events—Wegman has made his home
his studio, adorning it with yards of fabric, hanging backdrops, bolts
of colored material, huge, mural-like paintings-in-progress, and an ongoing accumulation of eclectic ephemera—thrift-store chairs and tables, tacky bric-a-brac, tossed-out bits of scenery and architecture.
What was once prop in a particular shot of the dog might remain as
furnishing. What was introduced as furnishing might suddenly serve in

a portrait. It all contributes: Nothing is sacred to the home or to the studio, to the man or to the dogs. But despite the mercuric, eccentric trappings of Wegman's photographs, the Weimaraner establishes a common point of identity. Like the vanishing point of perspective, *there* is Fay beneath it all, through it all; *there* is Fay offering herself as the known constant from which variation is created, the recognition from which surprise is made possible.

The anthropologist Jay Ruby‡ proposes that a dog's name and a snapshot are linked to a human in the same manner: both encourage a story, prompt the person to retell their conceptions. Both the dog's name and the family snapshot possess *specific* associations—an inherent set of circumstances, a narrative triggered by its mere mention or presentation. On the contrary, a human name, like a work of art, is connected to us by *general* associations—neither requires further elaboration to satisfy our expectations. They are accepted at face value (nothing more is required of the artist or the named individual), triggering, instead, our own personal associations or interpretations.

The dramatic power of Wegman's work results from being both family snapshot and work of art, both the specific and the general, the intriguing story and the engaged archetype.

The bright truth, spread like the emulsion across each photograph (something lost from sight when the image itself is perceived), is that the dog is such a familiar presence in such an increasingly unfamiliar culture that it is becoming easier to see ourselves, and surprise ourselves, in this theatrically costumed dog, this undisguisable beauty of a dog, than in our own complicated portrayals. The dog is holding our place in the picture. The dog is telling us a story about the way we imagine ourselves, mirroring back our feelings in a way that seems to disclose them for the first time.

If Wegman has caught—and been captured by—public attention

‡Jay Ruby, as cited in *Between Pets and People.*

in regard to dogs and photography, he is but the artist among the perennially infatuated professionals, amateurs, journalists, and family members with little interest in photography other than its ability to prompt memory's specific stories. The fashion and portrait photographer Richard Avedon writes in his essay "Borrowed Dogs" about the care with which his own family's snapshots were taken in his early childhood. "We made compositions. We dressed up. We posed in front of expensive cars, homes that weren't ours. We borrowed dogs." Nearly every picture taken of his family included a different dog, borrowed from someone. "It seemed a necessary fiction that the Avedons owned dogs. Looking through our snapshots recently, I found eleven different dogs in one year of our family album." His very choice of the word "fiction" connects photograph to story, image with what it tells about us. Avedon goes on to suggest that behind each snapshot was "some kind of lie about who we were" and that this "revealed a truth about who we wanted to be."

Just as in photography, the dogs in these collected stories reveal truths about who we are or think we are or want to be. While not as celebrated as Wegman's dogs, the dogs of these stories provide familiar constants, points of perspective. They offer a chance for self-portraiture, as Wegman has said of his work, without the egotism and nervousness of being in front of the lens, on camera, in public.

The poet Mark Strand ennobles this idea when he says, "We seem to be our friendliest, our liveliest, our most vulnerable, in short our best, when there is a dog at hand ready to restore us to ourselves."[*]

MORE THAN A FAMILIAR, LESS THAN A FATE

Ready to *reveal* us to ourselves, I might add. And so to the revelatory commission of the stories in *The Company of Dogs*. A preeminent and

---

[*] In a review of *The Dog Book* by Ruth Silverman.

impassioned presence of dogs in current storytelling prompted this com-
pilation. But beyond detecting mere presence, I sensed that the dog
was not only textural (realistic), but mythical, metaphorical, symbolic,
critical, auguring. The dog seemed variously elevated to the status of
child, parent, self—other, transitional object, witness, conscience,
moral, god, Nature—something other than pet or employee.

In Ethan Mordden's "The Complete Death of the Clown Dog,"
the lone act of a childhood circus features a small talking dog, a poodle
whose moot trick consists of two replies "Tell these folks . . . who you
are" "*Clown . . . dog.*" "Who is the *clown dog?*" "*Me.*" Returning
home from college at Christmas, the speaker finds that the clown dog
has died, the circus dispersed. And from this small loss, he realizes
what the dog had known and even said all along: "clown . . . dog.
Me." "You don't grow old yourself as fast as old things grow old because
even as you age you're still there but the other things are gone . . .
what you might call completed." The young man understands this
passing of time, of places, of his younger self, and comes to realize,
through the agency of the clown dog, that "you remember the old
things, and the other place, and suddenly you realize how much you
miss them. And this tells you how you have your own completion to
accomplish." *Clowning* around with the human, the dog has drawn a
human response.

Similarly, in David Updike's "Out on the Marsh," a young man
returns home to the childhood dog he had always considered a "peer"
to find that the dog has grown old without him. Having advanced
more quickly in the same interval of time, the dog bears significance
beyond its independent years.

In both stories, the dog is not merely a familiar—a constant
companion—but a family relation to whom a person looks for a sense
of recognition. Beyond the kind of recognition mythologized in Argus's
lone greeting of Odysseus upon his return, the dog bears its own lifespan
as some notion of what our human years will ultimately endure. Since

a dog's full life—ten to fifteen years—passes in roughly a seventh of our own, its life is an afforded measurement by which our own time may be marked. Its life is a perceivable span of memory, an apprehendable term: just about the length of childhood and child rearing, the occupancy of a particular house or, maybe, a town, some soured marriages, some careers, and so many other human durations. The dog can serve in fiction by metonymy: a part to stand—stand in—for the whole.

The presaging of mortality is but the extreme and most august role that dogs assume in our stories. "Lying Doggo," the title of Bobbie Ann Mason's story, is a perfect example of an appropriation from the canine world that registers the human. The title's concept is implemented as the wife in this story worries that the dog's dying will create "a milestone in her marriage to Jack, a marriage that has somehow lasted almost fifteen years. She is seized with an irrational dread—that when the dog is gone, Jack will be gone too."

In "Dog Life" a story by Mark Strand not included in this anthology, a husband turns casually to his wife and admits to her that he used to be a collie. Having confessed to this prior incarnation, the husband hopes his wife "would understand his having been a dog was not his choice, that such aberrations are born of necessity and are not lamentable." The husband explains that sometimes "the fury of man's humanity will find its finest manifestations in amazing alterations of expectedness. For people are only marginally themselves." In the morning, the husband and wife awakened as if nothing had happened. "What he had told her would be something they would never mention again, not out of politeness, or sensitivity for the other, but because such achievements of frailty, such lyrical lapses, are unavoidable in every life."

By the author turning to the dog, by the husband turning into the dog, the story/life managed a needed frailty, lapse, marginality. The story of altered expectedness thus altered the reader's expectedness (the reader's ability to know it already and dismiss it). The role of dog permitted a substitution of empathy for sympathy and provided, to all parties, a rare connection amid human exasperations.

LE CHIEN, C'EST MOI

The essayist Edward Hoagland† furthers this dissolution of boundaries between the species: ". . . to really enjoy a dog, one doesn't merely try to train him to be semihuman. The point of it is to open oneself to the possibility of becoming partly a dog." The idea, he suggests, is to "rediscover the commonality of animal and man—to see an animal eat and sleep that hasn't forgotten how to enjoy doing such things—and the directness of its loyalty."

This will toward the animal-like, toward dogginess in particular, is a confession that appears repeatedly in current fiction. Sometimes this is dreaded, sometimes this is desired. Lee K. Abbott writes: "I would not want to be one of those memoirists who begin a recollection by saying, 'Attention, people, there is a dead dog in these pages,' but, alas, I am and there is." As his narrator puzzles through the story "from the higher ground of time and distance," his wife, who is suing him for divorce, helps him to understand that "we dare not treat our pets —the cats and dogs, even the reptiles only the odd truly love—with more irony, or indifference, than we treat ourselves." She confirms the truism "that you can tell much about a person by the way he treats his animals: brutes for brutes . . . lapdogs for the lovely inside." The dogs that share our houses are "our analogues": "Us without the fret-filled, over-large brain. Us would we only bound and bark and fetch when the urge strikes us."

In the popular movie based on Reidar Jönsson's book, *My Life as a Dog*, an orphaned child, entranced and haunted by the idea of the

---

† "Dogs and the Tug of Life," Edward Hoagland.

famous Russian dog cosmonaut Laika, abandoned somewhere in space, is forced to move to the home of his uncle and aunt. There he comes to grieve for his mother's death only when the lie about his family dog crystallizes: like Laika, his little dog was never expected to return. And when the kind and deceiving uncle tries to console the child who is holed up in their impromptu doghouse of a cottage, the boy startlingly leaps at the windows, snapping, barking, growling protectively.

Our possible identification with the dog may be more an identification with a part of ourselves we have trained to hide beneath a human reflection. John Berger‡ suggests that "the pet offers its owners a mirror to a part that is otherwise never reflected."

And it is not always an attractive part of ourselves that is reflected in the dog's returning gaze. Perhaps it is a reluctance to see this reflection *and* a yielding to it only under the pressure of storymaking that might account for this prevailing preoccupation with dogs in contemporary fiction. In a John Updike story a dog is the final bearer of the sad and perennial news about the losses our lives attempt to assimilate. The dog's death follows the loss of other "distant friends"—his first wife's second husband and an elderly woman whose home he and his wife had frequented in happier days. The dog is a "witness" from those prior occasions, a witness to that precarious self. "The deaths of others carry us off bit by bit," Updike writes. "In truth—how terrible to acknowledge—all three of these deaths make me happy, in a way. Witnesses to my disgrace are being removed." The dog does not simply lose its own life, but takes with it aspects of its human's life. The dog's tangentiality creates sufficient distance so that the human can turn and see himself affected—encircled and contained by such losses.

So, too, in Gary Gildner's "Junhy" and in Bobbie Ann Mason's "Lying Doggo" and in so many stories that I found: the age, vitality, and mortality of the human protagonists is measured by their canine

‡John Berger, "Why Look at Animals?"

companions. And when the dog's life approaches its end as in Wright Morris's "Victrola," or Jack Matthews's "The Immortal Dog," the age of both dog and man are such equivalents that the dog's death is more like a suicide pact, an expiration shared between companions.

In Elizabeth Tallent's story "Keats," her separating characters insist that the "dog is definitely not negotiable," but that is, indeed, the most recognizable term of their predicament. Arguably, it is the clearest term as well, since the relationship to the dog is unclouded by nuance and vocabulary, unresponsive to the embittered difficulties of the couple's new lives. Maxine Kumin signals the lucidity a dog can confer in "The Neutral Love Object" when she explains, "Once at a cocktail party a psychiatrist had told her that people make their dogs into neutral love objects, a repository for all the *unspoken* passion at work in the yeasty ferment of a family." The emphasis on "unspoken" is mine: dog as perfect acoustics, friend upon whose silence our words are returned.

THE YELP OF ITS OCCASION

Like a title, a dog's presence in a story can be prismatic. Like a title, it can announce "the cry of its occasion," as Wallace Stevens wrote. "The yelp of its occasion," we might modify for present purposes. And we, as readers, attend to the dog's presence nearly as instinctively as we do to a baby's crying. (Indeed, the comparison is more than coincidence when one thinks of the reinforcing match between a dog's retention of its infantile behaviors and physiognomy—what is termed "neoteny"—and a human's response of nurturing behavior and perpetual "motherese.") When a dog barks at a figure still out of human hearing range, when a dog sniffs at something we cannot smell, evidence is detected and announced that comes, if it comes at all, much later to human senses. The dog's strong connection to nature and to its own instinctual powers confers a superhuman sensitivity. Additionally, the dog's senses respond without barriers of language or dilutions of repressive self-consciousness. Clarity and vulnerability are what the dog proffers—just what we've learned to withhold from one another.

In Antonya Nelson's "Dog Problems," the dog is but one of the tragic predicaments within the couple's uneasy attempts at sorting through their present situation, but it is the dog's irremediable and passive plight that earns (almost for contrast) our immediate sympathy. The dog's fate, clearer and more vulnerable, concentrates our attention on the venial human ineptitude.

Unwarranted or just, absurd or tragic, responsible or wanton—each term is unsparingly sharper in our relationship to dogs, while in human relationships these same qualities are overwhelmed and inundated, jeopardized by such human ploys as impatience, self-protectiveness, or jadedness, and compromised by the onslaught of daily traumas (personal, local, global) to which we have become inured. Even in the commonplace, nonfictional arena of the nightly news, as we listen to the broadcast of burning houses, car wrecks, and torrential weather, it is the unexpected mention of a dog, cat, or a barnyard animal into some calamity that suddenly pins attention to an otherwise generic and impersonal news item. The vividness of our responsibility (even if it is neglected) in regard to these creatures is what works to elicit a viewer's—or, in fiction's domain, a reader's—most earnest response.

The last chapter of Milan Kundera's *The Unbearable Lightness of Being* brings the characters Tomas and Tereza to the country. The political upheavals of Czechoslovakia, the torment of their ineffable and profligate love (tensions of public and private worlds), are left behind as a new life commences in a realm of pastoral simplicity. Not coincidentally, what deciphers the revolution's white noise of events and announces its personal implications is the presence of dogs. Tereza recalls a brief filler in the newpaper from a decade ago. All the dogs in a particular Russian city "had been summarily shot. It was that inconspicuous and seemingly insignificant little article that had brought home to her for the first time the sheer horror of her country's oversized neighbor."

THE LEASH CONNECTING US

More acutely, it is the aging dog Karenin's death in the last chapter that most emotionally charges the characters with the deeper, more sympathetic comprehension of their joined lives. In an odd moment, Tereza realizes that "Her home was Karenin, not Tomas. Who would wind the clock of their days when he was gone?"

This echoes and amplifies our concept of the dog as available measurement for human time. While it may be hard to celebrate the quotidian elements of our ongoing time with dogs, Kundera renders this complicity with its tragic and lyrical potency in this ticking image—another connotation for the term "watchdog."

Kundera proceeds to suggest that people living in the country with animals retain an access to Nature, even the primordial Nature, Paradise. Just as the dog's leash connects it to us, so another length connects the dog to nature. When Tereza stumbles on the oddity that the "dog's menstruation made her lighthearted and gay, while her own menstruation made her squeamish," Kundera provides the answer that "dogs were never expelled from Paradise. Karenin knew nothing about the duality of body and soul and had no concept of disgust." This accounts for why Tereza felt so easy with the dog. This is the danger, Kundera continues, in turning "an animal into a *machina animata*, a cow into an automaton for the production of milk. By doing so, man cuts the thread binding him to Paradise and has nothing left to hold or comfort him on his flight through the emptiness of time."

Kundera then reasons that the human/canine bond exceeds that which is even possible between man and wife: Tereza's love for Karenin asked nothing of the dog. Their bond was free from the questions of

degree and balance with which humans plague themselves. Tereza wonders if "all the questions we ask of love, to measure, test, probe, and
save it, have the additional effect of cutting it short." Her affection
did not transform or deprive the dog, but simply provided "the elementary language that enabled them to communicate and live together." Their love was, *a fortiori*, voluntary and free from overbearing
duties and fealties. Finally Kundera writes of the relationship's greatest
virtue: "No one can give anyone else the gift of the idyll; only an
animal can do so, because only animals were not expelled from Paradise.
The love between dog and man is idyllic." And what is this idyll but
repetition: the circle, cycle, ring, return of the everyday that has, itself,
recurred throughout our discussion. "And therein lies the whole of
man's plight," Kundera concludes. "Human time does not turn in a
circle; it runs ahead in a straight line. That is why man cannot be
happy: happiness is the longing for repetition."

A life with dogs is repetition. When we merge our own frenetic
lines with the dog's cycles, we participate in a restoration of Paradise,
joy's circle.

A PASTORAL WITH DOGS

A literary use of this propitious circle is the pastoral, a convention that
implies the world in a governable piece of it (village, island, ship,
pasture). Extending well beyond the domain of shepherds and allego-
ries, a pastoral maintains the romantic concept of a limited, controlled
oasis of simpler ways and means. In a pastoral, an author writes of the
world on a lucid, smaller scale, and a reader accedes to this. The laws
of humans, of nature, and of God are all present in less confused and
complex manners. In so many contemporary stories, a central dog
renews this pastoral contract.

Whereas I can impose this pastoral genre on most of the stories in
The Company of Dogs, Michael Martone's "Seeing Eye" constructs an

explicitly pastoral setting: a picturesque town where guide dogs are trained, and the whole population participates—voluntarily and involuntarily—in the public walking/training of guide dogs. Families board the dogs at night. The city's children grow to love and then to give up each guest. The streets are lined with extra fire hydrants, subway escalators that lead nowhere, and many other necessary distractions for a guide dog's lessons. Even the mail carrier, Martone's speaker, is part of the training. The human/canine relationship has staged the town: it is the town's building codes, the subject of town meetings, its weather. And as the carrier delivers the mail and encounters the training dogs, she is metamorphosed into the "seeing eye" through which we understand the townspeople's lives. Martone's pastoral world of seeing-eye dogs guides each of us toward insight.

ONE NATION, UNDER DOGS

If "Seeing Eye" is a generous example of this pastorality, it does corroborate the impression I had collecting these stories: our entire country is one pastoral setting unified by the persisting presence of our dogs. David Leavitt senses this in "Chips Is Here": in his story's Long Island, as in the rest of the country, there are people in every house "with cats and dogs, and stories to tell: the time Flossie fell four stories . . . the time Rex disappeared for weeks . . . the time Bubbles was mangled . . . They would tell you, if you asked them, how they had to put Darling to sleep; how Fifi went blind. . . ." His list—*the* list—goes on.

The substantiation for this pastoral came to me from the responses I received to queries soliciting stories for *The Company of Dogs*. So many individuals, most of whom had no pretentions to being fiction writers, sent me a story about a companion animal. Almost all were that other kind of "story"—a true account—about a real dog. Moreover, the majority of these submissions—columns, personal essays, reminiscences, letters to the editor—concerned a family dog that, after so many devoted years, had to be euthanized. Many included photographs or slides of their dogs, not merely to illustrate the story but to confirm what I came to understand was the essential character of the story: the enduring presence of the dog's absence. As though the interiors and fashions hadn't already divulged the passing years, handwritten dates revealed that the snapshots had been taken decades earlier; yet the stories were newly typed as though the loss was as unfaded as the fresh typewriter ribbon. Few contributions demonstrated any interest in or need for the artifice of fiction. Few adopted conventions (like the pastoral) to coax language back into experience. They were readers' responses, not writers', generated from genuine feeling and not from the passion to engender feeling once again.

Each day that the mail brought another of these stories reminded me of the woman in Amy Hempel's story who wears a charm bracelet with the "name tags from all of her former pets." The idle brushing of her hand against the dog would cause the bracelet to jingle. Whether or not the daily sound would call forth a painful memory or a cherished image, Hempel doesn't—needn't say. The lost lives are inscribed upon the human day as indelibly as the animals' names on the metal tags.

But these submissions did encourage me. They did inspire me with their prolonged sense of compassion. Just as sheaves of unshared poetry hide in the drawers of countless houses that harbor no one claiming to be a poet, the lasting memories of our companion animals are just as widely and privately concealed. I pledged to myself that my selection of stories would be kindred spirits to those submitted and unsubmitted memories, a public forum for the sharing of those individual sorrows.

TO SPEAK AT LAST FOR THE SPEECHLESS

The poet Richard Howard suggests that one reason why we are so haunted by our deceased dogs is because "dogs are already silent, and so become ghosts all the more quickly." In "The Death of the Dog and Other Rescues," Susan Kenney depicts this presence as yet another kind of "watchdog," a preoccupation we sense as an actual occupying. "What I've learned about the dead," she writes, is that "it is not always their absence that haunts us. So I still hear the clink of a chain collar against a porcelain bowl, the skittering of toenails across a wooden floor, the thump and sigh of a weary dog flopping his old bones down next to my chair." Those sounds from the dog's comparatively speechless world continue to resound in all the places where habit, expectation, and familiarity have stationed the dog.

Curiously, previous anthologies of stories with dogs seldom mention the word "death" in a title. Yet contemporary authors frequently undertake the harsher responsibility of a dog's mortality. (One can hardly entertain the idea that a dog's death is of only recent significance.) Short story collections by contemporary authors show that when an author has written a story in which a dog dies, the story appears, with few exceptions, as the final piece in the book. The dog's loss is culminating and cumulative, focusing, as in the pastoral, the transpired stories' complex of human divagations.

Earlier collections, by way of contrast, typically named stories with dogs for the dogs themselves, the dog's breed or its work, thus emphasizing a focus on the dog's life. This new mention of the dog's death ("the yelp of its occasion") signals, I suspect, not a forsaking of a dog's replete life, but a struggle to admit the final accompanying human loss simultaneous with the dog's death. And yet this accounts for only part of the reason so many dogs die in our contemporary fiction.

BREAKING UP THE HEART

Is there an appropriate, excessive or necessary level for our grieving over a companion animal? Such a question further complicates our lives and these stories. And because we know in advance that our dogs will have shorter lives than ourselves, even our way of aging them by "dog years"—approximately seven for every human year—is an attempt to reassure ourselves that their time with us is long and productive . . . and human.

But as I have maintained, we are just beginning to articulate without embarrassment our emotions for these and other creatures. Just as in a human/human relationship, writers find it most difficult to describe joy and happiness in human/canine interaction. Writing of the rewarded love and satisfied needs that a dog offers, preciosity, anthropomorphism, silliness, bravado, and so many other weaknesses stand ready to dismiss the story from a reader's empathies. We are crushed with ambivalence: wanting to confer human dignity and *personality* upon a dog, and at the same time wanting to insist on its animal, less sentient nature. We want to justify our love and devotion and yet permit the creature its fate as a dog. Indeed, what other than the denial of a dog's "humanity"—its soul, feelings, ethical rights, and even its ability to feel pain—has permitted us to exploit dogs in research, product testing, and cruel or inhumane inventions?

Psychiatrist Aaron Katcher proposes a further reason for the unsettling, latter-day inability to speak emotionally about dogs. And this is part of the risk these stories have undertaken. "Unconsciously or deliberately we either avoid befriending the animals we intend to harm, or we fabricate elaborate and often mythological justification for their suffering that absolves us of blame." Katcher argues that the saddest thing is that this "self-deception" has established itself as such a long-standing practice that "we are scarcely aware that we are doing it anymore. The myths have become reality, the fantasies, fact." Rather than impugn "our supposedly objective, utilitarian attitudes to other species, or the morality that governs our callous exploitation of animals and nature, we tend to ridicule or denigrate those who take the opposing view." Those who "display emotional concern for animal suffering, or the destruction of the environment, or the extinction of wild species are often treated as misguided idealists." As for concern about an animal's welfare, this we dismiss as suspect, wasteful, and inconsequential when compared to so many other issues. Thus, we are all—writers, especially, in the public exposure of print—"damned with the accusation of sentimentality, as if having sentiments or feelings for other species were a sign of weakness, intellectual flabbiness or mental disturbance."

With such reservations numbing the tongue's ability to confess the dog's prodigal slice of the heart's pie, a dog's death affords one unabashed chance to express, at last, something of this depth, temporarily cleared of the guilt of sentimentality. A dog's accidental or languishing or even peaceful death lowers the threshold of our reservations and supports a retelling in fiction. Then the audience of people who have lived with dogs, and even the people who have not, can nod in empathic assent: Yes, we know that degree of loss.

Freud elaborates this when he suggests that humans are freer to grieve unaffectedly over the loss of an animal, because people are not as ambivalent in their relationship to their animals as they are toward human members of their family.

And so our mourning is a reservoir of such considerations. And do we not, as well, mourn the self that was expelled from the natural, paradisiacal world into which the dog invited us with its cycles of happy familiarity? Do we not mourn our return to the human timeline of linearity?

It comes as no surprise to find that the poet Rainer Maria Rilke was painfully aware of our vulnerability to dogs. Having been asked to adopt a friend's dog, Rilke reluctantly admits that dogs "touch me so deeply, these beings who are entirely dependent on us, who we have helped up to a soul for which there is no heaven." I admit to wincing at that line. It appears to lie at the heart of the stories compiled here:

an unresolvable hope that all our commitment and kindness and responsibility and love will possess a futurity—a hope we extend into our own lives but find unbearable to discuss.

The pain of the dog's proposed adoption continues to burden Rilke. "Even though I need all of my heart, it is probable that this would end, end tragically, by my breaking off little pieces from the edge of it at first, then bigger and bigger pieces toward the middle (like dog biscuits). . . ." And as the bewildered dog pines for his previous provider, Rilke admits that he would, "after hesitating for a little while, give up my writing and live entirely for his consolation."

This figure of a person breaking up a heart like dog biscuits, feeding it in small fragments to an ill-comprehending creature, suggests that the heart alone—not the mind, nor the tongue, nor any other organ of communication—is the only means we can employ in our relationship with dogs, the only connection we have to this human/canine, pastoral world. The stories in *The Company of Dogs* reveal those occasions when we share such broken, heartfelt knowledge with one another.

ON MY BEHALF AND MORE

So, rather than see myself as a scholarly editor content to trace the new visibility of the dog in literature, and rather than see myself as an animal-rights activist who can espouse unimpeachable data about this ethical and environmental debacle, I'd prefer to see myself as someone whose increasing awareness and concerted education urge me toward the endeavor of this anthology, someone who is hoping to conjoin a group of writers who have endorsed a growing concern by donating their singular talents; someone who is eager to demonstrate that a considerable amount of concrete good can be done—the donation of this book's profits to agencies that provide direct care for animals at risk and in distress—by people who are willing to say, yes, the world is overwhelmed with problems, but here is at least one request I can honor, one problem that can be solved. No, none of the writers I've assembled would say that dogs are the most urgent problem facing civilization. But none would be deluded into thinking that ranking diminishes a problem.

We are, all of us, so rarely afforded the chance to contribute personally, significantly, lastingly, and to use a talent that can exceed the writing of checks or letters. It is therefore a particular honor to have the occasion of this collection in which a company of writers has contributed not only to dogs but to people who care about dogs. Although I express a gratitude to each author that is, alas, only personal, I offer it as though on behalf of each dog that has enriched these stories, each dog that will be benefited by them.

—*Michael J. Rosen*

Seeing Eye

MICHAEL MARTONE

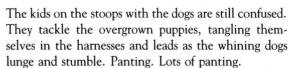

The kids on the stoops with the dogs are still confused. They tackle the overgrown puppies, tangling themselves in the harnesses and leads as the whining dogs lunge and stumble. Panting. Lots of panting.

"It's the Mailman Lady," the kids shout. I kind of throw the mail their way with just enough velocity for the postcards to strip away from the bundle, startling the dogs, who soundlessly bark at the spinning

3 7

envelopes. The kids hang on, use their sweaty faces to hold an animal back, grope for a purchase of fur and skin.

"Letter carrier," I say over my shoulder. Each stride a sidewalk square. The next stoop of the rowhouse has another dog, another kid already mixing it up. The dog's ears are pointing my way. It's stepping all over the kid. And now the whole block of children and animals senses me. "The Mailman Lady," they howl. The dogs bob and focus, then snap and tumble with the kids, slough them off, cock themselves again. The dogs know. The kids are still confused, don't know what to make of me. Never seen one of me before. The dogs are attentive to ancient messages. The uniform. The territory. I smell just as sweet.

I'm a letter carrier in a town whose main industry is raising dogs. Guide dogs for the blind. Shepherds and retrievers mostly. Big brains and bones. Steady mutts with substantial paws, plodding beasts. Slobberingly loyal. Obedient, of course. Easy to clean. It's still a mystery to me just how the training works. The school is on another route, but I've seen the Quonset huts, the kennels, the field of striped obstacles at the school. Every year the newspaper does a feature story with a page of pictures of the graduating dogs staring into the calm faces of their new masters. I only know the puppies come here to this bedroom community and are parceled out to families who keep them just like pets. After a while you'll see the dog in the station wagon. A mom is driving, dropping her husband off at the platform, the kids at school. The dog commutes to work also, comes home for the night, a pillow to a pile of kids in front of the TV.

I run into the older dogs, already on the special lead, as volunteers walk them around the town. There isn't a street where you won't see a couple of pairs plowing the sidewalks. The sighted volunteers, waving to each other, nudge their dogs around a corner. They slug their way through a cul-de-sac. At the corners, there are patient instructions.

They wait for the light to change and for the scramble bell to sound. The dogs walk through the aisles of the stores downtown. They wait in packs for the special bus that distributes them in the neighborhoods. In fact, the town is overly complicated for its size, presenting to the dogs every possible distraction. Too many cats. Dummy fire hydrants. Revolving doors in the butcher shop. The park has been landscaped in levels. Stairs lead by fountains and reflecting pools. I see the dogs taking cab rides. There is an escalator leading down to a subway station with turnstiles but no trains. They take the elevator back to the surface, where there are flower carts, news kiosks, street singers, three-card-monte games, people selling watches spread out on towels, and other volunteers who pretend to be drunk and passed out on benches. Everywhere there are trees. Lots of trees. And people who have signed up to be people today walk their dogs and eat ice cream, read newspapers they then throw in the white wire trash bins scattered everywhere on the avenues. The dogs slog through it all as a car, slow enough to chase, cruises by blowing its horn. I'm part of this too, I know, though the mail I deliver is real. My satchel is strapped to the back of this tricycle cart, and I slalom through the plodding dogs and trainers on the street. The dogs sniff the wheels of the cart. The walkers, for a second tense, lose the strange connection with the animal. My cart speeds up, pulls me along. Up ahead, a wailing fire truck skids around the corner on its way to an imaginary fire.

Along with the letters, we all carry a repellent. It comes in a canister with a pump action like a purse-size cologne. It is standard issue with the uniform and fits neatly in a leather holster. At Brateman's, the store that carries all the uniforms, I attracted a crowd of men—cops and fire-fighters, other postal workers, meter readers—as I tried on the new uniforms. The skirt, the shorts, the dusty blue acrylic cardigan still patchless but with stamped buttons. The baseball cap, the pitch helmet. I'd step out from the dark dressing room, wire hangers jingling, and the men stopped talking with the clerk who was, sucking on pins. They leaned on the glass cases of badges, whistles, and utility belts and watched me look at myself in the mirrors. There were piles of canvas coveralls on the floors, boxes of steel-toed shoes. I tried on a yellow slicker. "How does that feel?" the clerk asked, his mouth full of pins. It felt slick already with sweat. A sheriff's deputy twirled through a stand of string ties. The men talked under their breaths, examined a handcuff key. A dog and trainer glided through the racks of khaki shirts. I came out in pants that I had rolled up. I have always liked the stripe, that darker shade of blue, and the permanent crease that lets me fold everything back into the shape it started with. The clerk soaped the altered cuffs. In the dressing room, I stood there in the dark, my new clothes folding themselves into neat piles. I listened to the damped voices of the men outside, the dog whining, then yawning, and scratching, panting outside the door. The clerk made out the bill, punched the register. I had clothes for every weather and season, a week of shirts and calf-length socks. Shoes. At last he added on the key chain and the repellent in its shiny case. "To keep the boys away," he said. I smiled, thanked him, poised over the charge slip ready for the total. I knew it would take at least two trips out and back to the car to load the uniforms.

The mural above the Postmaster's door in the lobby is being restored to the way it looked when it was painted during the Depression. Scaffolding hides most of it now. The painters move deliberately in the rigging, scooting on their backs or stomachs. It seems to me they are too close to the work. The mural is about the guide dogs. The dogs are marching, leading a parade of blind workers. In the background are ghostly St. Bernards, border collies, and bloodhounds, all the working dogs working. The sky rolls with clouds. The rolling hills gesture like a cursive hand. The road they walk is like a signature, too. The painter signed his name in braille, the code of bumps shaded to make it look raised on the flat wall.

In the lobby, the county association for the blind runs the news concession selling candy bars and newspapers, stationery supplies and maps of the city's streets. They let Mabel, who mans the stand, smoke behind the counter. Her dog, a black Lab, curls around the stool, the stiff lead angling upward like a harpoon. Mabel's eyes are a kind of nougat. She never wears glasses. Smoking artlessly, she picks the tobacco off her tongue. It stays on her moist fingers.

My final job of the day is to clear sidewalk boxes outside the station in time to make the last dispatch. She hears me breezing through the lobby with the carton filled mainly with the metered mail in bundles.

"I always know it's you," she says. "You walk on your toes. I can't smell you." She feels her watch on her wrist. "Same time every day, too." I run through the lobby to the back with the mail. On my way out again, I stand by her stand untucking my shirt, letting myself cool down.

After weeks of this routine I say to her without thinking, "You're the only blind person I know." It isn't that she looks at me, of course. The dog on the floor does look up. She pauses and cocks her head.

"You can see, can't you?" She waits for me to answer yes, begins the elaborate ritual of lighting another cigarette. "I don't know too many blind people either. It's not like we run in packs."

The Postal Service has a secret. There is only one key that opens everything. It only makes sense. We can't be walking around with a ring of keys for all we have to open. The banks of boxes in apartment lobbies open at once with the key. The corner collection boxes. The green relay boxes. The padlocks we use. The box at the end of the glass chute between the elevators in the old hotels. Same key. In that way a substitute on the route already has all the keys needed. One key.

I guess it is not much of a secret. If you worked for the post office you would know, or if you even thought about it some, you could guess. There it is at the end of that long chain. One key.

They make a big deal about the key at the office. *Do Not Duplicate* is stamped on it twice. I find I am always fingering the key, my hand in the pocket with it as I walk. In cross-section it has an S shape. It has several deepening grooves and bristles with teeth. I want it not only to open up the boxes of the post office but to turn in every lock, a true skeleton key, opening all the houses on my route. Inside I could arrange the mail further, piles for each family member, on the marble mantel or the little table by the door. As it is, I find myself looking into houses through the mail slot, holding up the brass flap to see the slice of floor and the envelopes and flyers splayed out randomly there. I feel the cool air rush out in the summer. Adjusting my line of sight, I can see walls of framed pictures of grown children who send the postcards I've read from all the islands, the color envelopes thick with pictures of grandkids. Clocks hang on the walls. Coats on racks. And sometimes one of the dogs—I've heard it bark in the back of the house—will come clicking on the linoleum. Huffing around the corner of the entry hall, he is ready to blow the door down from the inside. A snarl and chomp. The flap on the mail slot is already back in place. That's when that black nose points through the door, the nostril blinking, opening and closing, trying to take in all the smells of me. The fear, the loneliness, my own secret combination of nerves.

Years after the trained dogs leave this city, their owners bring them back. They leave with a new dog.

I'm out at the airport picking up the orange bags of overnight mail when a dog and its owner will come limping across the tarmac. One of the props of the plane they flew in on still revs while the little trucks, run on propane, weave around with baggage and fuel. The dog and the man were the last down the metal stairway, led by an attendant to the terminal. The dog's muzzle is white. Its tongue is out, slipping off to the side of its mouth. There is no color left in the dog's eyes. The dog's almost blind. Its head is down. The shoulders roll. Someone from the school meets them. They wait in the van as the luggage is stowed. I can see the dog's head for a second next to its owner. It shakes itself and collapses beneath the window.

And I sometimes read the notes on the postcards they write home, postcards of the school, a color photograph of a German shepherd at attention rigged out and ready to go. The notes are about Spike or Lady, how the dog took the flight, how the dog is off its food, how the dog seems to remember this place. The writing is little and cramped or big as if magnified. The ink smears on the coated glossy stock of the card. They always love the town, the children on the street. The new dog will take some getting used to. "Buster is making new friends with all the retired pooches." On and on. It's too much to bear. I read these cards and think of losing them someplace or sending them out on the wrong dispatch. By the time they make it home, the writer will have returned to his or her life. "Oh that. I'd forgotten I'd sent it. It's just what I told you."

I read these cards in the new white trucks with the right-handed drive and no windows in the back. You have to use the mirrors to see and everything is distorted.

My family never writes but calls. My mail is window mail, stamped with the odd denominations of the definitive issues, the transportation series. Each stamp is a special class. Every one's soliciting. The stamps depict all these obsolete forms of movement. Canal boats, milk wagons, stagecoaches, pushcarts, carretas, railroad mail cars, a wheelchair with hand-cranked transmission. Bulk rates, presorted, ZIP-plus-4 discounting, carrier route sorting. When it isn't bills, it is charity, nonprofit dunning. Tandem bicycles, steamships, dog sleds. I read my name through the plastic window on the envelope. I try not to imagine what lists I am on, what those lists say about me. My family calls when they have to with important family news. "The mail takes too long to get there," they say. I am too far away to do anything with the news I get. I sign a sympathy note or write a check during the commercials on TV.

I get other calls in the evening or in the morning as I am dressing for work. I answer, and there is silence on the line for a second or two, then the disconnection. This happens often. I shout hello, hello into the static. I can't seem to not answer the telephone. You never know. It could be news. For a while I just picked up the phone without saying a word, listened hard to the silence and then to the line going dead. I have to sort my route first thing in the morning. I go to bed early. In the dark the phone rings. I let it ring for a long time. When I answer it, there is that moment of silence and that soft click. Just checking. Just checking. There is nothing to be done. I leave the phone off the hook and wait through the warning alarms of the phone company, the recorded message telling me to replace the phone in its cradle. And then even that gives up.

I have a screened-in porch, and in the summer I sit on the swing as the neighborhood gets dark. With the light out, the kids who come through collecting for newspapers, cookies, band uniforms, birth defects, can't see me through the gray mesh. I stop rocking. They rattle the screen door and peer in. Their dogs are circling in the quiet street. Positioning themselves at the foot of the dying oak trees, they crane to look up at the roosting starlings. I let the kids wonder for a bit if I am home, then I go to answer the door. It gets darker. The street lights come on. The wheezing birds wind down, and the locusts begin to saw. Across the street the lawn sprinklers start up, and the water pools in the street, a syrup on the blacktop. The bug traps sizzle, the blue light breaking into a cloud of sparks. Mosquitoes aren't attracted to the light. I know at least one is on the porch hanging in the still air, sniffing out the heat I'm giving off. Shadows of cats shoot under a parked car. A blind man comes up the street with a new dog. He is talking to the dog. Commands, encouragements, suggestions all just below my hearing. I can just make out the gist of things, the cooing and the nicker. A few paces back a trainer from the school walks in the wet grass, skips over the concrete walks. He turns all the way around as the tags along making sure no one is following.

Once a month the magazines arrive and the clerks will break into a few copies, never from the same address, leaving them scattered on the tables in the break room. After a few days they put the handled magazines in shrink-wrapped bags labeled with a form. Checked explanations for the condition of the enclosed: *Destroyed on conveyor. Fire damaged. Automatic equipment error.* And sometimes someone will go the extra distance, tear a few pages, pour on some liquid smoke. Customers suspect. They always suspect. I am stopped on the street, asked about the handling codes stamped on the back of the envelope. A C6 floats in the sky of a sunset on a card from Florida. And *NB* in red tumbles into it. What's this? The bar code embossed beneath the address like stitches closing an incision. "You read the mail, don't you?" I'm told. "I don't have time." I try to explain. "Things get lost. Overlooked," I tell them.

The men at the station like to think they are the first in town to see the pictures in the magazines. One will turn the pages when the other two have said they are through. Their free hands are wrapped around the steaming coffee cups, a tether to the table, as their heads float from one cluster of pictures to the other. I'm stuck with the cover girl. I look for the hidden rabbit's head. This time a tattoo. It could be the run in her stocking. The inky smell of the after-shave ads leaks into the room. Business return cards collect on the floor by the men's feet. They'll forget after a while that I am watching them. Forget to whoop and point. They'll forget to turn the magazine my way, holding it the way grade-school teachers do when they read to the class. They'll forget and their eyes will skip and flutter over the pages, the beams crossing and focusing. At last their eyes will be the only movement.

The dogs who don't guide, the pets, the ones too friendly, who can't refrain from jumping up and licking your face, the surly ones broken when they were puppies. We all have our routes. The dogs shuffling through each stop read the streets and hedges and utility poles. These dogs know when something is new. The trash can, the parked car, break up the picture in their heads. River pilots and the river. Their noses scour out a new channel, revise the map they carry in their bones. They pull their owners along the cluttered streets. These dogs see through their memory.

I hate to surprise an unleashed dog while he's intent on his rounds. I turn down an alley. A mutt is snapping at a pair of cabbage butterflies. His muzzle draws little circles in the air, tracking the flitting white wings. His eyes are crossed. I can hear his teeth snip. The butterflies are like a little whirlwind, scraps of alley paper. Now they tumble around the dog's body, and the dog begins to turn back on his tail, his wagging, until he dives into his own fur on his flanks, collapses and rolls, barks and paws at the insects hovering above his belly. Then, upside down, he sees me watching him. Instantly he is on his feet, pivoting on his nose. His eyes never leave mine. He is growling but backing up. His embarrassment is human, shuffling his feet, clearing his throat. He shrugs his shoulders, scratches his ear, then changes the subject, woofing right at me. I have the repellent out of its case. My arm is straight out, and I am aiming for the eyes. The dog circles, barking, trying to convince the backyards that he knew all along I was there. He takes a few steps closer, the skin on his face tight and his body rigid. It frightens me that I can read him so easily, how the gestures of people inform his every move. But still, I don't know dogs. There is no way for me to enter into his thinking, foolish of me for even thinking, at this moment, that there is a way to explain everything, a way to connect. I think of the spritz of chemical, its sting. I think of the one cord of muscle in my forearm used only when I squeeze the trigger or beat an egg. And just then the dog's eyebrows arch and his jaw relaxes and he starts to pant, a kind of laugh.

Now that the mural in the lobby of the office has been restored, it is much harder to see the dogs, the blind workers. It's as if they bleached the images away. The phantom working dogs have disappeared into the background of sky and clouds now all blended into a hazy yellow soup. Perhaps the paints were cheap during the Depression, unstable out of the tube. Or maybe the restorers didn't know when to quit stripping off age and went under into the rough sketch, the outlines, the patches of mixed paint. The workers seem less uniform but more tubercular. They find their own way. The dogs they hold on to now look hairless. I think it's a shame but that's just because I knew the mural before. If I'm here long enough, I'll have to get used to it the way it is. I'll forget the old painting, the gray dust the marching kicked up in the picture and the dust itself layered on like shellac.

I almost tell Mabel about the new painting but I think better of it. Her booth was built in the fifties. It looks like a wrecked spaceship in the marble lobby. Blond wood, goosenecked metal lamps, streamlined steel cash register. The aluminum dashboard candy rack is enamelplated with extinct brands. I hear the physical plant people talk on break about her concession. What to do with Mabel is the problem. She sits behind the counter touching piles of different things, tightening stacks of bubble gum, riffling town maps. After a while she'll reach down and touch her dog on the floor.

During the Depression drifters scrawled messages on light poles indicating what houses were good for a handout. There were arrows on the sidewalks, a soaped X on the brick by the mailbox. So I've heard. Now I just see the kids' games boxed out in colored chalk or maybe a name scraped on the sidewalk with a quartz rock from a gravel drive. I never walk on them and they last.

It's a sad town. The kids are always giving up their dogs. Their mothers give them Popsicles and they sit quietly together on the porch gliders, pick at the unraveling strands of the wicker furniture.

"Hey, Mailman Lady," one of them says. "My dog left." What can you say?

I say, "I don't know too much about dogs."

The kid says almost at the same time, "He went to help a blind person."

"Well, you've got to be happy about that, right?"

"I guess."

It goes on this way, a cycle of mourning visiting most houses on my route. In the summer the child, collapsed on the lawn, stares up at the sky. In the winter he is chewing snow. The kids get a new dog soon, but it is a chronic ache like a stone in my shoe.

On the corner I take out the one key to open a relay box. Inside, the bundles of mail have been delivered to me for the last leg of my route. I try not to think about the messages I am delivering. I file the mail into my cart, stand in a forest of telephone poles, streetlights, fire alarms, police call boxes. The square is crawling with dogs.

The dogs find ways through the crowded streets. They don't stop when children pet them. They ignore each other. They don't see me. They don't bark. They keep going.

The Complete Death of the Clown Dog

ETHAN MORDDEN

In Hanley, West Virginia, close on to Wheeling, where I lived when I was little, there was a poky little circus run by Hopey Paris. Most places don't have their own circus on the premises, not even a little one like Hopey's, which had almost no animals and a busted trapeze and these admission tickets that must have been printed up before the Civil War. You couldn't even read what they said on them anymore. In Hanley we figured it was O.K. to have this circus, though most

of us didn't care about it one way or the other. Anyway, you never knew when Hopey was going to put his circus on, because he ran it by whim. Also, he owned the dime store. I expect what he got out of the dime store he plowed back into keeping the circus going, since he didn't own anything else.

It was like this about having the circus: Some night in light weather, mostly at the tip end of summer, when everyone would just sit around and wait for something cool to happen, Hopey would come up from his end of town and find a crowd on the steps of wherever it was they were . . . someone's porch, whoever had beer. He'd wait about three lulls, nodding and shaking along with the gist of things as they got said. Then he'd go, "Guess I'll have to have the circus tonight." And everyone would get everyone else and go on over, because, look, what else is there to do? You go to the circus.

What a funny circus—but how much do you want for free? Hopey handed out the admission tickets in a little booth at the entrance and you would take your seat inside the tent, which stood in Hopey's back yard, hanging on by a thread to these old poles. It wasn't a big tent, of course, but, as it is said, size isn't substance. And then Hopey would come in with a whip and this hat he got somewhere to be a ringmaster in. You'd want to think he would look pathetic, wouldn't you? Hopey Paris trying to hold down a circus all by himself in Hanley? He didn't, though. He didn't look much like anything. But he did have a star attraction, the clown dog.

It's crazy about dogs—how some can do things and some can't. I knew a dog once that caught softballs in the air if you threw them underhand. Then he'd go racing off with the ball in his teeth and you'd have to trap him and pry the ball out with a stick. That was his trick, I guess is how he looked at it. And my father had a dog named Bill who was quite a hero in his day. Bill ran away finally and never came back.

But the clown dog sure was prime. He had this costume—a yellow coat sort of thing with polka dots, which he wore fastened around his middle, and a red cone hat with a little pom-pom at the top. Whether the circus was on or off, and in all weathers, never, never did you see the clown dog out of costume. And his trick was he could talk. That dog could really talk.

This was why we would always come back to see the same old one-man circus, with no animals or clowns except one animal-clown, like that was all you needed to call it a circus. The tent was hardly alive at all, the big-top tent itself. But you always had to go back, because you wanted to see how the trick was done. Because no dog, not even a circus trick dog, can talk. But the thing about tricks is whether or not you can figure them out. That's the art of tricks, right there. And the clown dog, though he often roamed around his end of town like any other dog, free in the sun, except he was dressed—the clown dog would never do his talking except in the circus. This was probably the deal he made with Hopey, who was, after all, his master. You'd suppose that they must have come to terms on something that important.

That's what's so funny. Because, speaking of dogs, my father never did come to terms with his dog, Bill, though he would try, hard as stone, to make that dog his. He trained it and trained it. It must have run near on to two years of sessions in Sunshine's field, and Bill just didn't ever submit and be trained. My father was a ferocious trainer by the standards of any region, but he couldn't get Bill to obey even the most essential commands. And he never could teach him not to chase around the davenport, especially late at night, when Bill most felt like a run. "I will have that dog behave," my father said, and I recall how he looked, like behavior was just around the corner. But Bill would not be suppressed. Sometimes he would come when you called, sometimes not. But even when he did come he had this funny look on him, as if he was coming over just to find out why you persisted in calling his name when it had already been established that he wasn't about to respond.

Bill was a mutt, not like the clown dog, who was a poodle—a very distinct breed. You can't miss a poodle, especially in a polka-dot coat and a cone hat with a pom-pom. But Bill was just another dog you might know, kind of slow for his race and disobedient but generally normal, except once when he was The Hero of '62. They called him that because he accidentally bit this management scud who was getting on everybody's nerves at the factory the summer before the strike.

McCosker, I think this guy's name was—one of those mouthy hirelings absolutely corrupted by a little power. He had been tacking up a notice by the front gate—some mouthy, powerful thing about something else you weren't supposed to do. He was just busy as anything tacking away and being hated by the people who were standing around watching. Suddenly Bill bounded over to where McCosker was. I guess maybe Bill thought he saw something to eat near his foot, but McCosker took it for some stunt and he made a sudden move and Bill got thrilled and bit him.

It was a tiny little bite on the ankle, kind of in passing, but McCosker screamed like he was being murdered and all the men cheered and patted Bill. And they all shook my father's hand, and mine, too. So Bill was The Hero of '62.

This is a funny thing. Because all Bill had done was what a dog will do every so often, whereas the clown dog was truly some kind of dog. Everybody said so. You just could not tell in any way that he wasn't talking when Hopey Paris brought him on for his circus turn. Now, that was a trained dog if ever there was one. Yet nobody ever called the clown dog a hero. And the clown dog never ran away, either, which Bill did once. Once is all it takes.

I guess you have to figure that a dog that goes around in circus clothes isn't going to earn the respect of the community. Besides him being a poodle, which is not one of your heroic breeds of dog. But I liked him, because he was the first thing I can remember in all my life. Hunkering back down in my mind as far as I can go, I reach a picture of the clown dog talking in the circus, and the polka dots, and the hat. I wonder if he ever had a name, because he was always known as the clown dog that I ever heard, and I don't recall Hopey ever calling to him. Sometimes Hopey would act like that dog was this big secret, cocking an eyebrow and looking cagey if you asked after him, as if everyone in town hadn't seen the circus a hundred times.

I expect the clown dog must have liked me, because he used to follow me around some days with his coat and his dumb little hat. He looked so sad. I guess he sensed that he was supposed to be a secret, because he tended to hang back a little, like someone who has already been tagged out of a game and is waiting for the next thing to start. I don't recall that he even barked. And he never gave in to us when we tried to get him to talk out of the circus.

Of course we had listened, with all the concentration of adolescents, to the exact words Hopey used in the act, when the clown dog would speak, and we would try these words on the clown dog ourselves—imitating Hopey's voice even, and standing the way he stood, to be an imperial ringmaster. But we couldn't make it happen; never did the clown dog utter a word out of his context, the circus. It was the strangest thing.

I was just thinking that I would have hated to be around Bill someday if someone tried to get him into a hat with pom-poms.

I was at college when Bill ran away, so I only know about it second hand, from stories. I couldn't help thinking it was presumable that in the end Bill would take a walk one day and not come back. It was presumable. But still I was surprised to hear of it. It was Easter, when I was a freshman, and the first sight I got of home when I got off the bus was my father cutting the grass with the Johnsons' lawnmower and Bill nowhere to be seen. I knew something was wrong then, because Bill never missed a chance to play dogfight with the Johnsons' lawnmower, which always enraged my father. Bill would growl at it, for starters, lying way off somewhere, and slowly creep toward it, paw by paw. Then he'd run around it, fussing and barking, and at last he'd get into rushing it, like he was going in for the kill, only to back up snarling at the last second.

So when I saw the lawnmower and no Bill I thought he must be sick, but my father said he had run off, maybe as far back as October sometime. I listened carefully to this, though he didn't talk carefully, not ever in all his life that I knew him. Whatever he was thinking when he spoke, that's what he'd say, as tough as you can take it. He didn't expect Bill back, he said, and he didn't miss him. He said it, and I believe him.

"No," he said lazily, because he is lazy. "I don't miss him. You run away from home and don't come back, nobody misses you at all. That's the rule."

I don't know of any rule saying you don't miss a runaway dog, even if he never come back. If he's of a mind to run, there's usually a good reason. My father used to say, "There's always a reason for something, and sometimes two."

That was one of his wisdoms. He had wisdoms for most things that came up in life—lawyers, school, elections, working. He had his wisdoms for Bill, too, even when it was really clear that that dog was born to go his own way in a nice wisdom of the animal kingdom.

I can see why that dog took off, anyway, because my father wasn't any too easy to get along with, especially when proclaiming one of his wisdoms. But despite what he said and how he looked saying it, I suppose he really did love that dog. Or he wanted to love it, which would be the way people like my father express affection. It must have threatened to tear him up some when Bill deserted him.

That was a bad time, too, with the strike coming sooner or later but sure as doom. I wasn't around for the strike. I was sixteen when I finished high school, and I could still have been young some more and not done much of anything with myself, but I had more ambition than to work in the factory or pump gas on Route 16. So I went to college on what you might call a soccer scholarship. My father always poked fun at me for playing soccer. "What kind of sport is that for a man, chasing a ball around with your feet? You look like a bunch of giant bugs" was his view of it. But soccer took me to college, on a full scholarship. It's true, I guess; soccer isn't much of a sport, and this wasn't much of a college. But one wisdom might be that college is college. Anyway, I went.

I came home for Easter because I was only two states away—one long bus ride. Besides, they closed the dorms on me—they were painting—and I had to go somewhere. That first night, Thursday, when I came home and saw the lawnmower and learned that Bill had run away, I was standing in the yard with my bag, like a salesman, and I decided to walk around town instead of just being home. Because I already knew about home, but I felt mysterious about Hanley—that it was a place filled with riddles that ought to be solved, even by someone who had lived his whole life of sixteen years so far in it.

I thought maybe I would take a look over to Hopey Paris's circus, in case that should be going on. Or maybe I would talk Hopey into doing his show just for me, because it was extremely rare that the circus would happen this early in the year. I had an idea that Hopey favored me over some others of my generation there in Hanley because I had always been the keenest of all to see the clown dog and figure out how he talked, and Hopey was pleased to be appreciated, even by kids.

He liked to think (I'm guessing at this) that his circus, starring the clown dog, which he celebrated as The Talking Dog of the World— that his circus was what kept the town from feeling too complete. You might suppose that a town with a circus is more complete than most, but instead I sense that it is less complete, and therefore more open and more free. Because a circus is magic. And having its own private circus reminds the town of all the other magic things it doesn't have.

It puts the town a little in touch with another town, a secret town that is the ghostly image of itself, a kind of myth in a mirror. Now, so long as the town is aware of its ideal twin, it will wonder about itself, and never think it knows everything there is to know, and not pretend that it is complete. Which I think is all to the good. So no wonder I liked to watch the clown dog's act. And that's why I went over to Hopey Paris's circus on my first night back from college—to watch the ghost dance by me again. Even after all those years, I still didn't understand how the clown dog did his trick.

This was the act. Hopey comes in with his whip and his hat and he stands in the ring. "And now we take great pride and the most highly principled pleasure"—this is exactly what he said every time— "in presenting for your delectation and enlightenment the one and only clown dog—The Talking Dog of the World!"

And out from behind a flap of the tent, in his coat and pom-pom hat, the clown dog would trot in. And he would sit on his hind legs looking expectantly at Hopey. That same old coat and hat. That poor little clown dog. Or I guess maybe he was well off, even if no one called him a hero.

In any case, Hopey would say, "Tell these folks here assembled who you *are*"—like that, with everything on the "are." And—I swear to God—the clown dog would answer, as if he was going to growl first. But no, it was this funny talking—"Clown . . . dog." Like that, broken up into words. It was a high voice, tensely placed, like the sounds puppets make on television. And of course we were looking madly from the clown dog to Hopey and back, to see that trick.

Then Hopey would say, "Who is the *clown dog?*" And the clown dog would answer, "Me." Something screwy would happen in his mouth, as if he were biting a fly or had bubble gum. And his head would tilt. But he talked, all right, and that was some trick. Just these two questions were all the talking, though. Because then Hopey would shout, "Leap, clown dog!" and the poodle just leaped right into Hopey's arms and licked his face. That was the whole act, and that was also the whole circus.

I miss that circus, for it is miles away from me now. All my youth and adventures in Hanley seem remote, rare things to savor, like slides of ruins in a stereopticon—though I keep my memories somewhat close to me by writing about them, as you can see. I write to preserve (even to rescue) them. But when I went home that Easter I didn't have the circus in mind as something you ever lose hold of, because I didn't realize about growing old. Now, that is a term for you—"growing old." And it, too, has a trick: it contains the thought that things vanish. They function, and they pass, and you also pass along, and perhaps you come to the big city here (as I have), and you learn a new function, like writing, and think about who you are. And somewhere in there you remember the old things, and the other place, and suddenly you realize how much you miss them. And this tells you how you have your own completion to accomplish.

I didn't reckon on any of this at the time, back in Hanley on my Easter vacation. I was just out for a stroll. I should have stopped and seen everything the way a camera sees, marking it down, so when I grew old everything that was there wouldn't have vanished even in completion. I just wanted a little peace.

The thing was that if I was sixteen the clown dog must have been well on to thirteen or fourteen. He just never acted old, so it was not something to realize. Fourteen is old for a dog, and that's near as long as a dog can last without vanishing, even if he still acts spry and bouncy and leaps into your arms when you tell him. So I just went up to Hopey's door and knocked, thinking he'd be there like always, and maybe Hopey would rustle up the circus just for me in honor of my coming back from college on my first holiday.

The house was lit inside, but no one answered, so I went around to the back, where the tent was. Except there was no tent there now. You could see the tracks in the dirt where it used to be, all the time before, and some of the bleacher seats were still there, a little wrecked, like someone had been trying to take them apart and then suddenly changed his mind. And as I stood there wondering, I heard Hopey's back door open. I turned and saw him in the doorway, so I asked him where the circus had gone to.

"My little clown dog passed away," Hopey said, "so I cut down the tent and dissolved the circus."

It happened in October, he said, which would have been only a few weeks after I left town for school. I didn't know what to tell him without making it seem like I was holding another funeral, and I was worried about words because I got distracted thinking about the clown dog's little hat and how sad he looked in it sometimes. You know how touchy it can be, lurking about a place and looking like a stranger. And what if I asked how did it happen and only made Hopey feel worse? I didn't ask. I must have stood there for a whole minute trying to get my mouth around a sentence.

"He liked you, you know," Hopey said suddenly. "Perhaps you suppose that I was busy in the store, but I knew who his friends were. He was a pickety chooser, but he had exquisite taste in people. Didn't you think so?"

"I think he was a shy little fellow," I said.

"Yes, that he was."

"I'm sorry, Hopey. I came over especially to see him again." Now that I'd found my tongue, I expected he would break down or get very quiet, but he was just so calm. The clown dog used to follow me around, I wanted to say. We tried to make him talk. But we never hurt him.

"Since he liked you," said Hopey, "do you want to plumb the mystery of how he talked?"

I had to smile now. "It was a trick, wasn't it?"

"It was a tip-top trick," Hopey replied, "because nobody knew how it was done. Bet I shouldn't spoil it for you after all this. Should I? Do you want to know?"

"I think I ought to plumb the mystery, if he liked me, after all."

"He didn't like everyone," said Hopey. "But I believe he was exceptionally popular in the town."

"I guess he had to be," I said. "No other circus dog that I heard tell of has ever been the headline attraction."

"Well, he certainly was that. And he led a rich life. He was The Talking Dog of the World."

Hopey asked me about college then, and I told him, and after a while there was this natural space to say goodbye, so I left. Hopey forgot to tell me the trick and I forgot to remind him that I should know it, but I didn't think it was fitting to go back there just then, and before I was halfway home I was glad I didn't find out.

You'd think I would be unhappy to learn that the clown dog had died, but in a way that conversation with Hopey was the only nice thing that happened that whole vacation. My father was in a terrible mood the whole time, spitting out wisdoms like he was on a quota system and falling behind. He kept talking about the strike that everyone knew was going to happen, and finally, a few days before I was due to go back to school, he asked me didn't I think my place was here with the people I'd known all my life instead of at some college?

It seemed to me that the place to be during a strike was as far from it as possible, and college would do for that as well as any. And that's what I told him. So he said if I felt that way about it I might as well get going right now.

"Just like Bill," he said.

I was waiting for that. I didn't have anything prepared to say back to it, but I knew it was coming. I don't care. It was meant to hurt me, but it didn't, though I must admit it began to gnaw on me after a while . . . because I hoped it was true.

I really did.

"Just like Bill," he said, but he meant more like "Go vanish."

"Just like Bill"—because I was leaving him, too. Well, there's always a reason for something, and sometimes two. I never went back to Hanley, either; maybe Bill did, after I left, but I won't. I have heard those words often since in my mind, *Just like Bill*, in just the way he said it, looking so smug that he had doped it out at last, made the simple sum and added another wisdom to his collection. I could accept it if I had to, but the truth is I am no way like Bill, all told. I am not like anyone. Whenever someone asks who I am, I say, "Me," just like the clown dog did, because it cheers me to remember him, and to think back on how I could have heard the trick if I had wanted to, which is as close as anybody ought to get. That was a strange, but fine, animal.

Dog Problems

ANTONYA NELSON

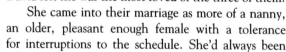

You always heard that dogs could smell fear; this dog could smell love. Whenever people were touching, embracing, kissing, she would be there, offering her front paw or nose for a similar embrace. She horned in on several moments a day. And there were times when David felt she was the most loved of the three of them.

She came into their marriage as more of a nanny, an older, pleasant enough female with a tolerance for interruptions to the schedule. She'd always been allowed to sleep in the bedroom, right next to Adrienne, but David, in their first year of marriage, had felt he wasn't having enough things his way. Not that Blanche bothered him at night: most nights he couldn't have said one way or the other whether she was in the room, but he wanted to be able to choose, and so he chose the backyard.

She went with only the mildest of sighs, aware, David was sure, of her own innocence in the situation. Every night Adrienne stood with her in the yard telling her good night. They'd play a halfhearted game of fetch, both of them conscious that though two had gone out, only one would return to the bedroom. Sometimes, in the black hours of the early morning, Adrienne would suddenly wake and, before David could move, be out the door, her robe swinging around her, worried about Blanche.

His family had had a dog while he was growing up, but he didn't have very clear memories of it. Sergio, he was named, a big drooling oily kind of dog who spent most of the time digging an enormous tunnel under the toolshed. The backyard stank of him. It was always someone's chore to feed him, a chore that was as odious and regimented as emptying the trash or plunging the bathtub.

On the other hand, Adrienne had gotten Blanche in high school, named her from *Streetcar* and taken her everywhere. She was a treat, not a chore. In college, Blanche smoked pot, had an ear pierced, sported a Magic Marker Picasso on her broad back. Blanche wore a bandana and rode in the bed of many boyfriends' trucks. She was a pal, a dog everyone loved, a dog who mostly seemed to take care of Adrienne instead of the other way around.

Blanche had meals twice a day, just like Adrienne. Breakfast was dog chow with powdered milk and warm water; dinner, dog chow with boullion and more warm water. She was eleven years old, her teeth could no longer chew hard food, and the rest of her system wouldn't digest canned. Adrienne mothered her, spoiled her even. Blanche had only to sound a single yip in the morning and Adrienne was out of bed and on her way. David, still foggy with sleep, heard them through the heat vents, the cabinets opening, then shutting, the food rattling into the shallow tin pan that was Blanche's plate, the water running until it matched the temperature of Adrienne's wrist, just like any other child's food. And then Adrienne made her own breakfast, coffee and a heaped spoonful of crunchy peanut butter. After that, they went outside to sit in the sun. Blanche retrieved the newspaper, every day except Sunday, when it was too large for her teeth to hold.

Later, if Adrienne remembered, she would come back to bed for a few moments, roll next to David in her robe, and nudge backwards into his rib cage and stomach. She called it invading the fetus. When they were first married, five years ago, she came back to bed every morning, sometimes more than once, eager for him to wake. Now, she seemed to prefer being alone. Well, not strictly: there was Blanche, of course.

Today, however, Adrienne graced his frontside with her backside, bumping up against his erection with the crease between her buttocks. "Howdy," she said. Then, "Come on, Blanche." The dog heaved herself onto the bed, always careful to stay on Adrienne's side of it, and curled into Adrienne. "Three spoons," Adrienne said, completely happy.

After she had left for work, David called in sick.

"You're not really sick," his partner, Robinson, said. "Not really, right?"

David was annoyed: he would have told Robinson the truth, that he was just down, tired of going to work, feeling a need to remain in his terry-cloth bathrobe—except Robinson tried to outguess him first. Instead, he said, "No, I woke up with the runs. Plus a toothache." Two inconsistent symptoms were better than two normally complementary ones, headache and fever, for example.

"Drag, man."

"Yeah."

"Okay. I'll be at the Stivaks', shoveling rocks, in case you get well later on."

The Stivaks. A whole swimming pool, cabaña, and archaic heat pump to landscape around. Also, the son had allergies. David and Robinson had already had to dig up a Palo Verde tree, its root system some sort of world's record. A kid with allergies had no business in the desert. "Fat chance," David said.

Robinson laughed. "You ain't sick."

"I got the runs, believe me."

"Okay, okay." Robinson would be looking up at the sky, thinking about heat, imagining the day over instead of beginning. "Bye." He said it like a sheep, *bah*.

They hung up. David, free for the day, took a tour of the house. Blanche followed, toenails clicking. She was half golden retriever, half husky, lumpy and round with fur like a bear rug. The white on her muzzle was creeping toward her ears, soon to take over her honey back and tail. She sat down on David's feet at Adrienne's dresser, a small reminder that he was not supposed to be opening Adrienne's little boxes, fingering her trinkets.

Adrienne collected and David threw away. That's how he would have categorized them today, looking at her junk. Though she was twenty-six, the filler in the boxes could have been a high school girl's. It was one notch higher than Cracker Jack fare, one notch lower than valuable. Stuff, and about twenty little boxes full. Everyone in her family was an accessory to this crime; stuff boxes were all they could ever think to give her, every Christmas and birthday rounding up a few more, every vacation they'd send one to her. Hawaii, Fiji, Japan . . . David jumped. Blanche barked out the window at two girls jogging by. They looked toward the noise, and David, without thinking about it, shied behind the curtains: caught at his wife's boxes.

"Hush!"

Blanche pulled her front paws off the windowsill and dropped to her haunches, obedient.

"Shake." She shook.

"Lie down." She lay.

"All the way down." She lowered her chin to the floor, eyes on him.

"Okay, Blanche, here's the clincher: fix me a Denver omelet." She continued watching him, not batting an eyelid, humorless, as David had always contended. They both perked up when they heard the front door open.

"Blanche?" Adrienne shouted. "Hey, Blanche." David considered hiding, spying on the two of them; what was it they did alone, anyway? But it was too late—there was Adrienne at the doorway. She grabbed her throat when she saw him.

"Oh, you scared me!" She stepped backwards. "What are you doing here?"

"I called in sick. I got the runs." It was a handy illness, amazingly vivid for being just one word.

She wrinkled her face. "Can I do anything?"

He shrugged. "Just don't feel like working."

She nodded, her heavy breathing moving her chest.

"What are *you* doing here?" he said.

"Well, on the way to the bus I saw this dog, a little black and brown dog, in the street. I mean, there was traffic . . ." She headed toward the kitchen, telling the story over her shoulder. David followed, just like Blanche. Adrienne was in the Tupperware cupboard, rummaging through the lids. ". . . I called to it, but it wouldn't come, so I turned my back and then it came. One of *those* kinds of dogs. Not like you, big Blanche." Blanche smiled, flattered.

Adrienne pulled out a custard keeper, then dove back in for its top. "So I had to coax it backwards, you know, pretending I wasn't interested, until it was out of the street. It could have been a stray

except it was wearing a collar. But it was *so* thin." She'd uncovered a
lid and was now filling the custard keeper with Blanche's dog pellets.
Blanche whisked her tail on the floor, licked her chops. "No, baby,
not for you." Abruptly the tail stopped. "So I turned around. I thought
I would just look in the paper real fast and see if there was a lost-and-
found ad, but then, you won't believe this, on the way home I saw a
notice on the telephone pole for a little black dog with tan markings.
I couldn't believe it." She shook her hair out of her face, snapped the
lid on, burped it. "326-0775. I'm going to call. Then I'm going to feed
it till whoever owns it gets there. What do you think?"

David blinked into the blank space the end of her story had made.
He thought that nothing like that would happen to him on his way to
work, that if he saw a dog he wouldn't think twice, but he said, "I
think that's a good idea."

Disappointed, mildly disappointed in his answer, but too happy in
her busyness to be disappointed for long, she picked up the phone,
singing, "Three two six oh seven seven five," and dialed. She hooked
the receiver between her shoulder and chin and pulled Blanche to her,
ruffling her face. "Oh, come *on*," she told the phone. Finally, she hung
up. She pursed her lips, shook the Tupperware of dog food, and then
calmed Blanche, who'd thought she'd seen a second chance at the
pellets. "Well, I'll feed it, anyway. And I'll just call later. But what if
it goes back in the street? Maybe I should bring it here and put it in
the pen. But what if it has rabies?" She worked through these while
David watched. "I'll call from work, tell them the dog is in this neighborhood and they can come get it. After all, it's lived this long without
my help." Satisfied, she kissed Blanche, then David, took her dog food,
and left.

The house was quiet again, nothing to indicate she'd been there
at all. David wished he had gone to work. He wished he had volunteered
to join her with the stray. He wished he had anything besides watching

"Donahue" to do. It was in this boredom that he decided to give Blanche a bath. She stank, as always, and Adrienne would appreciate it. Besides, bathing her would absolve some of his growing guilt at sticking Robinson with the Stivaks' rocks.

First he took his own shower, before the tub got filthy. Blanche lay on the bathmat, ignorant of what was coming, and tried to lick his legs when he got out. Apparently, Adrienne allowed this for, try as he might, he'd never been able to break the dog of it. True, her tongue felt nice, soft and caressing, but still, wasn't this how they gave you worms?

"Okay, Blanche. Bath time," he said. She crawled under the sink, trying to get small, trying to become heavier, trying to cling to the tile with her nails. "Out. Now." He pulled and she pulled. He almost gave up, almost felt sorry enough and respectful enough (after all, she was nearly eighty years old) to quit, but Adrienne would love to have her clean, would love him for cleaning her.

"Out!" he said, and yanked her onto the bathmat. He then slid the dog, on the mat, to the tub and hefted her in.

David had had an uncle who lived with David's family for as long as he could remember. Uncle Festes. Infestes, David and his brothers called him. Festes was a cheerful, doddering, mostly harmless alcoholic who took great pains to hide his affliction from the family. They all knew anyway. He would come into the kitchen after a night on the town and say, regretfully, apologetically, shaking his head sorrowfully, "Bottle problems." That was it.

If David's one sister, Leticia, whose job it was to fix breakfast, should burn something, which happened frequently, Festes would say, "Toast problems," and shake his head, sadly but without anger. What could you do? he seemed to say. Some nights, because there were too few beds and not nearly enough space to hold them all, they would fight. There were "P.M. problems."

David hadn't thought of his Uncle Festes in a long time. While scrubbing Blanche's hand-sized paws, he thought *dog problems.* Adrienne had gone out and found one, and here he was with his own. It was a good approach, a basically safe one. Shrug your shoulders and take the problem by the hand.

He hadn't dressed after his shower, figuring, correctly, that he would only have to change again after a round with Blanche in the tub. They both rested leaning against the wet porcelain in their respective corners, waiting for the bell that would send them back to the fight. Blanche threatened to shake her wet fur, and David responded by lifting the squeeze bottle of flea shampoo to her nose. There was something satisfyingly masculine about wrestling naked with a wet dog. David could get his teeth into this, he thought. For her part, Blanche kept her tail out of the water, staring straight ahead at the hot and cold faucets and blinking like a tortured prisoner when he rinsed.

David left the bathroom as Blanche stepped out; matron from the tub, she could attend to her drying off by herself. He put his bathrobe back on, beginning to believe he did have the runs. And a toothache, he reminded himself, reaching for his jaw. He mixed a Bloody Mary and opened the bathroom door.

Blanche stood dripping on the bathmat. She hadn't shaken, and that alarmed David. He set down his drink, which then fell over. The glass rolled on the carpet of the hallway, the cubes slid on the tile of the bathroom floor. The Bloody Mary formed a stain. Blanche trembled, then ceased, then trembled again, her eyes at David's waist, not accusing, not forgiving.

"Shake, buddy." David stepped into the humid room and pulled several towels from the racks, draping them over her. She vibrated beneath his palms. Drool formed a long strand from the corner of her mouth to the floor. "Oh, Christ," David said. "Oh, Christ. Come on, come on." He'd decided to take her outside in the sun, warm her up, and dry her off. A bath wouldn't kill her, he told himself, luring her step by wet step through the house and out the back door, a bath wouldn't kill her.

She stood as before, this time on the redwood deck David and Robinson had built in an off-week. Despite the sun, her back and legs quivered, her tail drooped. What had happened in the five minutes it had taken to pull on his robe and mix a drink? "Fuck," he said. "Come on Blanche, pal, shape up." The dog wouldn't even meet his eyes. He would have to call Adrienne. The thought of calling her was worse than the sight of the dog before him, two strands of drool now connecting her with the deck.

He dragged the phone onto the porch and dialed, twice incorrectly. Blanche didn't listen as he told her help was on the way, soon Adrienne would be there. But Adrienne hadn't come in yet; her boss was wondering, herself, where she could be. For a second, David wondered: where was Adrienne anyway? Then he remembered the stray. Then Blanche. He said, "Tell her to call me. It's an emergency at home. Dog problems."

"Oh dear," said her boss. "Not Blanche?"

David resented this: she knew the dog? He'd never even met Adrienne's boss, and yet here she was, familiar with their dog. He wanted to ask if she knew his name as well. "Yeah," he said, "Blanche. Maybe you can tell me what to do. She's all quivery . . ."

"No, no, I don't know a thing about animals. I rely on the veterinarian, I'm afraid."

"Well, tell Adrienne to call."

Blanche had knelt, all four legs buckled, as if suspended in mid-jump. She panted. She looked like she was doing a push-up, like she was a lizard.

* * *

At the vet's, a thousand things occurred to him, most of them having to do with Adrienne's blaming him for what had happened to her dog, whatever that would be. The vet, instead of escorting the two of them into a cubicle, had called her assistant and taken Blanche to the back, leaving David in the waiting room, pacing like an expectant father in a B movie. Now he played out a few scenarios: Blanche died, Adrienne wept and wept and never recovered. David would then discover, as he probably subconsciously had known all along, that she loved the dog more than him. And why not? She'd had her longer, grown up with her, confided to her all her secrets. Another scenario: Blanche died and David disappeared, caught the next train out, leaving the dog corpse with the vet and Adrienne with a mystery.

David stood before a colorful cartoon poster. It told how to brush a dog's teeth, beginning with a paper towel or soft cloth and just rubbing, eventually moving up to toothpaste and a soft-bristled brush, graduating into meat-flavored paste you could order, see below. David snorted. He wondered how Adrienne would read this: funny or serious?

From the back he heard Blanche yelp. This could be good or bad. Her bark aroused in him a sudden sympathy; she wasn't such a bad dog, really. It was just Adrienne's fixation on her that bothered David. Under any other circumstances she would have been a fine animal, good company and smart to boot. She did exactly what Adrienne said, always. If Adrienne were here now, in fact, he was willing to bet she could command Blanche to be well and the dog would obey.

David's stomach rumbled. He looked at his watch: 1:30. The time surprised him, though which way he could not say. Did it feel earlier? Later? He was hungry, his diarrhea and bad tooth long forgotten. He peered around the corner of the front desk and called out the vet's name. Nothing. He checked his watch again. Still 1:30. He slipped out the door.

* * *

Taco Tico would give him diarrhea, he decided, and that would be justice. He ate his burritos, sauce oozing down his chin. He thought about Adrienne's million pictures of Blanche, every stage of the way. First, Blanche changed the most, grew through puppyhood while Adrienne stayed the same, her high school hair stringy and close to her head. Then Blanche stayed the same for a few years while Adrienne changed, went from chubby to thin, then settled for medium, her hair growing longer, getting stringier, then shrinking against her head, getting permed, then growing into medium also. There was a picture with the two of them in earrings, Adrienne both sides, Blanche only one. For a while they both stayed about the same. Then Blanche got grayer, chunkier, shorter, if that was possible. Her tongue hung out more and her eyes got wider. Her face turned white. Her legs bowed. She looked a little desperate. Adrienne remained tall, medium, smiling, hair and eyes the same: young, basically.

David dropped his tray into the trashcan accidentally and left it there.

Back at the vet's, nothing had changed. He considered tapping the bell on the desk, then thought he'd rather not know, really, if something had changed. Eventually the doctor emerged, pulling a rubber glove from her hand as if she were a real doctor. David felt scorn, then corrected himself. She *was* a real doctor. Even vets wore gloves. He waited for her to speak.

"We'll keep her overnight and see what we can do. She's had a stroke."

David drove home, Blanche's leash beside him on the front seat. If Adrienne had come home while he was gone, she would have put two and two together: spilled drink, bathroom a wreck, car gone, dog gone. But she wasn't there, the mess was still intact. He cleaned up, wiping the tub smooth, washing Blanche's honey hairs and sand down the drain, throwing all the towels in the machine after he soaked Bloody Mary out of the carpet with them. The phone rang; David's heart leaped over a few beats.

"Hey, how's the boy?" It was Robinson, calling from the Stivaks' pool house phone.

"I'm all right. But my wife's dog had a stroke." David undressed while they talked, wanting to get back to his bathrobe for some reason.

"I thought that was a human problem."

Human problems, David thought. "Nope. It can be a dog problem, too."

"Well," Robinson said, then didn't follow up.

"I'll see you tomorrow, for sure," David said. "I know I'll be better."

"Okay. Sorry about your dog, man."

"Yeah."

"Bah."

When he heard Adrienne's key in the lock, he realized he shouldn't be in his bathrobe. How would she believe he'd taken the dog to the vet if he was wearing his bathrobe? He grabbed his clothes from the hamper and ran into the bathroom just as she called for Blanche.

At four-thirty they both sat in the familiar waiting room, Adrienne's fingers dug into David's wrist. There was no word on Blanche. The clinic was supposed to close at six, but the doctor would stay with Blanche all night if necessary. David had listened without really believing it: the vet would stay all night for the dog. It didn't surprise Adrienne a bit.

"What happened to the stray?" he asked, to distract her.

She was staring at the toothpaste poster, uncomprehending. "Oh, it's really pretty interesting," she said, not interested at all. Her eyes were miserable from crying, her face contorted. She was ugly, David thought briefly.

"Tell me," he insisted.

She took in a lungful of air. "Well, I found the dog again, but he was running down this alley. I followed him and he ran into this yard. I didn't want to go in, you know, in case somebody was home, but . . ."

"Go on."

"So I squatted down and I called him, tempting him with dog food." She stopped to calm her tears. Blanche's dog food. David patted her with his free hand. "But he wouldn't come, so I threw some to him. He ate it and I threw more, each time getting it closer and closer to me. Then this cat showed up, this huge cat, bigger than the dog, and she started eating the dog food. You should have seen this yard. I couldn't believe it. What a mess, junk everywhere, toys, wood, a red wagon full of limes: that was the weirdest thing—that wagon full of limes." She snuffled. From one of the cubicles an old woman and man emerged, the woman carrying a black tom, his fur mangled.

"Oh Spike, Spike, Spike," she cooed while the man looked over her shoulder, patting the cat's ridged ear.

The man smiled at them. "If you can't have kids, you have pets," he explained. They paid the receptionist, who would not look David in the eyes.

"So there's the cat and the dog in the yard," David prompted, "with the wagon."

Adrienne watched the couple. "They're so old," she said when they left. "And they love that cat." She sighed, her tears starting up again.

"Come on, Ade, what about the stray?"

"Well . . ." She took a deep breath, enough to finish off the story. "The surprising thing is that the dog and cat got along. So I thought, 'He lives here. He found his way home and I was just following when it happened.' By then I'd come farther into the yard. I knocked on the door and nobody answered, which made sense, because nobody had answered when I called on the phone either, so I figured here he was, home. There was even a leash tied around the tree, and an empty dog food bowl." She stopped.

"Hmm," David said. An empty dog food bowl, he thought.

"So. So I tied him to his leash, left him the rest of Blanche's food, and walked on to work. The end, I'm thinking. I'm thinking, while I'm walking, what a good deed I've done, how I hoped if anybody ever found Blanche out loose that they'd bring her some food and leave her back in her yard with her cat. If she had a cat."

David laughed, involuntarily. He reached around Adrienne. It occurred to him that if Blanche died he would have a chance, a real chance, at becoming the thing that Adrienne loved most. The thought raced through his blood.

"And I was also thinking how you would like it if I helped this dog, you know? I was thinking about that poem, 'A thing of beauty is a joy' and so on, I don't know why. It doesn't make much . . ." She lifted her toes off the floor, breathed wetly. "Sense. I was thinking helping was a thing of beauty, but it was conscious, which kind of ruins it maybe . . . Anyway," Adrienne went on, stronger. "Here's part one of the weird stuff. I call this number from work. Three two six . . . and so on, and this German guy answers. Very old, deaf practically. I say, 'You lost a dog,' and he says, 'Yes?' and I go, 'Well, I tied it up outside your house.' He says nothing. Then he says, 'The voman vill be happy.' I go, 'What?' He goes, 'The voman next door vill be happy.' Turns out they live in a duplex, she doesn't have a phone. Well, I ask him what's his address, and it's the wrong one. It's like half a mile from where I tied the dog up."

"Really?" The plot thickened.

"Really. So I tell why I tied his neighbor's dog up at the wrong house, explaining about the cat and the tree, but who knows what he's understanding, and then I give him the address of the house where the dog is tied up. He can go over there himself and get it, I figure. 2015

East 8th, I tell him. Then I say I'll call back later. Okay, so that's the end of it. I forget the whole thing and work. I was late so I have a lot to catch up on . . ."

"I called you."

"Yeah?"

"She didn't tell you?"

"She wasn't there when I got there. Early lunch. You called about Blanche?" she said.

"Uh huh."

"Oh."

"Go on. What happened next?"

"Anyway, so I forgot all about it until after work. Since it was on the way, I decided I'd stop by and see what was up with the dog. Well, I gave that German man the wrong address—it was on *7th* Street, not 8th. 2015 *7th*. God, I thought, what is he going to think? He probably went to the wrong backyard and everything. So I went up to this house, the right house, and the front door was open. Somebody was home. And I wondered what they thought about that dog tied to their tree, you know? I worried that maybe they'd called the pound or something. I looked through the screen and there was this girl, maybe twelve, sitting in a swivel chair staring at the wall. I swear to God, there was nothing around her, nothing she could have been doing. Just staring at the wall." Adrienne sniffed.

"Staring at the wall . . ." David coached.

"I knocked. She kind of came to, really spacy. I told her the whole thing, you know. 'You don't know me, but . . .' She said, 'Just a minute. Let me go see if there's a dog there.' She left me on the porch and went out the back. Pretty soon she returns. She says, I swear to God, 'I think that's our Paco.' I say, 'That's *your* dog?' She says, get this, 'I think so. I think that's Paco. Come on in and I'll look again.' So I come into this house, you wouldn't believe it. Junky, but like it's still being constructed, pieces of the walls are missing, a globe on the table, a broken telephone, and dog bowls, which kind of reassures me. I go into the kitchen and out the back door. She's squatted on the ground, holding up the dog's paw—he's still there, tied to the tree, the cat's still walking around—and the girl's checking him out. 'Yeah, I'm pretty sure this is Paco.' What a case, I'm thinking, doesn't know her own dog. Well, I leave my phone number and name. What else can I do? The dog looks happy enough. She says her mom will call me. I'm starting to figure that maybe it *is* the same dog, but with two different owners or something. Maybe they haven't had it long enough to remember what it looks like . . ."

The front bell rang, a boy and his cat came in. The receptionist hustled them into the cubicle the old man and woman had come from. The cat cubicle, David thought. It was nearly closing time.

"What then?" David prompted, gently.

"As I'm walking out the door, she says, 'This has been a strange day. All day long strange things have been happening.' "

"Whoa," David said. Adrienne had cheered a little in the telling, but then the vet came out of the other cubicle, the dog cubicle. She motioned with her finger for Adrienne, who recognized the woman's expression, just as David had. Blanche had died.

They drove home the long way, avoiding the rush hour traffic of main thoroughfares. Adrienne cried and cried; David's eyes teared in response. The vet wouldn't let Adrienne take Blanche home. There was some law about city burials.

". . . and I never let her have puppies, I got her spayed so early on . . ." She cried harder, confessing other non-sins.

"Let's drive by that stray's house," David suggested. "What'd you say, 8th Street?"

"7th." She wiped her nose on her arm. "Oh, David, I've had her so long."

"I know," he said, hoping in some vague way that he did.

They pulled into the alley. Adrienne pointed out the notice on the phone pole: "Missing dog, small, black with tan markings, red collar. Reward. 326-0775."

"This house," she said, then, "No, one more." A woman with a red bathing cap was emptying her trash across the alley, watching them suspiciously. "This is it," Adrienne said. She had to lean over David to look.

In the backyard, sure enough, was the dog, sitting under a tree, tail curled around him, looking content. Even if he did have another home, he seemed perfectly happy at this one. There were no lights on inside, though a few other lights had gone on next door. Beside the house, with her back to them, seated a few feet from the red wagon full of limes, was a woman. She was playing a blue accordion.

They lay in bed, dinner foregone. Adrienne was beyond crying. She said nothing, clung to David and shivered, then ceased, the way Blanche had earlier. He hadn't told her about the bath (how could that be the cause, he worried, endlessly, how could that possibly be the cause?), hadn't told her he wasn't really sick. He ran his tongue over a tooth that really had begun hurting; inside, he felt loose enough to have the real runs.

"I won't be able to sleep," Adrienne had said, but eventually she did, still clinging to David.

In his dreams, when he finally slept, he saw Blanche, outside for her nightly stool. She circled, as was her habit, for a moment in the corner of the yard, her designated area. She cast a sad but resigned eye at David, who always watched when he took her out, curious. Her legs fanned, her honey-colored fur pale in the dark yard, she lifted her head. The expression on her face had always struck him as oddly peaceful—odd, because it was obvious that she was in pain.

David thought now, dreaming and yet close to waking, that he had willed her death, that he had killed her in order to save himself. He saw Adrienne as a vessel, capable of holding only a limited amount of love. Blanche had syphoned off her share and now it was his turn. He held his wife in his arms, sure that she radiated sufficient heat for the two of them.

Keats

ELIZABETH TALLENT

We live on the money from a movie that never got made. Dennis's memories of L.A.—palm trees like enormous decaying twigs; the liquid sapphire of swimming pools; hamburgers eaten in the cushioned depths of a producer's Cadillac—have narrowed, I think, throughout three years of wistful frugality. It was all right, he told me once, while he was still a bachelor.

"What are you now?" I asked.

"I mean," he said, "while I was still living alone."

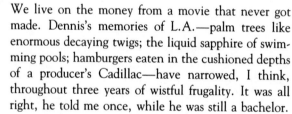

His script was about a feral child. Oddly, that year there was another film made about a feral child; it got excellent reviews. "It looks as if we've been beaten to the punch," his producer told him, the night of the hamburgers. He was stroking the tomcat that went with him everywhere, in the Cadillac. "No one leaves L.A. with their illusions intact," he said. The cat licked the lid of the Styrofoam hamburger box until it was quite clean. There was an unhealed cut, the depth of a dime, in his left ear.

Still, with the money he'd made, Dennis bought this house with its steep roof and shadowed stairways; from a narrow window at one end of the attic you can see part of the Golden Gate Bridge. More exactly, you can see a single fawn-colored upright, and, rarely, an arc of shining cable. In the back of the house there is a porch with wide panels of rusting screens. Some of the screens are torn, and swallows fly in and out. We are lucky to have this house, Dennis says, because it is impossible to buy in this neighborhood anymore. It was once a banker's summer house—the downstairs rooms are small, the carpentry neat and curiously spare, although one of the bannisters ends in the whorled petals of a rose. The plaster of the ceilings is flawed in places because of a small earthquake a decade ago. Inside the kitchen cupboard is tacked a pamphlet: "Plan Your Earthquake: Or How to Reduce Seismic Hazards." On the dusty shelves you find: a flyswatter so ancient its mesh has a burnished, coppery glint; a plastic Boy Scouts of America flashlight with a cracked lens; several onions with flaking golden skins, threaded with green shoots; nineteen cans of Little Friskies cat food, in various flavors; a tin of Star Olive Oil; a can of Band-Aids; a bottle of Nature's Blend Vitamin C in 1000 mg. tables, the label showing a remote yellow sun. If these are earthquake preparations, it is hard to decipher Dennis's logic. The vitamin C, at least, seems brave.

Before I came, he lived alone in this house for two years. The first time he left me by myself, I went through each of the empty rooms, staring at the cracks in the plaster, opening the drawers of the dressers.

Before he lived alone, he was married. Opening a closet in one of the downstairs bedrooms, I found perhaps fifty pairs of shoes arranged on the floor, each pair placed toe to toe: espadrilles, ballet shoes, slippers, Dr. Scholl's remedial sandals. The shoes were as scrupulously aligned as Muslims facing Mecca; many of them had the sort of spindly heels that suit only very long-legged and beautiful women. I stared at the shoes for a long time. Something, perhaps a mouse, had woven a small nest in the injured fabric of a red Adidas.

Sometimes Dennis tells me that we have to begin to watch our money. "Even if it means cutting some corners," he says. I am not certain which corners he means. It is true that I left my husband for him, and that I am spending a small fortune in long-distance telephone calls to Cheyenne, but that is because of Keats.

"I could tell you were going to leave me," my husband says. "You hated Cheyenne, didn't you? You were never really happy after we left Chicago."

"I didn't hate Cheyenne."

"I knew you'd leave," he says. "I just didn't know it would be so soon."

"It wasn't soon enough to keep us from doing a lot of damage to each other."

"Sometimes you are so transparent, Holly," he says. "You really want me to think this is somehow my fault."

"I don't want you to think it's your fault—"

"I can tell you one thing," he says.

I am eating a slice of Anjou pear at Dennis's kitchen table. The kitchen table is painted black; the black is thick as lacquer, and in places it has chipped away, showing the white paint beneath. One half of the pear is lying in a saucer near my elbow. I cradle the telephone receiver between my shoulder and jaw. "What thing is that?"

"Keats is definitely not negotiable."

A small knife rests against the saucer. Along the blade there is a sliver of wet pear, so thin it is nearly invisible, turning dark along one grainy edge. "John Keats is my dog, too," I whisper.

"You're the one who left him," my husband says. "You've been gone nearly three months now. Why are you whispering?"

"I was the one who took him to get his vaccinations."

"I know you did," he says. "When he was a puppy."

"Not only when he was a puppy," I say. "Without me, Keats would never have gotten his parvo virus shots in time, this spring."

"Oh," my husband says. "Was it only spring?"

There is a pause. I imagine wind blowing against creaking telephone wires, and the thick blue glass of the insulators on top of the slanting poles along a highway somewhere in Wyoming. "I held Keats," I say. "The needle was nearly as long as my finger. The vet had awkward hands, and he was humming to himself. Keats's ears were folded back against the nape of his neck."

"Never a good sign," he says.

"I put one arm around his chest and held him as hard as I could. His heart was thumping."

"I can barely hear you," my husband says.

I shift the telephone receiver to my other shoulder, turning in the straight-backed wooden chair. Dennis's orange tomcat watches me from the windowsill. I am wearing only a black Danskin swimming suit and one wooden clog. The other wooden clog is in the attic, at the foot of the mattress where Dennis has fallen asleep. I am whispering because Dennis is an insomniac. When I woke this morning, he said, "I could sleep like that when I was twenty-four." "Like what?" I said. He is thirty-eight. "Like a stone," he said. When I laughed, he kissed me, wetting my upper lip. "Would you like to go for espresso, Princess?" I said I would. In the small cafe, he leaned over the rickety table, smoothing the sports pages of the San Francisco *Chronicle*, holding my hand. Sometimes he toyed with the fingers, bending or straightening them. A red-haired waitress poured espresso, black as ink.

"The absence of baseball is boring, but not as painful as I would have thought," he said. "Did you know I was once the Harvard short-stop?"

"No," I said. "You were?"

"Sure," he said.

After we came home from the cafe, I was surprised to find he wanted to make love; after we made love, I was startled when he put one arm across his eyes and fell immediately asleep. In the cafe, he had had two cups of espresso, each with five spoonfuls of sugar. I listened to his breathing, which was light and even, his eyelashes dark against his shadowed cheekbone. "I didn't even know you could catch," I whispered. The planks of the floor creaked below my bare feet. I was afraid to risk even the small wooden *tock* the clog would have made when I fished it from below the fallen quilt.

The tomcat stares. His eyes are large, light green with darker rims. There are ash-colored flecks within the iris. Dennis believes that these flecks correspond to battle wounds.

"You know what I think about California as a place for dogs," my husband says.

"No."

"I think Wyoming is heaven for a dog, compared with California."

"That's not true."

"I know you're in the midst of a Mediterranean fruit fly crisis."

"That's not even here. That's in a different county."

"They're probably raining chemicals on your roof at this very moment," he says. "They like to use helicopters in heavy urban areas, right? Why would I send my dog into a second defoliation?"

"Listen. I can hold the telephone out the window. You can hear for yourself that there are no helicopters." Luke was a photographer in Vietnam; sometimes, when he is startled, his fingers go quickly to his chest, as if to the lens cap of an invisible Nikon. Now he is working for a newspaper in Cheyenne, photographing the waist-high wheat in the fields, various high-school beauty queens, and any deer that wander into the city, dazzled by the neon signs above the bars and the lights of the traffic. The old yellow house he chose for us to live in—we had moved rather hastily from Chicago, so that he could take advantage of the newspaper's offer—was set in the plains, far out in the wheatfields. It was a twenty-minute drive into Cheyenne. Near the house there was a steep bank, formed by the intersection of two irrigation ditches, where I would sit in the cattle-tamped grass with Keats, stroking his back and reading David Mamet plays.

"All I really need is a chance to be with Keats for a while," I say.

"Come home, then, if that's what you need."

"I can't, Luke."

"You can't?"

"I can't. You know I can't."

I close my eyes. The telephone is cool against my cheekbone. Suddenly I realize I am no longer whispering.

"How much does Keats really need?" I say. "There are sticks to throw in California. I can buy him organic dogfood. We even have a lawn."

"I don't want to hear about anything you have."

"It's not very big," I say, thinking this will please him.

"Keats needs room to run," he says.

For the second time, we fall abruptly silent.

"Last night I was scratching Keats on the belly," he says. "We were watching *Casablanca*."

"You've seen *Casablanca* fifteen times," I say. "You must know it by heart."

"I like the things I know by heart," he says.

The tom shifts his weight so that his toes rest more precisely on the edge of the sill.

"I found something below his rib cage, below that spot which is shaped like Baja," Luke says. "You know the one I mean?" Keats is a Dalmatian, leggy and slender, with a wide forehead and a dry pink curve of tongue that you glimpse between his incisors when he yawns; even the delicately striated roof of his mouth is marked with black spots. The night we brought him home Luke and I gave him a bath. Keats was round-eyed with apprehension, and his slick skin smelled of the straw in the kennel. His claws made a light nicking sound, skidding against the curved porcelain sides of the tub. I held him between my knees while Luke dried him with the hair dryer. He was no larger than a housecat, and shivered violently. All three of us were awkward with one another, until Keats fell asleep with his spine in a beautiful arc, the vertebrae showing clearly, his nose tucked beneath one paw. Luke and I stayed awake for a long while, watching him breathe. Some of his spots were like small islands, others like petals, others the size of nickels, perfectly round.

Now the tomcat lifts one paw, running his tongue down the bone of the foreleg. He never takes his eyes from me.

"I know," I say.

"I found a sort of lump the size of a thimble, and it nearly made my heart stop. I thought Keats had cancer of the stomach. I probed around with my fingers, and it was only a wad of bubblegum stuck in his fur."

The tom gives me a steady, critical stare.

"What is that supposed to prove?" I say.

"It proves I could get very upset if I thought anything was wrong with Keats," Luke says.

"No," I say. "I was talking to a cat."

"A cat?" he says. "There's a cat there?"

"Two cats."

"How can you even talk to me about bringing Keats there?" Luke says. "He would *hate* it."

With one fingernail, I scratch at the black paint of the table. The tom's ear swivel forward at the sound. I wonder silently whether Dennis is still asleep or not.

"Holly," Luke says. "I can't talk anymore right now. A woman is coming to clean the house."

"The house? Why does the house need cleaning?"

"I threw a little party," he says. "The police came. There are ashes in the Oriental rugs."

"The police came?"

"Only two of them," Luke says. "The older one admired Keats tremendously. He threw Keats's old green tennis ball for him, and Keats caught it in the air. They didn't stay for very long. They just asked us to turn down the George Jones." He inhales. "Did you know I started smoking again?"

"Oh, Luke," I say. "You did?"

"I did. My only hope is that the capillaries have more or less rejuvenated by now. It seems unlikely, though. Do you know the odd thing about it, Holly? Now it feels as if I had never quit smoking at all."

"Did you know you can get specially constructed boxes for dogs on certain flights?" I say. "No one even has to touch him."

"When I think about it at all," Luke says, "I imagine him freezing in a dark corner that smells of oil and ozone. I can barely stand that long a flight myself, and I always ask for a window."

"If you feel like that, the vet could give him some sort of gentle tranquilizer."

"You know he doesn't trust vets," Luke says. "I really don't want to put him through that trauma right now."

I shake my head silently, as if Luke could see.

"Parvo virus," he says. "Wasn't that the one where all the dogs died so mysteriously?"

"Yes."

"Mysteriously fast?" he says. In the long-distance silence that follows, I can hear clearly the strike of a match.

I have climbed the long flight of stairs to the attic. The attic is white, with long white exposed beams from which hang crimson and gold and black paper kites. The kites turn slowly on their lengths of string; the struts are of bamboo, the tails of rags. In some of the rags you can still recognize a woman's stocking, or the sleeves or rounded collar of a dress. "Clara cannibalized things," Dennis told me once. His ex-wife's name is Clara Wu; she is tall and Chinese. She left Dennis to live with an architect in Milan. Perhaps fifty of her paintings—nearly identical Oreo cookies, two feet in diameter, on white or indigo backgrounds—are stacked face-forward in the rear of a downstairs closet. The paintings still smell of linen and oil, although in places the canvas is beginning to sag from the light wooden frames. Dennis told me once in a tone of self-reproach that he ought to have known something was going wrong in the marriage: in the last few months they were together, she began painting an arrowroot biscuit a neighbor's child had left on their kitchen counter. Her brushstrokes were small and preoccupied; she complained of the unfamiliar textures of the light. "She was a forager," Dennis said. The architect is rich.

Dennis opens his eyes and stares at me. His second cat—a tortoiseshell female with a certain rueful prowess in turning her round skull against the bone of your ankle, and dark-yellow eyes—observes me from the end of the mattress. Some nights, she tries to sleep on Dennis's chest. Her weight wakes him with a thrust that carries his shoulders from the bed, fists clenched; Dennis's father died of angina, knee-deep in a stream, while panning for gold. One night Dennis showed me the gold his father had sifted from the stream, a packet of fine grains that stuck to the lines in the palm of his hand. "It was a tourist trap in the Sierras," Dennis said. "It cost him fifteen dollars. For what? For this. Not even enough to fill a tooth." He poured the grains back into the plastic bag, and wound the rubber band around it tightly. His father had been with a twenty-four-year-old woman, in the stream.

"You've been talking to him again?" he says. He lifts his hands, palms outward, thumbs touching. From the beginning, he has taken a series of imaginary movies of me—rising from the bathtub, eating a croissant, inserting my contact lenses.

"He wanted me to know he's keeping Keats."

"He can't tell you that," Dennis says. "He has no right." He sits up in bed, a long-legged man, unshaven.

"Why can't he?" I am willing to be reassured. Suddenly I wish Dennis would put his arms around me. He scratches his chin thoughtfully. "Isn't possession nine-tenths of the law?" I say.

"Not in California," he says. "You ought to know that by now. You ran away from home."

"It's different in Wyoming," I say. "It's very pure. If the dog lives in your house, it's your dog. And it was always Luke's house."

"You couldn't have helped that," Dennis says. "It's difficult for a Chekhovian actress to find work in Wyoming. Stay like that. The light's in your hair. This could be the opening shot, you know? With the credits running down the Matisse poster over your left shoulder."

I shake my head. "You ruined it," he says. "Holly, I can't understand why you two can't work out something a little more realistic. It's not as if there are huge sums of money involved, or dramatic changes of fortune. You left him three months ago. He keeps his Fiat, you get your tatami mats sent through UPS. Almost the only thing you have to agree on is the dog." When I am silent, he kisses my shoulder. "I know it's not exactly a divorce settlement," he says. "More of a predivorce contract, but it would prove you had been doing some serious thinking in the right direction."

"I hate the word 'contract.' "

"I can tell," he says. "What else did you talk about?"

"Not very much. Smoking."

"Smoking? I thought neither of you smoked."

"He used to, when we first met. I think he does again, now."

He lifts my wrist. "You're getting bony," he says. "You can't keep living on pears and espresso. Men won't follow you through the streets any longer."

"Is it bony?" I stare at my own wrist, and his dark chin.

"So Keats is the point of the disagreement," Dennis says. "Isn't that so? And he ought to let you have Keats, because Keats is your dog. Isn't that so? You always talk as if Keats is your dog."

"He is," I say. "The distinctions sometimes blur."

"Not unless you let them blur."

"You've only lived with cats. It's different. Cats are much cooler. They don't mix things around, or tamper with the evidence."

He turns his face away and scrapes his jaw along the back of his hand, as if to gauge the extent of his need for a shave. "I suppose you could steal Keats."

"I thought of that," I say. "I could drive up in a disguise and hide him in the pickup. Luke doesn't know you have a pickup. I could smuggle Keats out of Wyoming."

"I'll come with you," Dennis says. "We can be outlaws together." I scratch my knee; he is watching.

"I think there must be fleas," I say.

"In my house?" he says. "There's no way."

"They could come in on the cats."

"I doubt it," he says. I hold my knee up for him to see—the swelling is oval beneath a fan of small blond hairs. In the center there is the innocent tea-colored crystal of a newly formed scab.

. . .

Sometimes, out of the corner of my eye, I imagine that I see Keats. It can happen to me anywhere. Once, on University, I thought I saw the quick forward tilt of his shoulders, dodging a Volkswagen van, but it was only a small black child, carrying a flute, who had crossed against the light. Another time, at the kitchen table, I thought I felt the rasp of his paw on my shin; it was Dennis, bending to retrieve a chopstick. When I couldn't eat the rest of my food, he put his arms around me. "What's wrong?" he said softly. "What is it? Don't you like sushi, Princess?"

Dennis and I met in a hallway at the Cinematographer's Festival. Luke had come at the suggestion of his editor, who wished, he said, to explore the possibilities of videotape. Inside the darkened auditorium, they were showing a Charlie Chaplin film I had seen before. When I whispered this to Luke, he only nodded. "I want to stay," he said. "Don't worry, I'll find you." Dennis was in the hallway, leaning against the wall. When he saw me, he lifted his hands and framed an oblong of air. "Those eyes," he said. I was blinking, still making the transition from darkness to fluorescent light; he had caught me off guard.

"What eyes?"

"Your eyes," he said. "You ought to be in *The Cherry Orchard*. Not here. Anywhere but here."

"I've been in *The Cherry Orchard*."

"Pure intuition," he said. "It goes with my great sense of timing. Would you like to go for quiche? There's a quiche bar down the street, exclusively patronized by gay men wearing chaps."

"I can't," I said. "I'm waiting for someone." I sounded oddly apologetic.

"Would you like a cup of coffee, then? There's a machine down the hall." The coffee was darkly bitter; the cream came from the machine in a sudden, magical dollop. "Do you like San Francisco?" Dennis asked. "Have you walked across the bridge yet?"

"No."

"It's beautiful. You've got to do it," Dennis said. "It makes you believe in the existence of angels."

"Why?"

"I don't know, exactly," he said. "Something about the combination of great height and subtlety, or even the fine line between awe and vertigo. It's an odd bridge. Jim Jones once held a suicide-prevention rally on it, and he ended by saying, 'I can sort of see why people do it.' "

"Can you?"

"Can I what?"

"See why people do it?"

"No," he said. "I just think it's a great bridge." We stood talking, keeping our voices low. When Luke emerged from the auditorium, his hands in his pockets, we were still in the hallway, sitting cross-legged on the floor against a wall. Dennis had pulled a quarter from my ear, touching the lobe lightly, to demonstrate his sleight-of-hand. "Are you dazzled?" he said. Luke was frowning as I stood to leave. Dennis framed the air again. I shook my head abruptly. "You moved," Dennis accused.

"That's nothing new," Luke said. "She always moves. She makes a terrible subject." They stared at each other. Late that night, in the hotel room, Luke whispered against my cheek. "I thought that guy liked you. I thought that you liked *him*." When I did not answer, he turned away and lay on his back, staring at the ceiling. "We can do Chinatown tomorrow, if you want to," he said.

"I've seen Chinatown," I said.

"You know what?" he said. "I thought that movie would go on forever."

*　*　*

It is Saturday, nearly a week since I talked to Luke; it is raining lightly, and a bamboo rake lies where it has fallen in the misty yard. I stare at it through the kitchen window. Dennis has gone to play basketball, lacing his high-tops with care.

"Holly?" Luke says. He can tell it is me, even before I say anything, by the blur of the static. "Keats and I were just out hunting rabbits. I can barely keep up with him. Did you know I've been smoking nearly two packs a day?"

"Isn't that dangerous?" I say. "How could I have known that?"

"It's been so long since you telephoned," he says. "I thought you would hear a sort of roughening in my voice. I could get to sound like Bogart in *To Have and Have Not*, and it would win you back." He exhales slowly. "We didn't catch any rabbits, you know."

"Oh."

"That's like you, to say 'Oh,' " he says. "I know you'd hate it if Keats ever caught a rabbit."

"I wouldn't hate it. I would just be afraid he'd get bitten."

"He won't get bitten. He did go after a fox late last night, though. We were driving on the highway about an hour north of the house, in the grasslands, and there was a fox crouching over a dead rabbit on the shoulder of the road. You could see the reflection of the headlights in the fox's eyes. Keats took off across a field after him."

"Did he catch him?"

"He didn't really get anywhere near, as far as I could tell," Luke says. "The fox was beautiful, with black catlike feet and big ears. I've never been so close to one before. He took off like a shot."

"Keats came back?"

"After he'd been gone about an hour. There was a full moon, so I just sat on my jacket near the truck and waited for him. When he came back he laid down on the ground and panted until his tongue was dripping. After we got to the house I pulled the burrs from his paws with the tweezers you left in the medicine cabinet. He hated it."

"He always hates it."

"How are you otherwise?" he says. "I have a sore throat."

"You do?"

"I even took an aspirin," he says. "I haven't taken an aspirin in years. It didn't go very well with the tequila."

"What tequila?"

"The tequila I was drinking last night," he says. "While I was waiting for Keats to get back from chasing his fox. You should have seen the moon."

There is something wrong with the engine of Dennis's Toyota. It makes a sound like an old man swallowing, waspish and frail, whenever you go over forty-five. We drive slowly off the highway, onto the shoulder. Dennis polishes the windshield with a rag. "This is the only thing I know how to do with cars," he says. "I've spent my whole adult life learning how to avoid knowing anything about the inside." He taps the hood with his fist. "Be good," he says. Clearly, the sound worries him. His finances are carefully calibrated, the strategies listed on three-by-five index cards. I stole one of the cards one evening, and examined it: a series of sums in Dennis's careful printing, listing the costs of painting the house—materials, labor, time. At the bottom of the card he had written: "It seems unlikely that I will paint the house before 1985, when it will be absolutely necessary." I closed my eyes, still holding the index card. I liked the way the paint was unfurling from the wooden shutters, in curls as tight to the touch as an Airedale's. It made me sad to imagine the fresh white walls of 1985.

At the toll booth, he finds he has forgotten his wallet. I hand him a crumpled dollar; he smooths it against the dashboard before handing it to the woman in the booth. She smiles at him. I imagine that she thinks him unusually handsome, and that she is bored with the Sunday traffic. We cross the San Rafael bridge slowly. The wind cuts across the bridge at an angle; I am afraid that the linen cloth tucked into the wicker picnic basket will be blown away. Below, there are islands and oil freighters in shades of charcoal, their shadows falling depthlessly beside them. "Isn't it a beautiful morning?" Dennis says.

"Very beautiful."

"It was a beautiful idea to come to the beach, wasn't it?"

"I think so," I say. I smile sideways at him.

"We always have beautiful ideas, so far," he says.

His fingers rest lightly on my bare shoulder, except when he is changing gears.

On the beach, there is a blind woman with a Labrador retriever. The dog watches closely as the woman wades forward into the sea until the waves wash against her knees. The dog whines. About a hundred yards away, a man is reading the *Chronicle*, propping it open against one tower of a sand castle. The sand castle is perhaps seven feet wide, with a Chartres-like cathedral, airy towers and flying buttresses. There is a channel of sea water surrounding it; the sports pages fan open across the moat. The man's elbow is quite near a small bridge with splintered Popsicle-stick railings. He has a white belly and broad shoulders. His shadow falls across the page of newsprint sharply, like a cutout.

"There isn't a child in sight," Dennis says. "Is there?"

"No."

"So whose sand castle is it, the man's or the woman's?"

"You could ask him."

"I hate to interrupt any man serious enough to read the *Chronicle*'s sports pages during a baseball strike. Look at the light on the beach. You can see everything. You can see the red hair on that man's knees. Look, you can see the freighters."

The black dog sits, panting, on the shore. The woman has left her shoes near his front paws. "I envy that woman with her dog," I say.

"He's very beautiful, isn't he?" Dennis says. The dog's chest is drying into black spines encrusted with salt. Sometimes he yawns, noisily, anxiously; his tail thumps the sand near her shoes. The woman is now ten yards from shore. She is wearing a black swimming suit. One strap has slid nearly all the way down her shoulder. I can tell that Dennis fears for her: in a moment, her breast will be exposed, and the man at the sand castle isn't even watching.

We are sitting in a hollow between two dunes. My knees are cold, and I have been drinking Pinot Noir. The curves of the dunes are as flawless as white silk. The spread picnic cloth gleams with the sand that has collected in its folds; there are wet plastic spoons, crusts of bread, and the stones of peaches. "Look, Holly," Dennis says. He is lying on his stomach. He traces a series of tracks in the sand with a small twig. "A gull?" he says. "A sandpiper?"

"A sparrow?" I say. "Look how perfect each track is."

"Three toes on each foot," Dennis says. He covers the track gently with the palm of his hand, like a man trapping a moth, and smiles up at me. "I feel so lazy." He lies back and closes his eyes. When I lie down beside him, he takes two of my fingers and presses them against the hollow of his throat, between the tendons. "Hear my heart beating?" he says. "One of the associates of the film company I worked with had a heart attack last month. He was thirty-four. He was on the telephone when it happened. The person on the other end of the line wouldn't take him seriously."

I kiss him. Because he has not shaved, the kiss makes a small rasping sound. I turn my jaw until it rests against his. "Keats has two parallel lines between his eyes," I say. "It gives him this worried look."

"Holly," he says. "I've been hearing about Keats all the time lately. Listen to me: I know you want your dog. I *understand* you want your dog. All right? Please? I'm only human."

There is a light wind, even in this hollow.

He turns, keeping his jaw against mine. His chest is dark, the nipple a puckered, faintly darker oval. The spiral of his inner ear is close to my eyelid; I can see the grains of sand inside. The concavity in the center of his chest rises, falls, rises again. He is asleep. His hand lies near my chin, the fingers splayed; there is sand beneath his fingernails. I feel the steady rise and fall of his rib cage, and press myself closer to his body. The backs of my teeth still taste of Pinot Noir, and there must be sand in my swimming suit, but for a long while I do not move, feeling myself as well hidden as a fox in the curve of a ditch.

"I want to try it one more time," I say. "Please?"

Dennis rests the inside of one wrist along the top of the steering wheel, and steers that way; the highway is straight here. He reaches to touch my hair, running his fingers through it without really looking at me. He sighs. "O.K.," he says. "You're the princess."

I dial the numbers in a lighted booth near the highway. The glass of the booth rattles whenever a truck goes by; there is a heart scratched into the aluminum of the coin slot, but no names are scratched inside the heart. In the distance, over some low brown hills, there is a truck stop, its lights only now coming on. Dennis leans against the Toyota, looking away from the telephone booth.

"Holly?" Luke says. "It's dark. I must have fallen asleep."

"Luke, I wanted to tell you that if you can get Keats onto an airplane for me, I would keep him for two weeks—or a little longer if we could agree on that—and then I'll pay for his flight back to you. I thought that if we could divide his time equally between California and Wyoming, it would be fair."

"Confusing for Keats," Luke says. "Would he go on like that for the rest of his life, or what?"

"I'm only thinking about the near future," I say. "I only want to see him."

"What time is it?"

"I don't know. About nine o'clock, I think."

"Your time or my time?"

"Yours."

"I had a slight accident," he says.

"You did?" I touch my tongue to the backs of my front teeth. "Luke?"

"It wasn't anything serious," he says. "I was driving into Cheyenne, and I nicked the rear bumper of the car ahead of me. It was a Cadillac. I didn't even think anyone in North America drove Cadillacs anymore, you know. It was like running into a fucking black dinosaur. I fractured the windshield, though, when I hit."

"When you hit?"

"My forehead," he says. "Please don't cry. It's all right. Holly, really, it's all right. I even went and saw a doctor about it."

"You did?"

"The man in the Cadillac drove me to the emergency room in the hospital," he says. "He was concerned about my skull, I think. He kept looking to see whether or not my eyes were dilating, and quoting to me the number of synapses in the brain. He'd been reading Carl Sagan the night before, in some hotel room. I forget what the number was. Actually, he was from California. 'My intuition told me I should never have tried to drive through Wyoming on the way to Cincinnati,' he said. 'But I have always had this nameless longing to see antelope.' That was his word, 'longing.' He felt terrible, even though the whole thing was my fault. His Greenpeace bumper sticker was all smashed up. I told him my wife is in California."

"The doctor in the emergency room said it was all right for you to go home?"

"He did, but he said I should keep kind of quiet for a while," Luke says. "I suppose I didn't think it was going to hit me like this. I was lying down watching a movie, and Keats had his chin on my knee, just sort of watching me. Then I went out like a light. I can't tell how long I've been asleep."

"It's probably about nine o'clock now," I say.

"The movie started about three, I think," he says. "I forget what movie."

My shoulder is against the wall of the booth. Suddenly, I feel the cool pane of glass against my skin, and realize it is dark. The floor of the booth is gritty beneath my clogs. Torn pages flutter in the telephone book on the ledge before me. I close my eyes.

"I feel like a ghost of myself," Luke says.

I think of Keats, the curious arching trot he would adopt whenever he had to navigate through stubble; often, in the wheatfields, the grass was simply over his head.

Lying Doggo

BOBBIE ANN MASON

Grover Cleveland is growing feeble. His eyes are cloudy,
and his muzzle is specked with white hairs. When he
scoots along on the hardwood floors, he makes a sound
like brushes on drums. He sleeps in front of the woodstove, and when he gets too hot he creeps across the
floor.

When Nancy Culpepper married Jack Cleveland,
she felt, in a way, that she was marrying a divorced
man with a child. Grover was a young dog then. Jack

had gotten him at the humane society shelter. He had picked the shyest, most endearing puppy in a boisterous litter. Later, he told Nancy that someone said he should have chosen an energetic one, because quiet puppies often have something wrong with them. That chance remark bothered Nancy; it could have applied to her as well. But that was years ago. Nancy and Jack are still married, and Grover has lived to be old. Now his arthritis stiffens his legs so that on some days he cannot get up. Jack has been talking of having Grover put to sleep.

"Why do you say 'put to sleep'?" their son, Robert, asks. "I know what you mean." Robert is nine. He is a serious boy, quiet, like Nancy.

"No reason. It's just the way people say it."

"They don't say they put *people* to sleep."

"It doesn't usually happen to people," Jack says.

"Don't you dare take him to the vet unless you let me go along. I don't want any funny stuff behind my back."

"Don't worry, Robert," Nancy says.

Later, in Jack's studio, while developing photographs of broken snow fences on hillsides, Jack says to Nancy, "There's a first time for everything, I guess."

"What?"

"Death. I never really knew anybody who died."

"You're forgetting my grandmother."

"I didn't really know your grandmother." Jack looks down at Grover's face in the developing fluid. Grover looks like a wolf in the snow on the hill. Jack says, "The only people I ever cared about who died were rock heroes."

Jack has been buying special foods for the dog—pork chops and liver, vitamin supplements. All the arthritis literature he has been able to find concerns people, but he says the same rules must apply to all mammals. Until Grover's hind legs gave way, Jack and Robert took

Grover out for long, slow walks through the woods. Recently, a neighbor who keeps Alaskan malamutes stopped Nancy in the Super Duper and inquired about Grover. The neighbor wanted to know which kind of arthritis Grover had—osteo- or rheumatoid? The neighbor said he had rheumatoid and held out knobbed fingers. The doctor told him to avoid zucchini and to drink lots of water. Grover doesn't like zucchini, Nancy said.

Jack and Nancy and Robert all deal with Grover outside. It doesn't help that the temperature is dropping below twenty degrees. It feels even colder because they are conscious of the dog's difficulty. Nancy holds his head and shoulders while Jack supports his hind legs. Robert holds up Grover's tail.

Robert says, "I have an idea."

"What, sweetheart?" asks Nancy. In her arms, Grover lurches. Nancy squeezes against him and he whimpers.

"We could put a diaper on him."

"How would we clean him up?"

"They do that with chimpanzees," says Jack, "but it must be messy."

"You mean I didn't have an original idea?" Robert cries. "Curses, foiled again!" Robert has been reading comic books about masked villains.

"There aren't many original ideas," Jack says, letting go of Grover. "They just look original when you're young." Jack lifts Grover's hind legs again and grasps him under the stomach. "Let's try one more time, boy."

Grover looks at Nancy, pleading.

Nancy has been feeling that the dying of Grover marks a milestone in her marriage to Jack, a marriage that has somehow lasted almost fifteen years. She is seized with an irrational dread—that when the dog is gone, Jack will be gone too. Whenever Nancy and Jack are apart—during Nancy's frequent trips to see her family in Kentucky, or when Jack has gone away "to think"—Grover remains with Jack. Actually,

Nancy knew Grover before she knew Jack. When Jack and Nancy were students, in Massachusetts, the dog was a familiar figure around campus. Nancy was drawn to the dog long before she noticed the shaggy-haired student in the sheepskin-lined corduroy jacket who was usually with him. Once, in a seminar on the Federalist period that Nancy was auditing, Grover had walked in, circled the room, and then walked out, as if performing some routine investigation, like the man who sprayed Nancy's apartment building for silverfish. Grover was a beautiful dog, a German shepherd, gray, dusted with a sooty topcoat. After the seminar, Nancy followed the dog out of the building, and she met Jack then. Eventually, when Nancy and Jack made love in his apartment in Amherst, Grover lay sprawled by the bed, both protective and quietly participatory. Later, they moved into a house in the country, and Nancy felt that she had an instant family. Once, for almost three months, Jack and Grover were gone. Jack left Nancy in California, pregnant and terrified, and went to stay at an Indian reservation in New Mexico. Nancy lived in a room on a street with palm trees. It was winter. It felt like a Kentucky October. She went to a park every day and watched people with their dogs, their children, and tried to comprehend that she was there, alone, a mile from the San Andreas fault, reluctant to return to Kentucky. "We need to decide where we stand with each other," Jack had said when he left. "Just when I start to think I know where you're at, you seem to disappear." Jack always seemed to stand back and watch her, as though he expected her to do something excitingly original. He expected her to be herself, not someone she thought people wanted her to be. That was a twist: he expected the unexpected. While Jack was away, Nancy indulged in crafts projects. At the Free University, she learned batik and macramé. On her own, she learned to crochet. She had never done anything like that before. She threw away her file folders of history notes for the article she had wanted to write. Suddenly, making things with her hands was the only endeavor that made sense. She crocheted a bulky, shapeless sweater in a shell stitch for Jack. She made baby things, using large hooks. She did not realize that such heavy blankets were unsuitable for a baby until she saw Robert—a tiny, warped-looking creature, like one of her clumsily made crafts. When Jack returned, she was in a sprawling adobe hospital, nursing a baby the color of scalded skin. The old song "In My Adobe Hacienda" was going through her head. Jack stood over her behind an unfamiliar beard, grinning in disbelief, stroking the baby as though he were a new pet. Nancy felt she had fooled Jack into thinking she had done something original at last.

"Grover's dying to see you," he said to her. "They wouldn't let him in here."

"I'll be glad to see Grover," said Nancy. "I missed him."

She had missed, she realized then, his various expressions: the staccato barks of joy, the forceful, menacing barks at strangers, the eerie howls when he heard cat fights at night.

Those early years together were confused and dislocated. After leaving graduate school, at the beginning of the seventies, they lived in a number of places—sometimes on the road, with Grover, in a van— but after Robert was born they settled in Pennsylvania. Their life is orderly. Jack is a free-lance photographer, with his own studio at home. Nancy, unable to find a use for her degree in history, returned to school, taking education and administration courses. Now she is assistant principal of a small private elementary school, which Robert attends. Now and then Jack frets about becoming too middle-class. He has become semipolitical about energy, sometimes attending anti-nuclear power rallies. He has been building a sun space for his studio and has been insulating the house. "Retrofitting" is the term he uses for making the house energy-efficient.

"Insulation is his hobby," Nancy told an old friend from graduate school, Tom Green, who telephoned unexpectedly one day recently. "He insulates on weekends."

"Maybe he'll turn into a butterfly—he could insulate himself into a cocoon," said Tom, who Nancy always thought was funny. She had not seen him in ten years. He called to say he was sending a novel he had written—"about all the crazy stuff we did back then."

The dog is forcing Nancy to think of how Jack has changed in the years since then. He is losing his hair, but he doesn't seem concerned. Jack was always fanatical about being honest. He used to be insensitive about his directness. "I'm just being honest," he would say pleasantly, boyishly, when he hurt people's feelings. He told Nancy she was up-tight, that no one ever knew what she thought, that she should be more expressive. He said she "played games" with people, hiding her feelings behind her coy Southern smile. He is more tolerant now, less judgmental. He used to criticize her for drinking Cokes and eating pastries. He didn't like her lipstick, and she stopped wearing it. But Nancy has changed too. She is too sophisticated now to eat fried foods and rich pies and cakes, indulging in them only when she goes to Kentucky. She uses makeup now—so sparingly that Jack does not notice. Her cool reserve, her shyness, has changed to cool assurance, with only the slightest shift. Inwardly, she has reorganized. "It's like retrofitting," she said to Jack once, but he didn't notice any irony.

It wasn't until two years ago that Nancy learned that he had lied to her when he told her he had been at the Beatles' Shea Stadium concert in 1966, just as she had, only two months before they met. When he confessed his lie, he claimed he had wanted to identify with her and impress her because he thought of her as someone so mysterious and aloof that he could not hold her attention. Nancy, who had in fact been intimidated by Jack's directness, was troubled to learn about his peculiar deception. It was out of character. She felt a part of her past had been ripped away. More recently, when John Lennon died, Nancy and Jack watched the silent vigil from Central Park on TV and cried in each other's arms. Everybody that week was saying that they had lost their youth.

Jack was right. That was the only sort of death they had known.

Grover lies on his side, stretched out near the fire, his head flat on one ear. His eyes are open, expressionless, and when Nancy speaks to him he doesn't respond.

"Come on, Grover!" cries Robert, tugging the dog's leg. "Are you dead?"

"Don't pull at him," Nancy says.

"He's lying doggo," says Jack.

"That's funny," says Robert. "What does that mean?"

"Dogs do that in the heat," Jack explains. "They save energy that way."

"But it's winter," says Robert. "I'm freezing." He is wearing a wool pullover and a goose-down vest. Jack has the thermostat set on fifty-five, relying mainly on the woodstove to warm the house.

"I'm cold too," says Nancy. "I've been freezing since 1965, when I came North."

Jack crouches down beside the dog. "Grover, old boy. Please. Just give a little sign."

"If you don't get up, I won't give you your treat tonight," says Robert, wagging his finger at Grover.

"Let him rest," says Jack, who is twiddling some of Grover's fur between his fingers.

"Are you sure he's not dead?" Robert asks. He runs the zipper of his vest up and down.

"He's just pretending," says Nancy.

The tip of Grover's tail twitches, and Jack catches it, the way he might grab at a fluff of milkweed in the air.

Later, in the kitchen, Jack and Nancy are preparing for a dinner party. Jack is sipping whiskey. The woodstove has been burning all day, and the house is comfortably warm now. In the next room, Robert is lying on the rug in front of the stove with Grover. He is playing with a computer football game and watching *Mork and Mindy* at the same time. Robert likes to do several things at once, and lately he has included Grover in his multiple activities.

Jack says, "I think the only thing to do is just feed Grover pork chops and steaks and pet him a lot, and then when we can stand it, take him to the vet and get it over with."

"When can we stand it?"

"If I were in Grover's shape, I'd just want to be put out of my misery."

"Even if you were still conscious and could use your mind?"

"I guess so."

"I couldn't pull the plug on you," says Nancy, pointing a carrot at Jack. "You'd have to be screaming in agony."

"Would you want me to do it to you?"

"No. I can see right now that I'd be the type to hang on. I'd be just like my Granny. I think she just clung to life, long after her body was ready to die."

"Would you really be like that?"

"You said once I was just like her—repressed, uptight."

"I didn't mean that."

"You've been right about me before," Nancy says, reaching across Jack for a paring knife. "Look, all I mean is that it shouldn't be a matter of *our* convenience. If Grover needs assistance, then it's our problem. We're responsible."

"I'd want to be put out of my misery," Jack says.

During that evening, Nancy has the impression that Jack is talking more than usual. He does not notice the food. She has made chicken Marengo and is startled to realize how much it resembles chicken cacciatore, which she served the last time she had the same people over. The recipes are side by side in the cookbook, gradations on a theme. The dinner is for Stewart and Jan, who are going to Italy on a teaching exchange.

"Maybe I shouldn't even have made Italian," Nancy tells them apologetically. "You'll get enough of that in Italy. And it will be real."

Both Stewart and Jan say the chicken Marengo is wonderful. The olives are the right touch, Jan says. Ted and Laurie nod agreement. Jack pours more wine. The sound of a log falling in the woodstove reminds Nancy of the dog in the other room by the stove, and in her mind she stages a scene: finding the dog dead in the middle of the dinner party.

Afterward, they sit in the living room, with Grover lying there like a log too large for the stove. The guests talk idly. Ted has been sandblasting old paint off a brick fireplace, and Laurie complains about the gritty dust. Jack strokes the fire. The stove, hooked up through the fireplace, looks like a robot from an old science fiction movie. Nancy and Jack used to sit by the fireplace in Massachusetts, stoned, watching the blue frills of the flames, imagining that they were musical notes, visual textures of sounds on the stereo. Nobody they know smokes grass anymore. Now people sit around and talk about investments and proper flue linings. When Jack passes around the Grand Marnier, Nancy says, "In my grandparents' house years ago, we used to sit by their fireplace. They burned coal. They didn't call it a fireplace, though. They called it a grate."

"Coal burns more efficiently than wood," Jack says.

"Coal's a lot cheaper in this area," says Ted. "I wish I could switch."

"My grandparents had big stone fireplaces in their country house," says Jan, who comes from Connecticut. "They were so pleasant. I always looked forward to going there. Sometimes in the summer the evenings were cool and we'd have a fire. It was lovely."

"I remember being cold," says Nancy. "It was always very cold, even in the South."

"The heat just goes up the chimney in a fireplace," says Jack.

Nancy stares at Jack. She says, "I would stand in front of the fire until I was roasted. Then I would turn and roast the other side. In the evenings, my grandparents sat on the hearth and read the Bible. There wasn't anything *lovely* about it. They were trying to keep warm. Of course, nobody had heard of insulation."

"There goes Nancy, talking about her deprived childhood," Jack says with a laugh.

Nancy says, "Jack is so concerned about wasting energy. But when he goes out he never wears a hat." She looks at Jack. "Don't you know your body heat just flies out the top of your head? It's a chimney."

Surprised by her tone, she almost breaks into tears.

It is the following evening, and Jack is flipping through some contact sheets of a series on solar hot-water heaters he is doing for a magazine. Robert sheds his goose-down vest, and he and Grover, on the floor, simultaneously inch away from the fire. Nancy is trying to read the novel written by the friend from Amherst, but the book is boring. She would not have recognized her witty friend from the past in the turgid prose she is reading.

"It's a dump on the sixties," she tells Jack when he asks. "A really cynical look. All the characters are types."

"Are we in it?"

"No. I hope not. I think it's based on that Phil Baxter who cracked up at that party."

Grover raises his head, his eyes alert, and Robert jumps up, saying, "It's time for Grover's treat."

He shakes a Pet-Tab from a plastic bottle and holds it before Grover's nose. Grover bangs his tail against the rug as he crunches the pill.

Jack turns on the porch light and steps outside for a moment, returning with a shroud of cold air. "It's starting to snow," he says. "Come on out, Grover."

Grover struggles to stand, and Jack heaves the dog's hind legs over the threshold.

Later, in bed, Jack turns on his side and watches Nancy, reading her book, until she looks up at him.

"You read so much," he says. "You're always reading."

"Hmm."

"We used to have more fun. We used to be silly together."

"What do you want to do?"

"Just something silly."

"I can't think of anything silly." Nancy flips the page back, re-reading. "God, this guy can't write. I used to think he was so clever."

In the dark, touching Jack tentatively, she says, "We've changed. We used to lie awake all night, thrilled just to touch each other."

"We've been busy. That's what happens. People get busy."

"That scares me," says Nancy. "Do you want to have another baby?"

"No. I want a dog." Jack rolls away from her, and Nancy can hear him breathing into his pillow. She waits to hear if he will cry. She recalls Jack returning to her in California after Robert was born. He brought a God's-eye, which he hung from the ceiling above Robert's crib, to protect him. Jack never wore the sweater Nancy made for him. Instead, Grover slept on it. Nancy gave the dog her granny-square afghan too, and eventually, when they moved back East, she got rid of the pathetic evidence of her creative period—the crochet hooks, the piles of yarn, some splotchy batik tapestries. Now most of the objects in the house are Jack's. He made the oak counters and the dining room table; he remodeled the studio; he chose the draperies; he photographed the pictures on the wall. If Jack were to leave again, there would be no way to remove his presence, the way the dog can disappear completely, with his sounds. Nancy revises the scene in her mind. The house is still there, but Nancy is not in it.

In the morning, there is a four-inch snow, with a drift blowing up the back-porch steps. From the kitchen window, Nancy watches her son float silently down the hill behind the house. At the end, he tumbles off his sled deliberately, wallowing in the snow, before standing up to wave, trying to catch her attention.

On the back porch, Nancy and Jack hold Grover over newspapers. Grover performs unselfconsciously now. Nancy says, "Maybe he can hang on, as long as we can do this."

"But look at him, Nancy," Jack says. "He's in misery."

Jack holds Grover's collar and helps him slide over the threshold. Grover aims for his place by the fire.

After the snowplow passes, late in the morning, Nancy drives Robert to the school on slushy roads, all the while lecturing him on the absurdity of raising money to buy official Boy Scout equipment, especially on a snowy Saturday. The Boy Scouts are selling water-savers for toilet tanks in order to earn money for camping gear.

"I thought Boy Scouts spent their time earning badges," says Nancy. "I thought you were supposed to learn about nature, instead of spending money on official Boy Scout pots and pans."

"This is nature," Robert says solemnly. "It's ecology. Saving water when you flush is ecology."

Later, Nancy and Jack walk in the woods together. Nancy walks behind Jack, stepping in his boot tracks. He shields her from the wind. Her hair is blowing. They walk briskly up a hill and emerge on a ridge that overlooks a valley. In the distance they can see a housing development, a radio tower, a winding road. House trailers dot the hillsides. A snowplow is going up a road, like a zipper in the landscape.

Jack says, "I'm going to call the vet Monday."

Nancy gasps in cold air. She says, "Robert made us promise you won't do anything without letting him in on it. That goes for me too." When Jack doesn't respond, she says, "I'd want to hang on, even if I was in a coma. There must be some spark, in the deep recesses of the mind, some twitch, a flicker of a dream—"

"A twitch that could make life worth living?" Jack laughs bitterly.

"Yes." She points to the brilliantly colored sparkles the sun is making on the snow. "Those are the sparks I mean," she says. "In the brain somewhere, something like that. That would be beautiful."

"You're weird, Nancy."

"I learned it from you. I never would have noticed anything like that if I hadn't known you, if you hadn't got me stoned and made me look at your photographs." She stomps her feet in the snow. Her toes are cold. "You educated me. I was so out of it when I met you. One day I was listening to Hank Williams and shelling corn for the chickens and the next day I was expected to know what wines went with what. Talk about weird."

"You're exaggerating. That was years ago. You always exaggerate your background." He adds in a teasing tone, "Your humble origins."

"We've been together fifteen years," says Nancy. She stops him, holding his arm. Jack is squinting, looking at something in the distance. She goes on, "You said we didn't do anything silly anymore. What should we do, Jack? Should we make angels in the snow?"

Jack touches his rough glove to her face. "We shouldn't unless we really feel like it."

It was the same as Jack chiding her to be honest, to be expressive. The same old Jack, she thought, relieved.

* * *

"Come and look," Robert cries, bursting in the back door. He and Jack have been outside making a snowman. Nancy is rolling dough for a quiche. Jack will eat a quiche but not a custard pie, although they are virtually the same. She wipes her hands and goes to the door of the porch. She sees Grover swinging from the lower branch of the maple tree. Jack has rigged up a sling, so that the dog is supported in a harness, with the canvas from the back of a deck chair holding his stomach. His legs dangle free.

"Oh, Jack," Nancy calls. "The poor thing."

"I thought this might work," Jack explains. "A support for his hind legs." His arms cradle the dog's head. "I did it for you," he adds, looking at Nancy. "Don't push him, Robert. I don't think he wants to swing."

Grover looks amazingly patient, like a cat in a doll bonnet.

"He hates it," says Jack, unbuckling the harness.

"He can learn to like it," Robert says, his voice rising shrilly.

On the day that Jack has planned to take Grover to the veterinarian, Nancy runs into a crisis at work. One of the children has been exposed to hepatitis, and it is necessary to vaccinate all of them. Nancy has to arrange the details, which means staying late. She telephones Jack to ask him to pick up Robert after school.

"I don't know when I'll be home," she says. "This is an administrative nightmare. I have to call all the parents, get permissions, make arrangements with family doctors."

"What will we do about Grover?"

"Please postpone it. I want to be with you then."

"I want to get it over with," says Jack impatiently. "I hate to put Robert through another day of this."

"Robert will be glad of the extra time," Nancy insists. "So will I."

"I just want to face things," Jack says. "Don't you understand? I don't want to cling to the past like you're doing."

"Please wait for us," Nancy says, her voice calm and controlled.

On the telephone, Nancy is authoritative, a quick decision-maker. The problem at work is a reprieve. She feels free, on her own. During the afternoon, she works rapidly and efficiently, filing reports, consulting health authorities, notifying parents. She talks with the disease-control center in Atlanta, inquiring about guidelines. She checks on supplies of gamma globulin. She is so preoccupied that in the middle of the afternoon, when Robert suddenly appears in her office, she is startled, for a fleeting instant not recognizing him.

He says, "Kevin has a sore throat. Is that hepatitis?"

"It's probably just a cold. I'll talk to his mother." Nancy is holding Robert's arm, partly to keep him still, partly to steady herself.

"When do I have to get a shot?" Robert asks.

"Tomorrow."

"Do I have to?"

"Yes. It won't hurt, though."

"I guess it's a good thing this happened," Robert says bravely. "Now we get to have Grover another day." Robert spills his books on the floor and bends to pick them up. When he looks up, he says, "Daddy doesn't care about him. He just wants to get rid of him. He wants to kill him."

"Oh, Robert, that's not true," says Nancy. "He just doesn't want Grover to suffer."

"But Grover still has half a bottle of Pet-Tabs," Robert says. "What will we do with them?"

"I don't know," Nancy says. She hands Robert his numbers workbook. Like a tape loop, the face of her child as a stranger replays in her mind. Robert has her plain brown hair, her coloring, but his eyes are Jack's—demanding and eerily penetrating, eyes that could pin her to the wall.

After Robert leaves, Nancy lowers the venetian blinds. Her office is brilliantly lighted by the sun, through south-facing windows. The design was accidental, nothing to do with solar energy. It is an old building. Bars of light slant across her desk, like a formidable scene in a forties movie. Nancy's secretary goes home, but Nancy works on, contacting all the parents she couldn't get during working hours. One parent anxiously reports that her child has a swollen lymph node on his neck.

"No," Nancy says firmly. "That is *not* a symptom of hepatitis. But you should ask the doctor about that when you go in for the gamma globulin."

Gamma globulin. The phrase rolls off her tongue. She tries to remember an odd title of a movie about gamma rays. It comes to her as she is dialing the telephone: *The Effect of Gamma Rays on Man-in-the-Moon Marigolds.* She has never known what that title meant.

The office grows dim, and Nancy turns on the lights. The school is quiet, as though the threat of an infectious disease has emptied the corridors, leaving her in charge. She recalls another movie, *The Andromeda Strain.* Her work is like the thrill of watching drama, a threat held safely at a distance. Historians have to be detached, Nancy once said, defensively, to Jack, when he accused her of being unfriendly to shopkeepers and waiters. Where was all that Southern hospitality he had heard so much about? he wanted to know. It hits her now that historians are detached about the past, not the present. Jack has learned some of this detachment: he wants to let Grover go. Nancy thinks of the stark images in his recent photographs—snow, icicles, fences, the long shot of Grover on the hill like a stray wolf. Nancy had always liked Jack's pictures simply for what they were, but Jack didn't see the people or the objects in them. He saw illusions. The vulnerability of the image, he once said, was what he was after. The image was meant to evoke its own death, he told her.

By the time Nancy finishes the scheduling, the night maintenance crew has arrived, and the coffeepot they keep in a closet is perking. Nancy removes her contact lenses and changes into her fleece-lined boots. In the parking lot, she maneuvers cautiously along a path past a mountain of black-stained snow. It is so cold that she makes sparks on the vinyl car seat. The engine is cold, slow to turn over.

At home, Nancy is surprised to see balloons in the living room. The stove is blazing and Robert's face is red from the heat.

"We're having a party," he says. "For Grover."

"There's a surprise for you in the oven," says Jack, handing Nancy a glass of sherry. "Because you worked so hard."

"Grover had ice cream," Robert says. "We got Häagen-Dazs."

"He looks cheerful," Nancy says, sinking onto the couch next to Jack. Her glasses are fogged up. She removes them and wipes them with a Kleenex. When she puts them back on, she sees Grover looking at her, his head on his paws. His tail thumps. For the first time, Nancy feels ready to let the dog die.

When Nancy tells about the gamma globulin, the phrase has stopped rolling off her tongue so trippingly. She laughs. She is so tired she throbs with relief. She drinks the sherry too fast. Suddenly, she sits up straight and announces, "I've got a clue. I'm thinking of a parking lot."

"East or West?" Jack says. This is a game they used to play.

"West."

"Aha, I've got you," says Jack. "You're thinking of the parking lot at that hospital in Tucson."

"Hey, that's not fair going too fast," cries Robert. "I didn't get a chance to play."

"This was before you were born," Nancy says, running her fingers through Robert's hair. He is on the floor, leaning against her knees. "We were lying in the van for a week, thinking we were going to die. Oh, God!" Nancy laughs and covers her mouth with her hands.

"Why were you going to die?" Robert asks.

"We weren't really going to die." Both Nancy and Jack are laughing now at the memory, and Jack is pulling off his sweater. The hospital in Tucson wouldn't accept them because they weren't sick enough to hospitalize, but they were too sick to travel. They had nowhere to go. They had been on a month's trip through the West, then had stopped in Tucson and gotten jobs at a restaurant to make enough money to get home.

"Do you remember that doctor?" Jack says.

"I remember the look he gave us, like he didn't want us to pollute his hospital." Nancy laughs harder. She feels silly and relieved. Her hand, on Jack's knee, feels the fold of the long johns beneath his jeans. She cries, "I'll never forget how we stayed around that parking lot, thinking we were going to die."

"I couldn't have driven a block, I was so weak," Jack gasps.

"You were yellow. *I* didn't get yellow."

"All we could do was pee and drink orange juice."

"And throw the pee out the window."

"Grover was so bored with us!"

Nancy says, "It's a good thing we couldn't eat. We would have spent all our money."

"Then we would have had to work at that filthy restaurant again. And get hepatitis again."

"And on and on, forever. We would still be there, like Charley on the MTA. Oh, Jack, do you *remember* that crazy restaurant? You had to wear a ten-gallon hat—"

Abruptly, Robert jerks away from Nancy and crawls on his knees across the room to examine Grover, who is stretched out on his side, his legs sticking out stiffly. Robert, his straight hair falling, bends his head to the dog's heart.

"He's not dead," Robert says, looking up at Nancy. "He's lying doggo."

"Passed out at his own party," Jack says, raising his glass. "Way to go, Grover!"

Reach for the Sky

JIM SHEPARD

Guy comes into the shelter this last Thursday, a kid, really, maybe doing it for his dad, with a female golden/ Labrador cross, two or three years old. He's embarrassed, not ready for forms and questions, but we get dogs like this all the time, and I'm not letting him off the hook, not letting him out of here before I know he knows that we have to kill a lot of these dogs, dogs like his. Her name is Rita and he says, "Rita, sit!," like being here is part of her ongoing training. Rita sits

halfway and then stands again, and looks at him in that tuned-in way goldens have.

"So . . ." The kid looks at the forms I've got on the counter, like no one told him this was part of the deal. He looks up at the sampler that the sister of the regional boss did for our office: "A MAN KNOWS ONLY AS MUCH AS HE'S SUFFERED—ST. FRANCIS OF ASSISI." He has no answers whatsoever for the form. She's two, he thinks. Housebroken. Some shots. His dad handled all that stuff. She's spayed. Reason for Surrender: she plays too rough.

She smashed this huge lamp, the kid says. Of one of those mariners with the pipe and the yellow bad-weather outfit. His dad made it in a ceramics class.

Rita looks over at me with bright interest. The kid adds, "And she's got this thing with her back legs, she limps pretty bad. The vet said she wouldn't get any better."

"What vet?" I ask. I'm not supposed to push too hard, it's no better if they abandon them on highways, but we get sixty dogs a day here, and if I can talk any of them back into their houses, great. "The vet couldn't do anything?"

"We don't have the money," the kid says.

I ask to see Rita's limp. The kid's vague, and Rita refuses to demonstrate. Her tail thumps the floor twice.

I explain the bottom of the form to the kid: when he signs it, he's giving us permission to have the dog put down if it comes to that.

"She's a good dog," he says helpfully. "She'll probably get someone to like her."

So I do the animal-shelter Joe Friday, which never works: "Maybe. But we get ten goldens per week. And everybody wants puppies."

"O.K., well, good luck," the kid says. He signs something on the line that looks like "Fleen." Rita looks at him. He takes the leash with him, wrapping it around his forearm. At the door he says, "You be a good girl, now." Rita pants a little with a neutral expression, processing the information.

It used to be you would get owners all the time who were teary and broken up: they needed to know their dog was going to get a good home, you had to guarantee it, they needed to make their problem yours, so that they could say, Hey, when *I* left the dog it was fine.

Their dog would always make a great pet for somebody, their dog was always great with kids, their dog always needed A Good Home and Plenty of Room to Run. Their dog, they were pretty sure, would always be the one we'd have no trouble placing in a nice family. And when they got to the part about signing the release form for euthanasia, only once did someone, a little girl, suggest that if it came to that they should be called back, and they'd retrieve the dog. Her mother had asked me if I had any ideas, and the girl suggested that. Her mother said, "I asked *him* if *he* had any ideas."

Now you get kids; the parents don't even bring the dogs in. Behind the kid with the golden/Lab mix there's a girl who's maybe seventeen or eighteen. Benetton top, Benetton skirt, straw-blond hair, tennis tan, she's got a Doberman puppy. Bizarre dog for a girl like that. Chews everything, she says. She holds the puppy like a baby. As if to cooperate, the dog twists and squirms around in her arms trying to get at the penholder to show what it can do.

Puppies chew things, I tell her, and she rolls her eyes like she knows *that*. I tell her how many dogs come in every day. I lie. I say we've had four Doberman puppies for weeks now. She says, "There're forms or something, or I just leave him?" She slides him on his back gently across the counter. His paws are in the air and he looks a little bewildered.

"If I showed you how to make him stop chewing things, would you take him back?" I ask her. The Doberman has sprawled around and got to his feet, taller now than we are, nails clicking tentatively on the counter.

"No," she says. She signs the form, annoyed by a sweep of hair that keeps falling forward. "We're moving, anyhow." She pats the dog on the muzzle as a goodbye and he nips at her, his feet slipping and sliding like a skater's. "God," she says. She's mad at me now, too, the way people get mad at those pictures that come in the mail of dogs and cats looking at you with their noses through the chain-link fences: *Help Skipper, who lived on leather for three weeks.*

When I come back from taking the Doberman downstairs there's a middle-aged guy at the counter in a wheelchair. An Irish setter circles back and forth around the chair, winding and unwinding the black nylon leash across the guy's chest. Somebody's put some time into grooming this dog, and when the sun hits that red coat just right he looks like a million dollars.

I'm not used to wheelchair people. The guy says, "I gotta get rid of the dog."

What do you say to a guy like that: Can't you take care of him? Too much trouble? The setter's got to be eight years old.

"Is he healthy?" I ask.

"She," he says. "She's in good shape."

"Landlord problem?" I say. The guy says nothing.

"What's her name?" I ask.

"We gotta have a discussion?" the guy says. I think, This is what wheelchair people are like. The setter whines and stands her front paws on the arm of the guy's chair.

"We got forms," I say. I put them on the counter, not so close that he doesn't have to reach. He starts to sit up higher and then leans back.

"What's it say?" he says.

"Sex," I say.

"Female," he says.

Breed? Irish setter. Age? Eleven.

Eleven! I can feel this dog on the back of my neck. On my forehead.

I can just see myself selling this eleven-year-old dog to the families that come in looking. And how long has she been with him?

I walk back and forth behind the counter, hoist myself up, flex my legs.

The guy goes, like he hasn't noticed any of that, "She does tricks."

"Tricks?" I say.

"Ellie," he says. He mimes a gun with his forefinger and thumb and points it at her. "Ellie. Reach for the sky."

Ellie is all attention. Ellie sits, and then rears up, lifting her front paws as high as a dog can lift them, edging forward in little hops from the exertion.

"Reach for the sky, Ellie," he says.

Ellie holds it for a second longer, like those old poodles on "The Ed Sullivan Show," and then falls back down and wags her tail at having pulled it off.

"I need a Reason for Surrender," I say. "That's what we call it."

"Well, you're not going to get one," the guy says. He edges a wheel of his chair back and forth, turning it a little this way and that.

"Then I can't take the dog," I say.

"Then I'll just let her go when I get out the door," the guy says.

"If I were you I'd keep that dog," I say.

"If you were me you would've wheeled this thing off a bridge eleven years ago," the guy says. "If you were me you wouldn't be such an asshole. If you were me you would've taken this dog, no questions asked."

We're at an impasse, this guy and me.

He's let go of Ellie's leash, and Ellie's covering all the corners of the office, sniffing. There's a woman in the waiting area behind him with a bull-terrier puppy on her lap and the puppy's keeping a close eye on Ellie.

"Do you have any relatives or whatever who could take the dog?" I ask him.

The guy looks at me. "Do I sign something?" he says.

I can't help it, when I'm showing him where to sign I can't keep the words back, I keep thinking of Ellie reaching for the sky: "It's better this way. We'll try and find her a home with someone who's equipped to handle her."

The guy doesn't come back at me. He signs the thing and hands me my pen, and says, "Hey Ellie, hey kid," and Ellie comes right over. He picks up her trailing leash and flops the end onto the counter where I can grab it, and then hugs her around the neck until she twists a little and pulls away.

"She doesn't know what's going on," I say.

He looks up at me and I point, as if to say, "Her."

The guy wheels the chair around and heads for the door. The woman with the bull terrier watches him go by with big eyes. I can't see his face, but it must be something. Ellie barks. There's no way to fix this.

I've got ASPCA pamphlets unboxed and all over the counter. I've got impound forms to finish by today.

"Nobody's gonna want this dog," I call after him. I can't help it.

It's just me now, at the counter. The woman stands up, holding the bull terrier against her chest, and stops, like she's not going to turn him over, like whatever her reasons are, they may not be good enough.

The Immortal Dog

JACK MATTHEWS

Four women are standing on the street in front, down beyond the spiraca, talking. One of them especially keeps looking up at the window where I am standing. Either she can't see me behind the window, or she is bolder than I would have thought.

It is chilly outside, and all four of the women are in housedresses. They hug their arms and shift from one foot to the other, and occasionally all glance up at my house. Their air is unmistakably that of people

123

moved by an accumulated exasperation, or by an emergency that has startled them out of their routines.

Finally, they decide on a plan and come in single file up the rock path, my long spikes of grass scratching at their naked ankles. They walk with their heads down and their lips set in determination. My dog and I watch them with what must be equal interest and, ultimately, equal incomprehension. He does not bristle or growl; but he sits on the floor, looking comfortably out the window as the four women approach—giving evidence of his size, this hairy bastard born of bitches immemorial, this tamed carnivore with yellow eyes.

It is the first one, a large woman with orange hair and white-rimmed spectacles, that leads them. She is a domineering and talkative woman, capable of injecting the loftiest humanitarian principles into the most pedestrian conversations. Her name is Mrs. Van Fossen, and now she is wearing loose mannish slippers on her feet, and a housedress that is too small, so that it emphasizes her heavy breasts and stomach.

When they appear at my front door, Mrs. Van Fossen raises her face regally, while the other women look nervously to the side and continue to hug themselves, as if in obscure consolation.

The doorbell rings, and still my dog does not growl, bark, or make the slightest move. When I walk to the door and open it, Mrs. Van Fossen simply utters my name, as it is the salutation heading a long and formal document she is about to recite from memory.

"Yes," I say.

"We have come to talk to you again," Mrs. Van Fossen answers.

"Yes, I see you have."

There is a pause, and then Mrs. Van Fossen continues: "We don't expect you to ask us in, or anything like that. But don't you think it would be better if you could just step outside for a few minutes? It's really very nice out here in the sun . . ." (I see one of the women rubbing both her arms to warm them as Mrs. Van Fossen says this) ". . . and I think we could discuss things better with all of us together."

"Yes," I tell them. "I'll come out. But I don't suppose you want me to bring the dog. Do you?"

Several of them glance at one another when I say this, wondering at my grim humor, but Mrs. Van Fossen is not intimidated. "You may bring him if you wish, of course," she says, "because it is your yard, after all. And it's not for ourselves that we have come to talk with you."

I nod and make my dog sit and stay. Then I go outside. I keep my house cold, so I always wear a sweater over a flannel shirt. My wife, who died last September, used to refer to this as my "uniform." It was one of the few jokes I remember my wife making, and, as you can see, it isn't much.

When we are outside in the bright sun, one of the women salutes me permanently, by putting her hand horizontally above her eyes and squinting at my chin. Two others stare at the dead flower stalks along the side of the house. They act like unwilling witnesses, I think, to the airing of a private grievance by Mrs. Van Fossen. But I know this concerns all of them; and even if I didn't, their leader makes this clear right away.

"It isn't just me," she says, "or just us four. It concerns the whole neighborhood. I don't know of anyone who doesn't agree with us."

"I don't either," I say. This seems to surprise her.

"What exactly do you mean?" she asks.

"Exactly what I said: you all seem to be together. But I am not particularly impressed by such things."

"I see. You don't believe in the democratic process then?"

"Not always."

"Well maybe you're living in the wrong country, if you don't believe in democratic principles. But never mind that; I want simply to impress upon you how out of hand this situation has gotten."

"He hasn't bitten anybody, has he?"

"Nobody said he has," Mrs. Van Fossen says, moving her hands up and down, as if on an invisible piano. I suppose she is trying to placate me—which shows how upset she already is, to imagine I need placating at this juncture, for I am very calm and know exactly where I stand.

"And I've been keeping him tied up," I tell her.

"Yes," one of the other women interrupts, "but he's always getting away from you. He broke loose last Friday and just about scared little Danny Grimlich to death."

"Fuck little Danny Grimlich," I say. "He had no business coming into my yard."

That obscenity shocks them for a few seconds, but Mrs. Van Fossen is not to be shocked for long; she has her mission.

"Your crude language won't intimidate us," she says (but I think the two flower-watchers are *precisely* intimidated). "The fact that you can't keep that animal chained is in itself a good indication that he's turned vicious and that . . ."

"Just what are you suggesting," I interrupt. "That I have him killed? 'Put to sleep' as you would probably phrase it?"

Mrs. Van Fossen stares at me unblinkingly through her glasses. "No," she says, "you're wrong there. I would say 'killed' just as you would. And the answer is yes, I think that is precisely what will have to be done if you can't find a home for him."

This is the first time I am uneasy. I see at this instant that it isn't just my dog, and all the disturbance in the neighborhood, that matter to her—but something else—me, personally, and her. This is to be a bitter contest, and neither the weapons nor the prize is clear. Even to her.

"So," I say, "you don't shilly-shally."

"No, I don't shilly-shally. We have given you all the time in the world. At first, we were polite. You can't say we weren't. Then we reported your dog, and the police came and made you put the dog on the leash. The police saw how dangerous that animal is."

All of the women nod in sober agreement, like schoolgirls acknowledging a moral truth.

"But even *that* hasn't worked," the woman who has been saluting my chin says. Her eyes flick up at mine, and I see a sullen and girlish resentment in them. They are red at the edges, as if she has been rubbing them with her knuckles.

"They're afraid of him because he's big and hairy," I say. "That's all. He isn't likely to bark or snarl at kids unless they come through my yard."

"The police," Mrs. Van Fossen says, pausing after the word, "agree that the animal is dangerous. It so happens that my husband has gotten in touch with a lawyer, and he says we can have the animal destroyed." She snaps her fingers. "Like that."

"But if those kids would only stay out of my yard . . . the fact is, they're trespassing, and . . ."

"You can't expect a four-year-old to understand property rights. Now can you? Surely . . ."

"No, but I expect their parents to have some idea of what property rights are."

At this instant my eyes start watering, and I am afraid they might think I am crying. But apparently the idea doesn't even occur to them. Mrs. Van Fossen has seen a chance to avow principle, and no stubborn old man with teary eyes is going to stop her.

"You don't seem to understand," she says, "that we are here dealing with two different orders of moral and legal right."

They all nod wisely at that, and I realize they have sung in this harmony before. Mrs. Van Fossen's hands go up and down on the invisible piano before her as her eyes plead and her voice announces: "These children are *human beings!*"

"I've never broken any law," I say. "And as for taking that dog to another home, he'd die. It's that simple. I once took him to a vet for three days when I had to make a business trip, and they could hardly get him to drink water. That dog would die. I know it."

"Then the course seems very clear," Mrs. Van Fossen said. "Sad as it may seem to you."

"I haven't broken any law."

"You keep coming back to that," Mrs. Van Fossen says, "but what you refuse to face is the fact that your dog is vicious, and everyone *knows* it is vicious. It is not a matter of opinion. Everyone in the neighborhood agrees that this is so. And he is so enormous that if he ever *did* have a chance to attack a child, why . . . he would *kill* it. Could you bear to have *that* on your conscience?"

"No, but then I don't . . ."

"Listen," one of the quiet ones says, "we know why you don't walk your dog."

I stare at her an instant. When I don't answer, she says, "You don't walk him because *you can't hold him anymore.*"

"You mean I'm too old. Is that it?"

"Getting old is no disgrace," Mrs. Van Fossen says. "And we know you are probably lonely and find comfort in having a pet. All we ask is that you get one that you can manage. Actually, you'll be happier with a pet like that."

They all nod at this, but my eyes are watering so much by now that I can't see the expressions on their faces.

When we finish talking, they walk away uttering the same old threats, and I go back in the house and sit down in my rocker, looking at my dog. It is hard to believe that others could be afraid of him—although he is indeed enormous. His thick hairy head and his little yellow eyes would terrify a child . . . especially if that child is short-cutting across my lawn to get to the school bus, or back home.

Kids are lazy beyond belief, I tell myself. But then I think about it awhile, and I have to admit that what those women have said is true . . . I mean about my not being able to hold him. He is too big for

me these days, and I am not stable enough on my feet to handle him
. . . even taking him out to his chain in my yard is an uncertain venture.

But he worships the ground I walk on. That's why I know I could
never send him away. He and I are in this thing together.

Several days have melted away, and even a whole week—during which
there are some phone calls from various people about the dog. And I
am astonished, in the way of old age, at how insidiously and swiftly
time passes, and how much happens beyond my knowledge, when I
seem to be spending only minutes puttering around the house, and
sleeping now and then. I think probably the house stinks, and at nights
I don't sleep well at all.

This morning a policeman delivered an injunction, and there are
names I have heard of only recently on this injunction. And I realize
that strange machineries have been put into operation, and that this
thing with my dog is no joke. That I am either going to have to put
him to sleep, or find another home for him.

I am no sentimentalist about the dog.

But he is too old to start over, and I sit in my chair thinking about
what I should do. As if sensing my trouble, he comes over and puts
his nose in my hand, which is resting limply from the arm of my rocker.

The day is overcast, and the women from the ranch house are all
inside. This morning, their children circumvented my yard, casting
long looks into my underbrush for the dog. But I kept him inside until
they were in school.

Still, I know this is only a truce. The women are convinced that
their children have the right to cross my lawn, for it is *a shortcut that
saves them almost one-eighth of a mile*, as one of them explained.

Mrs. Van Fossen has called twice within the past few days, saying
she is sorry. I can't figure out whether she is really sorry, or merely
trying to savor the full taste of her victory.

Then I stare at my dog awhile, and finally I begin to accept the fact that it is up to me to kill him. The thought that he would have to spend his last minutes in bewilderment and fear, with an indifferent man injecting death into his veins, in a place smelling of ether and the urine of a hundred strange dogs . . . this is something I can't tolerate.

So in the afternoon I buy some poison at the hardware store. That night it rains, and there is thunder and lightning, and my television set goes off. I hate the God-damned thing anyway. I don't know why I watch it so much.

Naturally I hesitate, and before I know it, three more days have passed. Now there is a policeman at the door, and he is telling me that I have forty-eight hours to take care of the dog, one way or the other. He says he will return the day after tomorrow, and, if the dog is still here, he will be forced to call the dog warden and have him take care of things immediately.

The policeman is young, large, and vague-looking. He seems to resent the position he's been forced into. Several times, he refers to the pressure the neighbors have been putting on the police to get rid of the dog.

He doesn't look at me at all during the conversation. He either stares at a black notebook in his hands, or gazes outward upon nothing as he speaks, or as I answer. Before he leaves, though, he does take a long look at the dog lying on his rug in the hallway.

"It sure is a big one," the policeman says, shaking his head. "No wonder he scares hell out of people."

"Fuck people," I say to the policeman, and he turns and stares at me soberly for an instant, and then grins a little—one man responding to the jocular obscenity of another. Only I have not smiled at all. I have not smiled for a long time. I'm not sure anybody would notice if I did.

When the policeman leaves, my eyes start watering again. I am not crying, although my hands are shaking and I am appalled at the ugliness of things. Outside, it is dark and absolutely still, like a damp cellar.

It is not quite time to feed him yet, but I make up my mind that if it is to be done, it must be done now. I go into the kitchen and pour myself a glass half-full of whiskey. Then I add a little water and stand there sipping it for a few minutes.

Then I fill his dish with food. At the sound of his dish clanking, he stands up and walks into the kitchen looking at me. I finish drinking my whiskey and put the glass on the counter. My eyes are still watering, but this has been happening so much lately that I have learned not to be bothered by it. I don't even wipe the God-damned tears away anymore.

My dog sits down and watches me as I take out the bottle of poison and pour half of it into his food. The man at the hardware store told me that it has no taste and causes a painless death normally within two or three hours. It is a systemic poison; I made sure of that. I told the man I did not want a corrosive.

I will have to pour myself some more whiskey before I can lower the dish of dog food to the floor. My dog sits patiently, watching me almost dispassionately. He must be aware that this is early for his feeding. At this time of year, I usually feed him at dusk. But part of the reason for this is that I don't want the neighbors to see me take him out to his chain.

I drink some of the whiskey, and then pick up the dish of dog food and put it on the floor. I walk over to the single chair at the breakfast table and sit down on it. The dog has not moved. He senses something wrong, perhaps; or is alarmed at what is happening to me, because I am suddenly crying with both of my hands over my eyes. I hear my sobbing come echoing back to me from the emptiness of the house, and then my elbow hits the glass of whiskey, knocking it over.

When I pull my hands away, I can see my dog standing before his bowl, his nose touching it as he investigates. He gives me an inquiring glance, and I hear myself trying to encourage him.

"Eat it," I say in a hoarse voice.

But my voice merely makes him pause. Once more, I start to cry —sounding like the child I was seventy years ago—dismayed at my confusion and awed by the terror and sadness that flood over me.

I try once more to tell him to eat it, but I can only gasp for breath from so much hard weeping. And when I do catch my breath, I see him gulping the food down.

I vowed that I would hold his head when he died, and maybe even drink the rest of the bottle of poison.

But when my dog finishes eating, I grab his collar and lead him to the door. For a few minutes, we stand there in the dirty light of evening and stare out upon the pastel-colored ranch houses, occupying a land that was once covered with oak, beech, and hickory, and populated by foxes and squirrels.

Then I lead him toward his chain. He lurches slightly, almost causing me to fall . . . and then again, causing me to let go of his collar. He runs off into the spiraea bordering my hill in back, and turns to stare at me as he lifts his leg and urinates upon some obscure target.

His eyes seem unnaturally yellow, and suddenly I hate that dog with an inexpressible fury. My hands are clenched as he trots up over the hill.

"He won't come back," I say aloud. "He won't come back."

Now I am sitting in my rocker, staring down at the section of the road where the four women last congregated before coming up to my house.

It is dark, now; and in front of the ranch houses, the electric carriage lamps are lighted.

Perhaps he will crawl into one of their front yards and die there. But I don't believe this will happen. He will crawl into some bushes somewhere, and the dog warden or sanitation department will officiate at the burial ceremonies tomorrow or the next day, between coffee break and lunch.

I turn the television set on and sit there watching aliens from another land joking with one another in a language that I recognize, but do not understand, about a world that seems to be a grotesque translation of all I have known.

Long after dark, I awake and realize that I have been sleeping in my chair. My neck is stiff, and I can hardly breathe. I go into the kitchen and take a little baking soda in warm water; then I return to the other room and sit down. I stare through the window and neighborhood, and see that all the carriage lamps but one are dark. The one that is burning is next to the Van Fossens'. I am not sure what time it is, but I think probably he is dead by now.

I go over to the sofa and lie down. Maybe they will leave me alone, now. Although that will be poor compensation for what is gone. As I lie there, I imagine the yard filled with screaming children—jostling against one another, almost suffocating in the warmth of one another's breath, scratching at my house with their fingernails, trying to break in. And in the distance, Mrs. Van Fossen stands with her arms folded, and her chin raised, saying, "After all, they are human beings. What else do we have, in the last analysis?"

Maybe I'll die this time. I drift off to sleep on the sofa. I am aware that the house stinks, but I don't know why. It is dirt, of course; but there is something else, too.

I am dreaming vaguely. There is an awkward and heavy old rowboat I bought years ago, when I was a boy, and I am trying to pull the boat up onto the bank of the river. But the river is strange—it seems to be filled with smoke and to have no bottom. Somewhere, a stick is banging monotonously against an empty tin can, and several birds hang like tattered rags from a limb that crosses just above my forehead.

Now I hear a scratching sound, and I realize it is my dog. He has come back home.

For a few seconds, I lie motionless as I listen to the scratching sound. He has come back home to die. Maybe I can comfort him in some way.

I get up and walk a few steps, then the room starts shaking and I have to grab onto the doorknob. The scratching has stopped. I am so weak I cannot walk any farther. I ease myself back into the sofa and lose consciousness. Once or twice, I hear the scratching at the door, and I smell the stink in the house but I cannot move.

I awake in the morning and find him lying beside the steps. I let myself down the steps one by one, painstakingly, so as not to fall. He came back instinctively, of course; but also, I think, because he was dying . . . and a still deeper instinct told him I would help him, make him feel better, perhaps, or even make him well. Or possibly save his life.

I lean over and sink down on one knee beside him, and his tail begins to wag slowly, thumping against a bare spot, where the grass will not grow. Then his eye is open, looking at me distantly; and when I feel his muzzle, he manages to lick my hand.

Maybe he is still dying. Maybe he is so big and strong, in spite of his age, that the poison can't work as fast as it normally would.

There is one thing: I can't let them take him away. So I go into the kitchen and pour some more whiskey, preparing myself for the thing I have to do.

This time I am tempted to join him, only I have to use the rest of the poison for him, so there is none left for me. When I am stronger, I will go to the hardware store and get some more.

Half-drunk, I carry poisoned food out to him once more; and now it is afternoon already, and I walk to the front window and see flies buzzing around his hindquarters. Nothing else of him is visible, but his dish is empty.

I cannot go out and look. It is sufficient for me to know that his suffering is over. Toward evening I do manage to go out, and I find the yard empty. The dish is still there, exactly as I last saw it. Parts of the bare ground look darker than others, as if they absorbed liquid. Blood? Vomit? I don't know. I can scarcely see. I turn back toward the house, which in its shameless unpainted state is like an enormous, misshapen animal, covered with silver hair.

I am cold. I go into the house and find my rocker. The television set is on, but I cannot remember turning it on. Maybe there is someone else in the house. I can't remember. Do I hear voices?

No. There are no voices.

Again, there is a scratching sound, and I arise from the sofa and go to the door. He has come back again. He is sitting there, waiting for me—his hindquarters paralyzed and his head swinging back and forth.

I am screaming at him to go away, to get out. I tell him he mustn't come back to me for help. I tell him to stay away because I am trying to kill him. I am raging at him. I don't know whether it is day or night. I hear him whine. The neighborhood is transfixed. Perhaps it is early morning. A breeze chills my arms and back. I am standing outside. He whines and drags his hindquarters after him as he tries to circle my legs.

The television is still on, and I am back inside the house. The dog is shut out, once again. Perhaps he is dying now.

Again I am sleeping, and then again I hear the scratching at the door. It keeps up; it doesn't stop. I go into the pantry and find my old revolver, which I haven't fired for fifteen or twenty years. And a box of shells that are twice that old.

I put two shells in the revolver and make my way out to where the dog is lying. I am speaking to him, because I don't want him to be frightened.

What is a dog, anyway? A curious and unnecessary atavism, a monstrous peculiarity of affection and obsequiousness.

I say these things to myself, and go out into the darkness and call his name. He lifts his head. His eyes look metallic.

Since the eye is a projection of the brain, I point my revolver at the eye, and the shot nudges my wrist back . . . but not sharply enough, not hard enough. And the sound wasn't right. The ammunition was defective.

And I am horrified to see him simply swing his head aside, and start to gulp convulsively. The eye has been shot out, but the God-damned animal is still alive, and staggers through the long uncut grass, and stumbles to its knees and nods its head as if in acknowledgment of some human truth; and then rises once more to stagger a little farther away.

Can't he die? It begins to seem impossible. He continues to move away from me, now hiccuping in the spiraea, where I cannot see him any longer. And then whining gently, as if dreaming something wistful, before a fireplace and surrounded by security and peace.

And finally disappears.

The policeman is talking to me, and I am telling him that the dog is gone. He is asking questions, but I cannot answer because I can see Mrs. Van Fossen, naked, sitting in the weeds of my yard, staring at me. And all around her are children with red eyes and pale faces. And they are scratching at the earth. And screaming.

The stink is stronger than ever. And it is night again, and the carriage lanterns are burning, and I hear scratching again. There is nothing on the television screen, except for a pearl-gray light.

Who turned it on? My rocker is rocking by itself. Rain is running down the window.

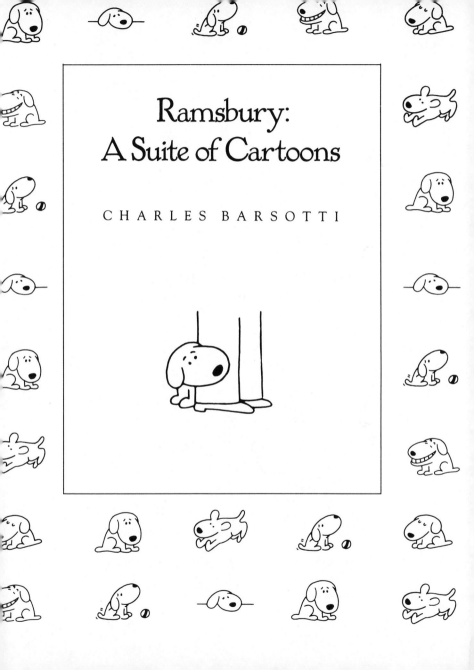

Ramsbury:
A Suite of Cartoons

CHARLES BARSOTTI

Charles Barsotti

"Well, perhaps 'guilty' is too strong a word."

"What the hell did you do with your day before I retired?"

"They feed me, I fetch.
It's a wonderful example
of a symbiotic relationship."

Charles Barsotti

*"Well, it's not as if you didn't give her
some cause to yell at you."*

DETERMINING WHO'S BOSS

"It's O.K. I'm not really in the mood, either."

"There are cat people and there are dog people and there are
people who are a little of both and people who are neither. Each
type of person can be nice in his own way, but generally speaking
you'll be better off sticking with dog people."

Charles Barsotti

"And a bag of peanuts."

"You're right, he is smiling. Now get him to stop."

"Oh, stop acting like a junior partner."

Charles Barsotti

"I'm back. Move."

*"Yeah? Well, I happen to know that you're
not supposed to be in here, either."*

At the Gates of
the Animal Kingdom

AMY HEMPEL

Ten candles in a fish stick tell you it's Gully's birthday.
The birthday girl is the center of attention; she squints
into the popping flash cubes. The black cat seems to
know every smooth cat pose there is. She is burning
for discovery in front of the camera.

Gully belongs to Mrs. Carlin. Mrs. Carlin has had
her since the cat was six weeks old and slept on the
stove, curled inside a saucepan warmed by the pilot
light. Mrs. Carlin has observed every one of Gully's

145

birthdays, wrapping the blue felt mice filled with catnip, wrapping the selection of frozen entrees from Mrs. Paul's, and photographing the birthday girl with her guests.

This year, Gully's guests include the Patterson boys, Pierson and Bret, fourteen and ten, and their cat Bert. Though it would be more accurate to say that Mrs. Carlin and Gully are the *boys'* guests, as the party is being held in the Patterson home.

Mrs. Carlin is staying with the boys for the week that their parents are away in an Eastern city for Mr. Patterson's annual sales conference. It is a condition of Mrs. Carlin's employment that Gully come with her. She had explained to Mrs. Patterson that one time a cat-sitter came to feed Gully, "and Gully—there is no other word for it— screamed."

To wash down the fish stick, Mrs. Carlin fixes Gully a tuña colada—the drained, chilled water that a can of tuna comes packed in. Then she serves the boys their dinner. The boys examine their plates with suspicion, and then with disbelief.

Between the two halves of the sesame seed bun, where there should have been catsup on a hamburger, rare, the boys see what looks like catsup on a cassette tape. It is actually tomato sauce on a slice of sautéed eggplant.

"Didn't our mother tell you what we eat?" says Pierson, the older boy.

"We eat hamburgers," says Bret. "We like hamburgers and smashed potatoes."

Mrs. Carlin tells them that *she* is making the rules now. She says, "Meat's no treat for those you eat."

She waits to let this sink in. "While I am looking after you," she tells the boys, "we will eat nothing with parents."

The boys look at each other so that Mrs. Carlin will see the look. They wish that Scooter were still alive to eat from their plates beneath the table.

In Alaska, begins the voice, *wild gray wolves are flushed from hiding and shot with rifles from low-flying planes.*

Mrs. Carlin loses her thought. She excuses herself from the table, and returns a moment later with a photograph album from her suitcase.

"Duncan's parties were always more lively," Mrs. Carlin tells the boys.

Duncan, asleep in another room, is her elderly long-haired dachshund, his muzzle gone white, a perfect widow's peak in the center of his narrow forehead. Duncan is another condition of Mrs. Carlin's employment.

Through the years, the photos show the dachshund born of a Christmas litter poised on a silver platter, an apple held slack in his mouth; Duncan, a hand-knit sweater covering his rump, heading down a snow-covered hill on a tobaggon; Duncan grinning at his "cake" of steak tartare, his guests straining their leads to reach their party favor chew-toys.

Mrs. Carlin thinks that reminiscing may be why the voice starts up again. This time what she hears is: *a veal calf cramped in a pen in Montana is forced to sleep on its feet.*

Mrs. Carlin asks the boys if they would mind eating alone. She goes to her room and takes two aspirin.

The boys look at Gully, still bent over her fish. Pierson spanks her lightly on the back; her body twitches, but the cat does not leave her dish.

"Takes a smacking and keeps on snacking," Pierson says.

Mrs. Carlin doesn't come out of her room until it is bedtime for the boys.

"We can have Ovaltine," says Bret. But Mrs. Carlin pours them glasses of plain milk, and gives them each a tablespoon of peanut butter to go with it.

"It stimulates your dreams" is what she tells them, and promises a trip to the Aquarium if they are good.

In their own comfortable room, in the Pattersons' soft bed, Gully and Duncan take their cat and dog places—Gully at the head, and Duncan at the foot of the bed. During the night, when Duncan stretches and moves to the other side, Mrs. Carlin's feet seek the warm place where he had lain.

She angles her face on a plane with the cat's, and breathes in the air that Gully breathes out—air that she thought would be warm but which is cool. She thinks about the woman who raised a lion that would suck the woman's thumb whenever something made him nervous. Mrs. Carlin imagines that every creature, including herself, will know this kind of love.

In a research lab in Eastern Pennsylvania, a hole is drilled in the head of a young macaque . . .

Mrs. Carlin draws Gully closer. She scratches the cat's stomach, then strokes the sleek flank that shines like a seal. She strokes the cat's fur for the cat's pleasure, then for her own, and back, and forth, until the pleasures run together and the two of them sleep through the night.

"The other sitters never took us on a field trip," says Bret.

Mrs. Carlin has taken the boys to the Aquarium. The boys are warming up to her—she keeps them entertained. She tells them what she knows about the animal kingdom—that twenty newborn possums will fit in a teaspoon, that snakes smell with their tongues, and horned toads shoot blood from their eyes. From Mrs. Carlin the boys have learned that emperor penguins sometimes ride an ice floe as far north as Rio!

That morning, Pierson complained of a stuffy head. Mrs. Carlin had told him it was sleeping with a pillow over his face that had done it. She told him what he had was called a "turtle headache," and Pierson had asked her if everything had to be animals.

Mrs. Carlin leads the boys to her favorite part of the Aquarium. It is a darkened hall with a green-lit tank that encircles the room. You stand in the center, in the hole of the doughnut, and turn to watch the hundreds of ocean fish swim around you. It is called the Roundabout, and it leaves you dizzy and reaching for the glass if you turn around too many times.

The boys study the reference cards with pictures of the fish. They claim to be able to match the following in the tank: the sting ray, of course, plus yellowtail, striped bass, red snapper, tarpin, and the seven-gill shark.

Always there are those few fish who swim against the tide. These are the ones that Mrs. Carlin follows. For her, the darkness and water and steady current of silent fins is immeasurably soothing. She gives herself over to the whirling sensation which, she believes, leaves her open to what she cannot control when it suddenly comes to her what day it is.

In North Atlantic waters off the Faroe Islands, it is the day of "Grindabod," the return of the pilot whales, when fishing boats herd the whales by hundreds towards the shore. There, fishermen swing grappling hooks into the whales' flesh to insure that the others will ignore their own safety; a whale will not abandon an injured mate.

Knives are drawn, and cleave through to the spinal cord. The whales thrash once more; in a sea of blood, they snap their own necks.

A handkerchief held to her mouth, Mrs. Carlin urges the boys out of the Roundabout. She forces herself to think of other things—the stiff velour of a Shar-pei's folds, the tumbling cubs of a cougar in the hills, Gully's paw holding down a Saltine cracker while her tongue scrapes the surface like a deer at a salt lick.

During the ride home, the boys poke each other and make fun of their teachers. They whine at Mrs. Carlin till she stops the car for ice cream. They eat it in the car, being quiet long enough to look out the windows and see lightning bugs spark the blue dusk.

"In South America," says Mrs. Carlin, a tremor in her voice, "the women weave fireflies in their hair."

And then one of the lightning bugs flies into the windshield. Mrs. Carlin has to sit up straight and lift her chin to see above the glowing smear that streaks her line of vision like a comet.

"Come here, Bert," says Bret. "Little Bert-Bert, little trout, little salmon."

Mrs. Carlin stands listening in the open doorway of Bret's bedroom where he is supposed to be dressing for school. He has lifted one side of his quilt and is calling for the cat under the bed.

"Where's that little naughty-pants? That furry soft furry darn thing?"

Bert stays under the bed.

Bret gives up, then sees Mrs. Carlin and knows that she has heard his string of endearments.

He tries to recover, says, "Dad calls him 'the cockroach.' "

His look suggests that someone else has overheard him like this, and will not let him forget it—his brother, Mrs. Carlin feels sure.

The night before, while the three of them watched television, Pierson had made fun of *her* when her eyes filled with tears during a cat-food commercial. The folks at Purina see me coming, was all that she could say as, privately, she was made aware that *at an animal shelter in Oklahoma, an attendant did not clean the feces off the bowl that he used to scoop dog food from a sack.*

Mrs. Carlin is not ashamed of what she has come to call "the Tender Vittles emotion." And she does not want Bret to be ashamed of showing affection. So she asks if he will help her groom Duncan.

Duncan lies across a pillow on Mrs. Carlin's bed; he doesn't move when Bret drags the brush across his back. When Bret brushes harder, Duncan closes his eyes.

"Takes a bruising and keeps on snoozing," says Bret, proud of the rhyme.

Mrs. Carlin laughs and smooths the dog's fur. "Takes an adoring and keeps on snoring," she says, and props Duncan up. She shows Bret how to draw the wire bristles gently down the dog's hind legs. When she brushes the dog, her bracelet jingles lightly. The only jewelry Mrs. Carlin wears is this charm bracelet of name tags from all of her former pets.

Then she asks Bret to get Duncan's pills from the inside pocket of her suitcase.

Duncan takes lanoxin for his rackety old heart. Mrs. Carlin examines the small plastic bottle and—the Tender Vittles emotion—thinks how unbearably dear it is that her pet's medication is labeled "Duncan Carlin."

Bret watches Mrs. Carlin stroke the dog's white throat to help get the pill down. He says, "I wish Scooter could have lived forever."

Mrs. Carlin looks up quickly. She pictures a plastic bottle labeled "Scooter Patterson."

She says something that is meant to be of comfort. She says, "Try to remember that God is rubbing Scooter's tummy."

She is surprised when Bret starts to laugh.

In her mind, Mrs. Carlin says to Duncan and Gully: You have made my happiness for thirteen years. Gully and the three cats before her, Duncan and the two pups before him—she owes them her life. It is for them she writes checks and Congressmen to try to protect the animals she will never know.

Mrs. Carlin gets the boys off to school, then stands distracted on the Pattersons' front lawn. She walks slowly to the mailbox that is empty of mail. Then she follows the gravel drive lined with ice plant back to the house, just missing the spot where a neighborhood dog has done his business.

Mrs. Carlin slips a section from the morning paper and moves to clean up the mess. But it proves, up close, to be a cluster of whorled bronze snails, glistening with secretion, stuck to curled dead leaves.

Mrs. Carlin carries the newspaper into the house and trades it for the car keys.

She drives with one finger on the wheel at six o'clock—what the Patterson boys call "the accident-prone grip." She is tired, and tired of the voices that are sometimes visions—marmosets whose eyelids are sewn shut with thick waxed thread. Mrs. Carlin is tired of knowing when a rabbit is blinded to improve the scouring power of a popular oven cleaner.

The Aquarium hasn't opened by the time Mrs. Carlin gets there, so she waits in her car.

She is tired of the voices. She says *no* to the voices. It occurs to Mrs. Carlin that the voices take a no-ing and keep on going.

She is the first visitor of the day. When the Aquarium is open, Mrs. Carlin has the Roundabout to herself.

The fish—do they never rest?—are streaming behind the glass. First, Mrs. Carlin spots the single humpbacked bluefish. From the shadow of a sting ray swim a pair of sand-tagger sharks.

She pivots just fast enough to track a school of amberjack the circumference of the tank. Then she plays a game with herself. She makes herself see the fish frozen in resin as in a diorama, feels *herself* the moving figure, the way, when a slow train starts, there is that disconcerting moment when it *could* be the landscape moving and not the train.

Then she lets the resin dissolve, freeing the fish to sluice through kelp and waves of their own kind.

Suddenly there is sound in the room. But not in the room—in Mrs. Carlin's head. She stands still and concentrates on what she seems to hear: *an infant gorilla, orphaned in Zimbabwe, makes a sound in the night like "Woooo, woooo."*

Mrs. Carlin leans against the glass tank for balance. They should limit your time in the Roundabout, she thinks. They should pull you out after so many minutes the way they do in a sauna.

And then she has a vision, clear as if she is there—a Korean family looking for a place to have a picnic. At a shaded clearing in a bamboo forest a mat is spread, a fire built up. The family's dog, a handsome blonde shepherd, is called by his master and gleefully runs to the call.

Mrs. Carlin sees the owner slip a noose around its neck. It is "Bok Day" in South Korea, "Land of the Morning Calm."

It is the picnic of death that Mrs. Carlin attends.

It takes two of this family to tug the dog to a height above the flames. The dog will be hung from a tree to strangle slowly as its fur singes over the fire. The point of slow death is to tenderize the meat.

There is an indescribable sound from the choking dog, and like a person who suffers the pain of an injured twin, Mrs. Carlin gasps and drops to the floor.

That is where the couple who come in from the Fossil Hall find her. The man touches two fingers to Mrs. Carlin's wrist, then touches the side of her neck. The woman calls for a guard, and stands back.

In Belize, the eyes of a fallen jaguar reflect the green of leaves.

Shooting Tookey

B A R B A R A   J.   D I M M I C K

The thin blue clarity of the sky had been thickening, almost imperceptibly, into a kind of cloudy fuzziness ever since noon, and now even the air itself seemed to be thickening, getting heavier, closer. With his sleeve, Tyler rubbed at the sweat and dirt on his face and neck. Sometimes, on an afternoon like this, a thunderstorm would sweep out of the northwest and around the high shoulder of the knob, then roil down the valley, flashing, booming, gusting with fat drops, or, on rarer days, pelting hail instead of rain. But first there would be a breeze, like a chill cellar draft, as though saved from the winter, preserved and yet somehow freshened, cleansed of darkness, and it would bring a goose-pimpling current of cool relief.

Still, if it would come, the breeze and then maybe the storm, it hadn't yet, and Tyler rested the handle of the shovel against his shoulder and looked down into the hole. He'd gone nearly a foot and a half already, saving out the rocks like his mother had told him, to keep the animals away after. Tyler wiped his eyes. Two feet at least, she'd told him, and knowing that it would please her, his doing it right the first time, he dug some more.

At the end, when the dirt began sliding back into the hole, he threw down the shovel, blade pinging as it hit the hardpan, and started scooping out the loose dirt with his hands. Then, all at once, he jumped up, yelping, and thrust one hand in the other armpit. He'd jammed a finger against a rock, pawing in the earth like that, like some animal. He stamped his feet, stamping away the pain, and spat with anger and disgust.

Where the hell was his old man, anyway? It was his old man's dog and where was the lazy bastard, anyways? Fishing maybe, or off to the feed store. No, probably down in the village, on the front porch of the grocery, squatting on the cool concrete with a beer in a paper bag and ogling the legs of the women who brushed past him on the steps.

It was deep enough, Tyler decided. Goddamn deep enough. And nursing his bruised finger, blowing on it, he went to fetch the boiled-out soup bone his mother had left on the porch for him to throw into the hole. As he skirted the lilac bush, his fingers making muddy prints on the parched white bone, he caught sight of Tookey, lying there in his special place under the lilacs. The setter's nose went up with interest at the bone, and feathers fanning, his tail thumped and brought down a shower of purple petals.

"Not now," Tyler said.

Tookey's tail drooped, then stilled.

Up around the back of the garden, Tyler tossed the bone into the grave. It rolled to one corner, and when it stopped it was covered with red earth. His mother had said Tookey would go in after the bone and they could do it then, when he was down in the grave, going for the bone. Tyler didn't think Tookey would, and then, unbidden, came an image of the dog in death, loose-lipped, as if for some reason blowing out a candle, but with red earth on his nose and on his pink and white tongue. There was a cold twist in Tyler's gut and he hoped suddenly, fervently, that Tookey wouldn't go for the bone.

He'd been a good dog. He was ailing now, but he'd been a pretty good dog. Tyler's father had fished him out of the creek, where someone had left him, the runt of the litter, for dead and drowned. Leave it to his old man to bring home a half-drowned pup instead of a stringer of fish. But the puppy had romped and frolicked with Tyler, tumbling on the grass and rolling on the kitchen floor, and they'd named him Tookey because that's what Tyler had called him—tookey, tookey, instead of doggy, doggy. Later, the few short times his father had worked a job and Tyler had been free to roam, it was Tookey who would tramp the woods and fields with him, sometimes climbing the ridges to the top of the knob. On those days, those private boy-and-dog days, Tyler, legs sprawled across a bed of moss, would lean back against a great white oak, the shallow elongated hollow in the trunk cradling his back, and he would look down at the farmstead. It seemed so small, so miniature, so neat even, and he felt free of the place then, but secure with the tree at his back and Tookey panting at his side. But when he did have chores, when he had to stay and tend the hogs and hens, Tookey would come along then, too, always lying in some cool spot, or when he had to work in the garden Tookey would gladly chase down clumps of weeds Tyler threw, same as the sticks and slivers when he chopped wood.

Tyler rinsed the bone in a pail near the henhouse, trudged to the shed for a scrap of newspaper, and then back up the hill. He lay the bone on the paper in the bottom of the hole. Now if Tookey went for it, he'd be going after a clean bone, even if all of them had long ago supped all the nourishment that could be boiled out of it.

His mother sat at the kitchen table, shuffling and reshuffling a deck of tattered cards, the deck that you had to remember the joker was one of the kings. She paused, patted her forehead with the inside of her wrist, then patted the wrist on her apron.

Tyler took the rifle from the corner behind the door. It was an Enfield, an old heavy infantry rifle his father had gotten in a swap, and he stood testing its balance. The barrel felt heavy, so heavy that it always seemed to nosedive, and he could only imagine how a good rifle, or maybe a shotgun, would feel in his hands.

"Tyler," his mother said.

He slid the bolt and checked the chamber. One shell. But that was all it would take. Somebody before had fooled with it, changed it around to a single shot. It might be good enough for scaring things off, like possums and bobcats, but still, Tyler didn't think it was good for much else.

"Tyler," his mother said again.

Jeezum, he wasn't deaf. He could hear her. "What? What is it? What do you want?" But then he heard the strange, shrill mockery in his voice and it shamed him. He felt sorry for answering back, bewildered that his dislike of the rifle in his hands had somehow led him first not to pay her any mind and then made him answer back.

"You understand, don't you?" she asked.

Soothing, he thought. She's trying to soothe me.

Well, he didn't need it. He understood all right. He understood his father had brought home a half-dead pup twelve years before and that that half-dead pup was now Tookey, and that there wasn't money for a trip to the vet's for the needle that would make him go to sleep forever. And he understood that his father, knowing that something had to be done, knowing that his wife—Tyler's mother—would take care of it somehow, had been out gallivanting more than usual lately, wanting not to be there. And all at once he understood this too: that his mother had accepted this duty, as she had accepted his father, and that her acceptance had first spawned him and then had, in some crazy convoluted way, involved him in the shooting of this dog.

He said nothing.

"It's because your father doesn't have the heart. And now that the others are away . . ."

The others were his little brother and sister, and they were at his grandmother's, where they would be reminded not to scuffle their feet against the rungs of their chairs and not to grab across the table. Still, suddenly, he wished he'd gone with them. It would have been easier to be a mannerly boy in that stuffy dining room than the bearer of this clumsy rifle.

Tyler cut her off. "Let's just do it, okay? We'll just do it."

"Wait," she said. "You look hot." She fanned the back of her neck. "You must be—out there digging and all." She got up. "You have a drink first, a nice cool drink."

"After," he told her. "I'll have something after."

It was all started now. The hole was dug, the bone in the hole, the rifle in his hands. And after a drink—of what? mint tea? sweetened vinegar?—he might not be able to go through with it. The wish to be away, to be with his little brother and sister, to not have to do this thing, was futile. He knew that. And he knew he desperately wanted to hurry up and finish the job, get it over with, before his old man came, before anybody came and saw that bone on its piece of paper.

Tyler whistled Tookey out from under the lilacs. His mother had the rifle in case he had to carry the dog up around back, but Tookey crawled out from under the bush and hoisted himself to his feet.

They rounded the shed and headed up the hill. The last of it was started, but to Tyler, his mother, still in her apron, seemed to carry the rifle as if it were her mop, as if it had no power of death. Only the throbbing of his bruised finger was real, and that was faint. He studied it as if it didn't belong to him and then squeezed the joint to make it pound harder and faster.

"You see," his mother said, "we really do have to do it."

Giddily, he looked back. Tookey's tail was barely waving, his body queerly hunched, and there were pale petals from the lilac, like scattered festoons, tangled in his coat. But when he saw how Tookey was trying to keep up, how game he was, instead of feeling pride for the dog, he remembered its fawning duplicity. He remembered that it was really his father's dog, and Tookey would only keep him company when his old man wasn't around, and that when Tookey heard that special whistle, he would desert Tyler, run off without even looking back. Tyler would always stand and point in the direction of the whistle, pretending to order the dog away pretending his desertion was really obedience. But if only Tookey hadn't always gone. If only once he had chosen Tyler.

"Give me the gun," he said.

"No, I'll do it." His mother's voice quavered into a kind of firmness. "I said I'd do it and I will."

She'd told him the day before about her plan to shoot Tookey, telling him the kindest way to kill a dog was to send it on one last retrieve and then shoot it on the run. But she didn't trust her aim and had come up with the bone-in-the-grave plan instead. Still, at the time, it had baffled and somehow saddened Tyler that his mother knew so much about such things—knew how deep to dig a grave, how to shoot and bury a dog.

Tookey lowered himself onto the mound of damp earth beside the grave, and, with tongue hanging, looked up at Tyler. He seemed cheerfully perplexed, as if lying on a pile of earth next to the cool updraft of the newly dug hole were some strange but intriguing entertainment.

Mechanically, Tyler pointed down into the grave. Tookey shifted his haunches, and with brow furrowed, cocked his ears, sighted along Tyler's arm, and sniffed toward the bone. Tail wagging, he inched forward. Tyler's hand, frozen in a point, seemed to him farther away

than the end of his arm, the pain in his finger even farther, the bone
and the grave miles beyond. And yet it was as though Tookey, in a
dizzily expanding void between Tyler's next breath and his next pulse
beat, would gladly belly that distance, belly away from Tyler, toward
that boiled-dry soup bone. But then he paused, his ears fell back, and
Tyler felt the warm slipperiness of Tookey's tongue on the back of his
hand. Rejoicing, he plucked a lilac petal from the fringe of Tookey's
ear and gave the thin, fleshy silkiness a gentle tug. Tookey hadn't gone
off. He had chosen him.

All at once, Tookey's ribs heaved and there was something like a
sharp catching in his chest. His tail stilled, his lips drew back, and he
coughed up some blood. Tyler's hand hung helplessly, wanting to caress,
to comfort, to possess. But the blood on the dog's lips made his own
throat feel tight, made his chest feel like caving in with loss, with
betrayal. He pointed furiously at the bone again and again. "Fetch the
damn bone," he wailed. "Fetch it, fetch it, fetch it."

Tookey rolled over onto his side, tail between his legs, quailing, and
in desperation Tyler knelt and tried to shove him away into the grave.

It was the click of the safety, cold and metallic, that quieted him
so that he could finally hear his mother's voice saying, "It's all right,
it's all right. Just get back."

And so he got back, stood behind his mother, and before he had
time to think or look away, she lifted the rifle and shot.

The dog screamed, more blood coming with the scream, and then,
trying to rise, to escape, it slipped feetfirst into its grave.

He had seen his mother drop the shot. The roar of the rifle echoed
in his ears, muddling his thoughts, but he knew she had dropped the
shot.

Hands trembling, rifle trembling, she fumbled in the pocket of her
apron for the second shell. Her fingers clutched and opened under the
thin cotton, and her lips twisted soundlessly, but it seemed to Tyler as
if the dog's moaning were coming from her mouth.

"We'll go away," she said finally, her voice low. "We'll go away and wait. He'll die."

Not his dog. His dog wasn't going to be left to die. His old man, his mother might do such a thing, but not him.

He took the rifle for himself and plucked the shell from his mother's pocket.

"Don't," she whispered. She grabbed the barrel of the rifle and set it shaking in his hands. "Don't. He'll die. He will die."

"Go back inside," he told her. And he thought he might have to slap her to get her to straighten up and wondered suddenly if he would, wondered how it would feel.

But she took her hand from the rifle, and with her shoulders hunched and her apron lifted for some reason to cover her bosom, she half ran down the hill.

Tyler stood with the rifle at his hip and waited until she was out of sight. Then, still filled with the horror and excitement brought by the thought of slapping her—slap her? his own mother?—he aimed at Tookey's chest and squeezed off a shot.

There was a crash of the rifle, the roaring echo, the brief muddle in his head, and then a profound silence.

Tookey was dead. The blood flowed freely, thick and dark, and somehow, in a way he didn't understand, Tyler felt better about this flow of blood than he had about the red sputum of Tookey's last days. It was as though something pent up had been loosed, as though he had been the one with the strength to loose it, and because of that, he felt a mysterious superiority, a freedom.

The screen door, springs zinging and jangling, slammed shut behind him, bounced open again and then finally bumped shut. His mother sat at the table dealing out a game of clockwork canasta. She looked up and called to him: "Tyler."

He put the rifle behind the door.

Again: "Tyler."

Jesus, don't start, he thought. Don't start this Tyler, Tyler business.

"Come here," she said, and holding out her arms for him, she began to weep.

He stood where he was, watched her tears run, but now, instead of the dog's moaning, he heard her own keening. He stood still, waiting for her to stop, waiting for silence, and he remembered the echo, then the stillness after the rattling crash of the rifle.

His mother let her arms drop and like a blind woman turned over the first card.

That damn game, he thought. That damn clock canasta. You never win because the last king always turns up at the wrong time. And now, watching his mother turn over the cards faster and faster, as if speed might help her beat the king, he felt the lure of the game, the lure that sometime—maybe this time—the cards would all come up in the right order.

"I'll have my drink now," he said, and going to the refrigerator, he took out a beer. It was the last one, and he took it on irrevocable impulse, in answer to the sudden instinct that there was something he had to prove, something to do with not waiting for cards to turn up right, not waiting for dogs to die.

"Tyler!" his mother cried. There was fright in her voice. "Your father . . . !"

His father never let him drink beer, saying, *When he pays for it he can have it, but he ain't having mine.*

Tyler twisted off the cap and snapped it into the sink. Then he met his mother's gaze, he lifted the bottle and took a log pull. But the beer was bitter and cold—so bitter, tears came to his eyes; so cold, a pain raked his scalp. His jaw tightened. Against the sweating bottle, his bruised finger began to throb again, and, with tears welling, he fled the kitchen.

He found himself looking down at Tookey's grave, down at the raw earth and at the blanket of stones he had pieced together when he had been so pleased at his cleverness with the stones, so full of wonder at his courage. He had even reached into the grave and brushed some of the lilacs from Tookey's coat, taken the knuckled bone and tossed it off into the woods. But he had lost that, lost the feeling of courage, the feeling of strength, and as if to prove he had once had it, as if to get it back, he drew at the bottle again, but the beer was sharp in his mouth and he spat it off to one side of the grave.

Tyler wiped his mouth, and then, almost as an afterthought, scrubbed the rest of his face dry with his sleeve. There would be no storm. The sky was still heavy, the air still heavy, but there would be no cool breeze, no pelting rain, no clearing off after.

So he sat for a long time, thinking of nothing, until at last he saw the long plume of dust drawn by his father's truck and heard the muffled banging of the rotted tailgate. Then from the yard came that shrill but melodiously fluctuating whistle. And all at once, he realized that Tookey would have bounded off, that Tookey hadn't chosen him.

The whistle came again, this time the last notes full of questions: *Where are you, Tookey? Can't you hear me, Tookey? Ain't you coming?*

No, he ain't, Tyler thought with a brief but bitter gladness. He ain't coming. But maybe it wasn't within a dog's ken to choose to answer or not to answer the whistles of the one it loved best.

Tyler studied the beer in the bottle, studied the broken circle of frothy bubbles inside the amber-brown glass, and he thought of his mother, alone in the kitchen where he had left her, had chosen to leave her, and where she couldn't help herself but to play the game, couldn't help herself but to wait for his father. He lifted the beer, about to drink, but the whistle came again, forlorn now. He pulled the bottle away and paused, looked toward the house as if a whistle might somehow track him down, find him out. Very quietly, he set the bottle down, careful not to break it, paused again, and then, after listening one last time, he headed up toward the knob, where he would lean against his oak, where he would not be able to hear, except in his heart, his father's calls and whistles.

A Story of a Girl and Her Dog

ALIX KATES SHULMAN

I

Lucky Larrabee was an only child, and unpredictable. At eight, she was still trying to sail down from the garage roof with an umbrella. She never ate ice cream without a pickle. She was afraid of nothing in the world except three boys in her class and her uncle Len who patted her funny. She brought home every stray dog in the neighborhood. She upset the assistant principal by participating in the Jewish Affair.

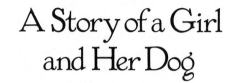

Naturally her parents worried, but they adored her nevertheless and all the more.

There is little Lucky, wearing red anklets with stripes down the sides and poorly tied brown oxfords while everyone else has on loafers, her hair hanging down in strings, her chin thrust out, absolutely refusing to sing the words Jesus or Christ. Why? Two Jewish girls in her class will not sing, and though she has never been Jewish before, Lucky has joined them. She says it is a free country and you can be anything you like. I'm a Jew, she says and will not sing Jesus.

Everyone knows she's no more Jewish than their teacher. It is ridiculous! But she insists and what can they do? She is ruining the Christmas Pageant. They'll get her at recess, they'll get her after school, they'll plant bad pictures in her desk, they'll think of something. But it won't work. Incorrigible little fanatic!

Okay. She doesn't have to sing. But will she just mouth the words silently during the program please? No one will have to know.

No, she won't. If they try to make her, she swears she'll hold her breath until she faints instead. Perhaps she'll do it anyway! Perhaps she'll hold it till she's dead! That'll show them who's a Jew and who isn't.

Is something wrong at home, Mrs. Larrabee? Does Lucky eat a good enough breakfast? Get enough sleep? She is very thin. Has she grown thinner? Not meaning to alarm you, but Lucky has been unusually sullen in class lately—doesn't participate in the class discussions as she used to, doesn't volunteer her answers, no longer seems interested in current events, spends too much time daydreaming, picking at scabs, being negative. She doesn't seem to be trying. Her fingernails. Is there any known source of tension at home? The school likes to be kept informed about these matters as we try to keep parents informed about progress at school. Don't you agree, parents and teachers ought to be working closely together in harmony, for the benefit of the child. The only concrete suggestion the school can make at this time is some companionship and diversion for Lucky. Another child perhaps, or a dog. Meanwhile, we'll just keep an eye on her. Thank you so much for coming in. These conferences are always helpful in any case, even if they do no more than clear the air.

As the Larrabees had been half considering buying a dog for Christmas anyway, they decided it would do no harm to seem accommodating and took the step. They waited until a month had elapsed after the Christmas Pageant so Lucky would not suspect a connection, and then, piling into the new family Nash, backing out of the cinder drive, they drove straight out Main Street beyond the city limits and continued on into the country to buy a dog.

2

Naturally, Lucky was permitted by the concerned Larrabees to pick out the pup herself, with only one restriction. It had to be a boy dog, they said, because if they took home a girl dog, sooner or later they would have to have her spayed, which would be cruel and unnatural and would make her into a fat, lazy, unhappy bitch, or they'd have to let her have babies. For keeping her locked up during heat (also cruel and unnatural) couldn't be expected to work forever; creatures have a way of eluding their jailors in quest of forbidden knowledge—witness the fate of Sleeping Beauty, Bluebeard's wives, etc., and the unwanted litters of the neighborhood bitches. And if they let her go ahead and have her babies, well, either they'd have to keep the puppies (a certain portion of which could be expected to be females too), generating an unmanageable amount of work, anxiety, and expense, even supposing they had the facilities, which of course they did not. Or they'd have to wrench the pups away from their mother (equally cruel and unnatural as well as a bad example for a child) and worry about finding a decent home for each of them besides. No, no, it could be any pup she chose as long as it was male.

The seven mongrel puppies from which she was permitted to choose one were to her untutored eyes and arms indistinguishable as to sex unless she deliberately looked. So she was perfectly happy to restrict her choice to the four males, though she did feel sorry for the females who, it seemed, were condemned to suffer a cruel and unnatural life or else bring on like Eve more trouble than they were worth—particularly since cuddling them in the hollow between her neck and shoulder felt quite as wonderful as cuddling the males. But such, she accepted, was family life.

She chose neither the runt she was temperamentally drawn to but upon whom her father frowned, nor the jumper of the litter over whom her mother voiced certain reasonable reservations, but instead picked from the two remaining males the long-eared, thoughtful-eyed charmer who endeared himself to her by stepping across three of his siblings as though they were stepping stones in order to reach her eager fingers wiggling in the corner of the box and investigate them with his adorable wet nose. Curiosity: the quality her parents most admired in Lucky herself. He sniffed and then licked her fingers in a sensual gesture she took for friendship, and although she continued to examine all the pups for a considerable time, picking them up and cuddling them individually, deliberating at length before rendering her final decision, she knew very early the one she would take home. It pained her to reject the others, particularly the runt and a certain female who tickled her neck lovingly when she held her up and was pure when she peeked underneath. But by eight Lucky had already learned through experience that one could not have everything one wanted, that every choice entailed the rejection of its alternatives, and that if she didn't hurry up and announce her selection, much as she enjoyed playing with all the puppies, she'd provoke her father's pique and lose the opportunity to decide herself.

She named the dog Skippy because of the funny way he bounced when he walked. An unimaginative name perhaps, but direct (a quality she instinctively valued) and to her inexperienced mind, which did not know that the dog would stop bouncing once it got a few months older, appropriate. Her parents thought she might have selected a name with more flair, but naturally they said nothing.

3

The day of Lucky's brightening (her word, for no one ever taught her another) seemed like an ordinary late-summer Saturday. Unsuspectingly, she was just finishing a treasured bath, where she had spent a long time sending the water back and forth between the sides of the tub to simulate ocean waves. She was studying the movement of the water, its turbulence, its cresting at the edges and doubling back, trying to imagine how the process could possibly illuminate, as her father declared, the mysteries of the ocean's waves and tides; and afterward when her brain had grown weary of encompassing the continental coasts, which she had never seen, the earth and the moon, she filled her washcloth with puffs of air which she could pop out in little explosions into the water, sending big bubbles rippling through the bath like porpoises.

Up through the open bathroom window drifted the familiar sounds of her father setting up the barbecue in the backyard and her mother bringing out the fixings on a tray. Next door Bertie Jones was still mowing the lawn while from the Jones's screened-in porch the ballgame droned on. Summer days; dog days.

Lucky climbed reluctantly from the tub, now cold, and examined herself in the mirror. Whistle gap between her front teeth, a splash of freckles, short protruding ears, alert: Lucky herself. If she had known what delights awaited her in the next room, she would not have lingered to peel a strip of burnt skin from her shoulder or scratch open a mosquito bite. But she was a nervous child who had never, from the day she learned to drop things over the edge of her high chair for her mother to retrieve, been able to let well enough alone. Three full minutes elapsed before she finally wrapped herself in a towel and padded into her bedroom where Skip, banished from the backyard during dinner preparations, awaited her with wagging tail.

"Skippy Dip!" she cried, dropping to her knees and throwing her arms around him. She hugged his neck and he licked her face in a display of mutual affection.

She tossed her towel at the door, sat down on the maple vanity bench, made a moue at her freckle face in the mirror, and in a most characteristic pursuit, lifted her left foot to the bench to examine an interesting blister on her big toe, soaked clean and plump in her long bath.

Suddenly Skip's wet little nose, as curious as on the day they had met, delved between her legs with several exploratory sniffs.

"Skip!" Lucky giggled in mock dismay, "Get out of there," pushing his nose aside and quickly lowering her foot, for she did know a little. Skip retreated playfully but only until Lucky returned (inevitably) to the blister. For like any pup who has not yet completed his training, he could hardly anticipate every consequence or generalize from a single instance. You know how a dog longs to sniff at things. When Lucky's knee popped up again, exposing that interesting smell, Skip's nose returned as though invited.

Suddenly Lucky felt a new, intriguing sensation. *"What's this?"*

She had once, several years earlier, felt another strange sensation in the groin, one that had been anything but pleasant. She and Judy Jones, the girl next door, had been playing mother and baby in a game of House. As Lucky lay on the floor of that very room having her "diaper" changed by a maternal Judy, the missing detail to lend a desired extra touch of verisimilitude to the game struck Lucky. "Baby powder!" she cried. "Sprinkle on some baby powder!"

"Baby powder?" blinked Judy.

"Get the tooth powder from the bathroom shelf. The Dr. Lyons."

In the first contact with Skip's wet nose, Lucky remembered her words as if they still hung in the room. She didn't stop to remember the intervening events: how Judy obediently went to the bathroom but couldn't find the Dr. Lyons; how after finally finding it she could barely manage to get the tin open. Lucky's memory flashed ahead to the horrible instant when the astringent powder fell through the air from a great (but not sufficiently great) height onto the delicate tissue of her inner labia and stung her piercingly, provoking a scream that brought her poor mother running anxiously from a distant room.

But the sensation produced by her pal Skippy was in every respect different. It was cool not hot; insinuating not shocking; cozy, provocative, delicious. It drew her open and out, not closed in retreat. No scream ensued, only the arresting thought, *What's this?* Like the dawning of a new idea or the grip of that engaging question, What makes it tick? If she had had the movable ears of her friend's species, they would have perked right up. *What's this?* The fascination of beginnings, the joy of the new. Something more intriguing than a blister.

She touched Skip's familiar silky head tentatively, but this time did not quite push it away. And he, enjoying the newness too (he was hardly more than a pup), sniffed and then, bless him, sniffed again. And following the natural progression for a normally intelligent dog whose interest has been engaged—as natural and logical as the human investigator's progress from observed phenomenon to initial hypothesis to empirical test—the doggie's pink tongue followed his nose's probe with a quizzical exploratory lick.

4

What would her poor parents have thought if they had peeked in? They would have known better than to see or speak evil, for clearly these two young creatures, these trusting pups (of approximately the same ages when you adjust for species), were happy innocents. They would probably have blamed themselves for having insisted on a male pup. They might even have taken the poor animal to the gas chambers of the ASPCA and themselves to some wildly expensive expert who would only confuse and torment them with impossibly equivocal advice until they made some terrible compromise. At the very least, there would have been furious efforts at distraction and that night much wringing of hands.

Fortunately our Adam and Eve remain alone to pursue their pragmatic investigations. The whole world is before them.

5

The charcoal is now ready to take on the weenies. Mrs. Larrabee kisses her husband affectionately on the neck as she crosses the yard toward the house. She opens the screen door, leans inside, and yells up the stairs, "Dinner."

"Just a minute," says Lucky, squeezing her eyes closed. One more stroke of that inquisitive tongue—only one more!—and Lucky too will possess as her own one of nature's most treasured recipes.

Waves and oceans, suns and moons, barbecues, bubbles, blisters, tongues and tides—what a rich banquet awaits the uncorrupted.

Victrola

WRIGHT MORRIS

"Sit!" said Bundy, although the dog already sat. His knowing what Bundy would say was one of the things people noticed about their close relationship. The dog sat—not erect, like most dogs, but off to one side, so that the short-haired pelt on one rump was always soiled. When Bundy attempted to clean it, as he once did, the spot no longer matched the rest of the dog, like a cleaned spot on an old rug. A second soiled spot was on his head, where children and strangers liked to

172

pat him. Over his eyes the pelt was so thin his hide showed through. A third defacement had been caused by the leash in his younger years, when he had tugged at it harder, sometimes almost gagging as Bundy resisted.

Those days had been a strain on both of them. Bundy developed a bad bursitis, and the crease of the leash could still be seen on the back of his hand. In the past year, over the last eight months, beginning with the cold spell in December, the dog was so slow to cross the street Bundy might have to drag him. That brought on spells of angina for Bundy, and they would both have to stand there until they felt better. At such moments the dog's slantwise gaze was one that Bundy avoided. "Sit!" he would say, no longer troubling to see if the dog did.

The dog leashed to a parking meter, Bundy walked through the drugstore to the prescription counter at the rear. The pharmacist, Mr. Avery, peered down from a platform two steps above floor level—the source of a customer's still-pending lawsuit. His gaze to the front of the store, he said, "He still itching?"

Bundy nodded. Mr. Avery had recommended a vitamin supplement that some dogs found helpful. The scratching had been replaced by licking.

"You've got to remember," said Avery, "he's in his nineties. When you're in your nineties, you'll also do a little scratchin'!" Avery gave Bundy a challenging stare. If Avery reached his nineties, Bundy was certain Mrs. Avery would have to keep him on a leash or he would forget who he was. He had repeated this story about the dog's being ninety ever since Bundy had first met him and the dog was younger.

"I need your expertise," Bundy said. (Avery lapped up that sort of flattery.) "How does five cc.'s compare with five hundred mg.'s?"

"It doesn't. Five cc.'s is a liquid measure. It's a spoonful."

"What I want to know is, how much vitamin C am I getting in five cc.'s?"

"Might not be any. In a liquid solution, vitamin C deteriorates rapidly. You should get it in the tablet." It seemed clear he had expected more of Bundy.

"I see," said Bundy. "Could I have my prescription?"

Mr. Avery lowered his glasses to look for it on the counter. Bundy might have remarked that a man of Avery's age—and experience— ought to know enough to wear glasses he could both see and read through, but having to deal with him once a month dictated more discretion than valor.

Squinting to read the label, Avery said, "I see he's upped your dosage." On their first meeting, Bundy and Avery had had a sensible discussion about the wisdom of minimal medication, an attitude that Bundy thought was unusual to hear from a pharmacist.

"His point is," said Bundy, "since I like to be active, there's no reason I shouldn't enjoy it. He tells me the dosage is still pretty normal."

"Hmm," Avery said. He opened the door so Bundy could step behind the counter and up to the platform with his Blue Cross card. For the umpteenth time he told Bundy, "Pay the lady at the front. Watch your step as you leave."

As he walked toward the front Bundy reflected that he would rather be a little less active than forget what he had said two minutes earlier.

"We've nothing but trouble with dogs," the cashier said. "They're in and out every minute. They get at the bars of candy. But I can't ever remember trouble with your dog."

"He's on a leash," said Bundy.

"That's what I'm saying," she replied.

When Bundy came out of the store, the dog was lying down, but he made the effort to push up and sit.

"Look at you," Bundy said, and stooped to dust him off. The way he licked himself, he picked up dirt like a blotter. A shadow moved over them, and Bundy glanced up to see, at a respectful distance, a lady beaming on the dog like a healing heat lamp. Older than

Bundy—much older, a wraithlike creature, more spirit than substance, her face crossed with wisps of hair like cobwebs—Mrs. Poole had known the dog as a pup; she had been a dear friend of its former owner, Miss Tyler, who had lived directly above Bundy. For years he had listened to his neighbor tease the dog to bark for pieces of liver, and heard the animal push his food dish around the kitchen.

"What ever will become of him?" Miss Tyler would whisper to Bundy, anxious that the dog shouldn't hear what she was saying. Bundy had tried to reassure her: look how spry she was at eighty! Look how the dog was overweight and asthmatic! But to ease her mind he had agreed to provide him with a home, if worst came to worst, as it did soon enough. So Bundy inherited the dog, three cases of dog food, balls and rubber bones in which the animal took no interest, along with an elegant cushioned sleeping basket he never used.

Actually, Bundy had never liked biggish dogs with very short pelts. Too much of everything, to his taste, was overexposed. The dog's long muzzle and small beady eyes put him in mind of something less than a dog. In the years with Miss Tyler, without provocation the animal would snarl at Bundy when they met on the stairs, or bark wildly when he opened his mailbox. The dog's one redeeming feature was that when he heard someone pronounce the word *sit* he would sit. That fact brought Bundy a certain distinction, and the gratitude of many shop owners. Bundy had once been a cat man. The lingering smell of cats in his apartment had led the dog to sneeze at most of the things he sniffed.

Two men, seated on stools in the corner tavern, had turned from the bar to gaze out into the sunlight. One of them was a clerk at the supermarket where Bundy bought his dog food. "Did he like it?" he called as Bundy came into view.

"Not particularly," Bundy replied. Without exception, the dog did not like anything he saw advertised on television. To that extent he was smarter than Bundy, who was partial to anything served with gravy.

The open doors of the bar looked out on the intersection, where an elderly woman, as if emerging from a package, unfolded her limbs through the door of a taxi. Sheets of plate glass on a passing truck reflected Bundy and the notice that was posted in the window of the bar, advising of a change of ownership. The former owner, an Irishman named Curran, had not been popular with the new crowd of wine and beer drinkers. Nor had he been popular with Bundy. A scornful man, Curran dipped the dirty glasses in tepid water, and poured drops of sherry back into the bottles. Two epidemics of hepatitis had been traced to him. Only when he was gone did Bundy realize how much the world had shrunk. To Curran, Bundy had confessed that he felt he was now living in another country. Even more he missed Curran's favorite expression, "Outlive the bastards!"

Two elderly men, indifferent to the screech of braking traffic, tottered toward each other to embrace near the center of the street. One was wearing shorts. A third party, a younger woman, escorted them both to the curb. Observing an incident like this, Bundy might stand for several minutes as if he had witnessed something unusual. Under an awning, where the pair had been led, they shared the space with a woman whose gaze seemed to focus on infinity, several issues of the *Watchtower* gripped in her trembling hands.

At the corner of Sycamore and Poe streets—trees crossed poets, as a rule, at right angles—Bundy left the choice of the route up to the dog. Where the sidewalk narrowed, at the bend in the street, both man and dog prepared themselves for brief and unpredictable encounters. In the cities, people met and passed like sleepwalkers, or stared brazenly at each other, but along the sidewalks of small towns they felt the burden of their shared existence. To avoid rudeness, a lift of the eyes or a muttered greeting was necessary. This was often an annoyance for Bundy: the long approach by sidewalk, the absence of cover, the unavoidable moment of confrontation, then Bundy's abrupt greeting or a wag of his head, which occasionally startled the other person. To the young a quick "Hi!" was appropriate, but it was not at all suitable for elderly ladies, a few with pets as escorts. To avoid these encounters, Bundy might suddenly veer into the street or an alleyway, dragging the reluctant dog behind him. He liked to meet strangers, especially children, who would pause to stroke his bald spot. What kind of dog was he? Bundy was tactfully evasive; it had proved to be an unfruitful topic. He was equally noncommittal about the dog's ineffable name.

"Call him Sport," he would say, but this pleasantry was not appreciated. A smart aleck's answer. Their sympathies were with the dog.

To delay what lay up ahead, whatever it was, they paused at the barnlike entrance of the local van-and-storage warehouse. The draft from inside smelled of burlap sacks full of fragrant pine kindling, and mattresses that were stored on boards above the rafters. The pair contemplated a barn full of junk being sold as antiques. Bundy's eyes grazed over familiar treasure and stopped at a Morris chair with faded green corduroy cushions cradling a carton marked "FREE KITTENS."

He did not approach to look. One thing having a dog had spared him was the torment of losing another cat. Music (surely Elgar, something awful!) from a facsimile edition of an Atwater Kent table-model radio bathed dressers and chairs, sofas, beds and love seats, man and dog impartially. As it ended the announcer suggested that Bundy stay tuned for a Musicdote.

Recently, in this very spot—as he sniffed similar air, having paused to take shelter from a drizzle—the revelation had come to Bundy that he no longer wanted other people's junk. Better yet (or was it worse?), he no longer *wanted*—with the possible exception of an English mint, difficult to find, described as curiously strong. He had a roof, a chair, a bed, and, through no fault of his own, he had a dog. What little he had assembled and hoarded (in the garage a German electric-train set with four locomotives, and three elegant humidors and a pouch of old pipes) would soon be gratifying the wants of others. Anything else of value? The cushioned sleeping basket from Abercrombie & Fitch that had come with the dog. That would sell first. Also two Italian raincoats in good condition, and a Borsalino hat—*Extra Extra Superiore*—bought from G. Colpo in Venice.

Two young women, in the rags of fashion but radiant and blooming as gift-packed fruit, brushed Bundy as they passed, the spoor of their perfume lingering. In the flush of this encounter, his freedom from want dismantled, he moved too fast, and the leash reined him in. Rather than be rushed, the dog had stopped to sniff a meter. He found meters more life-enhancing than trees now. It had not always been so: some years ago he would tug Bundy up the incline to the park, panting and hoarsely gagging, an object of compassionate glances from elderly women headed down the grade, carrying lapdogs. This period had come to a dramatic conclusion.

In the park, back in the deep shade of the redwoods, Bundy and the dog had had a confrontation. An old tree with exposed roots had suddenly attracted the dog's attention. Bundy could not restrain him. A stream of dirt flew out between his legs to splatter Bundy's raincoat and fall into his shoes. There was something manic in the dog's excitement. In a few moments, he had frantically excavated a hole into which he could insert his head and shoulders. Bundy's tug on the leash had no effect on him. The sight of his soiled hairless bottom, his legs mechanically pumping, encouraged Bundy to give him a smart crack with the end of the leash. Not hard, but sharply, right on the button, and before he could move the dog had wheeled and the front end was barking at him savagely, the lips curled back. Dirt from the hole partially screened his muzzle, and he looked to Bundy like a maddened rodent. He was no longer a dog but some primitive, underground creature.

Bundy lashed out at him, backing away, but they were joined by the leash. Unintentionally, Bundy stepped on the leash, which held the dog's snarling head to the ground. His slobbering jowls were bloody; the small veiled eyes peered up at him with hatred. Bundy had just enough presence of mind to stand there, unmoving, until they both grew calm.

Nobody had observed them. The children played and shrieked in the schoolyard as usual. The dog relaxed and lay flat on the ground, his tongue lolling in the dirt. Bundy breathed noisily, a film of perspiration cooling his face. When he stepped off the leash the dog did not move but continued to watch him warily, with bloodshot eyes. A slow burn of shame flushed Bundy's ears and cheeks, but he was reluctant to admit it. Another dog passed near them, but what he sniffed on the air kept him at a distance. In a tone of truce, if not reconciliation, Bundy said, "You had enough?"

When had he last said that? Seated on a school chum, whose face was red with Bundy's nosebleed. He bled too easily, but the boy beneath him had had enough.

"O.K.?" he said to the dog. The faintest tremor of acknowledgment stirred the dog's tail. He got to his feet, sneezed repeatedly, then splattered Bundy with dirt as he shook himself. Side by side, the leash slack between them, they left the park and walked down the grade. Bundy had never again struck the dog, nor had the dog ever again wheeled to snarl at him. Once the leash was snapped to the dog's collar a truce prevailed between them. In the apartment he had the floor of a closet all to himself.

At the Fixit Shop on the corner of Poplar, recently refaced with green asbestos shingles, Mr. Waller, the Fixit man, rapped on the glass with his wooden ruler. Both Bundy and the dog acknowledged his greeting. Waller had two cats, one asleep in the window, and a dog that liked to ride in his pickup. The two dogs had once been friends; they mauled each other a bit and horsed around like a couple of kids. Then suddenly it was over. Waller's dog would no longer trouble to leave the seat of the truck. Bundy had been so struck by this he had mentioned it to Waller. "Hell," Waller had said, "Gyp's a young dog. Your dog is old."

His saying that had shocked Bundy. There was the personal element, for one thing: Bundy was a good ten years older than Waller, and was he to read the remark to mean that Waller would soon ignore him? And were dogs—reasonably well-bred, sensible chaps—so indifferent to the facts of a dog's life? They appeared to be. One by one, as Bundy's dog grew older, the younger ones ignored him. He might have been a stuffed animal leashed to a parking meter. The human parallel was too disturbing for Bundy to dwell on it.

Old men, in particular, were increasingly touchy if they confronted Bundy at the frozen-food lockers. Did they think he was spying on them? Did they think he looked *sharper* than they did? Elderly women, as a rule, were less suspicious, and grateful to exchange a bit of chitchat. Bundy found them more realistic: they knew they were mortal. To find Bundy still around, squeezing the avocados, piqued the old men who returned from their vacations. On the other hand, Dr. Biddle, a retired dentist with a glistening head like an egg in a basket of excelsior, would unfailingly greet Bundy with the words "I'm really going to miss that mutt, you know that?" but his glance betrayed that he feared Bundy would check out first.

Bundy and the dog used the underpass walkway to cross to the supermarket parking area. Banners were flying to celebrate Whole Grains Cereal Week. In the old days, Bundy would leash the dog to a cart and they would proceed to do their shopping together, but now he had to be parked out front tied up to one of the bicycle racks. The dog didn't like it. The area was shaded and the cement was cold. Did he ever sense, however dimly, that Bundy too felt the chill? His hand brushed the coarse pelt as he fastened the leash.

"How about a new flea collar?" Bundy said, but the dog was not responsive. He sat, without being told to sit. Did it flatter the dog to leash him? Whatever Bundy would do if worst came to worst he had pondered, but had discussed with no one—his intent might be misconstrued. Of which one of them was he speaking? Impersonally appraised, in terms of survival the two of them were pretty much at a standoff: the dog was better fleshed out, but Bundy was the heartier eater.

Thinking of eating—of garlic-scented breadsticks, to be specific, dry but not dusty to the palate—Bundy entered the market to face a large display of odorless flowers and plants. The amplitude and bounty of the new market, at the point of entrance, before he selected a cart, always marked the high point of his expectations. Where else in the hungry world such a prospect? Barrels and baskets of wine, six-packs of beer and bran muffins, still-warm sourdough bread that he would break and gnaw on as he shopped. Was this a cunning regression? As a child he had craved raw sugar cookies. But his euphoria sagged at the meat counter, as he studied the gray matter being sold as meatloaf mix; it declined further at the dairy counter, where two cartons of yogurt had been sampled, and the low-fat cottage cheese was two days older than dated. By the time he entered the checkout lane, hemmed in by scandal sheets and romantic novels, the cashier's cheerfully inane "Have a good day!" would send him off forgetting his change in the machine. The girl who pursued him (always with pennies!) had been coached to say "Thank you, sir!"

A special on avocados this week required that Bundy make a careful selection. Out in front, as usual, dogs were barking. On the airwaves, from the rear and side, the "Wang Wang Blues." Why wang wang? he wondered. Besides wang wang, how did it go? The music was interrupted by an announcement on the public-address system. Would the owner of the white dog leashed to the bike rack please come to the front? Was Bundy's dog white? The point was debatable. Nevertheless, he left his cart by the avocados and followed the vegetable display to the front. People were huddled to the right of the door. A clerk beckoned to Bundy through the window. Still leashed to the bike rack, the dog lay out on his side, as if sleeping. In the parking lot several dogs were yelping.

"I'm afraid he's a goner," said the clerk. "These other dogs rushed him. Scared him to death. He just keeled over before they got to him." The dog had pulled the leash taut, but there was no sign that anything had touched him. A small woman with a shopping cart thumped into Bundy.

"Is it Tiger?" she said. "I hope it's not Tiger." She stopped to see that it was not Tiger. "Whose dog was it?" she asked, peering around her. The clerk indicated Bundy. "Poor thing," she said. "What was his name?"

Just recently, watching the Royal Wedding, Bundy had noticed that his emotions were nearer the surface: on two occasions his eyes had filmed over. He didn't like the woman's speaking of the dog in the past tense. Did she think he had lost his name with his life?

"What was the poor thing's name?" she repeated.

Was the tremor in Bundy's limbs noticeable? "Victor," Bundy lied, since he could not bring himself to admit the dog's name was Victrola. It had always been a sore point, the dog being too old to be given a new one. Miss Tyler had felt that as a puppy he looked like the picture of the dog at the horn of the gramophone. The resemblance was feeble, at best. How could a person give a dog such a name?

"Let him sit," a voice said. A space was cleared on a bench for Bundy to sit, but at the sound of the word he could not bend his knees. He remained standing, gazing through the bright glare at the beacon revolving on the police car. One of those women who buy two frozen dinners and then go off with the shopping cart and leave it somewhere let the policeman at the crosswalk chaperon her across the street.

A Folio of Photographs

WILLIAM WEGMAN

The Year of the Dog

ROBERT FOX

How could I ever have believed I would write this piece, I who have never been able to order my thoughts? A nervous incapacity has hindered my speech and Parkinson's disease has robbed control of my fingers. Yet, God is kind of the afflicted and I am able to record this for posterity as witness to His greatness.

*   *   *

Thimbleberry's madness was so openly discussed that he himself put up a neatly stenciled road sign, exactly two miles from his home, that read, "Madagascar Mental Health Clinic, 2 mi." He was commonly known as a harmless old eccentric, although the "Angelic Demons," claiming he was a Peeping Tom, rode up to his house on motorcycles, smashed several windows and punctured the tires of his bicycle. They performed this mischief one night when their girlfriends didn't appear at an appointed cave.

"They couldn't have done it if I was home," Thimbleberry said. "They would have been scared the moon might turn them into donkeys. She does that, you know. Will turn you into stone just like herself from the waist down—cry all you want, she won't set you free. She threatened to do it to me once—I was up on the hill watching her with my telescope—and she wanted to come down stay awhile, threatened me if I didn't but I said, 'Why sure,' and we had a grand old time and then she went back up in the sky."

"She didn't leave you any gifts?" I asked.

"No, no," he said and stopped in his work. He was pouring a path of concrete from his side door to the middle of his freshly cut lawn. "She threatened to turn me to stone, but she had a good time, she did, and commanded that I pave a walk, a real pretty one, from my home to hers." He laughed as if there were a joke somewhere, and it might have been on me because I was willing to listen.

He made three perfect squares of pavement and embellished them with impressions from a gear, a pair of pliers, a row of stars from a toy deputy badge, and signed it all with a handprint.

Later on, he began other walks, equally as elaborate, from his front and back doors, and they too ended as abruptly. "She didn't say which way she wanted to come in," he said.

*   *   *

I loved to spend time at Thimbleberry's, listening to his rhythmic, even if somewhat nasal, intonations. After a time he came to trust my visits and invited me in. I sipped instant coffee while he would stitch together a shirt for himself—front and back out of ladies' shifts and sleeves out of summer curtains. He sewed carefully, saying little, and was himself amused at what he had chosen for the front: a pair of huge red strawberries. What astonished me—and what I found of most interest—was not Thimbleberry's haphazard existence, his sparse furnishings, but his collection of books. (In my active days I operated a second-hand store, where I prized above all, not the romances loved by the ladies, but the dusty, voluminous aggregations of men's wisdom.)

"So you love books, do you, Normal?" he said upon espying my delight.

My trembling hands fondled his volumes—books of ancient Chinese, Arabic and Hebrew wisdom, side by side with home medical dictionaries and practical methodologies. They were in no order, their covers warped, spines dried and some with pages curled from the rain.

No inside cover or flyleaf was free of his calculations, done in a penmanship archaic even in my time, and all of which I could not decipher, but for the larger articulation of his name and birthdate.

On one of my visits, I noticed a handsome puppy cavorting about on his lawn, near the abrupt end of one of his walks. Thimbleberry explained that the dog was a gift from one of his neighbors. Then he said, "It'll be comforting to have him around. This is The Year of the Dog."

I rummaged my brain for what allusions I could, and came up with none save something about a Dog Star and the Dog Days of August. We were presently in the month of August, and contrary to Dog Days, we were beneficiaries of an abundance of rain. Thimbleberry could see that I was at a loss to discern his meaning and he bade me follow him inside. The old stairs between his walk and the door were uneven and I stumbled.

"I better make new steps, too," he said. "Don't want her tripping her way in—some welcome—make a hell of a mess she will, spill her milk all over."

He took up several of his books one at a time and read from them, reasonably it seemed, yet in symbols that were unintelligible to me. While he spoke, my eyes fell upon various letters of rejection from near and distant colleges. I read their polite terms of denial and reflected that Thimbleberry was just too old for them, for he certainly had the brains.

"Well, what do you think of that, Normal?" he said, catching me by surprise. I am able to make use of my nervous disorder in such situations. By adding a little extra impetus to my shakes, I can mean yes or no, according to the preferences of the other person.

"Pretty fascinating, ain't it?" he said.

If only I was able to understand the symbols he employed, which by means of his voice seemed to conduct disputations of their own. For what he had vaguely predicted has begun to happen, and in no way can I understand the explanation he had propounded so readily.

It commenced with the sunset turning into the soft, wrinkled belly of a female dog. Then the various lawns assumed the colors and textures of dog coats—long- and short-haired, one color and dappled. All the foliage, including the tallest and oldest trees, was likewise adorned with a plumage of tails. Oh, if I could have only rushed to Thimbleberry's right then and shared this wondrous moment with him, for who would have believed that everything in one's environment could be transformed into the canine? But alas, my condition prevented me from setting off in the increasing darkness, and ruing my physical state, and thinking that the very stars themselves must be the eyes or claws of dogs, I went to bed.

* * *

Needless to say what I discovered when I awoke. Let it suffice that my journey to Thimbleberry's next day was my easiest ever, and I noticed along the way that the grass and foliage had returned to their original condition; it was only I who was changed.

At this moment I sit panting next to Thimbleberry's leg while he records this occurrence at my behest. Will I ever be restored to my former condition, like the foliage, I do not know, and Thimbleberry is unable to say. I can only hope that his pup, who has gone off, does not return while I am in this state, for my years make it impossible for me to defend against youthful jealousy.

The Neutral Love Object

MAXINE KUMIN

On the way over to the Island they composed the kind of grouping commonly sought by fashion photographers. One of those faintly insolent, terribly insouciant family sets you see from time to time in *Vogue* magazine, Sue Swanson thought. The still-youthful mother and father, athletic and well nourished; the married daughter who improves on them both in profile, with the wind lifting and tunneling through her long brown hair; the European son-in-law with his brief beard and ever so slightly down-turning mustache. And of course the dog, the obligatory panting golden retriever obediently sprawled at his master's feet. The difference being, she noted silently, that we are pretenders in this glossy, and our golden is one-half ancestry unknown.

A few other late vacationers lounged at the rail, lifting already tanned faces to the September sun, but they had the top deck of the ferry pretty much to themselves. After the *Cranston* had delivered its three right-of-way hoots and the ship had settled into a vigorous bobbing motion, Sue began unpacking the picnic basket Bertrand had carried up from the station wagon parked in its allotted slot below. Ham and cheese sandwiches for Douglas, her husband, and for Bertrand, her son-in-law, Bertrand's with Dijon mustard. For Cindy and herself, the penitential yogurt. Potato chips for the men. Carrot sticks for the women. For the men, chocolate cupcakes. Apples for all. Biscuits for Agamemnon, who had been denied breakfast as a precaution against seasickness. He dispensed with these in one gluttonous swipe and waited slavishly for the sandwich crusts and cake crumbs that were also his birthright.

Once at a cocktail party a psychiatrist had told her that people make their dogs into neutral love objects, a repository for all the unspoken passion at work in the yeasty ferment of a family. And she had smiled passively, agreeing with him. So they had. They were, furthermore, the kind of family that gives its animals royal, heroic, mythological names. There had been Castor and Pollux, Cindy's dapple-gray ponies; Oedipus and Caesar, Peter's pygmy goats of one summer. Melissa's cat had been named Cleopatra, her one surviving kitten, Cassandra. And, in this case, fourteen years of Agamemnon, who had as a puppy slept in one child's bed after another, transported from place to place with his wind-up clock wrapped in a towel, his teddy bear, and his teething bone. Cindy had been eight, Melissa six, and Peter four when he came into their world. The trouble was, he would not live long enough. The trouble with love was, it could be outlasted.

Someone else's apricot poodle was loose on deck. Two children bounded after it, their matching suede jackets flapping. They called "Heather, Heather!" in angry little bursts. The dog was finally cornered piddling on an exhaust vent and borne away as it yipped piteously.

"Someone ought to put the *laisse* to them," Bertrand remarked.

"Leash," Cindy said. "*On* them."

It was the fifth correction of the day, Sue thought. But why am I counting? I suppose he's just as hard on her French. And then the Thurber cartoon came into her head: When did the magic go out of our marriage?

But the sun was soothing, the illusion of open sea restful. She dozed finally, tipped back in one chair, her feet braced on another, the thrum of the engines jarring her cheekbones, and woke with a mild headache.

"There's Gardiner's Light," Douglas called from the rail. His hair blew forward from the crown, revealing a developing bald spot. "That's where you throw a penny overboard if you want to come back."

"On the way over?" Cindy was doubtful. "I thought only on the way back." Her tone said plainly, *If you've had a good time.*

"On the way back seems logical," Sue said. And then, for no reason, "I love islands."

Douglas came over and put his arm around her. "The mind is an island."

"Yours, maybe," she told him. "Mine is nothing but a cranberry bog at this point."

They were all so tired, after what was to have been a joyous summer. For Bertie had gotten his *agrégation* and Cindy had finished her provisional year teaching and they had agreed to forsake Geneva, beautiful in that season, to spend the summer in Boston. And then the phone call: Cindy, ashen calm, coming to find her in the garden squatting in the carrot row. *Now, Mother, sit down a minute? Goggy fell down a flight of stairs and broke her hip? In Lake Forest? It's her next-door neighbor, a somebody Ashendon?*

Weekly flights to Chicago ensued. Her mother appeared to be cheerfully mending in a convalescent home. Sue brought her potted plants, needlework, magazines, pictures of the grandchildren. And then pneumonia. The double anniversary party—their twenty-fifth, Cindy and Bertie's first—hastily called off. Bleak hours in the hospital, waiting to be allowed the thirty-minute visit. Bleaker ones in between in the airport. A stroke. Specialists. Dozens of telephone calls recklessly placed person-to-person at the peak hours. And finally, grudgingly, mercifully, death entered, imposing more responsibilities. Meanwhile, in Boston, Cindy bought Peter a suit for the funeral. Melissa came back from her American Friends'-sponsored summer on an Indian reservation. Bertie slept in her mother's vacant house until Douglas, who had been in Panama supervising the installation of a power line, returned. Coward that she was, she would not stay in her childhood bedroom without him. "Too many ghosts" was all she said.

"Everybody's mother has to die sometime," Melissa said, meaning to be reasonable. "In the Navaho culture they *celebrate* the deaths of the parents. They *rejoice* that their spirits have gone to join the ancestors."

"Lissa," Peter said, fingering his new haircut. "Do me a favor. Take a deep breath, okay? Now see how long you can hold it."

And then the house was put on the market and Bertie and Peter, during a record heat wave, hauled away all the detritus of her mother's long widowhood.

She grieved as quietly as possible. She had been an only child, a late arrival, and she was only ten when her father died. Her mother took over his real estate office and drew a vital energy from it. It was as if she had saved something of him by keeping his business alive. She had never encouraged intimacy between mother and daughter, and they lived side by side inside their baggy sweaters with the thermostat set low. Explaining to Douglas, trying to keep the tears out of her voice, Sue said, "It was serene. Chilly, but serene. I never questioned it."

Now she thought, *But I left too soon.*

The stresses had opened little cracks in everyone. Not the least in Agamemnon, who had been kenneled for three days and had neither eaten nor drunk water the entire time. "You should have started when he was very young," the vet said reproachfully. Now Melissa had returned to Oberlin with her sand paintings, Peter with his duffelbag and guitar had entered Reed, and the last four of them were on their way —"Look! there it is!" Sue said—to the magical island where they had never been.

The harbor town was determinedly quaint. An absence of gaudy storefronts, no billboards, gas lamps on the still-cobbled main street. The shingled houses, uniformly unpainted, weathered to a silvery gray. Fat and disdainful seagulls sat on pilings or followed the lobster boats in and out of port. And everywhere an air of restraint, of self-sufficiency, Yankee pride or pluck. Bertrand was enchanted; it could have been Denmark, or the Frisian Islands. "It's so . . . un-American!" he congratulated.

The weather, miraculously, held. They were in the midst of a Bermuda high with spectacular sunsets and only thinly foggy mornings. The cottage boasted an immense, intricate television antenna but no television set. The beds were predictably lumpy, the blankets flimsy. There were no decent reading lamps. Agamemnon, normally allotted a cushion on the kitchen floor, was happy with the living room couch. Such is the fate of the rented summer house. On the bulletin board in the kitchen, a formidable list of instructions and caveats loomed. They scrupulously observed them all.

Renting a sailboat that late in the season was difficult; Douglas finally borrowed a trailer hitch from the real estate agent and hauled a catamaran from a boatyard at the far end of the island. "As long as I don't have to get in it," Sue said on inspection. "Double ditto," Cindy added. Tennis was available just across the way, provided they rolled the court themselves. The horses Cindy and Sue longed for seemed not to exist.

They were immediately segregated by their proclivities. Douglas and Bertrand played tennis in the morning; mother and daughter, mutually awkward at it, eschewed the game. Douglas played fiercely and competitively, serving overhand smashes that went wide of the mark, while Bertrand lazed at the baseline, acknowledging what he did not wish to return. Agamemnon lolled in the shade, occasionally stirring to chase a seagull.

At noon when the sun was strongest and the wind steady, the menfolk sailed bravely out of the harbor. Cindy and Sue swam, taking a martyred pleasure from the icy water. For the first few days the dog kept paddling out from ever-more-distant sandspits, always hoping that at this new launch the salt water would have mysteriously turned to fresh.

Sue and Cindy cycled. They pedaled for miles purposefully single file, dressed like twins in blue jeans and heavy white sweaters, each with her hair hidden under a bandanna tied gypsy style. They saved their breath for the hills, all attention riveted on the invented destination, for where, after all, was there to go?

Sue, always a little behind, driving her legs like pistons, made up the dialogues she did not dare to initiate: Do you still love him, your superior Swissman? Are the Alps as perfect as that? Have you left us forever? And received her wishful answers: We are thinking of a divorce. We are thinking of making a baby. Bertie has a mistress, Bertie has joined the Communist Party. We are thinking of coming back to the States forever.

Once, the little general store in Quinig was open; they bought ice-cream cones and sat in a dusty booth eating them. Another time they passed a roadside farm stand, presided over by a gaunt elderly woman who assured them she would have fresh corn—the last of the crop— the next day. The next day she said the raccoons had gotten into it.

"Twelve miles for some mythical corn," Cindy lamented.

"Never mind," Sue said, determined Puritan. "It's *good* for us."

By default they picked rose hips and beach plums and wild grapes and made an overabundance of jelly, filling all the cottage glasses and mayonnaise jars.

"It's sick," Cindy said, squeezing the cheesecloth bag with her purple hands. "Positively neurotic and sick."

"I know," Sue said miserably. "I can't help it." And they picked ticks off the dog after each expedition.

At night they worked by turns on an enormous irritating jigsaw puzzle which gradually pre-empted eating space at the dining room table. From time to time Douglas read them facts from an ancient edition of the *Encyclopaedia Britannica*. Everyone wrote letters. "Oh, God, you know what? I started to send a postcard to Goggy," Cindy confessed.

The phone, of course, never rang. Of course, no one came to call. There were three outside edge pieces missing in the puzzle. One night they drove into town and had dinner at the Captain's Table overlooking the ferry slip. Since neither of the men was wearing a jacket and tie, they were seated far from the view. Bertrand, sulking, ordered a twenty-dollar bottle of wine.

"I think it's horse meat," Douglas said of the steak.

"The next one who complains gets to wash the dishes," Sue said, trying.

The problem was, they had a checklist of forbidden topics and they had run out of comfortable small talk. Some of the things they could not talk about included: early marriages, particularly those that take place between foreign exchange students and the daughter of the host family; Cuba, China, or the overthrow of the Allende government in Chile; baptisms, bar mitzvahs, last rites, or circumcisions; America's diminishing oil resources, America's Indians, the American military establishment, Arab-Israeli attitudes, or the Palestinian guerrilla movement; Swiss neutrality in all wars; Swiss bank accounts; Swiss reluctance to grant women the vote. Even Watergate, which they all agreed on, had a way of edging them nastily over the abyss.

This left: pornography, pantsuits, athletics, animals.

Agamemnon had taken to howling at night. They took turns getting up to beat him with a newspaper.

"There's a bitch in heat somewhere on this island," Cindy declared. "His glands get the message even if his legs are too old."

"It's the last thing that dies," Douglas said, leering a little for effect.

"Tomorrow let's take him to the clams," Bertrand said. "It's not too hot at the beach now, is it? I'll bring the termos of drinking water."

"Thermos," Cindy said. "Clamming. You say, 'Let's take him clamming.' "

"Please," Sue began. She was going to say, "Please don't correct his English every minute," but tomorrow was their last full day together. Until when? Forever? "Please do, Bertie, that's a good idea. If he gets some real exercise, maybe it will take his mind off the call of the wild."

The soft-shells were plentiful and illegal. They lugged away two guilty bucketfuls and gathered up their tools. Cindy and Bertrand took turns calling, "*Aggie! Come on, Aggie, that's a good dog!*" Douglas walked half a mile down the sandspit, but there was nothing. No blob of blond fur on the horizon.

"He knows his way back to the house," Sue said matter-of-factly. "You'll see, when he's tired enough, he'll show up."

Although they managed to finish all the steamers laced with butter and Douglas drank the clam broth, proclaiming it the best part, the absence of Dog pervaded their farewell feast.

Over the dishes Sue said to Cindy, "I don't know what to do. I don't see how I can just leave tomorrow not knowing what's happened to him."

"Oh, God, I know. I feel terrible. But if we don't take the ten o'clock ferry, we won't make our afternoon plane. And Bertie would have a fit; he starts at the university the day after. You know how the Swiss are. Punctual as their watches."

The whole year loomed ahead like a perpetual twilight. "Well, we'll have to wait and see," Sue concluded. "Face the east and pray, or something."

Nobody slept. She heard first Douglas, then Cindy, slip out of the house; she heard the flap-flap of Cindy's thongs on the macadam strip that divided their cottage from the beach-side; she heard their separate, unaccompanied returns, and the murmur of voices from Cindy and Bertie's room. With the first light she rose, dressed, and half trotted the mile to the clam beds. The wind had sharpened; a high gray cloud bank was billowing in from the open sea. No one.

They had coffee and toast and packed the car. Bertrand hiked over to the open fields where she and Cindy had gone for beach plums. He came back shaking his head.

Cindy went along the strip of cottages that formed their little settlement. Most of them were boarded up for the winter, but she knocked at the inhabited ones and left their name and city phone number, in case. At nine o'clock, Douglas dialed the island SPCA and gave them a description.

In their bedroom, facing each other over the stripped and sagging mattresses, Douglas said, "Be reasonable. You can't just stay on here for days and days, waiting for a missing dog to show up."

"But suppose he comes back? Suppose he comes back tonight and the house is closed up and there's no one here?"

"Don't you want to see your daughter off? It's for a whole year. Sue, he was a very old dog. Get your priorities straight. He had a long and happy life. He never suffered. He probably just went off somewhere in the marshes to die."

She noticed that he spoke in the past tense and hated him for it. Hypocrite. Liar. So much for allegiances!

At the ferry slip, Cindy and Bertrand stationed themselves like a ment; Swiss neutrality in all wars; Swiss bank accounts; Swiss reluctance to grant women the vote. Even Watergate, which they all agreed on, had a way of edging them nastily over the abyss.

This left: pornography, pantsuits, athletics, animals.

Agamemnon had taken to howling at night. They took turns getting up to beat him with a newspaper.

"There's a bitch in heat somewhere on this island," Cindy declared. "His glands get the message even if his legs are too old."

"It's the last thing that dies," Douglas said, leering a little for effect.

"Tomorrow let's take him to the clams," Bertrand said. "It's not too hot at the beach now, is it? I'll bring the termos of drinking water."

"Thermos," Cindy said. "Clamming. You say, 'Let's take him clamming.'"

"Please," Sue began. She was going to say, "Please don't correct his English every minute," but tomorrow was their last full day together. Until when? Forever? "Please do, Bertie, that's a good idea. If he gets some real exercise, maybe it will take his mind off the call of the wild."

The soft-shells were plentiful and illegal. They lugged away two guilty bucketfuls and gathered up their tools. Cindy and Bertrand took turns calling, "*Aggie! Come on, Aggie, that's a good dog!*" Douglas walked half a mile down the sandspit, but there was nothing. No blob of blond fur on the horizon.

"He knows his way back to the house," Sue said matter-of-factly. "You'll see, when he's tired enough, he'll show up."

Although they managed to finish all the steamers laced with butter and Douglas drank the clam broth, proclaiming it the best part, the absence of Dog pervaded their farewell feast.

Over the dishes Sue said to Cindy, "I don't know what to do. I don't see how I can just leave tomorrow not knowing what's happened to him."

"Oh, God, I know. I feel terrible. But if we don't take the ten o'clock ferry, we won't make our afternoon plane. And Bertie would have a fit; he starts at the university the day after. You know how the Swiss are. Punctual as their watches."

The whole year loomed ahead like a perpetual twilight. "Well, we'll have to wait and see," Sue concluded. "Face the east and pray, or something."

Nobody slept. She heard first Douglas, then Cindy, slip out of the house; she heard the flap-flap of Cindy's thongs on the macadam strip that divided their cottage from the beach-side; she heard their separate, unaccompanied returns, and the murmur of voices from Cindy and Bertie's room. With the first light she rose, dressed, and half trotted the mile to the clam beds. The wind had sharpened; a high gray cloud bank was billowing in from the open sea. No one.

They had coffee and toast and packed the car. Bertrand hiked over to the open fields where she and Cindy had gone for beach plums. He came back shaking his head.

Cindy went along the strip of cottages that formed their little settlement. Most of them were boarded up for the winter, but she knocked at the inhabited ones and left their name and city phone number, in case. At nine o'clock, Douglas dialed the island SPCA and gave them a description.

In their bedroom, facing each other over the stripped and sagging mattresses, Douglas said, "Be reasonable. You can't just stay on here for days and days, waiting for a missing dog to show up."

"But suppose he comes back? Suppose he comes back tonight and the house is closed up and there's no one here?"

"Don't you want to see your daughter off? It's for a whole year. Sue, he was a very old dog. Get your priorities straight. He had a long and happy life. He never suffered. He probably just went off somewhere in the marshes to die."

She noticed that he spoke in the past tense and hated him for it. Hypocrite. Liar. So much for allegiances!

At the ferry slip, Cindy and Bertrand stationed themselves like a pair of Ancient Mariners and stopped each boarding passenger. "Pardon me, but have you seen a big golden retriever anywhere?" Douglas took a last turn through the village, cruising down the side streets, peering into backyards, while Sue called halfheartedly, "Aggie, Aggie! Come on, that's a good dog!"

It was too cold to stand out on deck, so they huddled together as apathetic as refugees in the deserted salon, where water sloshed underfoot. No one spoke. Bertrand, who had never had a dog of his own and had walked Agamemnon every morning of the year he had lived with them as a student, put his head in his hands and began quietly to weep.

Sue put her arm around him. He hugged her and cried against her neck.

"Don't, son," Douglas said in a strange and furry voice.

"It's all right, Daddy," Cindy told him, lifting her face. Tears shone on it. "Remember, in Shakespeare? 'For God's sake let us sit upon the ground / And tell sad stories of the death of kings.' It's all right to cry."

And thus together the family mourned Agamemnon.

Distant Music

ANN BEATTIE

On Friday she always sat in the park, waiting for him to come. At one-thirty he came to this park bench (if someone was already sitting there, he loitered around it), and then they would sit side by side, talking quietly, like Ingrid Bergman and Cary Grant in *Notorious*. Both believed in flying saucers and health food. They shared a hatred of laundromats, guilt about not sending presents to relatives on birthdays and at Christmas, and a dog— part Weimaraner, part German shepherd—named Sam.

She was twenty, and she worked in an office; she was pretty because she took a lot of time with make-up, the way a housewife who really cared might flute the edges of a piecrust with thumb and index finger. He was twenty-four, a graduate-school dropout (theater) who collaborated on songs with his friend Gus Greeley, and he wanted, he fervently wanted, to make it big as a songwriter. His mother was Greek and French, his father American. This girl, Sharon, was not the first woman to fall in love with Jack because he was so handsome. She took the subway to get to the bench, which was in Washington Square Park; he walked from the basement apartment he lived in. Whoever had Sam that day (they kept the dog alternating weeks) brought him. They could do this because her job required her to work only from eight to one, and he worked at home. They had gotten the dog because they feared for his life. A man had come up to them on West Tenth Street carrying a cardboard box, smiling, and saying, "Does the little lady want a kitty cat?" They peered inside. "Puppies," Jack said. "Well, who gives a fuck?" the man said, putting the box down, his face dark and contorted. Sharon and Jack stared at the man; he stared belligerently back. Neither of them was quite sure how things had suddenly turned ominous. She wanted to get out of there right away, before the man took a swing at Jack, but to her surprise Jack smiled at the man and dipped into the box for a dog. He extracted the scrawny, wormy Sam. She took the dog first, because there was a veterinarian's office close to her apartment. Once the dog was cured of his worms, she gave him to Jack to begin his training. In Jack's apartment the puppy would fix his eyes on the parallelogram of sunlight that sometimes appeared on the wood floor in the late morning—sniffing it, backing up, edging up to it at the border. In her apartment the puppy's object of fascination was a clarinet that a friend had left there when he moved. The puppy looked at it respectfully. She watched the dog for signs of maladjustment, wondering if he was too young to be shuttling back and forth, from home to home. (She herself had been raised by her mother, but she and her sister would fly to Seattle every summer to spend two months with their father.) The dog seemed happy enough.

At night, in Jack's one-room apartment, they would sometimes lie with their heads at the foot of the bed, staring at the ornately carved oak headboard and the old-fashioned light attached to it, with the little sticker still on the shade that said "From home of Lady Astor. $4.00." They had found the lamp in Ruckersville, Virginia, on the only long trip they ever took out of the city. On the bed with them there were usually sheets of music—songs that he was scoring. She would look at the pieces of paper with lyrics typed on them, and read them slowly to herself, appraisingly, as if they were poetry.

On weekends they spent the days and nights together. There was a small but deep fireplace in his apartment, and when September came they would light a fire in the late afternoon, although it was not yet cold, and sometimes light a stick of sandalwood incense, and they would lean on each other or sit side by side, listening to Vivaldi. She knew very little about such music when she first met him, and much more about it by the time their first month had passed. There was no one thing she knew a great deal about—as he did about music—so there was really nothing that she could teach him.

"Where were you in 1974?" he asked her once.

"In school. In Ann Arbor."

"What about 1975?"

"In Boston. Working at a gallery."

"Where are you now?" he said.

She looked at him and frowned. "In New York," she said.

He turned toward her and kissed her arm. "I know," he said. "But why so serious?"

She knew that she was a serious person, and she liked it that he could make her smile. Sometimes, though, she did not quite understand him, so she was smiling now not out of appreciation, but because she thought a smile would make things all right.

Carol, her closest friend, asked why she didn't move in with him. She did not want to tell Carol that it was because she had not been asked, so she said that the room he lived in was very small and that during the day he liked solitude so he could work. She was also not sure that she would move in if he did ask her. He gave her the impression sometimes that he was the serious one, not she. Perhaps "serious" was the wrong word; it was more that he seemed despondent. He would get into moods and not snap out of them; he would drink red wine and play Billie Holiday records, and shake his head and say that if he had not made it as a songwriter by now, chances were that he would never make it. She hadn't really been familiar with Billie Holiday until he began playing the records for her. He would play a song that Billie had recorded early in her career, then play another record of the same song as she had sung it later. He said that he preferred her ruined voice. Two songs in particular stuck in her mind. One was "Solitude," and the first time she heard Billie Holiday sing the first three words, "In my solitude," she felt a physical sensation, as if someone were drawing something sharp over her heart, very lightly. The other record she kept thinking of was "Gloomy Sunday." He told her that it had been banned from the radio back then, because it was said that it had been responsible for suicides.

For Christmas that year he gave her a small pearl ring that had been worn by his mother when she was a girl. The ring fitted perfectly; she only had to wiggle it slightly to get it to slide over the joint of her finger, and when it was in place it felt as if she were not wearing a ring at all. There were eight prongs holding the pearl in place. She often counted things: how many panes in a window, how many slats in a bench. Then, for her birthday, in January, he gave her a silver chain with a small sapphire stone, to be worn on the wrist. She was delighted; she wouldn't let him help her fasten the clasp.

"You like it?" he said. "That's all I've got."

She looked at him, a little startled. His mother had died the year before she met him; what he was saying was that he had given her the last of her things. There was a photograph of his mother on the bookcase—a black-and-white picture in a little silver frame of a smiling young woman whose hair was barely darker than her skin. Because he kept the picture, she assumed that he worshiped his mother. One night he corrected that impression by saying that his mother had always tried to sing in her youth, when she had no voice, which had embarrassed everyone.

He said that she was a silent person; in the end, he said, you would have to say that she had done and said very little. He told Sharon that a few days after her death he and his father had gone through her possessions together, and in one of her drawers they came upon a small wooden box shaped like a heart. Inside the box were two pieces of jewelry—the ring and the chain and sapphire. "So she kept some token, then," his father had said, staring down into the little box. "You gave them to her as presents?" he asked his father. "No," his father said apologetically. "They weren't from me." And then the two of them had stood there looking at each other, both understanding perfectly.

She said, "But what did you finally say to break the silence?"

"Something pointless, I'm sure," he said.

She thought to herself that that might explain why he had not backed down, on Tenth Street, when the man offering the puppies took a stance as though he wanted to fight. Jack was used to hearing bad things—things that took him by surprise. He had learned to react coolly. Later that winter, when she told him that she loved him, his face had stayed expressionless a split second too long, and then he smiled his slow smile and gave her a kiss.

The dog grew. He took to training quickly and walked at heel, and she was glad that they had saved him. She took him to the veterinarian to ask why he was so thin. She was told that the dog was growing fast, and that eventually he would start filling out. She did not tell Jack that she had taken the dog to the veterinarian, because he thought she doted on him too much. She wondered if he might not be a little jealous of the dog.

Slowly, things began to happen with his music. A band on the West Coast that played a song that he and Gus had written was getting a big name, and they had not dropped the song from their repertoire. In February he got a call from the band's agent, who said that they wanted more songs. He and Gus shut themselves in the basement apartment, and she went walking with Sam, the dog. She went to the park, until she ran into the crippled man too many times. He was a young man, rather handsome, who walked with two metal crutches and had a radio that hung from a strap around his neck and rested on his chest, playing loudly. The man always seemed to be walking in the direction she walked in, and she had to walk awkwardly to keep in line with him so they could talk. She really had nothing to talk to the man about, and he helped very little, and the dog was confused by the crutches and made little leaps toward the man, as though they were all three playing a game. She stayed away from the park for a while, and when she went back he was not there. One day in March the park was more crowded than usual because it was an unusually warm spring-like afternoon, and walking with Sam, half dreaming, she passed a heavily made-up woman on a bench who was wearing a polka-dot turban, with a hand-lettered sign propped against her legs announcing that she was Miss Sydney, a fortuneteller. There was a young boy sitting next to Miss Sydney, and he called out to her, "Come on!" She smiled slightly and shook her head no. The boy was Italian, she thought, but the woman was hard to place. "Miss Sydney's gonna tell you about fire and famine and early death," the boy said. He laughed, and she hurried on, thinking it was odd that the boy would know the word "famine."

She was still alone with Jack most of every weekend, but much of his talk now was about technical problems he was having with scoring, and she had trouble following him. Once, he became enraged and said that she had no interest in his career. He said it because he wanted to move to Los Angeles and she said she was staying in New York. She said it assuming at once that he would go anyhow. When he made it clear that he would not leave without her, she started to cry because she was so grateful that he was staying. He thought she was crying because he had yelled at her and said that she had no interest in his career. He took back what he had said; he told her that she was very tolerant and that she often gave good advice. She had a good ear, even if she didn't express her opinions in complex technical terms. She cried again, and this time even she did not realize at first why. Later she knew that it was because he had never said so many kind things to her at once. Actually, very few people in her life had ever gone out of their way to say something kind, and it had just been too much. She began to wonder if her nerves were getting bad. Once, she woke up in the night disoriented and sweating, having dreamed that she was out in the sun, with all her energy gone. It was stifling hot and she couldn't move. "The sun's a good thing," he said to her when she told him the dream. "Think about the bright beautiful sun in Los Angeles. Think about stretching out on a warm day with a warm breeze." Trembling, she left him and went into the kitchen for water. He did not know that if he had really set out for California, she would have followed.

In June, when the air pollution got very bad and the air carried the smell that sidewalks get when they are baked through every day, he began to complain that it was her fault that they were in New York and not in California. "But I just don't like that way of life," she said. "If I went there, I wouldn't be happy."

"What's so appealing about this uptight New York scene?" he said.

"You wake up in the night in a sweat. You won't even walk through Washington Square Park anymore."

"It's because of that man with the crutches," she said. "People like that. I told you it was only because of him."

"So let's get away from all that. Let's go somewhere."

"You think there aren't people like that in California?" she said.

"It doesn't matter what I think about California if I'm not going." He clamped earphones on his head.

That same month, while she and Jack and Gus were sharing a pot of cheese fondue, she found out that Jack had a wife. They were at Gus's apartment when Gus casually said something about Myra. "Who's Myra?" she asked, and he said, "You know—Jack's wife, Myra." It seemed unreal to her—even more so because Gus's apartment was such an odd place; that night Gus had plugged a defective lamp into an outlet and blown out a fuse. Then he plugged in his only other lamp, which was a sunlamp. It glowed so brightly that he had to turn it, in its wire enclosure, to face the wall. As they sat on the floor eating, their three shadows were thrown up against the opposite wall. She had been looking at that—detached, the way you would stand back to appreciate a picture—when she tuned in on the conversation and heard them talking about someone named Myra.

"You didn't know?" Gus said to her. "Okay, I want you both out. I don't want any heavy scene in my place. I couldn't take it. Come on—I really mean it. I want you out. Please don't talk about it here."

On the street, walking beside Jack, it occurred to her that Gus's outburst was very strange, almost as strange as Jack's not telling her about his wife.

"I didn't see what would be gained by telling you," Jack said.

They crossed the street. They passed the Riviera Café. She had once counted the number of panes of glass across the Riviera's front.

"Did you ever think about us getting married?" he said. "I thought about it. I thought that if you didn't want to follow me to California, of course you wouldn't want to marry me."

"You're already married," she said. She felt that she had just said something very sensible. "Do you think it was right to—"

He started to walk ahead of her. She hurried to catch up. She wanted to call after him, "I would have gone!" She was panting.

"Listen," he said, "I'm like Gus. I don't want to hear it."

"You mean we can't even talk about this? You don't think that I'm entitled to hear about it?"

"I love you and I don't love Myra," he said.

"Where is she?" she said.

"In El Paso."

"If you don't love her, why aren't you divorced?"

"You think that everybody who doesn't love his wife gets divorced? I'm not the only one who doesn't do the logical thing, you know. You get nightmares from living in this sewer, and you won't get out of it."

"It's different," she said. What was he talking about?

"Until I met you, I didn't think about it. She was in El Paso, she was gone—period."

"Are you going to get a divorce?"

"Are you going to marry me?"

They were crossing Seventh Avenue. They both stopped still, halfway across the street, and were almost hit by a Checker cab. They hurried across, and on the other side of the street they stopped again. She looked at him, as surprised but as suddenly sure about something as he must have been the time he and his father had found the jewelry in the heart-shaped wooden box. She said no, she was not going to marry him.

It dragged on for another month. During that time, unknown to her, he wrote the song that was going to launch his career. Months after he had left the city, she heard it on her AM radio one morning, and she knew that it was his song, even though he had never mentioned it to her. She leashed the dog and went out and walked to the record shop on Sixth Avenue—walking almost the same route they had walked the night she found out about his wife—and she went in, with the dog. Her face was so strange that the man behind the cash register allowed her to break the rule about dogs in the shop because he did not want another hassle that day. She found the group's record album with the song on it, turned it over and saw his name, in small type. She stared at the title, replaced the record and went back outside, as hunched as if it were winter.

During the month before he left, though, and before she ever heard the song, the two of them had sat on the roof of his building one night, arguing. They were having a Tom Collins because a musician who had been at his place the night before had brought his own mix and then left it behind. She had never had a Tom Collins. It tasted appropriately bitter, she thought. She held out the ring and the bracelet to him. He said that if she made him take them back, he would drop them over the railing. She believed him and put them back in her pocket. He said, and she agreed, that things had not been perfect between them even before she found out about his wife. Myra could play the guitar, and she could not; Myra loved to travel, and she was afraid to leave New York City. As she listened to what he said, she counted the posts—black iron and shaped like arrows—of the fence that wound around the roof. It was almost entirely dark, and she looked up to see if there were any stars. She yearned to be in the country, where she could always see them. She said she wanted him to borrow a car before he left so that they could ride out into the woods in New Jersey. Two nights later he picked her up at her apartment in a red Volvo, with Sam panting in the back, and they wound their way through the city and to the Lincoln Tunnel. Just as they were about to go under, another song began to play on the tape deck. It was Ringo Starr singing

"Octopus's Garden." Jack laughed. "That's a hell of a fine song to come on just before we enter the tunnel." Inside the tunnel, the dog flattened himself on the back seat. "You want to keep Sam, don't you?" he said. She was shocked because she had never even thought of losing Sam. "Of course I do," she said, and unconsciously edged a little away from him. He had never said whose car it was. For no reason at all, she thought that the car must belong to a woman.

"I love that syrupy chorus of 'aaaaah' Lennon and McCartney sing," he said. "They really had a fine sense of humor."

"Is that a funny song?" she said. She had never thought about it.

They were on Boulevard East, in Weehawken, and she was staring out the window at the lights across the water. He saw that she was looking, and drove slower.

"This as good as stars for you?" he said.

"It's amazing."

"All yours," he said, taking his hand off the wheel to swoop it through the air in mock graciousness.

After he left she would remember that as one of the little digs he had gotten in—one of the less than nice things he had said. That night, though, impressed by the beauty of the city, she let it go by; in fact, she would have to work on herself later to reinterpret many of the things he had said as being nasty. That made it easier to deal with his absence. She would block out the memory of his pulling over and kissing her, of the two of them getting out of the car, and with Sam between them, walking.

One of the last times she saw him, she went to his apartment on a night when five other people were there—people she had never met. His father had shipped him some 8mm home movies and a projector, and the people all sat on the floor, smoking grass and talking, laughing at the movies of children (Jack at his fourth birthday party; Jack in the Halloween parade at school; Jack at Easter, collecting eggs). One of the people on the floor said, "Hey, get that big dog out of the way," and she glared at him, hating him for not liking the dog. What if his shadow had briefly darkened the screen? She felt angry enough to scream, angry enough to say that the dog had grown up in the apartment and had the right to walk around. Looking at the home movies, she tried to concentrate on Jack's blunders: dropping an Easter egg, running down the hill after the egg, going so fast he stumbled into some blur, perhaps his mother's arms. But what she mostly thought about was what a beautiful child he was, what a happy-looking little boy. There was no sense in her staying there and getting sentimental, so she made her excuses and left early. Outside, she saw the red Volvo, gleaming as though it had been newly painted. She was sure that it belonged to an Indian woman in a blue sari who had been there, sitting close to Jack. Sharon was glad that as she was leaving, Sam had raised his hackles and growled at one of the people there. She scolded him, but out on the street she patted him, secretly glad. Jack had not asked her again to come to California with him, and she told herself that she probably would not have changed her mind if he had. Tears began to well up in her eyes, and she told herself that she was crying because a cab wouldn't stop for her when the driver saw that she had a dog. She ended up walking blocks and blocks back to her apartment that night; it made her more certain than ever that she loved the dog and that she did not love Jack.

About the time she got the first postcard from Jack, things started to get a little bad with Sam. She was afraid that he might have distemper, so she took him to the veterinarian, waited her turn and told the doctor that the dog was growling at some people and she had no idea why. He assured her that there was nothing physically wrong with the dog, and blamed it on the heat. When another month passed and it was less hot, she visited the veterinarian again. "It's the breeding," he said, and sighed. "It's a bad mix. A Weimaraner is a mean dog, and that cross isn't a good one. He's part German shepherd, isn't he?"

"Yes," she said.

"Well—that's it, I'm afraid."

"There isn't any medication?"

"It's the breeding," he said. "Believe me. I've seen it before."

"What happens?" she said.

"What happens to the dog?"

"Yes."

"Well—watch him. See how things go. He hasn't bitten anybody, has he?"

"No," she said. "Of course not."

"Well—don't say of course not. Be careful with him."

"I'm careful with him," she said. She said it indignantly. But she wanted to hear something else. She didn't want to leave.

Walking home, she thought about what she could do. Maybe she could take Sam to her sister's house in Morristown for a while. Maybe if he could run more, and keep cool, he would calm down. She put aside her knowledge that it was late September and already much cooler, and that the dog growled more, not less. He had growled at the teenage boy she had given money to to help her carry her groceries upstairs. It was the boy's extreme reaction to Sam that had made it worse, though. You had to act calm around Sam when he got like that, and the boy had panicked.

She persuaded her sister to take Sam, and her brother-in-law drove into New York on Sunday and drove them out to New Jersey. Sam was put on a chain attached to a rope her brother-in-law had strung up in the backyard, between two huge trees. To her surprise, Sam did not seem to mind it. He did not bark and strain at the chain until he saw her drive away, late that afternoon; her sister was driving, and she was in the back seat with her niece, and she looked back and saw him lunging at the chain.

The rest of it was predictable, even to her. As they drove away, she almost knew it all. The dog would bite the child. Of course, the child should not have annoyed the dog, but she did, and the dog bit her, and then there was a hysterical call from her sister and another call from her brother-in-law, saying that she must come get the dog immediately—that he would come for her so she could get him—and blaming her for bringing the dog to them in the first place. Her sister had never really liked her, and the incident with the dog was probably just what she had been waiting for to sever contact.

When Sam came back to the city, things got no better. He turned against everyone and it was difficult even to walk him because he had become so aggressive. Sometimes a day would pass without any of that, and she would tell herself that it was over now—an awful period but over—and then the next morning the dog would bare his teeth at some person they passed. There began to be little signs that the dog had it in for her, too, and when that happened she turned her bedroom over to him. She hauled her mattress to the living room and let him have his own room. She left the door cracked so he would not think he was being punished. But she knew, and Sam knew, that it was best he stay in the room. If nothing else, he was an exceptionally smart dog.

She heard from Jack for over a year—sporadically, but then sometimes two postcards in a single week. He was doing well, playing in a band as well as writing music. When she stopped hearing from him—and when it became clear that something had to be done about the dog, and something had been done—she was twenty-two. On a date with a man she liked as a friend, she suggested that they go over to Jersey and drive down Boulevard East. The man was new to New York, and when they got there he said that he was more impressed with that view of the city than with the view from the top of the RCA Building. "All ours," she said, gesturing with her arm, and he, smiling and excited by what she said, took her hand when it had finished its sweep and kissed it, and continued to stare with awe at the lights across the water. That summer, she heard another song of Jack's on the radio, which alluded, as so many of his songs did, to times in New York she remembered well. In this particular song there was a couplet about a man on the street offering kittens in a box that actually contained a dog named Sam. In the context of the song it was an amusing episode—another "you can't always get what you want" sort of thing—and she could imagine Jack in California, not knowing what had happened to Sam, and, always the one to appreciate little jokes in songs, smiling.

Where Is
Garland Steeples Now?

LEE K. ABBOTT

Every time Garland told the story, which, according
to his sister, Darlene Neff, was so farfetched and shifty
an item that it couldn't be true, he gave its hero, the
dog, a new name. Garland's first week back after dis-
charge, those medals of his—the Army Commendation
Medal, the Good Conduct Medal, the NDS medal,
and that unit citation for valor from the Republic of
Vietnam—still untattered, the dog was called Chester
Sims, supposedly after a spec four known to Garland

2 1 3

up in the MR3 with the 18th ARVN. In April, however, a month after Garland had begun working at that 7-11 which was practically in sight of Arlington Stadium, the dog was known as Mr. Eddie and had only three legs, the absent one reportedly blown off clean in a place identified as the Crescent of Fertile Minds. In June, before Garland started the bank-robbing he became famous for, the dog was Spike or Marvin, and its story—from the time it was met and loved and then murdered by Garland—took nearly thirty minutes of telling. Ivy Parks, Darlene Neff's neighbor, heard that the dog was named Nick Carter, after Garland's favorite reading matter, and was supposed to be as big as the enemy itself and, what with toothsome grin and mange, probably rabid. In July, on the day he brought home the gleaming Roadmaster, its engine a masterpiece of brightwork, Garland told his boss, Mr. Hemsley, that his dog was named Tiger and that, like all stories, Tiger's was part joy and part trouble, the whole of it unhappy as Xmas in Russia—not a word of which Hemsley believed on account of Garland's goofy grin and the way his eyes turned dark whenever he reached the passages about being able to speak canine, a fact he illustrated by going "Aarrff" and "Woof" and "Grrrr" until the story was not English at all but only bark, ardent growl and gesture that looked like four-legged distress.

After a time, though, everybody, from Darlene's husband, Virgil, to Ike Fooley who lived down the street, to Bonnie Suggs, the First Federal teller to whom he told it while pointing a big old cannonlike gun—everybody knew it as Garland H. Steeples's story, "The Dog of Vietnam," a narrative he told a thousand times in 1971, always mentioning how he was on loan to the 1/26, Hotel Company, in particular a fivesome of ethnic savages who billed themselves as the Detroit Pistons (because of their affection for basketball and place of national origin), who high-stepped around Firebase Maggie dressed up in these abso-fucking-lutely outrageous tailored outfits they'd gotten on Nathan Road in Hong Kong (black leaf-patterned camouflage suits so tight they were

skin itself, with matching boonie hats). "I was truly happy," he told Darcel Worthy, a man who'd come into the store one night looking for ginger ale and Cheez Whiz. "I had me a mission in this life," Garland said, "and folks around to help me do it. Plus, I was eighteen, which means I was permanently optimistic." He had his mind right, he said; he was not terribly aggravated by peacecreeps nor otherwise upset about the downscale living and dying that took place when Victor Charles sought his destiny and Uncle Sugar aimed to resist. Truth to tell, he was some excited by all that NVA bang-bang and the hardware by which, including CAR-15 and beautimous Claymore mine, he endeavored to hush it. "I was gonna do my two years, get loose of that place and go back to the world an adult."

Anyway, Garland would say, having established time, place and central character, into Firebase Maggie one day walked this dog—here G's eyes would get all misty and quite unfocused from the memory of it all—with mussed hair like a twenty-dollar streetwalker and an expression that said, "I could be forty thousand years old, but screw you anyway, GI." That animal, someone said, brought to mind such words as *scourge* and *mishap*. "It was a Vietnam dog, all right," Garland told his brother-in-law. "It had floppy ears, one practically chewed right to the bone, and you could tell it just loved being around the smells and wealth of us. I knew right then I had to have me that animal." It took nearly twenty minutes for the beast to take the pressed meat Garland offered, what with its disposition being more wary than trusting; then the two of them went back to G's hooch and shared a cornflake bar while the human one introduced the animal to the CO and an E-8 master sergeant named Krebs; Garland pointed out that beyond the bangalores and perimeter wire and artful maze of land mines lay an almost impenetrable jungle in which lurked a shitload of high-principled cutthroats who rode bicycles and who would like nothing more than, given their usual diet of rat and rice, to feast upon haunch of dog or backbone filet. "So what do you say, Vietnam dog, how 'bout you and me becoming pals?" While the animal appeared to debate the question, Garland cast about for more convincing arguments. "The way I look at it," Garland said, "you are alone and I'm alone, which means that we ought to be together having fun. Loneliness ain't for the kind we are." Whereupon that critter, so the story went, lay its muzzle on its forepaws and seemed to ponder for a time; then, with an affirmative noise, it leaped aboard our boy, leaving sloppy lick marks all over his cheeks.

It was, according to Darlene Neff's recollection, the sort of love as was had between Pancho and Cisco, Tonto and the Lone Ranger —Garland and his grungy sidekick as inseparable as white on chalk. They went everywhere together—latrine, commo tent, even on a dark-of-night extraction near Hill 199 when a Chinook warrant officer, trying to evade heavy ground fire, almost pitched them into outer space. "I told that dog everything about me," Garland confessed to Billy Pickering, the boy who delivered the *Times-Herald*. "I showed him pictures, too: me at Disneyland, me at high-school graduation, me pissing into the Grand Canyon." He even read to that dog, its favorite passages being those when Marc Bolan, the Executioner, blasted the bejesus out of the lowdown evil other guy. He taught that dog how to sit up, how to roll over like a drunk, and how to cross its front legs like a Frenchman named René. He taught him how to beg like you were being done a favor; and once, after some three-star action in Recon Zone Hood, he got that furry creature high on Cambodian weed and they staggered off to eyeball the stars and make up miracles to astound the in-country gangsters they had occasion to deal with.

"Oh, that was some smart animal," Garland used to tell the other clerk, a wide-hipped Big Springs woman named Colette. Why, he took that dog one time into the big airbase at Da Nang, made it walk right up to Mr. Bob Hope and shake his Hollywood hand, Garland later coming up on stage to take a bow for having such an intelligent and well-mannered companion. Yet that dog could be plumb feisty too.

One time, so the story went, it bit the rear end of a larcenous Friendly, which prompted a blizzard of directives up and down the chain of command—which resulted, so rumor had it, in MACV itself, in the estimable person of General William Westmoreland, saying it favored and did encourage man–pet love as a morale booster, as essential to a given hombre's welfare as letters from home or exotic R & R.

The trouble started, Garland told the ticket-taker at Six Flags, when his dog—then called Buster or, if female, Sally—chewed through its leash and somehow found its way to Garland's side, forty klicks into the murk-filled hinterlands. The TL, a Philly delivery man who liked to be called Bigfoot, was all for shooting Buster. He said "Shit" and "Goddam" and "Ain't this a crock?" and twice flicked the safety off his Sixteen with the full intent of vaporizing the entire hair and teeth and scrawny, pest-ridden hindquarters of him who was one man's best friend. Garland was outraged: "You don't touch my dog," he yelled. "Touching my dog will get you killed many times!" A COM/SIT report which surfaced after the war said an hour's discussion followed, during which it was reported that because LURPs in II Corps were supposedly bringing along skivvy bar girlfriends (not to mention those Highway 14 Rangers who'd taken a Saigon rock 'n' roll band named Teenage Wasteland into the Ir Drang Valley), it seemed okay to bring along old Shep or whatever the hell his name was. "He's got to watch his ass," the TL said. "I don't want to hear no squealing or nothing."

According to EYES ONLY paperwork out of the GVN, the murder and Garland's subsequent ill-will began the night he went into the bush with the Detroit Pistons to bury several Black Boxes on a so-called high-speed trail down which Charlie and his ilk were conveying ordnance so sophisticated it was feared that Uncle Ho himself would soon be following in an Airstream house trailer with Bar-B-Que and Magnavox color TV. Garland said the night was pure Alfred Hitchcock: pale moon, inhospitable flora, fauna such as might have been invented by Dr. Frankenstein, not to mention an E & E route they all believed led right past the open door of the Hanoi Politburo. Buster was there, too, half dipped in lampblack to give him that dangerous Hell-I-don't-care evil look it took humans only twenty minutes to acquire over there. Everything was fine for a time, the good guys being sneaky and expert, the six of them, men and dog, stopping for a while to eat and catnap, then there was a crackling noise in the woods, a six-sided shiver of recognition, and the TL tumbled over in a heap, a big hole where his chest used to be, which was followed by scrambling, jumping and diving. According to the Governor of Texas, who'd heard it from the TBI, who'd gotten their information from the Tarrant County sheriff whose deputies had interviewed the guard and two tellers at the Citizens' Bank on Cedar Street, the ATL took it in the neck, and one by one, in a storm of tears and rendered hearts, all the other Detroit Pistons fouled out, there being now in the whole wide world only two creatures to worry about: a dog that could have been named Butch and a Van Nuys (CA) PFC named Garland H. Steeples whose insides and sense of self were all scrambled on account of fear and a handful of U.S. Army methamphetamine.

"I didn't move for an hour," Garland said in the holdup note he gave to the girl at the Quik-Mart in Richardson. It was a seven-page document in which, his handwriting cramped with hysteria, Garland said he and his mutt huddled in a hidey-hole while all about them flocked deadly sons-of-bitches got up in gray pith helmets and regular greens. "That dog and I were doing some heavy communicating," he wrote. "I was saying *Scoot down, scrunch up, pull that branch over you*; and that dog was saying in body language *Stop leaning on me, let go of my neck, watch your elbow.*" The man at the Texaco station, which Garland stuck up the last time he was in the state, said that Steeples and his dog had a real primary thing going in that hole: they were one breath, one heartbeat, one desire. They could see little, smell nothing but their own stinks and hear nothing but Haiphong gobbledygook. "I could sing to you," Garland said. That dog gave him one dark eyeball and the chin tilt a rich man uses to convey impatience and distaste. "How about this?" Garland wondered, doing several lines of—almost inconceivable in this situation—"Soul Xmas in Bethlehem." His voice, a whisper really, had all the charm of dirt. "I know some others," he said. Around them, they could hear crackling undergrowth and native chitty-chat. "Dog," Garland began, "I believe we're gonna die." He felt the animal looking at him with intense concentration, its eyes like tiny wet marbles; it was then, Garland swore, that he plainly heard that dog talk. It said, "Steeples, why don't you just shut up for about five minutes and let me think." If they had been somewhere else, Garland proposed, that canine would have been smoking a Havana cigar and wearing La Dolce Vita sunshades. Old Bowzer then said, "How'd I get myself into this pickle?"

(This was Darlene Neff's favorite part, wherein her brother and this humanoidlike dog crouched face to muzzle in a jungle mud pit, exchanging opinions. "Garland said that dog sounded like Walter Cronkite," she told her neighbor one day. "Said that dog was smarter than some teachers he'd known. Said he had no problem seeing that dog driving a Buick or opening a Sears account." Even after he was long gone, Darlene liked to describe Garland's face every time he came to this spot in his adventure: it was a miserable, fraught-filled expression, what it was, as if he were again in that distant world, a place of darkness and terror and heat in which it was entirely possible that persons much influenced by loneliness and imminent doom might indeed strike up a relationship with rotted tree stump or far-off fleecy cloud.)

Here it was, then, Garland remembered, that his amigo, Old Yeller, actually barked—a sound so loud and alien in this place it was like a spotlight shining in his eyes—and he found his hands clamped immediately around that dog's snout. "You're trying to get me killed," Garland said. Through the leaf growth, our boy could see the enemy frozen with curiosity. "Steeples," that dog said, "what the hell are you doing to my neck?" Garland brought the dog's face to his own. "If I let you go," he whispered, "don't yell no more, okay?" The animal seemed to take a long time to consider. "Boy," the dog said, "you ain't learned much about me, have you?" Yet as soon as he was released the dog started to take off, the racket he was making loud enough to be heard on the moon. Garland grabbed him by the throat. "What're you doing?" The dog eyed him suspiciously: "I am leaving here and you, 'bye." Garland clamped his hands over the jaws again. It was a moment, he remembered, as still as death itself: two creatures, one with a big brain and no hope, the other with eons of instinct and four legs for running. "Honest," Garland said once, "I was inside his brain. I knew where he came from, which was Long Binh, and that its old momma was the dog equivalent of a three-dollar business suit." It was thinking dog thoughts: bone and hank, piss on bush and fly on out of there. Garland could almost see himself through the animal's eyes: a skinny work of American manhood, some pimpled, its cheeks completely tear-ravaged. "You're about to do something mean, ain't you?" that dog said. "Dog, you are some first-rate animal, you know." The dog affected the aspect, yes, of supreme disinterest: "I could've been a lot of things in this world." Garland could see the bad guys pressing in from near-abouts, all of them evidently waiting for the next peep or telltale howl. He tried explaining that there was nothing else he could do—life was a pisser, it seemed, ignorant of him and his desires. "I'd like to live, plus you're an orphan—and a dog besides." Whereupon that dog, Garland had to admit, tried to talk him out of it, tried appealing to our boy's sense of fair play, of loyalty; said it aimed to go on down to My Khe, heard there was a whole pack of poodles down there, all named Fifi or Babette, with painted toenails and French-cut hair; said it was scraggly, sure, but in the long view offered by such as Monsieur Descartes just as valuable as Lassie or Rin Tin Tin himself. Garland shook his head; he was truly sorry. "Well, then," the dog said, "go ahead and do it, you old son-of-a-bitch." Whereupon that dog composed himself into a sterling example of insouciance and turned on in its eyes a light such as might emanate from that vast afterworld they both knew about.

"So I started squeezing," Garland wrote in a letter to the Dallas *Morning News*. He threw his whole weight, all 176 pounds, into his grip, one arm around the head in a Kung Fu–inspired move the Army had guaranteed to incapacitate utterly. That dog, Garland reported, was thinking airy thoughts the whole time—about getting a bath with GI soap, about having commissary chopped steak in the Philippines, about having maybe even a Washington, D.C., backyard to cavort in. It didn't squirm or struggle or shiver a bit. Though it was still dark, Garland could sense the NVA folks milling about like customers at a circus; and he could feel, as old Buster got short of breath and his eyes rolled up partways, things giving loose inside himself as well—his heart thudding, his stomach doing a flip, his lungs filling up with some awful liquid he assumed was related to having to do unfortunate deeds for the best of reasons in the worst of times. "I don't know how long it took," Garland wrote, " 'cause the next thing I knew it was morning, the enemy had melted away like mist, and I was holding this limp, crushed friend to my chest."

After he was gone for about four months, you heard this story often and with considerable conviction, it now having entered the popular imagination. It was told by a KINT DJ and appeared in the CB cross-talk on I-10 or up around Odessa. Darrell Royal, then coaching the Longhorns and in Houston for a cookout, told a high-school running back named Scooter that it, the story, was pure-D invention—wish and whine from those of mashed spirit. You heart it in Goree, at the VFW hall in Heron, at Mildred's Diner. It was heard at the Flying R dude ranch in Big Bend country once, all its grit removed, the story itself as slick and unfelt as glass. You heard it gussied up or nude as an oyster. Were it woman, a legislator from Huntington County once said, it would be named Sheree or Debbi-do, a being that looked good with a cocktail or a water bed. Once, Cappy Eads, a one hundred percent look-alike for Santa Claus himself, heard it from the My Sin saleswoman at Neiman-Marcus who'd heard it from her neighbor who'd heard it from her nephew who'd gotten it from a wild-haired East Dallas youth. Cappy said that old Tramp's story was only cheek and shinbone, the bulk and organ of it removed, the murder itself taking place in a thousand middle-class bedrooms, Garland no more than a shade or Vincent Price ghoul from the netherworlds. Sometimes, in fact, Garland wasn't in the story at all, his place taken by an equally unfulfilled round-eyed youth; and sometimes it wasn't a dog which died, but a crawly-grimy piece of work which looked like a vision drunks weep over; and sometimes the story itself took a whole day and much whiskey to tell, its moments, from getting to losing, spirited, mean and epic enough for silver screen or drive-in movie.

After a year or so, it left Texas for the rest of North America. In Florida, you heard it as "Another Story of Fate and Circumstance," the human no longer a boy but an adult named Dalrhymple or Poot, the dog a specter called forth from the lower waters by tribulation and shared failure. In South Carolina, it had a dozen episodes, including one in which that *Canis familiaris* took up a Parker Bros. ballpoint and, after some cogitation, wrote its name and several sentences of the complex-compound variety. At Frank J. Wiley Junior High School in Chaney, Nebraska, it produced a dozen essays, foremost of which was written by Oogie Pringle, Jr., who, at the honors assembly, recited the whole thing, devoting particular attention to those sections in which the dog, some cleaned up for this telling, and on the verge of everlasting darkness, was saying "Okay" at the very instant the protagonist, Garland H. Steeples, was crumbling to dust in his frozen, desperate and wracked heart.

The story was told last, it appears, by the famous West Coast psychic

Charlene Dibbs, in the studios of KNET Phoenix, who informed an audience of St. Vincent Gray Ladies that she, at this precise instant, was in mental contact with the notorious felon and veteran, Garland Steeples. It was a moment of dire expectation. She could visualize him now, she said, as if he were sitting across from her, his face darkened by three days of bristly beard, his clothes shabby and loose. "I see him as a hobo," she said, there being in her voice a lilt such as used by those fetched up by UFOs or victims of out-of-body travel. It was Garland H. Steeples, she said, who was living in reduced circumstances, most probably in a trailer park, him the uneasy guest of a woman named Rae Nell. "At this time," she announced, "I will try to invade his mind." There were many oooohhhs and aaahhhs as Charlene Dibbs set herself to this task, her eyes squinty with concentration. "May I have quiet, please?" she said. "I am getting interference." You could see she was doubtlessly picking up the troublesome thoughts of several naughty people, among them those in pain or about to be. "He is miles away," she said. There were mountains in his distance, she said, but mainly he lived in a flat, barren place—a place of winds and wild climates. "My, that boy is unhappy." It was here, everybody would one day remember, that Ms. Dibbs's face suddenly took on a strained, unlived-in look and she pitched forward in her chair until she had arranged herself in a crouch, alert and suspicious. She made sounds, too, throaty and wet, as if what was to be said was best put in grunts and groans. And then, in what came to be known as the climax of this story of man and dog, it came to pass that an army of viewers from Yuma to North Tucson saw Charlene Dibbs, as if by magic, transformed into one Garland H. Steeples, and you could see that he was out there—anywhere, everywhere—long of tooth and gleeless, as if he had centuries to wait, as if he again were in a deprived venue and again faced with the impossible choice between life and love.

Junhy

GARY GILDNER

One Sunday in July, in heavy humidity, a man and woman left off arguing and ate a chicken together. The chicken was baked with butter and rosemary and thyme, and the man and woman, as if suddenly set free, ate it with their fingers, sitting out on their porch, facing each other, under an old-fashioned ceiling fan that still worked. Their old golden retriever lay quietly panting on the floor beside them.

Everything looked to the man as before they had

started arguing—years before. Even the dog seemed younger. The man thought, After dinner, Buster, we'll go outside and play soccer. And in his mind they were already doing that. He was kicking the ball, the dog was running for it and nosing it back, and the man was guarding the goal. Over and over in his mind that scene replayed itself, until finally the dog, which was only a pup, after all, flopped in the wet grass, his head between his paws, and just looked at the ball—while the rising sun cast long, dark green shadows shaped like northern pike across the lawn.

The man could see all that in his mind as clearly as if it were a series of photographs. And then he heard himself say, "Do not squander your youth, Buster. In six or seven years you will be as old as I am." But maybe, he reflected, that wasn't the right thing to say on such a fine fresh morning that spoke so simply, so eloquently, of promise. Squatting down close to the puppy's face, he therefore tried another approach: "You and I, Buster Brown, are the men of the house," he whispered. "When you get a little older, that is, a little stronger, we'll go to the park and play soccer under the noon sun, on a sweet meadow, and all the girls who pass by will admire our fancy footwork."

Just then the golden retriever raised his head from the floor, in-terrupting the man's reverie, and studied an ant crawling toward his belly. The man saw it too and stepped on it, and the old dog lay his head back down, sighing.

"What was that?" said the woman.

"An ordinary ant," the man told her.

The woman nodded. "I hope the termites don't come back."

"Yes," he said, "I hope not too."

They were finished eating; the plates with the bones on them sat on the ledge beside their rocking chairs, catching the late sun. Using his thumb, the man eased his plate two or three inches away, to get the reflection out of his eyes.

"I wish I could give Buster these bones," he said.

"He's too old, the darling." The woman reached down and rubbed the back of her fingers along his tail, regarding him with a fond, sad gaze.

"Ten years ago he was a baby. Now he's practically an old man."

"He is an old man," said the woman.

"Remember when we'd watch him sleep?"

"Yes."

"Didn't we take a really good picture of him one time, sleeping?"

The woman nodded. "We took hundreds."

"I know we took a lot," the man said gently. "But I was thinking of one in particular. I wonder where it might be?"

"In a box somewhere. Along with everything else."

The man thought about hunting up the box, but then he thought of all the other pictures he'd see, of the two of them during the times when they had been happy, and he didn't want to see them. Not right now. He remembered taking a picture of her when she was sleeping— napping on the porch in the hammock, the sun sneaking through the sycamore leaves making bright speckles on her cheek. Remembering that, and how pretty she had looked, he felt his chest thicken. He got up and took the plates to the kitchen. He scraped off the bones into the garbage, then ran water in the sink. The woman came up behind him.

"Would you like me to look for it?" she said.

"No. I don't think so."

She put fresh ice in their tea glasses.

"How do you feel?" she asked him.

"Oh . . ." He paused, for he was not sure how he felt; rather, he did not know how to express it. "Better," he finally said, though that was not an answer that satisfied him.

"I do too," she said.

They returned to the porch and sat beside the dog, drinking their tea in silence. The black raspberry canes in the yard were already freckled white and curling, the silvery undersides of their leaves pushed up in a sudden hot draft. So many fading palms trying to signal *stop*, the man thought. After a while he saw himself walking into a party to which he was not certain he had been invited. He hesitated in the foyer, twisting the tail end of the green tissue paper that wrapped his gift roses, twisting the paper and wondering if he was standing on one leg like a heron, and if so, why? Then he felt a sharp pain in his right index finger—he'd pricked it on a thorn—the same finger that struck the *j, u, n, h,* and *y* on his typewriter. An instant after he realized this, a woman wearing a hat with a black veil came up and introduced herself. She was the hostess, she said; her name was Junhy. He was too astounded to speak—and against his ribs his heart knocked to be let out, to explain. She said, "Oh, your finger is bleeding. Here, let me help you," and she took the flowers, indicating he should follow her. But he could not follow her, for she had quickly disappeared among all the other flowers—baskets and vases of them—lining the walls of the foyer and spilling into the other room. And his tongue, useless, lay in his mouth like a dead minnow.

Groaning, the dog raised his head and looked at the man, as if wanting a word of some kind.

Finally the man returned from where he had been, heartsore, puzzled, and noticed the dog's long look. "What would you like, Buster? Tell me. Do you know what *I'd* like? What we haven't had in a long, long time? I would very much like, even though it's not the best day for it—I mean the best weather, for Sunday is the proper day—a baked chicken. With melted butter brushed on all the pieces, and just the right amount of rosemary and thyme sprinkled on them. Wouldn't that be delicious? And wouldn't you, faithful friend, wouldn't you really go for the delicious scraps?"

"Stop it. Oh please, please, please stop it," the woman begged—and when he looked up she had come back, and was smiling. He was sure of it.

Chips Is Here

DAVID LEAVITT

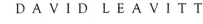

Here is why I decided to kill my neighbor:

On a rainy morning in midsummer, after several failed efforts, my cat finally managed to scale the fence that separated my yard from Willoughby Wayne's. The cat landed on all four feet in the narrow space behind a privet hedge. At first he sat there for a moment, licking his paws and acquainting himself with his new situation. Then, quite cautiously, he began making his way through the brushy underside of the hedge toward

228

Willoughby's lawn. Unfortunately for him, the five Kerry Blue Terriers with whom Willoughby lives were aware of the cat's presence well before he actually stepped out onto the grass, and like a posse, they were there to greet him. The cat reared, hissed and batted a paw in the face of the largest of the Kerry Blues, who in turn swiftly and noisily descended with the efficient engine of his teeth. "Johnny! Johnny!" I heard Willoughby call. "Bad dog, Johnny! Bad dog!" There was some barking, then things got quiet again.

A few hours later, after I'd searched the house and checked most of the cat's outdoor hiding places, I called Willoughby. "Oh, a young cat?" he said. "Orange and white? Yes, he was here. Needless to say I did my best to introduce him to my pack, but inexperience has resulted in their maintaining a very puppylike attitude toward cats; the introductions—shall we say—did not go well. I interceded delicately, breaking up the melee, then, for his own good, lifted the feline fellow over the fence and deposited him in the field adjacent to my property. I believe he was quite frightened by Johnny, and suspect he's probably hiding in the field even as we speak."

I thanked Willoughby, hung up and headed out into the field that adjoins both our yards. It was a fairly wild field, unkempt, thick with waist-high weeds and snarls of roots in which my dog, accompanying me, kept getting trapped. I'd be thrashing along, breaking the weeds down with a stick and calling, "Kitty! Here, Kitty!" when suddenly the dog would start barking, and turning around I'd see her tangled in an outrageous position, immobilized by the vines in much the same way she often became immobilized by her own leash. Each time I'd free her, and we'd continue combing the field, but the cat apparently chose not to answer my repeated calls. I went back three times that afternoon, and twice that night. In the morning I canvassed the neighbors, without success, before returning to comb the field a sixth time. "Still looking for your young feline?" Willoughby called to me over the fence. He was clipping his privet hedge. "I'm really terribly sorry.

If I'd had any idea he was *your* cat I most certainly would have hand-delivered him to you on the spot."

"Yes, well," I said.

"For whatever it's worth, it was right here, right here where I'm standing, that I lifted him over."

"Well, I've been meaning to ask you. He *was* all right when you handed him over, wasn't he? He wasn't hurt."

"Oh, he was perfectly fine," Willoughby said. "Why, I would never put an injured cat over a fence, never."

"No, I'm sure he's just hiding somewhere. I'll let you know when I find him."

"Do," Willoughby said, and returned to his clipping. The thwack of the clippers as they came down on the hedges followed me through the field and out of the field.

I'm not sure what it was, but the next day something compelled me to search Willoughby's yard. I waited until he wasn't home, then, like my cat before me, crept stealthily through a side gate. From their outdoor pen the Kerry Blues growled with suspicion. I circled the lawn until I was standing at the place where Willoughby was standing when he claimed to have put the cat over the fence. On the other side of the fence a thorny bush blocked my view of the field, and just to the left of it lay my cat, quite dead. I didn't make a sound. I went around the other way, into the field, and dug behind the bush, in the process cutting myself quite severely on the brambles. There was a gash running from the cat's chest to near his tail.

I picked up the carcass of my cat. His orange and white markings were still the same, but he was now just that—a carcass. I went to the house and got a garbage bag and shovel, and then I buried my cat in the overgrown field.

On the way home, climbing over my own fence, I decided to kill my neighbor.

At home I took a shower. The soap eased me. I felt no urge to confront Willoughby, to argue with him, to back him up against a wall and force him to confess his lie. I did not want to watch him writhe, or try to wriggle away from the forceful truth inhabiting my gaze. I simply wanted to kill him—cleanly, painlessly, with a minimum of fuss and absolutely no discussion. It was not a question of vengeance; it was a question of extermination.

Of course a shotgun would have been best. Then I could simply ring his doorbell, aim and when he answered, pull the trigger.

Unfortunately, I did not own a shotgun, and had no idea where to get one. Knives seemed messy. With strangulation and plastic bags, there was almost invariably a struggle.

Then, drying myself after the shower, I noticed the andirons. They were Willoughby's andirons; nineteenth-century, in the shape of pug dogs. He had loaned them to me one night in the winter. I'd lived next door to him for three years by then, but for the first two years I was living with someone else, and he hadn't seemed very interested in us. We'd exchanged the merest pleasantries over the fence. All I knew of Willoughby at that point was that he was exceedingly red-cheeked, apparently wealthy, and a breeder of Kerry Blue Terriers. It was only when the person I was living with decided to live somewhere else, in fact, that suddenly—at the sight of moving vans, it seemed—Willoughby showed up at the fence. "Neigh—bor," he called in a singsong. "Oh, neigh—bor." I walked up to the fence and he told me that one of his dogs had escaped and asked if I'd seen it, and when I said no he asked me over for a drink. I didn't take him up on the offer. One day my dog managed to dig under the fence to play with his Kerry Blues, and when she returned there was a small red Christmas tree ornament in the shape of a heart fastened to her collar. It hadn't been there before.

A few nights later a smoldering log rolled out of my fireplace, setting off the smoke alarm but bringing no one but Willoughby to the rescue. He was wearing a red sweatsuit and a jacket. I thought, Rambo the Elf.

"I must loan you a pair of andirons," he said happily as he looked down at the charred spot on my rug. "Firedogs, you know. I'll be right back."

"Ah—no need. I'll buy a pair."

"No, no, you must accept my gesture. It's only neighborly."

"Thanks very much, then. I'll come by and pick them up in the morning."

Willoughby beamed. "Oh, too eager, I am always too eager when smitten. Well, yes, then. Fine." But in the morning, when I woke up, the andirons were waiting on my doorstep, along with a piece of note-paper illustrated with a picture of a Kerry Blue Terrier. On it, in red pen, was drawn a question mark.

From the fireplace, now, I picked one of the andirons up. It was cold and slightly sooty, yet it felt heavy enough to kill. "Blunt instru-ment," I said aloud to myself, savoring the words.

My dog was sitting in the backseat of the car. Since the cat's disappearance this had become her favorite resting place, as if she feared above all else being left behind and was determined to make sure I didn't set foot out of the house without her being aware of it. Now, however, I was traveling on foot and figuring that anywhere I could walk was close enough not to pose a threat to her, she remained ensconced. It was a bright, sunny day, not the sort of day on which you would think you would think of killing someone. As I passed each house and turned the bend toward Willoughby's, I wondered when my resolve was going to lessen, when, with a rocket crash, I'd suddenly come to my senses. The thing was, it was the decision to kill Willoughby which felt like coming to my senses to me.

Halfway to his house a Jeep Wagoneer pulled up to the side of the road ahead of me. On the bumper was a sticker which read. "The Better

I Get to Know People, The More I Love My Dogs," and leaning out the driver's window was Tina Milkowski, the proprietress of a small, makeshift and highly successful canine-sitting service. She was a huge woman, three hundred pounds at least.

"How you doing, Jeffrey?" she called.

"Not bad," I said. "How are you, Tina?"

"Can't complain." She seemed, for a moment, to sniff the air. "Where's the Princess today?"

"Home. She's spending the afternoon in my car."

"Hope you left the windows open. Say, what you got there? Firedogs?"

"They're Willoughby's."

Tina shook her head and reached for something in her glove compartment. "He's a strange one, Willoughby. Never been very friendly. The dogs are nice, though. He give those firedogs to you?"

She pulled a stick of gum out of a pack and began chewing it ruthlessly. I nodded.

"I didn't know you two were friends," Tina said in what seemed to me a suggestive manner.

"We're not friends. In fact, I'm on my way to kill him."

Tina stopped chewing. Then she laughed—a surprisingly high, girlish laugh, given her hoarse, bellows-like voice.

"Now why do you want to kill Willoughby?"

"One of his dogs murdered my cat. Then he threw the corpse over the fence into the field. But he told me the cat was alive, that he'd thrown the cat alive into the field because he didn't know it was my cat, and for three days now I've been searching that field for my cat when the whole time he was dead. At least I hope he was dead. It's possible he threw the cat over injured and let him bleed to death, though I can't believe, I honestly can't believe . . ."

I believed Tina had seen her fair share of the crimes human beings commit against one another; for this reason, perhaps, it was the crimes human beings commit against animals toward which she brought her harshest judgment.

She narrowed her eyes. "Listen, honey, don't do anything you'll regret. Think of it this way. His dog kills the cat, he throws it over, he isn't even thinking, probably. He figures it was a wild cat, pretends it'll just disappear. Then you ask him, he never knew it was your cat, and he just makes something up. On the spur of the moment. Probably he's over in that church right now saying a hundred Hail Marys and praying to Jesus to forgive him."

"It was worse than that." I cleared my throat. "Look, there's no point in going into details."

"The doggy probably didn't know what he was doing. Sometimes they just act instinctually."

"I don't blame the dog. I blame Willoughby."

Tina chewed her gum even more ferociously. For a few moments we were silent, her Wagoneer idling, until I realized what it was she was waiting for me to say.

It was easy enough. I laughed. "Don't worry," I said, "I'm not *really* going to kill him. I'm just going to bring back his andirons and have it out with him."

"You sure you're all right? You want to come by for a cup of coffee and talk it over?"

"Really, it's okay. Anyway, Tina, do I look like a murderer?"

She smiled, and I saw how tiny her mouth was, lost in her huge face. "You don't look to me," she said, "like you could kill a deer tick if it was biting you on the face."

I was learning something about murder. Before—that is, before the cat—I had always assumed that when the thought of killing someone enters the mind, a sudden knowledge of its consequences rears up almost automatically in response, saving the would-be killer from himself by reminding him, in glorious technicolor, of all the cherished things he stands to lose. Today, however, no vision of jail cells or courtrooms or electric chairs entered my head. Nothing compelled me to replace the gun gratefully in its holster, the knife happily in its drawer, the firedog cheerily in its fireplace. The urge to kill had fogged every other feeling; walking down the street in its grip, I could see nothing but the immediate goal, and that goal was so clear, so obvious, it seemed so justly demanded, that the rest of the world, the world after the murder, the world of repercussions and punishments, receded and became dimly unreal. Indeed, as I approached Willoughby's house and rang his doorbell, I felt as if I were no longer a person; I felt as if I were merely a function waiting to be performed.

"Good afternoon," Willoughby said automatically as he pulled open the door; then, faced by mine, his face sank.

He looked down quickly. "I see you're returning my andirons."

"Yes," I said.

"Please come in." Willoughby led me into his living room. He was wearing a bright purple polo shirt and green shorts. I had one andiron in each hand, and what I hadn't counted on was having to put one down in order to kill him with the other one.

"I'll just take those from you," he said.

I allowed him to remove the andirons from my hands and replace them in his fireplace, along with several other sets.

"Have you found your little cat?"

"Yes. He was dead. Just where you threw him over."

Willoughby seemed to do some quick thinking, then said, "Oh dear, how terrible. I suspect one of these roaming dogs must have gotten to him. You know, with no leash law, this town is full of roaming, wild dogs. Most irresponsible of their owners, but I've always felt the folk here were a cretinous brood." He shook his head, turned from me, sat down on the edge of a settee.

"The corpse was at the exact spot where you told me you set him over the fence—alive."

"It is possible the dog—the wild dog—brought the corpse back after killing him, or—or did it right then—right after I—put him over." Willoughby coughed. "I am truly most terribly sorry about your cat. You know, Johnny really is very frightened of cats. He killed another—killed a cat once, another cat, that is. It was wandering in that field, and it attacked him. The cat attacked him. Viciously. He reacted in self-defense. With that cat, of course, the other cat, not with yours. In your case I interceded in the nick of time and removed the cat unharmed." He looked up at me. "Are you sure I can't induce you to take *some* libation?" he said.

"I'm going to kill you," I said.

Willoughby stood. "I'll call the police," he said. "I'll scream. My neighbor can be here in thirty seconds. My dogs are trained to kill. Believe me, I've dealt with thugs like you before and I know what to do. Many people have tried to take advantage of me, and none have ever succeeded. There's a gun in that drawer. There's a knife in the kitchen. I'm trained to kill. I know karate. I'm warning you. Stand back! Johnny! Johnny!"

His eyes were bulging. He stood pressed against a sliding glass door, as if pinned back, as if he were waiting for knives to land in a pattern around his body. Then he pulled the door open and ran out into the backyard. The dogs came leaping to him. He ran past them, toward the side gate that opened into the field, and then he ran out the gate, not bothering to close it. The dogs huddled around the open gate, but hesitated to follow their master through it.

I turned around and left Willoughby's living room. I closed his door behind me. I did not kill him, and I went home.

I did not know my cat well when he died. I had had him just over a month. But I liked him, and I was beginning to look forward to our life together. Not much distinguished him from other young cats. He was orange and white, and looking at him always made me hungry for those orange Popsicles with vanilla ice cream inside. He liked to romp around the house, to play with balls of string, to climb trees and to hide. For hours he and Johnny sat across the fence from each other, staring, not making a move. He climbed tablecloths, and the smell of tuna fish made him yowl with an urgent desire which I could not seem to talk him out of. At first he had been wary of my dog, but then they grew loving toward each other. He used to nip at her legs for hours, trying to get her to play with him, while she sat there unreacting, an enduring, world-weary matron. Sometimes he'd bat her face with his paw, and his claws would stick in her wiry fur.

When I got home from Willoughby's that afternoon my dog was still in the car. The paint on the driver's door, I noticed, was scratched from her nails. I got in and pulled out of the driveway. From where she was lying behind the backseat she lifted her head like the stuffed dog with the bobbing head my aunt kept in the back of her car in my childhood. She jumped onto the seat. I opened the back window a little, and she nudged her nose through the crack, sniffing the wind. We passed the empty field next to Willoughby's house, and I saw Willoughby on the side of the road, barefoot, red-faced and panting. I honked, and his mouth opened and he ran across the street. In my rearview mirror I watched him grow smaller and smaller until I turned a corner and he disappeared. Soon we were in open country—long fields where corn had been planted in narrow, even rows.

Once, on a snowblind winter night, I had heard Willoughby whistling. I stood up and went to the back door. There he was, just on the other side of the fence. "Jeffrey," he said, "are you really my friend?"

"Excuse me?" I said.

"I'm asking if you're really my friend," he said. "I must know, you see, because the Lord has seen fit to lock me out of my house, and I must rely upon the kindness of strangers."

"Wait a minute. You're locked out?"

"Afraid so."

"Have you lost your key?"

"No, I haven't lost my key."

"Is the lock broken, or frozen?"

"There's nothing wrong with the lock."

"Well, I don't understand then—"

"The *Lord* has seen fit to lock me out of my house. It is a test. I must throw myself upon the mercy of strangers, the kindness of strangers. I must be humble."

"Call a locksmith," I said, and went back inside.

A few hours later the phone rang. I let the answering machine pick it up. "Jeffrey, among the many things you may not ever forgive me for is calling you at this indecent hour," Willoughby said. "It's ten—or, rather, two o'clock." For a long while he was silent. Then he said, "Whenever you're ready, I'll be waiting. And my house is all alit by the Christmas tree."

When I got back from my drive that afternoon, the phone was ringing. "Excuse me," said a voice I didn't recognize. "Is this Mr. Jeffrey Bloom?"

"It is."

"Oh, hello. You don't know me, I'm your neighbor, Mrs. Bob Todd?"

"Hello," I said. I knew the house: a standard poodle, a children's pool and a sign in front that read, THE BOB TODDS.

"I'm sorry to bother you in the evening, Mr. Bloom, but Tina Milkowski told me what happened to your little kitty and I wanted to extend my sympathies. It's just monstrous what that Willoughby Wayne did."

"Thank you, Mrs. Todd."

"Willoughby has been a nuisance ever since he moved into the

Crampton place. Piles of money from his grandfather, and nothing to do with it. Now that was a man. Norton Wayne, he had character. But you know what they say, every family spawns one bad seed, and Willoughby Wayne is it. Always yammering on about his family tree. One poor couple, they were new at the club? They thought they had to be polite. I was at the next table, and I heard. Willoughby told them his family tree from 1612. Forty-five minutes, and he didn't even pause to take a breath. And those dogs. They bark like crazy, annoying the whole neighborhood. Then one day a few years ago he was leaving the club, and he hit a woman. He was *drunk*."

"My goodness," I said.

"And he's never married. I don't have to tell you *why*." Mrs. Bob Todd hiccupped. "Everyone says it's the Jews that are wrecking the neighborhood, but if you ask me, it's the old good-for-nothings like Willoughby. Nothing but trouble. Now I'm not rich but I've lived in this town my whole life, and I can tell you honestly, I think you Jewish people are just fine."

"Thank you," I said.

"Anyway, dear, the reason I'm calling is Tina and I have decided to take some action. This has just gone far enough, with Willoughby and those dogs, and we're going to do something about it. I've already complained to the dog warden, and now I'm going to start a petition to have Willoughby thrown off the board of the Animal Protection League. He has no business being on that board, given what he did, no business whatsoever."

"Mrs. Todd," I said, "really, this isn't necessary—"

"Oh, don't you worry. You won't have to lift a little finger. Your kitty's murder will be avenged!"

I was quiet. "Thank you," I said again. "You're very welcome," she said. "Goodbye." She hung up. I looked outside the window. My dog was flat on her back, being licked by an elderly Labrador named Max, neither of them deterred from this flirtation by the fact that one was spayed and the other neutered. And suddenly I remembered that I had an appointment for my own cat's neutering just the next week. I'd have to cancel it in order to avoid being charged.

I put the phone down. I was sorry I'd mentioned the whole thing to Tina Milkowski, and thus inadvertently begun the machine of vengeance rolling. Revenge anticipated is usually better than revenge experienced. (Then again, when I had wanted to kill Willoughby, it hadn't felt like revenge, what I'd wanted—or had it?)

I decided to clip a leash onto my dog and take her for a walk. It was the dog-walking hour. The Winnebago of our local mobile dog groomer was parked in Libby LaMotta's driveway, Libby pacing nervously alongside while within that mobile chamber her cocker spaniel puppy, Duffy, was given a bath. We waved. Across the street Susan Carlson had Nutmeg, her Manx cat, on a leash. We waved. Farther down the street Mrs. Friedrich was watering her plants. She often spoke wistfully about the "big, velvety balls" of which *her* cat, Fred, had finally to be deprived, once he'd sprayed too many sofas. We waved. Then I passed Mrs. Carnofsky, quite literally dragging her resistant Dandie Dinmont terrier behind her, unmoved by the scraping sounds the dog's paws were making against the pavement, the wheezing and choking as he gasped against the tug of his collar, determined to pull her back to a pile of shit a few feet down the sidewalk. "He won't budge," she said. Her blue-gray hair was exactly the same tint as her dog's. We did not wave.

As for Willoughby—just past midnight that night there was whistling at the fence. There he stood, in his elf suit, having somehow climbed through or over the privet hedge.

"Jeffrey," he said.

"What is it, Willoughby?"

"Why do you hate me so?"

"I don't hate you," I said honestly.

"If you don't hate me, then why are you persecuting me?"

I crossed my arms and turned away from him. "Look, I'm sorry I said I wanted to kill you. I was just angry. I'm not going to kill you. I apologize."

"Nadine Todd called me this evening and she said the most horrid things. She called me a monster and a drunk and worse. She's going to have me thrown off the board of the Animal Protection Society."

"I really didn't have anything to do with that, Willoughby—"

"The Animal Protection Society is one of my great loves. Disregarding the humiliation for the moment, you'll be taking away one of the few ways in the world in which I'm able to feel truly useful."

"I'm sorry," I said. "Really, I have nothing to do with it. Mrs. Todd is acting on her own."

He looked away. "I am lost and forlorn. I have nowhere to turn. I throw myself upon your mercy."

"Good night, Willoughby," I said, and went inside.

A few minutes later there was a knock on the door.

"Do with me what you will," Willoughby said, and threw his arms out at his sides, like Christ.

"Willoughby, it's past midnight."

"The Lord has directed me to you, Jeffrey. He has told me to throw myself upon your mercy. I must learn to be humble, to act humbly."

"Is it humble to barge uninvited into someone's house in the middle of the night? Is that humble?"

"I am a pathetic and desperate man," Willoughby said. He hung his head in shame.

"All right," I said. "Come in."

He smiled, then, came through the door gratefully, and sat down on the sofa. My dog ran up to him from where she was sleeping, barked, sniffed at his haunches. He reached down and stroked her neck. There was something incalculably gentle and expert about the way he stroked her neck, and I wondered for a moment if he suffered from a kind of autism: if, in lieu of his clumsy and imperfect relations with humans, he had developed an intricate knowledge of the languages and intimacies of dogs. There were people who, for all the affection they felt, hadn't the foggiest idea how to stroke a dog. They pushed the fur the wrong way, their hands came down rough and ungentle. I suspected Willoughby was like this with people, and always had been.

I brought him a cup of tea, which he thanked me for. The dog had crawled into his lap and gone to sleep. "This is not, of course, the first time that I've been the object of persecution and derision," Willoughby was saying. "Even when I was a little boy it happened. My parents for some reason insisted I attend public school. Another child circulated a petition which read, 'We, the undersigned, hate Willoughby Wayne.' I didn't understand why. I had tried to ingratiate myself to those children, in spite of the enormous gulf which separated us." Tears welled in his eyes. "The ancient Hebrews were cursed with the vice of avarice, and often I have felt the modern Hebrews have inherited that vice, yet in spite of this I feel deeply for the persecution they suffered at the hands of the Nazis, for I too have suffered such persecution." And like a litany he incanted: "I am a pathetic and desperate man."

I sat down next to him. "You don't have to be that way," I said.

"I am very set in my ways." His hand, I noticed, was on my thigh, following, even at this dark moment, its sly and particular agenda. I moved it away. The dog lifted her head, sniffed and jumped barking onto the floor.

"I'll call Mrs. Todd," I said. "I'll try to persuade her not to throw you off the board. But I can't guarantee anything. Now I have to go to bed."

Willoughby stood up. I handed him a Kleenex and he blew his nose. "I assure you," he said at the door, "that when I threw your cat over the fence, he was unharmed," and I realized that whether or not this was true, he believed it.

"Good night, Willoughby," I said.

"Good night, Jeffrey." And I watched him go out the door and head down the street. I was remembering how when I was digging the grave that afternoon, I'd kept repeating to myself over and over, "It's just a cat, just an animal, with a small brain, a tail, fur." Then I started thinking about the night my dog, spooked by thunder, bolted out the front door and ran. For three hours I'd driven through the neighborhood, calling her name, knocking on doors. Various sightings were reported in a direct line from Mrs. Friedrich's house, to the Italian deli, to the laundromat; then the trail disappeared. Finally I went to bed, making sure her dog door was open for her, while outside the storm railed on, and my dog, lost somewhere in it, struggled to make her way home. And what a miracle it was when at four in the morning she jumped up onto my bed—filthy, shivering, covered with leaves and brambles. Like the dogs of legends, she had found her way back.

I thought I'd *had* my brush with death then. I thought from then on I might be spared.

It must have been at that moment—when I was digging the grave, remembering how nearly I'd lost my dog—that the thought of murder came to me, growing more vivid with each thwack of the shovel against the stony earth. Really, I was no better than Willoughby; I just hadn't been alone so long.

"I am a pathetic and desperate man," I said to myself—trying the words on for fit—and, standing in the doorway, watched Willoughby stumble home, bereft in the starlight. All along the street, houses were dark, and inside of each of those houses were people with cats and dogs, and stories to tell: the time Flossie fell four stories and broke a tooth; the time Rex disappeared for weeks, then showed up one afternoon on the back porch, licking his paw; the time Bubbles was mangled under the wheels of a car. They would tell you, if you asked them, how they had to put Darling to sleep; how Fifi went blind, then deaf, then one day just didn't wake up; how Bosco could jump through a hoop; how Kelly swam underwater; how Jimbo begged, how Millie spoke, how Sophie ate nothing but tuna fish. The night was brisk, and somewhere distantly a dog barked. My dog growled, then barked in response. The distant dog barked back. This conversation, like mine and Willoughby's, might, I knew, go on all night.

Here is my story: when I was young, my family lived in Cleveland, and we had a dog named Troubles. Next door was a dog named Chips, and sometimes in the afternoon, when Chips wandered into our yard, my sister would yell, "Troubles, Chips is here! Chips is here!" and Troubles would leap up from wherever she was sleeping and bound into the yard to see her friend. Then we moved away to California, and Troubles got old and cranky and seemed no longer to like other dogs. Chips was still in Cleveland, or dead; we didn't know.

One day my sister had a friend over. They were going through the old photo albums from Cleveland, and my sister was telling stories. "All we had to do," I heard her saying to her friend, "was yell, 'Troubles, Chips is here! Chips is here!' and then—" And before she could even finish the story Troubles had leapt into the room once more, barking and jumping and sniffing the air. Something had lasted, in spite of all the time that had passed and the changes she had weathered, the trip cross-country, and the kennel, and the cats. My sister put her hand to her mouth, and tears sprang in her eyes, and like the young enchantress desperate to reverse the powerful incantation she has just naïvely uttered, she cried out, "Troubles, stop! Stop! Stop!" but it did no good. Nothing would calm Troubles, and nothing would dissuade her, as she barked and jumped and whined and nosed for that miraculous dog who had crossed the years and miles to find her.

Out on the Marsh

DAVID UPDIKE

I turned twenty-one a month or two ago, and I have been rather surprised lately to find myself suddenly conscious of my age. Twenty-one: that sounds very different from twenty right now, though I don't think I would have thought so a year ago. Against my better judgment, I now think of myself as standing at the edge of what presents itself as "the rest of my life," the previous twenty years being some sort of vague and distant warm-up. I am suddenly aware, I suppose, that my present actions are an indicator, a preview, of what's to come. I feel old.

At night, sitting under the dim yellow light of my desk lamp, I take from my wallet two photographs, from expired driver's licenses, of me at sixteen and at twenty. My hair has grown, my cheeks have broadened. Do I look older? Have I lost the question in my eye? I am handsome, I am told; I smile and look away. This picture of me at sixteen was on my first license, and I have always liked it. At the registry of motor vehicles, when it came time to turn my license in for a new one, I told the woman at the desk that I wanted to keep the picture, and she took a pair of large scissors, snipped it brusquely from the rest, and tossed it onto her desk with a flip of her chubby wrist. I have kept it with me since.

Have I become more sedate lately? I am home from college for spring vacation and spend my days puttering around the house and taking long solitary walks on the marsh with Mtoti, my dog. He has recently become my best friend, and I must admit I find his company entirely sufficient. A large red-haired golden retriever, he walks with a sway that suggests he should not eat so much. The other day we found a deer carcass, completely decomposed except for the fur and a foot, which he tried to sneak away from me to eat in the woods. I went after him and got the foot and threw it into the creek, only to have him grunt and grovel and wheeze in a vain and pathetic search through the mud. He walked right over it twice, but could not see or smell it through the water, so I pointed it out to him with a long stick, and he stole away with it back to the house and finished it under a tree on the lawn.

It is on these recent wanderings that I have become acquainted with Mr. Birch, not so much in conversation as by seeing him, a familiar, waving figure on the marsh—a mobile landmark—at all hours of the day, collecting old scraps of wood, gazing toward the horizon. He lives here on the marsh with his wife, along the road that runs from town to the ocean, in a small white house on a knoll hidden in the trees. They are both in their eighties, and in the winter, when the tide is high and the wind blows from the northeast, the neighbors worry for them, knowing that the road to their house is covered with water and the knoll the house sits on has become an island. But when the tide subsides, and we hurry over to see if everything is all right, we find them, invariably, fine, surprised and amazed by our concern.

Now and then the paths of our wanderings intersect, and Mr. Birch and I stand together briefly, looking out over the marsh, trying to think of things to say. I ask him questions mostly, about the weather or the birds, and he returns short, soft-spoken answers, and we set off on our different ways, glad to have had someone to talk to, relieved to be again alone. It is his distant presence I cherish most—the sight of his ancient and erect form gliding across the marsh in his aluminum motorboat, his arm raised in a wave, his collar flapping in the wind—and the sense that all I see and hear and love here is shared.

Mr. Birch spends much of his time working in the small yard next to his house. The other day, after watching him and Mrs. Birch climb into their tired green Rambler and drive over the bridge toward town, I walked up to the house and stood in the yard. I was struck there by the wonderful haphazard order of the objects he has collected and saved and arranged in a randomness I knew not to be random—a disorder I thought to be the highest form of order, a personal one, which only Mr. Birch understands. A buoy hangs by a rope from a lilac bush. The wheelbarrow is concealed, covered by a heavy piece of gray canvas, faded by the sun. Stumps double as stools, clothespins cling like birds to the line, a mattress dries in the sun. The grass is full but matted, padded by his step, and a beaten path bends through a gap in the bushes, marking his daily route between the house and the yard, between the yard and the marsh. I wonder if it has ever occurred to him that he alone has made this track—years of work, three decades of soft steps. Or at his age do you take these things for granted?

I met him recently on the road in front of his house and he pointed out two pine trees, forty feet high, that he and his wife planted from pots when they first moved here. We stood there marveling at their height, and I—and Mr. Birch, too, perhaps, as he leaned over to pet the dog—thought of what these trees implied about his age. It was a beautiful spring day, with a high, cool wind blowing through the tops of the trees. We said good-bye and I walked slowly over the bridge back toward my house. I had been out on the marsh for several hours that day, and Mtoti was tired and followed a few feet behind me. I turned to him and ran backwards, urging him on, clapping my hands, calling his name, and he worked himself into a run. On the lawn we stopped, and I bent down to hug him. In the afternoon light, I could see that the gray flecks of his muzzle had gone to white, and I realized that he had drifted into old age without my having noticed. I have thought of him all these years as my peer, but it is only now, in the blue light of spring, that I realize he has grown old without me.

Going to the Dogs

ROBERT GILLESPIE

Before they head downhill through the new snow for their afternoon pitchers of beer, Stoker wants to ship off the last alimony check—his ex-wife is marrying in a month—and he leaves the truck idling to keep the small cab warm. As he lopes back from the corner mailbox he can just see Louie Tucson's head, peppery and salty beard and hair, as if Louie had chinned himself on the dashboard. Beside him Stoker's husky gazes straight ahead like a driver who has picked up

2 4 9

embarrassing strangers, her mask white except for the black ridge along the snout and the little dark smudges like an athlete's under the eyes, the icy wolf-look melted down by her brown eyes. Kite looks as if she wears a black cap. Back in the cozy truck, Stoker pats his dog's crown.

"Kite all right?" Louie asks.

Stoker only says, "What," wheeling away.

"She saw a dog over there and didn't do anything ferocious, and she's shivering." Louie strokes her and she raises her head, snout pointing toward the roof of the cab, pressing back under his palm. She paws the air softly until Louie holds hands. Stoker rests his arm on her back, feels her lean away as usual.

"You good old dog," he says, steering carefully downhill with his right arm around her shivering haunch. "She stayed inside last night until almost six in the morning. Jesus, she's ten and a half years old, she's never spent a whole night in the house in her life. I let her out, she came right back in and got up on the bed. But she seemed OK later when we went out for the Christmas tree."

Stoker's dread, which admitting will only make worse, is that Kite is dying, will not make it through another winter. That morning, looking out at the white pasture in the light flakes, he'd thought of friends who buried their father in the woods above their cabin on the lake, of Lauren deep in the white cemetery they used to walk in with Kite winters ago, of his college roommate, dead twelve years of cancer, and of his parents and his ex-wife's parents, all gone into the snow. Even his old black cat, little life that he was, was buried beside the fallen-in barn. Seeing Kite rolling in the snow falling outside the kitchen window while he'd fried bacon and listened to Cat Stevens ballads, his neighbors' white house on the opposite hill beyond the dark row of apple trees, he soared into the sky because he shared this place with Kite, wasn't worrying whether she liked the white isolation of this life too or whether she was happy; and then on his snowshoes, in the woods in the falling snow, stroking her grizzled head, he knew as she did not that one day Kite too would go into the snow for good, and his eyes stung and then his throat hurt and he hugged her and mourned for them all.

Louie says, "You and Kite went out to get a Christmas tree this morning. You have presents to put under it for each other? Jesus, Stoker, the girls are right about you. You don't need to get married again, this dog sits up here on this seat like your wife."

"Ten and a half years to train her, too. You should've seen her this morning, Louie, leapfrogging around, that white tail curling up there, those old ears pointed. Then she took off back up the pasture. Just crapped out under the porch. I don't know what's the matter."

Downtown Waterville's Concourse parking lot is practically filled with the cars of Christmas shoppers, even though it snowed all morning and the temperature has dropped to ten degrees above zero, but Stoker cruises into an empty spot right beside Patricia Tucson's silver Datsun station wagon.

"Patricia went shopping in Portland this afternoon," Louie says, peering in at the cargo area of his wife's car.

Stoker reaches back inside the cab, pats his dog's head. She presses up against his hand. Almost in this same slot of this same parking lot, Lauren, furious that he was going through this routine with his dog, fists pounding her thighs, howled that if she drove off with Kite and never came back, Stoker, bum that he is, would miss the dog more than he would her. Stoker sees teeth, small, pointed. He sees the dark demanding ferocity of a face he has come to recognize as her own since that hot blue and gold August afternoon two months to the day before she killed herself, because he'd known long before that explosion that, impossible as her perceptions and demands were proving to be, about this she was absolutely right.

"I'll be back," he tells the dog. When he closes the door, Stoker's truck sounds tinny.

"Lend me three, Rockefeller," Louie says at The Pub door. "I'm buyin'."

Around the corner of the bar, Stoker is glad to be in The Pub again, leaving outside the spaces—the lakes, big and blue in summer, now white blanks—and the great dark fir trees in the snow. In The Pub he is warmly subterranean, windowless. He steps behind the bar and picks up two glasses from the rack, checking them against the light. He likes the barn-red walls, and the black ceiling and wall trim, the painting of three clowns and the old photograph of Pub waitresses posing in long dresses, pistols in hand, leaning against a 1934 Pierce-Arrow between men in suits and large-brimmed hats with shotguns looped in the crooks of their arms; he likes the mirror's black and gold pool, the overhead lighting through colored glass like a church, the earth tones. Stoker wouldn't mind if he never drank beer in another bar again; he wouldn't mind if he never again crossed the borders of the state of Maine.

"Stoker!"

Stained light, pitchers of beer, glasses, bags of chips and beer nuts, a crumbled heap on the big table in the center of the room—a birthday cake—and Jeannie Seashore's face framed by long red hair, floating up round-eyed, her mouth puckering.

"Jeannie! How *are* you?" Stoker tips backward as she jumps to hug him.

"Better'n nothin'." She lifts up and down on the balls of her Bean boots as if expecting to be picked up and kissed. She wears a red sweatshirt with "Hers" in white letters across the chest, and faded Levis. "It's my birthday. All the guys in the band and their old ladies're here."

Louie hugs her, waves to the party, and backs around to the next small table beyond. He's spotted his wife behind a pitcher of beer.

Stoker softly says, "Where you been? Come on over with us. What's happening?"

"Jeez, Stoker, you look like something out of the 1880's." She snuggles into his old buffalo coat and tickles his beard. "I gotta go to the Setters, be back in two shakes."

Stoker eyes Jeannie's Levi's, sees Lauren, her first time in The Pub, puzzled between the "Setters" sign on one toilet door and the "Pointers" sign on the other: "Which am I?" "If you could stand up and point it, you'd know," Stoker told her, his arm across her shoulder. He should have known better right then when she thought it wasn't funny.

"Hello, you handsome guys," Patricia Tucson says, helping Stoker unhook a coat button caught in a loop, looking in this light as if she's been weeks on a beach, honey hair and blue eyes. "We've got to stop meeting like this," she says, giving Louie a deadpan kiss on the mouth. "How about some hair of the dog?" She winks and smiles at him, filling his glass.

Louie hunches his shoulders and tilts his head as she kneads his neck.

Stoker says, "Jeannie sure is looking good."

"Last time we saw her," Louie says, "she looked like six pounds of shit in a five pound bag."

"Going to the dogs," Stoker nods at Louie. He was worried about Jeannie that night, frightened even, Jeannie drunk and weeping on his shoulder that he was the man for her. He passed her helplessly to the off-duty bartender, and cursing in his truck, wondering what he did to bring out the desperate worst in women in front of God and everybody, pounded on the steering wheel until Kite cowered in the corner. When he tried to pull her back to reassure her that it wasn't Kite he was angry with, he almost piled them both off the bridge into the river.

"She's still the best voice in the band," Patricia says.

Stoker watches Jeannie standing over a hungry-looking guy wearing a head band, his dark hair in a long ponytail. She is trying to look as sober and intent as she can with a floppy-brimmed denim hat on. When she waitressed at The Pub delivering pitchers of beer, vodka collinses, sombreros, Jeannie seemed to him unflappable and solid, given to ironic flips of the hip and to delays when whistled at by empty customers, and even after years Stoker still likes watching her. He likes watching all the women who work here. Little Sally with a flow of blond hair steers energetically and perfectly to her point with no waste motion, tossing off ripples that he bobs in while admiring the lines and bright colors of so sure a trim little craft; Annie, round as a stone, dark-haired and heavy-breasted with a Mona Lisa lift to her lips, wafts by as if she were balancing the tray not on her palm but her head, her feet shrouded in the voluminous billowing of her dark habit. In the kitchen Maureen makes pizza splendidly to order, her hair tied up in a draggly bun; watching her round white arms while she briskly chops onions and pats together hamburgers, he thinks of her as Mademoiselle of the French Revolution. And always behind polished wood and spigots there is Rocky, his heart's oldest favorite. The gods have sent blondes in yellow. Ministering Rocky, cheerfully unpossessed of college degrees, gap-toothed, high-hipped and long-legged, a little pouchy below the belt, a heart-piercingly handsome soft sort of voice; working with a construction company part-time when she is not working at The Pub, working almost all the time just to stay alive, a survivor who mixes drinks and tapes Sheetrock, a dry-waller: Rocky is real life to Stoker. Listening to her voice, low, a slightly gritty whisper as if there are husks on words and she shucks them off, he simply clams up. Down here below the streets drinking beer amongst these earth-toned walls, he sights another and then another shimmering palmy cocktail waitress, he honors and loves them, every one, he thinks someday he shall marry them all.

"Hi, Patricia." Jeannie bobs up breathlessly as if she's been running. Patricia pats the chair between herself and Stoker, and Jeannie bails in.

"What're you drinking?" Louie looks at Jeannie intently. "Gin? Vodka?"

"White wine. I'm staying off the hard stuff and the beer. But I just got lectured. I drank three bottles yesterday." She sputters gleefully. "And I don't even remember. That's why I put on all that weight last year. You know I didn't have my period for *months*? I was *really* screwed up. Boy. No more." She groans, rolls her eyes, laughs.

Louie leans over to Patricia, grumbling. She sits back.

"Don't be an old crosspatch about Portland. I wasn't led into fiscal temptation except just a teeny bit."

Jeannie giggles, and Stoker, sure she is about to bounce up and down in her seat clapping, pulls out a bill and deals it. Louie slaps his palm flat on the table, covering the face on the money.

"Daily bread," he says.

"Root of all evil," Stoker says.

Jeannie snorts, puts her arms around Stoker, and tells the group, "He's the grumpiest man in the whole world." She gives Stoker a big wet buss on the cheek. As he looks appropriately grumpy, she says, "D'ya hear the one about the woman whose husband died and she buried him in the dooryard, and every night she goes to the window and goes 'Good night Charles.' Every morning she gets up and goes 'Good morning Charles.' She met a guy and he came to the house that night and she goes to the window and she goes 'Good night Charles' like she always does. In the morning she gets up, she goes to the window, she sticks out her tongue and she goes *pppphhhlllaaugggh*."

When Jeannie laughs, a throaty *coo coo coo coo coo*, Stoker hears pigeons in the eaves.

"Humph," he says.

"Old grump." Jeannie punches him on the arm, and sniggers for Patricia. Louie snores loudly, his eyelids drooping sleepily. Patricia gives him a schoolmarm glare.

"I'm still having problems with my battery, Stoker," Jeannie tells him. "*Rrrr rrrr rrrr*. Nothing. It's all right, Stoker." She leans into him. "Stoker, it's not your fault, really."

"So can't Wheeler fix it?"

"Chester the molester?" She sniggers. "He just takes care of my basic needs."

Stoker watches Patricia walk to the bar for potato chips, watches Louie pass her with a look on his way to the Pointers. And here he sits listening to Jeannie, who seems to him to be forever in need, with black eyes from running, she maintains, into doors, calling herself "retarded." Stoker in front of The Pub in the fall when he'd bumped into Jeannie, up zoomed a denimed person on a Harley, hair long and scraggly down his poll so that, bald in front, he looked as if he wore a wig tilted back on his forehead. Jeannie wiggled and fidgeted as Wheeler, leaning toward him in the saddle, told Stoker, "You like this country, Bro?" raspily, slow, deep. "I like this country. It sure is good to be free around here."

Jeannie says, "You know I spent a week in the psych ward at Thayer?"

"Ohhh," Patricia says, dropping into the chair, "no Jeannie, we didn't know that, what *hap*pened?"

"I just freaked out. I was runnin' around the house yelling 'Jesus will save us, Jesus will save us.' We were havin' a party and the guys in the band were all there, they tried to calm me down but I ran next door. Some old woman and her creepy old man."

Stoker says, "How'd you get to the *psych* ward, for crissake."

"I locked myself in the bathroom, so they finally called an ambulance." She whinnies with gaiety. "You know it costs seventy-five dollars for an ambulance to come out there all the way to Chester's? I said, 'Boy, no sirens or I'm not going.' "

Patricia looks sadly at Jeannie.

"I wasn't eating too good, I guess, Patricia. And we did a *lot*ta rehearsing too. Things're much better now, though. I'm gonna stop goin' on the road trips, just do the gigs at home. Just concentrate on learning a few songs good and work on writing lyrics." Then she brightens up. "So long you guys." She laughs, waving.

The hungry-looking man helps a blond woman into a blue parka. The woman smiles, waving across the birthday table, and the man calls, "Thumbs up, Jeannie. Gotta go. We love you."

"What's Wheeler doing during all this?" Patricia wonders.

Jeannie studies her wine seriously. "Wheeler's lying low for a while. He's been seein' some dude's old lady and the dude's trying to get back at him with a drug bust."

Patricia winces: "Oh Jeannie, that's *awful*."

"Jesus, Jeannie!" Stoker tosses down the last of a beer. He looks down the room to Louie sitting at a table and laughing with four students, looks around for a waitress.

"How 'bout you, Stoker? Ladies at The Pub climbing all over you?" She bobs away from Patricia, sputtering through her lips.

"Women only go for my dog," he says.

"Is *that* why they call it a pointer?" Jeannie laughs, "*Hmmm hmmm hmmm hmmm*," and ogles him.

"I haven't pointed at a thing for over two years. It fell off."

Jeannie pats him on the knee, cooing.

Every afternoon, late, the lights over the bar dim, and the group is suddenly the evening crowd. Stoker, watching the bartender mix a gin and orange juice in the lowered light, breathes in deeply through his teeth, takes a long swallow of beer.

"Shit," he says. "Sex fucks things up."

"Old grump," Jeannie says. She snickers, leans over and gives him a big hug.

Patricia sighs, pointedly looking toward the clown picture. She stands up, glares down at him, says, "Stoker, that's so silly," and walks out toward the Setters.

"You still feel really guilty about Lauren, don't you?" Jeannie asks.

"We're not going to talk about that, OK? Christ, she was so screwed up, that crazy mother and that father, she changed moods so fast it was like watching a cloud go across the sun, just like that. You know she sat up one night, she wouldn't come to bed, the whole night, typing? Know what she was typing? Her name. Over and over all night long, she's typing her name. 'I am Lauren Thurenburg. Lauren Thurenburg is my name. Lauren Thurenburg lives here.' In the morning she wouldn't even admit she'd *done* it. Jesus, she had a fatal dis*ease*. She was born with it, she had to kill herself to get rid of it. But I was *there*, you know? I was part of her life. That makes me part of her getting dead."

"I felt awfully guilty when my brother died. I'd got him started on dope and all that shit." She takes a sip of the wine. "Stoker," she blurts, "I wish you loved me the way you thought you did. You probably didn't really love me." She snuffs, and smiles bright-eyed. "You've always been the man I loved."

"Oh shit. Oh dear." Smiling stupidly, hand lightly on her arm and wishing he were standing and shuffling his feet and scratching his noodle, feeling again the chill in his chest of her aggressive vulnerability, her aimless dependency on his total time, her inability to complete anything and her capacity to make him feel guilty for not liking it, her frantic peppiness, he says, "Jeannie, we were really drunk that night. I'd gazed upon you, nymph, for so long from afar."

"Anything important you say, you never *know* it, you bastard! Anything significant you say, you *never* know it!" She rubs the back of her hand across her nose, pulls out a cigarette, tapping the end on the table hard, her eyes shiny.

"So I should do anything with all those hard guys around?" he says, feeling justified in detesting the way women cry. He sees Patricia coming, and he lights Jeannie's cigarette, not wanting Patricia to hear.

"Stoker, you're such a jerk," Jeannie says. "You have so much to give but you just don't give nearly what you could." As Patricia sits, beaming on them both, Jeannie blows smoke away from the side of her face and says, "He thinks he's responsible for everybody and he catches shit because he's not good enough. This distance makes you irresistible, don't you know that, Stoker? I know lots of ladies who'd ball you under this table right now if you only asked."

Stoker, whose great aspiration is to be invisible, says, "Christ."

"Me first." She gargles high up in her throat.

"Who else?"

"Rocky thinks you're really cute-looking."

"Rocky? Jesus," he says, "she's holding down about three different jobs. She ever get off?"

"At least," Jeannie splutters, "six times a night."

He takes a long breath, his lips curling. If I can just keep free of desire, he tells himself, I might be dead, but I will not be in trouble.

"I'm not interested in just getting laid," he says.

"*Kinky!*" She draws the word out, licks her lips, blurts into laughter, rocks into him. "You're such an old grump, Stoker. You're the world's grumpiest man."

He lets out his breath. "I meant I can see a hardworking grateful little body with three kids to mother me and a nice big color TV football game and lots of cold Buds in the ice box. Maybe that's what I want. But I ain't lookin'."

"D'ya know you sigh a lot through your nose? Excuse me," she says, popping up, "I gotta pee. If Chester the molester calls, tell him I'm hanging around out front picking up a few pointers."

Watching her bounce away, he says, "Goodnight, Jeannie." Patricia stands up, leans over him, hugging his head.

"We're having a really simple soup and sandwiches for supper. Stop on over? Louie has a batch of papers to read so it'll be short, I promise."

When he nods she hugs him again, and then she is gone. Is it because he'd sell his country's secrets for a woman's flat hard belly and peppy little butt that he sits sipping beer until Jeannie bounds back? He tries not to watch, and settles for eyeing her backward in the mirror.

"Chester's not coming in so I gotta go." She snorts, making a gargling sound. "He needs me."

Trying not to sigh through his nose, Stoker raises up and puts his arm around her shoulders and pats her. She leans into him and he can't think of anything more upbeat to say than: "Don't stay away so long, Jeannie. We'll see you soon, OK? You're tops with us too."

"That's not my favorite position," she says. "Bye, Stoker." She shrugs, mousily pouting.

He drops coins into the tip jar, and waves on the way out the corridor into the cold.

Under the frosty light thirty yards from the dark edge of buildings around the parking lot, the cab windows of the truck are white ice. When he tries it, his door is locked. Around on the other side, the door also locked, worried, he gets the key in, the door open, and still he can't understand. Strips of ceiling liner hang like stalactites, and what is left of the left side of the benchseat looks like a snowstorm inside of the cab; foam rubber pebbles the right side and floor like hailstones. The driver's sun visor is chewed off. Both shoulder harnesses are gnawed off at the stump. The lining of both doors is shredded on the seat and floor, and both arm rests are thin plastic skeletons, all padding ripped away. A foot-long strip of dashboard is gnawed down to metal, and one hard plastic chunk of it, like topping on a cake, sits on the pile of foam and lining.

The dog jumps out past stunned Stoker, and runs across the parking lot until, over a pile of snow off at the edge, she squats and hunches convulsively. Fast after her, Stoker peers down into a steaming muddy puddle already freezing in the snow. After another hunching stop she wanders off through the cars, and he shouts her back; as she hops onto the seat, Stoker, piling in behind her, shouting "You dumb fucking *dog*!" loses his temper at last.

"What the fuck are you doing to my goddam fucking truck for crissake? Jesus Christ, *look* at it! Jesus, you fucking *ruined* the goddam thing. Look at it. Look at it!" From the seat he shoves shreds of plastic doorliner the size and color of pieces of toast. The dog cowers and her

eyes half shut. She puts out her paw and he slaps it away. "Goddammit, what were you fucking *think*ing of! You dumb fucking *dog*!"

He rants the four blocks to the Tucsons, and yanks her out of the truck in the driveway. By the time he gets to the porch, Kite is barking to be let inside for kitchen scraps.

"Don't give that damned dog a thing," Stoker calls. "She's already full," he explains to Louie, "she just ate the inside of my truck."

"She like those guys who eat whole automobiles, engine block and all? Jesus, you and that dog," Louie says, taking his beer through the basement door.

"Poor Kite." Patricia, leaning down, spatula in one hand, pets Kite's head with the other. The dog stamps all four feet, moaning happily.

"Go find your brain." Stoker boots her, a soft one on the rump, soccer-style, out of the kitchen. "Look at her, ears back, tail down, you'd never believe it was the same ferocious beast." He shouts after her, "Don't start in on any small children."

"Oh we could spare one or *two*," Patricia says. "They're all down in the basement fixing their cross-country skis. So what more did Jeannie have to say?"

"Jesus, Patricia, she talks about changing her life and being all better, but she's still hanging around with the same people, guys who treat her miserably, drinking too much. She's always broke anyway even when she *is* working, and now these guys are cutting her loose from the band. So what's different? Goddam woman. She just can't do a thing to help herself."

Patricia carefully slices ham onto a chopping board.

"You've heard of distress signals, Stoker? She wants you to notice she's hurting. Come rescue me. That's elementary."

"So what's new? Why can't Chester the molester or Wheeler the dealer or whatever his name is handle it?"

"Stoker, you get involved with a woman and then you start looking for a flaw, and so of course you find it, and then you feel trapped and you get mean to her. You think you're just a creampuff."

"I get mean so she'll go away and not torment me with her un-solvable problems," he says. "Besides, I'm not involved. Because I boffed her a couple of times, she's mine forever? Jesus, in this day and age?"

She slams the knife on the board and looks at Stoker as if she'd like to slice him instead.

"What about giving her Lauren's car, and I *know* you gave her the money to get it fixed too. And I *know* you offered her fifteen hundred dollars to go back to school because she *told* me. You think you're not involved?"

"Maybe I was laying up treasures in heaven. Jesus, that's oriental. What'd she think, I was buying her?"

"You know, you really do hope that the next girl who comes along isn't going to need a thing from you. She'd have to live in a plastic space bubble. Who'd want anybody like that?"

He says, "Jeannie's like that poor little kid in Houston. Even his mother couldn't touch him. He didn't have any immunity to anything."

Patricia nods at the ham. "Just don't be mean to her, that's all I'm saying, Stoker."

"Patricia, Jeannie doesn't need a carer like you, she needs black eyes, she needs to feel punished for being the screwed-up rich kid she knows she is. Dumb sonofabitch Wheeler's probably even got himself convinced he loves her when he's feeling so effectual, snapping wet towels at her butt, kicking her ass across the room. Jesus, her screwing up just gives the bastard the reason he needs to punch her so he can feel good, and she's fucked up enough to think he *does* care, so she keeps on screwing up." He drains his beer. "Intimacy is for shit. It's either be miserable in your own little castle or it's late night drunken recriminating tantrum phone calls."

"Seem to me a man so ol' and fulla years ought to have the right to just hang up." Louie rises through the basement door, converging with Stoker on the refrigerator, and in that moment Stoker despairs of all attempts at self-preservation as repulsively parasitical.

"Shit," Stoker says.

"Otherwise," Louie grins, handing over a Budweiser, "what good is being divorced?"

"Shit," Stoker says. "Last time I hung up on a woman she killed herself."

Patricia bobbles the ham slices, he thinks, a fraction, and he can't remember if he ever hinted even to her about Lauren's last terrible phone calls. He doesn't remember now, doesn't remember anything except Lauren's pitiable voice rising hysterically—"God took my mother away from me because I'm bad"—and his "Oh for Christ's sake!" "God doesn't love me, God doesn't love me," she kept crying. Stoker is still hanging up.

"Whyn't you fry this bacon while I do these chocolate chips. I haven't made any cookies for you in a long time." Patricia peers intently into the mixing bowl.

As she stirs beside the stove, Stoker turning over strips in the skillet, Louie tapdances to the refrigerator for another beer, then sidles up behind her. He slips both arms around her and nuzzles and growls at her ear. Stoker can't tell before he looks away whether his arms are across her breasts. She holds the beer can in her hand without moving.

Frying bacon, Stoker suddenly feels abandoned, embarrassed. Is it the display at this moment, Louie the loving man, or is it the vocabulary of affection, clumsy, boozy, trite, and a voice Stoker can't recognize? Their intimacy dismisses him. He is a person simply standing there frying bacon, out of it all, except that for a moment he looks for a hard sign of rebuff from her. Patricia stops her stirring, stands still, the way Kite does under caressing, but as Stoker observes them she seems to him to grow very quiet, like a planet inside the circling orbits and moons of Louie's arms, a celestial body floating silent and serene in its blue and red and green colors in black distant space. For just a moment and as if from a great way off as she slowly starts once more to stir the batter in her mixing bowl, Stoker has the impression that she is glowing.

Suddenly he is glad that Louie stands there and not himself, feels relieved that there is no one for him to have to care for. But why does he still feel trapped, angry, guilty, unwhole? Why does he feel he is watching something happening in Eden?

He puts the last piece of bacon on a paper towel, and goes out to the living room where Kite, lying on her left side, looks mountainous. Certain that what he really wants is to sock something, he gets down facing the dog. Her eyes move on him and she pants, her tongue drooping toward the carpet.

"Poor old girl." He puts his arm over her, nuzzles her. She snorts and moves her head away. Her breath is foul. When he strokes her tight stomach she raises a leg slightly. Her eyes open. "You look as if you're really in pain, sweetheart. You want to go see the doctor tomorrow?" She licks his hand, unusual for her to do, and her eyes close slowly down like a doll's.

If there is anything Stoker is sure of, it is that his dog likes and trusts him and that he is the most important person in her life. Kids and dogs and Stoker, they ask only for a steady sturdy consistency.

He hears, "Come on, let's eat, everybody"—Patricia, calling into the basement.

Like children the small towns go to bed first, the country road shuttering its lights as if turning down their wicks. Even Libby's store in Benton has shut down for the night by eleven-thirty. Beyond the village the houses thin out and dark spaces fill in, the pines closing down to the edge of the road. It is hard keeping his eyes open the last miles, until the clearing and the farmhouse perched high on the hill picked out in moonlight, and the old barn, its roof caved-in under the weight of skylighted snow, like the front of a castle. The dark house sits on its alp surrounded by a world of white. Stoker stands in the gleaming dooryard gawping at the moon high up, bright in the black and the millions of brilliant steady stars. Neither wife, family, nor job—and even in his house he is only a renter, as loosed from the world as he can get without blowing away. He watches the black gorges of the sky glittering silently and forever, peers down the bright pasture, and thinks he might just root in the snow like a white birch and listen and listen to the absolute stillness, his breath the only thing moving ever. But Kite is talking at him, anxious to get into the house.

"No Cycle-Four for you tonight, tubby, you already had your truck for dinner. Besides, I saw Patricia Tucson sneaking you scraps when I wasn't looking." He cracks out a can of beer. Kite laps up a long drink of water, slopping the floor as usual, and then silently, head slightly down and stepping carefully as if she were on ice, slips from the kitchen. She is not in the living room and he turns on the phonograph as he follows her into the bedroom. She is stretched out on her side across the thrown-back blankets.

He lies down beside her with his arm along her body, and for a few minutes he listens to Cat Stevens. She smells like popcorn and bacon. She smells like ice cream, until she pants.

"I'm sorry I got pissed at you, Kite. It's OK, babe. You couldn't help it."

When he nuzzles her, she sneezes in his face, and at this moment he knows that if some woman had torn up his truck he'd be furious, sure that it was a deliberate abuse of reasonable behavior he'd never forgive or forget. But Kite chewed up his truck, dashboard and shoulder harnesses and ceiling liner and doors, creamed his lovely truck, and here he is coddling the creature, comforting an upset that she knows nothing about, protecting her from all the confusing impulses flickering up from the fires below, protecting her from himself.

And he wonders, did Lauren have any more idea of what she was doing in her depressions than this dog, frantic to get out of her prison and chewing up the cab?

"You're a good old dog," he says.

He gets off the bed and heads for the kitchen. Kite jumps after him when she hears the back door, toenails tapping on the wide floor boards and skittering on tiles, getting out before he can shut her in. Down the trail they made in the morning she runs into the white night while he carries the long trailshoes off to a trampled area to strap them over his boots.

A dark spot in the snow takes shape. In the brightness he makes out the head of a deer, certainly not fresh, the skin gone, the antlers broken or chewed. He knows: Kite's work. Stoker feels sorry for the creature hunters killed and left, angry with Kite for dragging it home, and then, a load off his heart, knowing for sure that her problem is only intestinal and at worst only for another uncomfortable couple of days, strapped together, down the pasture he heads dropping one long foot in front of the other in easy loping strides. The trees along the stone fence shadow half of the pasture, and Kite, an eerie spot, floats in and out of the light like a dark ghost. The trees, and the wind eddies on the snow—as if they are etched on old silver, fuzzy and firmly at the edges—back shyly into the dark.

Near the end of the pasture they both stop, as if they have come to the bank of a dark river and are asking each other if they are ready to put in—ready to disappear into the alder and paper birch and pine that ring the far field around. He goes for the trees, remembering once pointing a course for East Benton into this stand of white birches with his compass, getting lost and returning on his tracks. This night's snow, heaped up higher for the moon and starlight, is so deep that the small firs and pines are buried, and he crosses over them as if he were on air, able to see absolutely clearly in the white light in the openings, floating with the tilts and dips of the earth, going for the gaps, sliding above the tops of these trees as if he were striding across the rooftops and chimneys of farmhouses. He has stepped above fire into the sky. He walks across such tundras of cloud as one sees from above them in aircraft, he feels that he hangs, a bird in heaven's wind, veering on his wings and floating from side to side for the brilliant universe. A maple looming out of so much whiteness in the bright night darkens as he comes on, and he knows startlingly that he will not get back into his body; his body will return home trudgingly backtracking on itself while he will be left out here in white and black spaces forever adrift between blue spruces and stars. In absolute silence he stops and hangs on, mitten against the maple, eagle-eyed, straining to catch hold of a sound, willing himself back around his bones until a branch cracks nearby with the cold and it seems as if the bright sharp stars and the moonlight must be ice clear through.

Kite slips up and sits in the soundless snow beside him. What is she hearing? He wonders how far it is to his neighbors, how far to summer evening chats across the stone fence as they look over the black-eyed Susans and the herds of Holsteins, their heads bobbing, rumps high as the sterns of galleons, going before the wind of late August across the long green summer pasture to the shade to get drunk on the apple trees along the fence line. The heifers look straight ahead as they walk as if they wore blinders, intent on the path they have made to a place they know to be good. They stand like boulders and chew. He always feels elated when he sees his neighbors' ski trails like a cowpath heading for the gap into the frozen-over cranberry bog where cattails are thick in the spring, and he knows why he has sat on the little log set upright like a throne beside the creek that cuts across this land. He is ready to stay on forever in these dark trees, forever feeling the contours of this earth he loves—the way a person mowing learns every dip and rise in the fields—from walking out across the stream and into the grass and snow and, always, into these trees. And so he knows again at this moment of intensest love the sharpest pang of loss. Not to be here! Lives that he has loved are *buried* in this land. It can only happen, this jag throwing in with the universe, he knows, in moments. Death is the place beyond the last little town, the stop with no bars and no people and no dogs, where the last windless campground is without water, without trees to hitch to, without stars.

"Kite," he says, the sound larger than life in the bitter bright night. She is peering straight ahead at something Stoker cannot see. When he bends down to throw an arm around her, the dog lurches, hops like a rabbit, and churns away through the timber in surges of snow.

He smiles in the bright silent dark, looking up through bare hard-woods for the Big Dipper and the pole star, thinking, Maybe aloofness is the medicine she inherited from the north, who knows? Maybe she keeps her distance not because she knew all along that fear is so much more corrosively painful than the absence of affection and love could ever be, but because she came out of the earth of the pasture and the blue air and the white water of the stream and the snow and the fire of the sun, came forth, out of all creation just like creation, only to be beheld and rejoiced in, a dog simply, simply to be loved by a man?

Brown oak leaves still on the trees stir with the sound of light rain on rocks. It takes so much longer, he thinks, to bring back a leaf and put it up than it does to bring it down. One leaf lies dark in the snow, a small body recently fallen, and he thinks, good night. Good night, he says to the sky, good night. He brushes snow over the leaf, thinking, I love this place, and I want to stay on to see the leaves go up again on the aspens waving in a breeze like thousands of little babies' hands, and the pale green needles of the balsams, and the sun come out in metallic bronze cold light after a dousing by fast clouds, and the hooves of the cattle smoothing a brown path through the cropped timothy green, and I want to feel the frost crisp and whiten the pasture grass of a late-spring dawn, and work all day in the dooryard feeling the sun climb up along the side of an early-June afternoon beyond the top of the sky into a more radiant exalted light than there ever is in the haying days of late August.

In a clearing of snow in the moon and starlight he hums Cat Stevens's "Morning Has Broken," and for the trek back along his fish-shaped tracks he thinks how, home at the kitchen phone, he'll call his ex-wife—just to say a check's on the way and if she needs anything, holler, she knows that, goodbye—and then, tomorrow, Louie may drop out with Patricia, or tomorrow, the next day, he'll give Jeannie a buzz, tell her hi, what's happening, thumbs up, or maybe cross trails with Rocky at The Pub even, just say hello, how you doing, how'd you like to maybe go snowshoeing out in the timber one day soon, you and me and the dog?

Flight

THOMAS McGUANE

During bird season, dogs circle each other in my kitchen, shell vests are piled in the mudroom, all drains are clogged with feathers, and hunters work up hangover remedies at the icebox. As a diurnal man, I gloat at these presences, estimating who will and who will not shoot well.

This year was slightly different in that Dan Ashaway arrived seriously ill. Yet this morning, he was nearly the only clear-eyed man in the kitchen. He

helped make the vast breakfast of grouse hash, eggs, juice, and coffee. Bill Upton and his brother, Jerry, who were miserable, loaded dogs and made a penitentially early start. I pushed away some dishes and lit a breakfast cigar. Dan refilled our coffee and sat down. We've hunted birds together for years. I live here and Dan flies in from Philadelphia. Anyway, this seemed like the moment.

"How bad off are you?" I asked.

"I'm afraid I'm not going to get well," said Dan directly, shrugging and dropping his hands to the arms of his chair. That was that. "Let's get started."

We took Dan's dogs at his insistence. They jumped into the aluminum boxes on the back of the truck when he said "Load": Betty, a liver-and-white female, and Sally, a small bitch with a banded face. These were—I should say *are*—two dead-broke pointers who found birds and retrieved without much handling. Dan didn't even own a whistle.

As we drove toward Roundup, the entire pressure of my thoughts was of how remarkable it was to be alive. It seemed a strange and merry realization.

The dogs rode so quietly I had occasion to remember when Betty was a pup and yodeled in her box, drawing stares in all the towns. Since then she had quieted down and grown solid at her job. She and Sally had hunted everywhere from Albany, Georgia, to Wilsall, Montana. Sally was born broke but Betty had the better nose.

We drove between two ranges of desertic mountains, low ranges without snow or evergreens. Section fences climbed infrequently and disappeared over the top or into blue sky. There was one little band of cattle trailed by a cowboy and a dog, the only signs of life. Dan was pressing sixteen-gauge shells into the elastic loops of his cartridge belt. He was wearing blue policeman's suspenders and a brown felt hat, a businessman's worn-out Dobbs.

We watched a harrier course the ground under a bluff, sharptail grouse jumping in his wake. The harrier missed a half dozen, wheeled on one wingtip, and nailed a bird in a pop of down and feathers. As we resumed driving, the hawk was hooded over its prey, stripping meat from the breast.

Every time the dirt road climbed to a new vantage point, the country changed. For a long time, a green creek in a tunnel of willows was alongside us; then it went off under a bridge, and we climbed away to the north. When we came out of the low ground, there seemed no end to the country before us: a great wide prairie with contours as unquestionable as the sea. There were buttes pried up from its surface and yawning coulees with streaks of brush where the springs were. We had to abandon logic to stop and leave the truck behind. Dan beamed and said, "Here's the spot for a big nap." The remark frightened me.

"Have we crossed the stagecoach road?" Dan asked.

"Couple miles back."

"Where did we jump all those sage hens in 1965?"

"Right where the stagecoach road passed the old hotel."

Dan had awarded himself a little English sixteen-gauge for graduating from the Wharton School of Finance that year. It was in the gun rack behind our heads now, the bluing gone and its hinge pin shot loose.

"It's a wonder we found anything," said Dan from afar, "with the kind of run-off dog we had. Señor Jack. You had to preach religion to Señor Jack every hundred yards or he'd leave us. Remember? It's a wonder we fed that common bastard." Señor Jack was a dog with no talent, loyalty, or affection, a dog we swore would drive us to racquet sports. Dan gave him away in Georgia.

"He found the sage hens."

"But when we got on the back side of the Little Snowies, remember? He went right through all those sharptails like a train. We should have had deer rifles. A real wonder dog. I wonder where he is. I wonder what he's doing. Well, it's all an illusion, a very beautiful illusion, a miracle which is taking place before our very eyes. 1965. I'll be damned."

The stagecoach road came in around from the east again, and we stopped: two modest ruts heading into the hills. We released the dogs and followed the road around for half an hour. It took us past an old buffalo wallow filled with water. Some teal got up into the wind and wheeled off over the prairie.

About a mile later the dogs went on point. It was hard to say who struck game and who backed. Sally catwalked a little, relocated, and stopped; then Betty honored her point. So we knew we had moving birds and got up on them fast. The dogs stayed staunch, and the long covey rise went off like something tearing. I killed a going-away and Dan made a clean left and right. It was nice to be reminded of his strong heads-up shooting. I always crawled all over my gun and lost some quickness. It came of too much waterfowling when I was young. Dan had never really been out of the uplands and had speed to show for it.

Betty and Sally picked up the birds; they came back with eyes crinkled, grouse in their mouths. They dropped the birds and Dan caught Sally with a finger through her collar. Betty shot back for the last bird. She was the better marking dog.

We shot another brace in a ravine. The dogs pointed shoulder to shoulder and the birds towered. We retrieved those, walked up a single, and headed for a hillside spring with a bar of bright buckbrush, where we nooned up with the dogs. The pretty bitches put their noses in the cold water and lifted their heads to smile when they got out of breath drinking. Then they pitched down for a rest. We broke the guns open and set them out of the way. I laid a piece of paper down and arranged some sandwiches and tangy apples from my own tree. We stretched out on one elbow, ate with a free hand, and looked off over the prairie, to me the most beautiful thing in the world. I wish I could see all the grasslands, while we still have them.

Then I couldn't stand it. "What do you mean you're not going to get better?"

"It's true, old pal. It's quite final. But listen, today I'm not thinking about it. So let's not start."

I was a little sore at myself. We've all got to go, I thought. It's like waiting for an alarm to go off, when it's too dark to read the dial. Looking at Dan's great chest straining his policeman's suspenders, it was fairly unimaginable that anything predictable could turn him to dust. I was quite wrong about that too.

A solitary antelope buck stopped to look at us from a great distance. Dan put his hat on the barrels of his gun and decoyed the foolish animal to thirty yards before it snorted and ran off. We had sometimes found antelope blinds the Indians had built, usually not far from the eagle traps, clever things made by vital hands. There were old cartridge cases next to the spring, lying in the dirt, 45–70s; maybe a fight, maybe an old rancher hunting antelope with a cavalry rifle. Who knows. A trembling mirage appeared to the south, blue and banded with hills and distance. All around us the prairie creaked with life. I tried to picture the Indians, the soldiers. I kind of could. Were they gone or were they not?

"I don't know if I want to shoot a limit."

"Let's find them first," I said. I would have plenty of time to think about that remark later.

Dan thought and then said, "That's interesting. We'll find them and decide if we want to limit out or let it stand." The pointers got up, stretched their backs, glanced at us, wagged once, and lay down again next to the spring. I had gotten a queer feeling. Dan went quiet. He stared off. After a minute, a smile shot over his face. The dogs had been watching for that, and we were all on our feet and moving.

"This is it," Dan said, to the dogs or to me; I was never sure which. Betty and Sally cracked off, casting into the wind, Betty making the bigger race, Sally filling in with meticulous groundwork. I could sense Dan's pleasure in these fast and beautiful bracemates.

"When you hunt these girls," he said, "you've got to step up their rations with hamburger, eggs, bacon drippings—you know, mixed in with that kibble. On real hot days, you put electrolytes in their drinking water. Betty comes into heat in April and October; Sally, March and September. Sally runs a little fever with her heat and shouldn't be hunted in hot weather for the first week and a half. I always let them stay in the house. I put them in a roading harness by August first to get them in shape. They've both been roaded horseback."

I began to feel dazed and heavy. Maybe life wasn't something you lost at the end of a long fight. But I let myself off and thought, These things can go on and on.

Sally pitched over the top of a coulee. Betty went in and up the other side. There was a shadow that crossed the deep grass at the head of the draw. Sally locked up on point just at the rim, and Dan waved Betty in. She came in from the other side, hit the scent, sank into a running slink, and pointed.

Dan smiled at me and said, "Wish me luck." He closed his gun, walked over the rim, and sank from sight. I sat on the ground until I heard the report. After a bit the covey started to get up, eight dusky birds that went off on a climbing course. I whistled the dogs in and started for my truck.

The Death of the Dog and Other Rescues

SUSAN KENNEY

It's a typical Saturday morning in October. Linnie's due at a birthday party at noon, but I've rushed into town with both kids to get sneakers, and we're late so I'm feeling pressed and a little cross at David, who had a fit in the shoe store because he couldn't find new sneakers that looked and felt exactly like his old ones; and I'm worried about the three other little girls I'm supposed to pick up, waiting all dressed up wondering what happened to us, and the little girl whose party it is thinking no one is going to come, so as I turn into the driveway I say over my shoulder to Linnie, "Now as soon as I stop the car you jump right out, run in, and get dressed as fast as you can, because we're late."

"I don't want to be late," she wails, tears jumping out of her eyes.

"Well, it's too late not to be late now, so just do it," I answer sharply. David is scrunched down in the back seat glaring at me in the rearview mirror, elbows jammed down on the new sneakers box with the old sneakers inside, not talking.

Phil looks up, smiling. He's out in his shorts mowing the lawn for what he fervently hopes is the last time of this long Indian summer we got in trade for the real summer that never came. It's so warm he's not wearing a shirt; he's finally gotten over his self-consciousness about the big scar from his operation, and his whole upper body is tan and greased with sweat, the scar looping up from his shorts and across his ribs with a little jog at the end like an upside-down hockey stick. The truth is, it's barely noticeable now, especially when he's tan. The dog is lying beside the driveway panting slightly in the heat; he bumps his tail on the ground as our wheels crunch down the driveway. He can't hear us because he's deaf now, but he feels our vibrations and turns his head in our direction as we pass, tail gyrating wildly. He's very old, fifteen, in fact, but the same foxy bright-eyed collie face he had as a young dog looks up expectantly to see who's here. Even now in his old age he is in truth a handsome dog, a rake, a pirate, an Errol Flynn of a dog. We've had him all our married life and even before, ever since he was a puppy almost too young to stand on all fours, his back legs not quite strong enough to hold up his rear end.

Phil waves briefly, cantilevers the mower around, and starts back down the grass. He's left the gas can and funnel at the edge of the driveway not far from the dog, who is also at the edge just off the grass, out of the way of the mower. As I yank on the brake and hop out of the car to open the kid's door I think how peaceful it all is, what a nice day we have here, and isn't everything going well?

But there's the party, and we're late. "Come on, Linnie, let's step on it. Crying doesn't get you anywhere."

"I don't know where the present is." She sniffles. I hold the back door open with one hand over her head to let her pass.

"I hate my new sneakers," David mutters, ducking under my arm. He has an additional grievance. "I want to go too. I never get to go anywhere."

"You weren't invited," I say from the middle of the cupboard where I've stashed the present for the birthday girl.

"Mom! Mom!" Linnie screams hysterically from upstairs. "I need you!"

"Just for the ride," David says glumly as I run upstairs to Linnie.

Inside of three minutes we are all running back out to the car. The doors slam, one, two, three, the motor roars, the radio blares, the kids are squabbling and I can't hear a thing, can't even think, and I jam the car into reverse and back up fast, bump, crunch, right over some hard but hollow object that crumples under my wheels. "What's that! What's that?" the kids holler, peering all around, and I look up through the windshield to see Phil, a horrified look on his face, waving frantically at me, gesticulating wildly as though we were in some terrible imminent danger. He's shouting at me, but the windows are rolled up and the radio is blaring and the kids are yammering so loud I can't hear him, so I try to read his lips as he pantomimes disaster, something about the door, but all the doors are shut, I heard them, and then I realize I must have run over the loaded gas can and we are going to catch fire and explode so, always quick to respond to danger, I shove the gear into forward and pull ahead crunch, crunch, buckle, away from the ruined gas can and the leaking gas so we won't explode, pull forward out of danger and turn off the ignition so we're safe. No one can say I don't react well in a crisis.

But Phil has really gone crazy now, dancing and whirling and hopping up and down, bending forward with his hands over his stomach as though he were going to throw up, then standing up with his eyes closed and flinging one arm out as if he were throwing a Frisbee in a gesture of what I take to be despair, and I watch him, puzzled, because haven't I done the right thing?

But of course not, because it's not the gas can that has gotten up, moved and flopped its old arthritic bones down in a heap behind the car where I never thought to look. It's not the gas can I have run over, crunching and crumpling it not once but twice, coming and going this bright fall day—it's the dog.

II

He was always a handsome dog. This line, a joke between Phil and me because it was so literally true, has for some reason always reminded me of my father. There is a photograph of the dog in his younger days lying on the lawn in what we always called his noble-dog pose, nose lifted, eyes staring off in the distance, a faintly ironic, tolerant, ever-so-slightly self-conscious expression on his face. There is a similar photograph of my father when he was very young and very handsome, dressed to the nines in white sharkskin coat and knickers, sitting in a lawn chair with his legs crossed, cigarette dangling casually from his fingers. He looks wonderful, one eyebrow cocked wittily, like a blond Robert Taylor without the mustache. Someone has just said to him, "Jim, you are a handsome dog," and he is regarding that person with a tolerant, amused, ironic smile as if to say, Yes, I know, but it doesn't really matter, that's just the way I am.

When Phil and I were first married and had no children, the dog went everywhere with us. People would stop us on the street and say, "Oh, what a pretty dog!" then mystify us by asking "Is he ugly?" and when we shook our heads, bewildered, not understanding at first that they meant his temper, not his beauty, they'd reach down to stroke his white ruff, his blond fur, scratch behind his foxy ears, admire his dainty paws. Cars would slow down, children across the street would tug at their mothers' sleeves and call out, "Look, a little Lassie! A little Lassie, see?" Actually he was not a little Lassie at all, except for his color and markings not even close. In fact he was a collie-shepherd mix with big limpid brown eyes and a wedge-shaped shepherd nose, pointy upright ears, and long but not really shaggy fur. But some genetic accident had made him look, as so seldom happens with mixed-breed dogs, as though he had got that way on purpose. We always thought he was a throwback to those first small wiry blunt-nose mountain collies before they were bred up to size with coats like llamas, torpedo noses, and beady little snake eyes on the sides of their heads. Because he was a crossbreed, we knew that there would never be another one quite like him. Even if he fathered puppies, which in his green and salad days running loose he certainly must have, he would not breed true.

We got him unexpectedly when he was very small, his whole litter abandoned in Phil's sister's dorm at college, brought home while we were visiting and given the bum's rush from Phil's mother's kitchen right into our car for the trip back up to school. And there he stayed for all our travels, at first so little he curled up under the seat with only his wedge-shaped nose sticking out in front; then, as he grew bigger, under my feet in the front footwell where as a grown dog he just fit and felt secure. In a paroxysm of graduate school cuteness we named him Collie Cibber after the eighteenth-century poet laureate and enemy of Pope, and in some ways he lived up to his name. He was a fop, a dandy, the only dog I've ever seen licking his fine white paws clean and then polishing his face just like a cat. He went everywhere with us, was well known, even legendary, on campus for herding students into our classes, nipping officiously at their ankles, rounding them up and ushering them through the door, then thumping down with a resigned and drawn-out groan across the doorway, stretching out on his back with his legs sticking up, underbelly exposed, and ostentatiously going off to sleep, punctuating my lectures with an occasional snore. When the bell rang at the end of class he invariably leaped bolt upright, startled and sleepy-faced, abashed, then recovered himself, shook down his fur, and stood sentry by the door as the students filed out. For years after the children came, first David, then Linnie, he refused to acknowledge their existence, would never come when they called or lift a paw to shake their hands as he did ours, suffered by no means gladly their mawlings and pettings. He was our first and in his eyes remained our only child, was one of us, never seeming to take in the fact that he was much the furriest and generally though not always ate and slept on the floor. And he was perfect, charming, bright, intelligent, yes, a handsome dog.

III

Ever since my father died suddenly away from home when I was twelve, I have felt that it was my responsibility to keep everyone around me safe. This has meant saving them when necessary, at the very least hovering somewhat officiously, a walking first-aid manual, rapid extricator and rehabilitator of lost causes. Phil has called this my rescuer complex, but, complex or not, I can't help believing deep down that whatever is lost can be recovered, what is broken can be mended, and what is gone replaced; at least it's worth a try. So over the years I have tracked down within minutes children missing from the school bus at the appointed stop, yanked out drowning ones before they could inhale a single drop of water, righted capsized sailboats, glued back together broken objects, recovered a single dropped earring of little real but great sentimental value from the middle of a well-used tennis court. Quick off the blocks, I have rescued no later than the third thump around the dryer a cat suicidally fond of sleeping in odd places. I have toughed it out with barely a murmur in countless waiting areas, emergency rooms, ICUs, stood close and watchful while my husband struggled through the numerous nearly fatal complications of a botched and messy operation for a tumor the size of a dumbbell in his belly, clutching his hand and muttering "Don't leave me" while I nagged the doctors with questions gleaned from medical textbooks—What does this mean? Have you checked that? What happens next, and are you positively absolutely sure?—determined not to lose him the way we did my father. Now I, who have weathered any number of these crises and near-misses without losing control, I, the cool, the calm, the take-charge person, leap screeching out of the car with my two hands simultaneously trying to cover my eyes, my ears, my mouth, run screaming hysterically into the house and up the stairs as fast and as far away as I can get, howling at the top of my lungs, "Oh, no, dear God, not the dog, please, not the goddamned dog!" In my carelessness and haste, I, the rescuer, the caretaker, have run over and killed my own dog.

I finally skid to a halt upstairs in the bedroom that overlooks the driveway. I creep over to the window, cautiously uncovering one eye, ready to leap back if it's too awful, and take a look.

Phil is bending over the dog, who is lying in some sort of heap in the middle of the driveway. Then Phil takes a step back and I stare in disbelief. The dog is not dead after all.

In fact, he is sprawled more or less upright in a version of his stately noble-dog pose, swinging his head around and looking a little dazed, obviously trying to figure out what hit him. He looks pretty much the same, and I can't quite believe it; can it be we've both been spared? Then I notice his hindquarters aren't quite right; they are askew and slightly flattened, one leg sticking out behind at an awkward angle. No, he has definitely been run over. I watch, holding my breath, expecting him to expire before my eyes, while Phil reaches forward. The dog sniffs at his hand, his tail starts to twitch, then gyrate slightly, whisking up a little cloud of gravel. He is wagging his tail. Wow, I think, that's a good sign, his tail still works, his spine must not be crushed. In the back of the car the children gaze in fascinated horror, their noses pressed against the rear window. I go into the bathroom and throw up.

But the dog is still alive. I have not killed him, at least not so far. He's hurt, of course, but what is broken can be mended. I splash water on my face and go downstairs, sidle over to the car; I still can't go near the dog. I yell to Phil that I'm going to take the kids on up to the Lanes' and to the party, that he should call the vet. As I back around past him he shakes his head as though to say, Don't get your hopes up. On the way up the road I consider the probability that, even though he is not dead, the dog is so badly hurt he'll have to be put to sleep when we take him into the vet's. How many dogs can get run over and survive? So this reprieve is only temporary; the reckoning comes soon.

When I arrive at the Lanes' house I am in a terrible state. The three little girls are lined up beside the driveway with their presents clutched to their smocked bosoms, looking anxious. I can hardly talk, but Joyce just nods; Phil has called ahead with the news. She is sympathetic; once she ran over a kitten, which proceeded to get up, shake itself, and dance loosely toward her with its crushed bones, then leaped straight into the air and died at her feet. She felt terrible for weeks, still dreams of it sometimes. "Come on, shove over," she says. "I'll drive."

Everyone piles into the car, and we drive back down the road and stop at the top of our driveway. I get out and she pulls away in the direction of the birthday party, but not before I hear Katie's shrill voice: "Did Sara really squash Cibber flatter than a pancake?" I walk down the drive, forgetting that with the car gone we have no way to transport the dog to the vet's eleven miles away.

The dog is still alive, breathing fast and whimpering, one leg stuck out behind at that funny angle, otherwise apparently intact, if a little flat. There is no blood, no splintered bone. "Sorry, old man, I didn't mean to," I say as I walk over to him. He does not bump his tail this time, only blinks up at me desperately, his breath rasping. Oh, oh, I think, progressive trauma; we're losing him. We've got to do something. I bend down and put a hand out toward him.

"Don't touch him," Phil says quickly. I look up to see that he is holding a towel to his neck, and there is blood congealing on his bare shoulder. He shrugs. "I wanted to get him away before you came back so you wouldn't have to see him, but when I tried to pick him up he whipped right around and bit me on the neck." He takes the towel away and I see the two deep toothmarks oozing blood, no more than an inch from Phil's carotid artery. "Do you fucking believe it?" Phil says by way of conversation. I shake my head; I fucking don't. I look back down at the dog, who is making impatient weeping noises like faint radar bleeps as if to say, Well, don't just stand there, do something. He peers around at his rear end and his front paws contract as he digs into the gravel, trying to stand up. Old as he is, this is not easy in the best of circumstances, and now it is clearly impossible. He shifts his front paws, gazes up faintly puzzled at the two of us, and groans.

"I'll get a blanket," I tell Phil, and run into the house, thinking about first aid for shock and keeping the victim warm.

"Do you think we can move him?" I ask Phil after I've covered the dog up.

"We'll have to," Phil says. "The vet can't make house calls; the trauma truck is in the shop. Besides, they don't come out this far."

So we have to drive the dog into town, but that's all right, because Phil will have to go to the emergency room anyway to get his neck sewed up. We need a car, and ours is gone to the birthday party. Just then our neighbor down the street arrives with his son. They have heard my screams and want to know if they can help. He and Phil and the son confer over the dog's head about what to do, and because they seem able to take care of everything, I wander back inside, out of earshot. But I watch out the window while the three of them tie the dog's mouth shut with an old nylon stocking, arrange him on a blanket sling, and hoist him into the back of our neighbor's brand-new Volvo station wagon. I peer out the window until they're out of sight, and when Joyce arrives with the car I drop her and David at her house and follow the others into town.

IV

And after all that, the dog is not only not dead, according to the vet he is not even dying, or in immediate danger of it. The vet on call, a short stocky woman with small hands, tells me there are no other contiguous eight inches of dog I could have run over without killing him outright. I have run over the pelvic arch, breaking it in three places, and there may be some kidney and bladder damage, some nerve and muscle bruising, but it's not too bad, considering. A close call, she says, and of course his age will be a factor in recovery, but they'll keep him under sedation and quiet for a few days until the bones can set—you can't put a cast on a dog's ass, or anyone else's, for that matter—and then we can take him home and go from there. So things are clearly not as bad as we first thought. "You're a lucky dog," she says as she gathers up the dog, his nose still tied shut, and starts out back with him. "You'd better get that seen to," she says casually over her shoulder to Phil, "before you bleed to death." Phil blinks and goes pale; he is no stranger to the possibility of bleeding to death. But of course she's only kidding. "Call us tomorrow," she shouts from the back room. "We'll probably know better then." And that's it; she and the dog are gone.

Phil and I stand there, flabbergasted. I can't believe it. A fifteen-year-old dog run over and squashed flat, and we can pick him up in a few days? It seems incredible, too good to be true, but naturally I'm relieved. Still, after our trip to the emergency room—five stitches, not a record, only average for us—as we drive home in the dark I prepare myself for the worst. The dog may not recover, he may not walk again, life may not be worth living to him as an invalid, a cripple. Phil has always been more adamant on this issue than I, especially since his illness; he is a confirmed quality-of-lifer. So I try to face up to the fact that we may finally have to make a decision we have been dreading these last few years as the dog has grown more stiff and feeble, the time when—if he did not die a sudden and natural death the way my first dog Barney did at fourteen, his age and mine, conveniently expiring in seconds on the living room rug—we would have to say the word and have him put to sleep. I have contemplated this and decided I would want to be there to see him out, the good old friend. The vet has not said anything about putting the dog to sleep, not even as a remote possibility, but just in case, I say to Phil as we drive along, "He's had a good life, at least there's that. He's been a happy dog. So if it *does* come to that it's not so bad." I hear a sniffle next to me, and look over to see the tears rolling down Phil's cheeks, along his jaw, and into the gauze bandage. Choked up but dry-eyed—lately I seem to have lost the knack of tears—I say, "Come on, you know, he's really just a dog." Phil nods, but I can tell it doesn't help one bit.

v

Still, rescued for the moment from the worst consequences of my own haste and negligence, I ponder this latest in a long series of other such near-misses and close calls, so many, in fact, that I have come to think of myself as some sort of lightning rod for disasters that don't quite happen, or turn out at the last moment not to be so bad. We are certainly no strangers to the odd laceration, the quick and bloody trip to the emergency room with thumbs held over pressure points, towels and ice packs pressed to rapidly rising lumps and contusions. Oddly enough, these stitches of Phil's are his first, not counting the ones from his operation. David at age ten has had his head split open twice, has put his hand through the glass storm door, cutting it badly in three places, and nearly taken the top of his thumb off within minutes of acquiring his new Swiss army knife. I am in second place with the scar—now barely visible—over my eyebrow from falling into the garbage can when I stepped on one of David's toy trucks, and Linnie is a distant fourth with two tiny stitches on the bridge of her nose where David whacked her accidentally last winter with the snow shovel. These are the near-misses—the eye not put out, the artery not sliced, the tendon unsevered—dreadful possibilities that you never think of until after it's all over, and you just wipe your brow and sigh deeply with relief that it wasn't worse. Even more unsettling are the close calls, those terrible calamities that somehow are revoked after you have accepted the reality of their happening, fully entered into the altered state of post-disaster consciousness, the ones that give you that strange sense of dissociation, as though you might be dreaming that they didn't happen because they are so awful, but in a little while you will wake up and find they have. So the children do *not* roll out and get smashed dead at 60 miles an hour through the back door of the station wagon I have carelessly left unlatched in my hurry to get somewhere. Thanks to a friend with quick reflexes who grabs her arm before she can pull it back through, Linnie does *not* lacerate and scar her hand for life after putting it through the other glass storm door panel we have not had the sense to replace after David's accident. And the tender skin at the back of David's knee is *not* after all impaled on the rusty barbed-wire fence six miles from help as in our panic we at first believed, but only pinched between two prongs, the skin hardly even broken, and even though after I have freed him he falls over in a dead faint from sheer fright, he recovers almost immediately.

So the dog run over but not killed is only the latest in a long list of these bizarre remissions, close calls, near-misses, lost causes not so lost after all. And I wonder sometimes what I have done to deserve this peculiar brand of good fortune, or if in fact it is a kind of test, a punishment, to be always coming up short of real disaster, always running to the rescue, always compelled to see what I can do. And do I keep at it because it somehow seems to work?

On the kitchen table among the other odds and ends I find this note printed in my daughter's hand. It's the beginning of a story she has to write for school. "A mother is telling her daughter to keep trying and not to give." That's as far as she's gotten, but it makes me wonder if I have done my children any favors by instilling—not only that but apparently demonstrating—this attitude of "keep trying and not to give." Whatever is broken can be mended, whatever is lost can be replaced, whatever is missing can be found, whatever is sick can be healed. It's all done with mirrors after all, and there's no such word as can't. But, I often wonder, by jumping on my horse and riding in all directions, usually to some, if not complete, avail, have I given them an impression of life that is not really true? How will they know, if and when the time comes, how to give? How will I? Sometimes in my worst daydreams I imagine a plane crash or shipwreck in the middle of a dark cold ocean, the four of us floating survivors with no hope of rescue, or a nuclear bomb blast not too near but near enough, so that it's just a matter of time before the death cloud hits. I imagine them clinging to me, looking at me, asking "What are we going to do?" And for once there will be nothing, absolutely nothing, I can do.

V I

Four days after the accident I go to pick up the dog. Our regular vet is there, the one who's taken care of the dog all these years. He's kind but not a sentimentalist, and when he sees me he just shakes his head. "I was sorry to hear what happened; I know how crazy you are about that dog."

"He's a good old friend," I say in a slightly choked-up voice. But I don't cry. After all, it's just a dog, and there are worse things than running over your own dog, particularly if the dog survives.

The vet brings the dog out, his mouth tied shut with a strap, puts him in the back of the car for me. The dog's eyes look wild and desperate; he growls at the vet, nudges him sharply with his tied-up nose; if it weren't for the strap he'd bite him for sure. "You'll have to tie his jaw shut whenever you move him," the vet says. "He's pretty strong for an old dog, and he sure knows how to use those teeth." He slams the door shut. "Give me a call in about a week, let me know how he's doing," he says through the window, then adds ominously, "if he's making any progress." That's it; I drive home with the dog.

The kids and Phil have set up a bed in the kitchen, a camp mattress, David's old sleeping bag, the smelly blanket the dog sometimes curls up on, and newspapers all over. The red plastic dog dish and a ceramic bowl for water—over the years he has become accustomed to drinking from the toilet bowl, but that's out of range for the time being—are neatly arranged at one end of the bed. I lug the dog in, protesting through his tied-up teeth, and lay him down, untie the strap from his nose. He just lies there panting, his head and chest erect, front paws parallel, looking from one of us to the other. He whimpers a little, then groans, staring up at me. But there is no way, I tell myself, that he could know I did it, just a sudden dark shadow, a heavy crushing weight, and pain. No, he couldn't know. But just the same I'll make it up to you, old man, I promise silently. I will make you better; I will make you well.

As it turns out, it's just as well I've made this solemn vow, because the dog will not let anyone else come near him, even to tie up his mouth. He growls and snaps at Phil and the kids if they so much as put a hand out. He will not let me pick him up with his mouth untied. Clearly unable to help himself, he snaps at me and then sinks his head down sheepishly, apologetic. He submits, blinking in humiliation, when

I come toward him with the nylon stocking, but lets me tie it around his nose and behind his ears, so I can pick him up.

At first he cries all night. For a while I sit with him, but I keep falling asleep in the chair, so I go upstairs and collapse into a stupor, in which I still hear him yelping and moaning faintly throughout the night. In the morning I find him at one end of his bed, as far as he can get from the puddles and piles of dog shit, looking up at me with that bright foxy look, shifting his front paws in restless expectation as though to say, Let's get on with it.

And get on with it we do. I learn to recognize a certain tone of whimper and restless scrabbling as a signal he wants to go out, so I tie his mouth, hoist him up—for an old arthritic bony dog he's still no lightweight—take him outside, where he does his business lying down. There are accidents, but fewer and fewer as we get our signals straight, and picking him up seems to hurt him less and less. He does not complain much, eats and slurps up water, and watches us all go in and out, following us with the old bright foxy look, still interested, so I can hardly believe what the vet has told us, that he's not only deaf but nearly blind. When I call the vet to tell him how things are going he listens carefully, then says the last thing I want to hear. "I'm worried about those legs. If he's not using them in a month, you may want to reconsider your options." I go all limp and wobbly at this, but the vet goes right on in his matter-of-fact voice. "Meanwhile, just let him take the lead, go at his own rate. If he wants to get better, he'll let you know."

Let him take the lead, I tell myself after I've hung up. Fine. What could be more reasonable? But I worry about the legs, about the dog's not walking, and what will happen then.

One morning in early November about three weeks after the accident, I come down early to find the dog all the way across the kitchen, squatting in front of the back door. He is straining upright, his back legs still sprawled awkwardly on the floor, scrabbling feebly. He looks at me, then points his nose up toward the doorknob and cries to be let out. Taken aback, I open the door and watch as he struggles through the opening, the two hind legs pushing like flippers behind. He gets all the way out the door and several feet beyond before he gives up. As I pick him up to lug him the rest of the way, he grunts and his nose grazes back against my cheek, but he does not bite me. Outside on the grass I stand him on his feet and hold his back end, and for the first time he pisses standing up, the way he did at first when he was a puppy, before he learned to lift one leg. I remember one time in particular when he jerked his leg so high he overbalanced, fell backward, and caught himself right in the eye. The next time I take him out and hold him up, he takes two faltering steps forward before his rear end keels over onto the ground. But I'm elated; he's walking, or will be soon, and when I call the vet to tell him, he says, "That's a good sign; that's good."

All through the next month as fall turns into winter I lug the dog out, following behind with one hand on either side of his skinny rear, holding it up as he staggers along. The legs both work now, though he still drags one, but I can't let him go, because the weight of his hips on the tottery old legs gradually tilts over the weak side and he goes down, subsiding slowly over to the ground the way he did when he was small. Then I have to set him back up again, but he will walk as long as I hold on, so I trot along behind him like a child playing train, eventually going all over the yard while he sniffs the snow for gossip, until finally my back can't take it anymore and I concoct a kind of sling for under his belly. Watching me trot after him, holding the contraption up, Phil shakes his head and says, "That's the first time I ever actually saw someone going around with his ass in a sling."

After a while the dog is strong enough to get around with me hanging onto the tip of his tail as though it were a leash. My in-laws come to visit, and my father-in-law sneaks out early one morning, takes a picture of me in my bathrobe, down vest, and rubber snow boots trailing around behind the dog in the snow, holding his tail up like a plume. My mother-in-law comments, "Such devotion, I never would have believed it. You're certainly making it up to him. But don't your feet get cold?"

I shake my head, although they do, but that is little enough to pay for this miraculous recovery, little enough as expiation for my sins.

VII

"Well, old man," I hear Phil murmur as he lets the dog out one morning the next fall, "you may outlive me yet." The dog looks back at him, then staggers out and down the porch steps, rickety on his old pins, but no more than any sixteen-year-old arthritic dog, to do his morning rounds. He has, according to the vet, recovered as fully as possible from the accident, but the effects of old age, weak kidneys and arthritis are creeping up on him, and he is getting frailer. A bad liver infection he contracted in the spring did not help much, and he has had several fits in the last few months, which the vet regards as warning signs of progressive terminal kidney failure. He has told Phil that it is just a matter of time; most dogs his size don't live past twelve, let alone sixteen. When Phil asks him what to do, the vet shrugs, says we'll know when it's time, that we will be able to tell when his life is not worth living to him anymore. So we watch and wait, but so far it does not seem the time has come and we think we'll let him have this one last summer, and when winter comes, then it will be time. He is as he was, if frailer, and in fact in the late summer after we change his diet the fits come less frequently. He still seems pleased to be alive, and it seems he'll go on forever, in his contracted world. He does not go out of the yard now, and he can't get up the stairs to sleep under our bed the way he used to, falling to his belly with a crash and thumping on

his elbows as far in as he could get. He sleeps downstairs now, on a blanket in the dining room next to my chair. He seems perfectly happy in this world of downstairs and around the yard, places he knows intimately by smell and feel, if no longer by sight and sound.

Anyway, it is Phil we're concerned with now. The tumor has recurred and the local doctors, at a loss, have at our insistence agreed to send Phil to a big cancer center in Boston to have his case reevaluated, to see if something can be done. The doctors here are worried about his kidneys—or rather kidney, since we now know that one was mistakenly removed during the operation in 1979. So Phil is home now, and we are waiting for a bed. When one is free, Phil's parents will come up to stay with the children, and Phil and I will drive to Boston. Phil is not hopeful, and thus his comment to the dog, not meant for anyone to hear. He knows I don't want to hear things like that, believing as always where there's life there's hope; his fatalism is balanced by my refusal, with what I consider to be ample precedent, to declare the game is over, at least in public and out loud.

Contemplating Phil's illness and what we have come to so soon, Phil not even forty yet, I see this as the apotheosis of a childhood fantasy, conceived not too long after my father died, while we were still living in Toledo, before my mother gave up on living by ourselves and we all moved back with my grandmother and my aunt in Skaneateles, in what I have come to think of as the house of widows.

In the street in back of us on River Road there was a big boy, a bully, head of a gang of children in a subdivision neighborhood—the Island Avenue gang. Although I played with many of the kids in the gang, I was never invited to belong, by virtue of my address as well as my timidity. The bully and his cohorts used to tease me unmercifully on the way home from school, and I was a natural and satisfactory victim, quick to respond and especially to cry. My mother told me I had to learn to fight my own battles, and the worst thing I could do was to talk back or cry. I must let them know they didn't bother me one bit. I was to turn the other cheek, as my father used to say, so one day I did just that, leaning back against the fence nonchalantly as they passed, chanting, "Sticks and stones will break my bones, but words will never hurt me," while rather prominently looking the other way. In an instant the bully had whipped off his leather belt and whacked me across the face with the buckle end. It laid the skin above my eye right open, narrowly missing my eyeball and, as my outraged mother later told the parents of the bully, nearly blinding me for life. Naturally I was forbidden ever to play with the Island Avenue hooligans again, those ruffians, and for a long time my mother drove me to school the long way around.

My fantasy was this: In one of my lonely walks through the woods of the abandoned filtration plant up the road, I would come upon the bully, laid out cold, having fallen from a high branch of one of the trees that had been allowed to grow up on the reserve. He lay there either unconscious or with a broken leg, or both. And of course it was up to me to save him, which I did in any number of ways, the most implausible of which involved my carrying him piggyback all the way to Island Avenue. The upshot always was that I would rescue him somehow, and become the heroine of the gang.

This, I now recognize, was the original formulation of my rescuer complex, a conversion into fantasy of my feeling that I should somehow have prevented my father's death, either by not letting him go away from home or by being there when the heart attack hit, so he'd know someone was there and wouldn't die. But I failed at this, and the conviction of my original powerlessness developed into an irresistible impulse to rescue everything and everyone in sight.

Certainly life has given me ample opportunity to exercise this impulse, but over the years I have gotten better at moderating it somewhat—take for instance my mother's last psychotic episode, in 1975, when she wound up in yet another paranoid frenzy in an Auburn motel. It was the seventh go-round since 1969—the second in a little over a year—and my sister had washed her hands of the whole thing and was on her way to Colorado. But instead of jumping in the car and driving ten hours to get there and take care of things, even though it was once again my turn, after pondering the problem for a while, I finally sent the motel owner a card with several phone numbers and the message: "In case of any trouble with Martha Gilead, please contact the following." Sure enough, three days later a social worker from the psychiatric ward at Auburn General called me with the news that my mother was there, they were putting her back on lithium, and everything was going to be just fine. We'd heard that many times before, but oddly enough this time they were right, or close enough. There have been one or two lapses since, but she has generally been getting better and better. She came through her mastectomy five years ago with no trouble, and even showed up unexpectedly when Phil was in the hospital for so long after his operation to help me with the kids, just like anybody else's mother. She's helping to put my sister Fran through medical school; last spring she took a bus down to see my brother and his family, and even went by herself into Philadelphia to see the Garden Show. She writes letters now which, if a little scrawly at times, are funny ha-ha, not funny peculiar, so that I sometimes feel I am getting glimpses of the way she must have been when she was young and first married to my father. I think I have a better understanding of what she must have gone through in her sad life, and it seems possible now that, after all these years, we may even have resumed that old uncomplicated childhood mother-daughter relationship so abruptly short-circuited nearly thirty years ago. So it seems that after all our combined efforts over the long haul, she is finally rescued for good.

But the situation with Phil makes all these other rescues seem like dress rehearsals, mere warm-ups. The doctors have told us he is dying, has perhaps six months, a year to live. If his words to the dog are any indication, he feels some parallel in their predicaments, though Phil is only thirty-nine, and the dog in people years is upwards of a hundred and two, and of course the dog is just a dog. But both of them are waiting for a sign that says, "It's time to give."

While we are waiting, we go about our business, to work, to school, or in Phil's case sailing, since he has taken a medical leave from the college. The days stretch on, the pathology reports crisscross the medical establishment, and one day I notice a growth in the dog's mouth that is interfering with his chewing. Since nothing else is going on at the moment, I load him in the car and take him to the vet's. It's the first time we've been there since his liver infection in the spring, and he quivers and trembles and looks pathetic, but acquiesces finally in his elderly dignified way.

This vet is horrified when he looks in the dog's mouth. "Oh, Jesus," he says, baring his teeth in a grimace of pained discovery. The growth is large and black, a piece of the dog's inner lip, looking like a giant slug of chewed-up licorice bubble gum. "Melanoma," the vet mutters. "Not good."

It doesn't sound good to me either. Melanoma is a cancer in humans, and a friend of ours has just died of it at the age of forty-one.

"Pretty advanced," the vet goes on. "He's probably got it other places, too. Why didn't you bring him in before?"

"Could it be something else?" I ask, ignoring his implication. The question's worked before. In fact, sometimes I think it works for everything except death itself.

"Nope," the vet says non-negotiably as he gets out his tools, a huge hypodermic and a vial. Suddenly I'm overtaken by a terrible suspicion.

"You're not going to put him to sleep, are you?"

"Of course," the vet says, holding up the vial and sucking the pale green fluid back into the huge needle.

"But, but . . ." I throw an arm protectively over the dog, who looks up at me curiously, the iridescent cataracts in his eyes catching the light, momentarily clouding the bright puppy look. "Just like that?

But . . . but we haven't even discussed it," I say desperately. The fact is, I'm not ready for this.

"What's there to discuss?" the vet says imperturbably. "If I don't put him to sleep for this, he'll squirm all over. I don't think you can hold him. And I've felt those teeth too many times before."

I stare at the vet. Dumb. Put him to sleep. Right. For the operation. He's going to remove the growth and send us on our way, reprieved again. I nod, and he grabs a front leg, jabs the needle in while I hold the dog's nose.

But there is not even time for a struggle, the odd snap; as soon as the needle hits his skin the dog goes limp, without even time to shut his eyes, which roll back and shine dully up at me, sightless under peaky eyebrows. He looks dead, and I think in horror that the vet has killed him, either by accident or—knowing me—by design.

"Is he dead?" I gasp.

"Of course not," the vet says as he turns toward an instrument that resembles a blowtorch. "Just out cold."

The blowtorch thing is in fact an electric cauterization needle, and the vet burns away the tumor while I hold the dog, his body limp as a fur rug, his head lolling, the tongue hanging to one side like a slab of veal. I count his teeth; some are missing, some broken. Dogs should not outlive their teeth, I think, such an indignity. But he's got plenty left. "When will he wake up?" I want to know.

"In an hour or so. He'll be pretty shaky for a while. You got any errands downtown?" The vet hangs up the electric scalpel, finished. The growth is gone, or near enough. "I can't promise you much in the long run, though. These things are generally lethal," he says, looking at me seriously. "It won't be long. You might want to talk it over with your husband. It may be time."

But when I pick the dog up later that afternoon he's wide awake and frisky, still the same old dog with his foxy, handsome face. He skitters across the floor in his eagerness to get out of there, staggers out to the car and hops into his place in the front footwell, next to my feet, and home we go. I don't mention to Phil what the vet told me; there will be time to do that later when we get Phil squared away himself. The dog's all right for the time being, and it's not winter yet.

VIII

And the end of the story is this:

It's been almost two weeks since Phil and I drove down to Boston to the hospital, but all the tests are in now, and the operation is scheduled for tomorrow. It's old home week in Phil's room, doctors coming over from the Institute: surgeons, endocrinologists, oncologists, nephrologists, radiologists, anesthesiologists, not to mention nurses, nurse's aides, student nurses, all wanting to wish him well. He's very popular around here—someone they can cure, or hope they can. And the phone calls come in from all over, too: Maine, Vermont, New Jersey, California. His hometown doctor has called, some friends have called, his sisters have called.

Phil lies there, his cheeks pudgy from all the fluids they've pumped into him to offset the anticipated effects of tomorrow's surgery. He's also chockful of Valium, grinning cheerfully. Besides the doctors, two friends are visiting; it's a three-ring circus. I haven't been here very long myself; in fact, I just got in from Vermont after spending two days with Phil's parents and the kids.

Finally everyone leaves, and then the phone rings again.

"You get it," Phil says. "I'm tired of talking." It's almost time for his body shave and the enema they've promised him to get his bowels whistle clean "just in case."

I pick up the phone. "Sara, is that you?" It's Phil's mother, and she sounds so upset I decide on the spot I'm not going to let her talk to Phil. But it's me she wants. "Listen, I'm sorry to bother you at a time like this, but it's about the dog. I don't know what's wrong, but he had a fit in the study and he's messed himself and all over the floor, poor soul, and he's lying in it and can't get up." In the background I can hear yelping and howling, shouting of several voices: Pop and the kids. "When we went to help him he tried to bite Pop," she finishes, her voice trailing off into a quaver. "We don't know what to do."

I stand there gripping the phone, thinking, I just don't believe it. The phone hums, the dog yelps, and I hear Pop's voice raised faintly: "No, no, don't go near him!"

The phone sniffles, clears its throat, waiting. "Sara?" I shut my eyes, my head buzzing angrily. They're asking *me* what to do, for chrissake? What do they expect, me to drive back up tonight and rescue the goddamned dog? Can't they deal with this themselves? It's the night befcre Phil's operation, and they can't cope with a stupid dog?

"I hate to bother you at a time like this," my mother-in-law repeats, "but we thought you should know."

For once I'm speechless.

"Sara?" my mother-in-law says timidly after a moment. Phil is looking at me, his head lifted off the pillow, alarmed.

"The dog is sick," I say with my hand over the phone. "They're all hysterical." Phil's head flops back, his eyes closed. He looks relieved. "I thought it was one of the kids," he says.

Meanwhile, not used to being stuck for an answer, I'm thinking furiously. It's eight o'clock at night. The clamor at the other end of the phone squawks in my ear; all hell has broken loose. "Okay, look," I say as calmly as I can to Phil's mother. "If you're afraid to go near the dog, call Punch next door or Joyce up the street—the dog knows both of them—and ask them to come and help you. See if you can get him in the car and take him straight to the vet's. Then call me back. Call me back no matter what."

They call me back ten minutes later. Nobody's home, not Punch, not Joyce, not even the vet. "Well, just shut the doors and leave him until tomorrow morning," I say at last. "There's nothing else anybody can do."

"Poor soul," my mother-in-law says. "I feel so bad for him."

"There's nothing I can do," I tell her, unable to keep the exasperation out of my voice any longer.

"I know, Sara, I know," she says wearily. "We just thought you ought to know. Can I speak to my son now?"

I hand the phone over to Phil, and that's the end of that.

Over the next couple of days I'm at the hospital constantly, during the eight hours of Phil's operation and his subsequent stay in the intensive care unit. I hardly think about the dog. When I call with the good news that the operation was an apparent success, they tell me almost as an afterthought that the man from the general store down the street came over the next morning to help Pop get the dog into the car, but at the last minute he got up and walked into the car under his own power, God bless him, so maybe things aren't so bad. But he cried all night, and they're all exhausted. They'll let me know what happens, and everything's under control.

Meanwhile, Phil is recovering but in a lot of pain, and both of us have to struggle with the horrors, remembering the other operation and its aftermath. But he amazes everyone with his rapid progress, his eagerness to get up and get going, back on his feet. I spend most of my time there. The nurses let me stay beyond the ten minutes at a time, because by now they know I won't scream and cry and faint into the forest of IVs and monitors around his bed, and besides, my presence seems to help. I don't cry at all; I haven't yet and I don't now, because things are looking up. One day runs into the next in ICU, but he makes rapid progress. One minute I am watching Phil, vacant-eyed and dopey, trying to stand up between two stocky nurses; the next time

I see him he's walked around the whole unit and is talking about sending out for a pizza. The nurses joke about not knowing what to do for him since no one ever eats real food in ICU. But they are short of beds in the step-down unit where Phil goes next, and they want to keep him in here one more day. So I leave for Cambridge, thinking how relaxed and jolly it all is, and how everything is going so well.

But when I get back to our friends' house where I'm staying there's a message: "Call home." And it's the dog. The vet has called that morning, Sunday, to find out what we want to do. The dog is suffering, sick and retching, can't stand up. I'm supposed to call him. "His life is a misery to him," my mother-in-law says sadly, and I can guess what it is the vet wants me to say. And so I call the vet.

"The dog is really in bad shape, full of tumors, advanced kidney failure," he says in his matter-of-fact, professional, but not unsympathetic voice. "There's no point in prolonging this. I hate to see him suffer this way."

He wants my permission; all I have to do is say the word—two words, actually: Do it. And I remember the times Phil and I talked about this, how we would want to be there, and my throat dries up and my tongue cleaves to the roof of my mouth, and I can't say anything at all.

"I've got to think about it," I say finally. "I don't know what to do." I explain to the vet what's going on down here, Phil still in Intensive Care, that I can't leave right now.

"He wouldn't know you," the vet says. "He's really out of it, doesn't know much of anything anymore." He pauses, waiting. "But it's entirely up to you."

Still I can't do it. I try to remember the last time I saw the dog, whether I even noticed him, patted him and said good-bye. It's a familiar feeling, this guilt, and I have to remind myself he's just a dog.

"I've got to think it over," I say finally in my crabbed voice, aware of the vet's silent disapproval on the other end. He thinks that this is sentimental bullshit, and in a way it is. "I can't decide now, I just can't," I tell him apologetically. "Let me sleep on it, and I'll call you in the morning."

And then I go to bed, but I don't sleep, and in fact this is the worst night I've spent since we came down to Boston. Somehow the dog's trouble has gotten lost in all this other business, but he's been such a good old friend and can it be there's no time to spare after all these years to see him out? I toss and turn, arguing with myself he's just a dog, he wouldn't know I was there, it's silly, stupid, a waste of time and energy. In the midst of all this, I remember the time not long ago when I took him in to have the growth removed and thought the vet had killed him, that he was dead just like that, right before my eyes. And I think that is how it would be, the first shot that puts him out instantaneously, with no pain, and then the second one that stops the heart. He'll never know what hit him. Not a bad death, so quick, so humane, and how can it be worth it for me to drive all the way back up there just for those few seconds? And have I made it up to him, I wonder in the dark? Did I really make him better, and was it worth it to him, even though it's come to this? And all the time I'm thinking this, I know it's not the dog I need to rescue; it's me.

In the morning I've made up my mind. I'm driving up. I call the hospital to get a report on Phil; he's been moved out of Intensive Care, his condition satisfactory, stable. I dial the vet's number to let him know I'm coming.

And the vet says, "I'm afraid it's out of your hands. The dog passed away in his sleep last night. I found him this morning. So it's all been decided for you."

"Thanks," I croak, barely able to hang up the phone. I cross over to the couch, bury my face in my hands, and start to cry—sudden loud, wet, uncontrollable sobs.

"Oh, my God!" my friend Jane shrieks as she stops dead in the doorway of the room, her hands flying to her face in a pantomime of anticipated horror. "Oh, my God, Sara! Oh, no! What's happened, what's wrong?"

Of course, seeing me crying, she thinks it's Phil. I look up at her, damp and trembling with these my first, my only, and my ancient tears, and say, "No, it's all right. It's just the dog. It's just the goddamned dog."

And this is what I've learned about the dead: It is not always their absence that haunts us. So I still hear the clink of a chain collar against a porcelain bowl, the skittering of toenails across a wooden floor, the thump and sigh of a weary dog flopping his old bones down next to my chair. I feel the presence of those old bones under my chair, under my feet. Under my wheels.

An Afterword

The dogs we cared for as children sometimes escaped through the backyard gate. Our housing development bordered a freeway. On the sad occasions when we didn't recover a missing dog, my parents comforted us with the assurance that the dog had found "a good home," a euphemism that doesn't last past childhood. Surprisingly, an unaccountable number of adults perpetrate this fiction each time a dog is abandoned on an outlying road, foisted on an animal shelter, or left behind in an apartment on moving day.

I live in a small stucco house with two retrievers in a neighborhood that, like most, is full of dogs. When we were first looking for a home, our realtor showed us a gutted, boarded-up duplex. We were startled to hear a dog offering a pair of token barks as we entered the house— a female golden retriever whose eyes could barely stand the sunlight that entered with us. A flap of cardboard covered a hole in the back door through which the dog could exit into a backyard serving as a junkyard; otherwise the dog was confined to complete darkness. Her affectionate exuberance was rivaled only by vain attempts to relieve her flea infestation. Our realtor tried to show us the house with her flashlight, but the fleas drove us out. Rid of the fleas, but not the misery of that dog, we contacted the out-of-town owners the next day. After the house was sold, we were assured the guard dog would go to "a good home."

Beyond this anthology, I've been doing a good deal of thinking about such "good homes" and about the continuous responsibility we owe this other species, the dog. (And for the sake of this collection and manageability itself, I will, for the moment, confine my thinking to dogs alone.) We've pulled canines out of natural selection; buffered them from predation, disease, and interspecies competition; bred them into capricious shapes that aren't always healthy or genetically sound; trained them to disregard so many protective survival instincts—and yet, as caretakers, we have offered in exchange an unconscionably reckless range of care. Americans have refashioned a complete spectrum of dogs: commodities, protective devices, expendables, social statements, victims, inconveniences, whims, tests, hobbies, tools, revenues, sports, menaces, rescuers, helpmates, hazards.

A quarter of the dogs in American homes will meet untimely ends. We have learned to fail animals in so many ways that we barely consider our betrayal. It doesn't take a veterinarian or an ecologist or, least of all, a dog lover, to see this. In how many homes does the dog suffer the blame for a human's failure in training? And because no one likes to be reminded of a failing, how many dogs are surrendered by people refusing to suffer their own culpability for the dog's problems?

The vividness of that trashcan painted with the words PREVENT LITTERS remains with me: a disturbing collusion of the playful and the pathetic, of "litter's" two meanings: what a cat or a dog gives birth to and what is discarded. I can imagine myself as one of the sign's third-grade creators; that kittens and puppies can pose a problem is inconceivable. I can view this as a realistic adult as well: the problem is still inconceivable, but for different reasons.

Having read the stories in *The Company of Dogs*, you've been furnished many such hard-hitting images, alloyed from the heart's aspirations and the intellect's reservations, from the feisty affection and troubled custodianship that we offer the loved dogs of our families. And as for the Introduction's earlier discussion of mortality, these stories render the question of the dog's soul moot: our life with dogs is their heaven on earth. Or it *should be*. Having no fear or foreknowledge of their death, dogs live in a present tense with no division of body and soul. Rilke articulates this in his "Duino Elegies": "Where we see the future, he [the animal] sees/all, himself in all, and whole forever."* But beyond this capacity it shares with other animals, the dog is the one living being that "has found and recognizes an indubitable, tangible, unexceptionable and definite god," or so Maurice Maeterlinck insisted.† The dog alone knows, concretely, to whom he can devote himself. "He has not to seek for a perfect, superior and infinite power in the darkness, amid successive lies, hypotheses and dreams. That power is there, before him, and he moves in its light."

The stories' impassioned focus on companionship is all the more poignant if we allow ourselves to consider this spiritual role; but the passion is still compounded if we simply consider the larger earthbound contexts—communal, environmental, and ethical—issuing unavoidably from our physical dominion on earth.

After many fraught hours and pages of foregone prose, I've declined a full or even partial enumeration of atrocious phenomena that might begin a specification of the crises. Evidence is everywhere apparent (one need only look instead of look away) and documented in volumes more suitable than this anthology, some of which are listed at the end of this book. But I did want to offer my own reader's version: how one person might respond. This anthology is one response. But beyond this. . . .

*Rainer Maria Rilke, *Duino Elegies*.
†Maurice Maeterlinck, "On the Death of a Little Dog."

When presented with some clear evidence of human neglect or exploitation, I am no more immune than the next person in feeling alternations of rage and helplessness, anguish and ignorance—however divorced from such evidence I delude myself (temporarily? entirely? comfortably?) into feeling. When I read that 70,000 kittens and puppies are born every day in America, I'm shocked—more like stunned or numbed. Then I read that 10,000 human beings are born every day in America. This starts to prick my distracted attention, but the predicament still remains in numbers at a vague, dismissable distance. But then I read further, and I find myself implicated in a simple and practical translation: "Even if every man, woman, and child in the country were to adopt an unwanted animal, they could never provide enough homes for them all."‡

The shopping-mall pet store signals something of the problem. Our capricious consumerism. We think of a dog like a fashionable article of clothing: something to select, try on, tie with a gift bow, exchange, hand down, wear out, discard. And our zeal for this enterprise seems insatiable. Nearly all the puppies offered at pet store chains (360,000 sold each year) are born of continuously bred females that are killed when their bodies begin to diminish in litter productivity. This occurs on puppy mills known for extreme crowding, malnutrition, inadequate veterinary care, and unsanitary conditions. Licensing, inspections, and prosecuting violators are low priorities for the USDA, and so high mortality rates, inhumane practices, and congenitally unhealthy animals have become the norm.

When I read that thirteen million unwanted cats and dogs are annually collected, and that only three million are adopted, I can't stop myself from performing that simple math. I can usually stop myself from imagining the euthanized remainder. Of these, I have come to realize that millions are shipped to rendering plants to be recycled into

‡Humane Society of the United States, "Close-up Report."

low-phosphate detergents and fodder for chickens and hogs. My imagination never completes the cycle that returns those dogs and cats to our laundry rooms and kitchen tables.

But some of our discarded animals live out even unluckier lives. In thirty-one states, pound seizure—the practice of releasing pound and shelter animals to laboratories—is still permitted; in five states, it is mandated by law. This means that someone can drive up to an animal shelter, pack a truck with animals, and sell their specimens for studies that can involve (to specify only a few ongoing forays) radiation poisoning, germ- and chemical-warfare agents, narcotic addiction, pain thresholds, assorted deprivations, burns, collisions, and miscellaneous maimings. Of course, many dogs are bred for this given purpose. But lost and stolen companion animals are even more ideal—trained, socialized, sensitive, trusting, well-adjusted, forgiving—that is, once a tracheotomy has been performed to keep the dogs from annoying the researchers by whining or barking.

Medical advances in the seventeenth century hinged on vivisection—experimentation on a live animal. That people were capable of nailing a dog's four paws to a table and, with nothing even resembling anaesthesia, slitting open its body to demonstrate how blood might circulate, is an atrocity that we could never justify. Replicating such a "discovery" is unfathomable to our current sense of ethics, however insular I suggest they may be. Yet, so many vivisections continue and are invented today that bear little difference to these earlier explorations, little more in the way of the fathomable.

If our awareness is still evolving, how much more of what presently seems essential will we (and not future generations, please) come to regard as gratuitous, primitive, heinous? How much more we could do if the very funds that perpetuate inexact and inhumane research were designated for furthering viable alternative tests.

However convenient or crucial animals may have proven in bringing us to this technological point (an arguable point, as in assessing the critical nature of our previous exploitations of blacks, immigrants, children, or women as certain work forces), our scientific and medical industries can now assess nearly every requisite action with cruelty-free trials—on computers, on cell cultures, on human placental tissues, and on less sentient tissues such as horseshoe crabs or the lining of a chicken's eggshell. And when animals cannot be *replaced* in a given medical trial, there are proven procedures to *reduce* the number of tested animals, and to *refine* the process to require less dosage, intensity, duration, restraints, anxiety, pain, and repetition. There is also an overwhelming mandate to employ the obvious but typically neglected measures of anaesthesia, antidote, and physical assuagement.

The late and outrageous fact is that too much of the data gathered from dogs and other creatures, meant to ensure human safety, have inflicted human suffering and death—an estimated two million Americans are injured or killed by products deemed "safe" through animal testing. (This is, of course, in addition to the suffering and death of twenty million test animals.)

Here is the achingly glorious paradox: In vivisection, we have looked to dogs for information about humans, and we have learned about the dog, its singularity and differences. In fiction, as this collection has intimated, we have looked at the dog for information about the dog—we have looked with that fixity of attention that earlier we called "love"—and we have learned about ourselves, our similarities and compatibilities.

How have we come this far and not accounted for the true costs of our progress? Only by employing the most active avoidance, the standard tactics that Hyam Maccoby* outlines as detachment, concealment, misrepresentation, and shifting the blame. Collectively they have hidden the disagreeable and difficult-to-condone; couched the affected creatures within a genericized, impersonal remove; placated a

* Hyam Maccoby, *The Sacred Executioner.*

public with euphemisms and gross unapprehensible numbers; and officially shrugged off each and every responsibility, until, ostensibly, not only is no one to blame but nothing is left worth blaming.

If we truly considered the literal dimensions of any given fact, would we be this late in responding to the consequences of so many of our collective actions? Mathematician John Allen Paulos has diagnosed us correctly: we suffer from "innumeracy"—a complete inability to comprehend numbers with rationality or accuracy. I'd say our determination *not* to comprehend arises from the fact that such awareness would demand immediate and personal reckoning.

Part of the solution must be to translate numbers and facts into perceivable notions. This is what fiction can do. Not that these stories were commissioned for this purpose, not that these authors are enlisted in this Afterword's broader design. No—all stories, at their most potent, move us toward greater sensitivity by the creation of a context in which blunt factualities assume pointedly individual implications. My hope is that *The Company of Dogs* will contribute to this growing context. And yet I know that a story's imagined world can only predispose us toward the difficult work of the real world (concepts not as diametrically opposed as they must remain here).

As people are persuaded—by advocates with hard facts, by artists who take them to heart—to face the real news about our custodianship and its consequences, more and louder voices will continue to demand revisions. The prodigality, carelessness, and oblivion are excruciating; yet the most unbearable, unimaginable aspect of these crises is that they're solvable. Unlike many of our seemingly incurable, unalleviated social and physical and economic disasters, the issues we've been discussing—animal overpopulation, negligence, exploitation, experimentation—can be rectified. They require comparatively little money and person power; they hardly disrupt human economy or livelihoods; they don't preclude the other necessary changes we must make to survive on this exhaustible planet.

To focus on dogs by design and necessity is finally an embarrassing selectivity. Dogs are easy targets, as I mentioned, for sympathy and indignation. Even foreign communities understand our supersensitivity to dogs. During the Olympics, officials in Seoul urged a ban on a typical South Korean dish, dog stew. Today, American tourists to Moscow are warned not to purchase fur hats on the street because a recent source of quick American cash has come from the stealing, skinning, and cap-making of family dogs. But even though I have claimed many exceptional qualities for this human/canine alliance, the dog is only one of all species on earth that humans have dominated, or even doomed. Each day dozens of species, plant and animal, are being lost forever. Not specimens, *species*—all members of one unique form of life on Earth. Extinction has become so much a part of human transaction that we assume it is a normal exchange, like that of carbon dioxide for oxygen that follows every human inhalation. And what makes us think that we humans can preserve our own exemption? Is it inevitable that we hunt down ourselves, exploit ourselves, prepare our own extinction?

More than two hundred years ago, the philosopher Jeremy Bentham posed the key question, insisting that the difference between humans and other species could have but one determinant: "The question is not, Can they *reason?* nor Can they *talk?* but, *Can they suffer?*" What we hold in common with the dog and so many other species under our capricious care is a capacity for suffering. Often quoted in animal rights essays and journals, his question makes me confront my own discomfort in the face of facts and statistics, in the wake of these compassionate stories. What can I do with those feelings? Well, the first thing is promise not to offer anyone a simpler solution than I've managed to offer myself. What follows this note is a list of books, professional organizations, and publications that clarify key issues. They can help to channel the sympathy and indignation.

But even questions as simple as "Well, what good can I do?" and "How can I help?" can't be stopped there. We can engage friends, family members, and all those unappointed people whose concern awaits a furthering dialogue. We can seek regional chapters of humane societies, local animal shelters, and any number of organizations that have mounted efforts toward increasing long-range public awareness or providing immediate care. In whatever arena—shopping mall, supper table, editorial, rally, neighborly chat—our emotions and questions and beliefs need to be put into practice. *Practice*, as in rehearsing, refining. We need not feel useless if we do not pledge all-consuming and unflinching activism. I'm grateful to those for whom this is possible. But I'm also learning to cast off some of this intimidation and some of its concomitant lethargy, and to take some pride in *working* ideas: the hard work of genuine understanding, the harder work that understanding urges.

I have singled out the dog and I have insisted that, as in these stories, the dog stands not only for its own individual presence but for all the other creatures in our lives. I am finally left with the idea that you and I and the rest of the people with whom we are to share our years on earth deserve responsible, informed, humane treatment. Let us recognize the litter our living makes and accept the requisite humility that can save us, and all the rest of creation, from ourselves. As James Thurber said, "Man is born to the belief that he is superior to the lower animals, and that critical intelligence comes when he realizes that he is more similar than dissimilar." Extending this theory, Thurber suggests "that Man's arrogance and aggression arises from a false feeling of transcendency, and that he will not get anywhere until he realizes, in all humility, that he is just another of God's creatures, less kindly than Dog, possessed of less dignity than Swan, and incapable of becoming as magnificent an angel as Black Panther."†

—*Michael J. Rosen*

†James Thurber, interview with Harvey Breit.

Contributors

Lee K. Abbott is the author of four collections of short stories, *The Heart Never Fits Its Wanting, Love Is the Crooked Thing, Strangers in Paradise* and, most recently, *Dreams of Distant Lives*. He currently teaches fiction at The Ohio State University.

Charles Barsotti is a regular contributor to *The New Yorker, Punch,* and *USA Today*. His cartoons are gathered in several collections, including *A Girl Needs a Little Action, Kings Don't Carry Money, C. Barsotti's Texas* and, most recently, a British publication, *The Best of Charles Barsotti*.

Ann Beattie is the author of seven books, most recently a new novel, *Picturing Will*. Her earlier books include *Love Always, Distortions, Chilly Scenes of Winter,* and *Falling in Place*.

Barbara J. Dimmick lives in the woods of Vermont and teaches writing in New Hampshire. She has coached riders, schooled horses, taught equine science for SUNY, and contributed regularly to national horse magazines. She is currently writing a novel.

Robert Fox is the author of *Destiny News* (short stories) and *The Last American Revolution* and *Confessions of a Dead Politician* (two novellas in one volume). Though currently dogless, he yearns for a new canine companion in Columbus, Ohio.

Gary Gildner's published books include *Blue Like the Heavens* (poems), *The Second Bridge* (a novel), *A Week in South Dakota* (short stories), and *The Warsaw Sparks* (a memoir). During 1987–88 he was a Fulbright lecturer at the University of Warsaw, Poland, and coach of the city's baseball team.

ROBERT GILLESPIE is associate professor of English and editor of publications at Colby College in Maine. His poems have appeared in many periodicals and anthologies and in his collection *The Man Chair*, published by Ithaca House. Larsen, his malamute, is four years old.

AMY HEMPEL is the author of two collections of short stories, *At the Gates of the Animal Kingdom* and *Reasons to Live*, both published by Knopf. Her stories have appeared in *Vanity Fair*, *Grand Street*, *Witness*, *New American Short Stories*, and *Mother Jones*.

SUSAN KENNEY is the author of two novels, *In Another Country* and *Sailing*, as well as a series of mystery novels, the most recent of which is *One Fell Sloop*. She teaches at Colby College.

MAXINE KUMIN's most recent book of poetry is *Nurture*, preceded by eight other volumes, one of which was awarded the Pulitzer Prize. Her work in fiction includes four novels, the country essays of *In Deep*, a collection of short stories, and several children's books. She lives and works on a horse farm in New Hampshire.

DAVID LEAVITT has published two novels, *Equal Affection* and *The Secret Language of Cranes*, and two collections of short stories, *Family Dancing* and *A Place I've Never Been*.

MICHAEL MARTONE has published three collections of stories, *Alive and Dead in Indiana*, *Safety Patrol*, and *Fort Wayne Is Seventh on Hitler's List*. He is editor of *Place of Sense: Essays in Search of the Midwest*, and Briggs-Copeland Lecturer on Fiction at Harvard University.

BOBBIE ANN MASON, a native of Kentucky, is the author of *Shiloh and Other Stories*, winner of the PEN/Hemingway Award for first fiction, and two novels, *In Country* and *Spence + Lila*. Her new book of stories is called *Love Life*. Her new puppy is named Max.

JACK MATTHEWS is Distinguished Professor of English at Ohio University and the author of sixteen books, the most recent of which are *Memoirs of a Bookman* and a volume of short stories, *Dirty Tricks*.

THOMAS MCGUANE is the author of nine books. His most recent is a novel, *Keep the Change*, published in 1989 by Houghton Mifflin. He lives with his family on a hay and cattle ranch in Southwestern Montana.

ETHAN MORDDEN, a regular contributor to *The New Yorker*, is the author of twenty-one books, most recently *Medium Cool: The Movies of the 1960s*.

Contributors

WRIGHT MORRIS is the author of more than thirty works of fiction, essays, memoirs, and photo-texts. His latest book is *Time Pieces: Photographs, Writing and Memory*, published by Aperture.

ANTONYA NELSON's collection of short stories, *The Expendables*, won the Flannery O'Connor Award for Short Fiction and was published this year by The University of Georgia Press. She lives in Las Cruces, New Mexico, with her husband, daughter, and golden retriever.

ALIX KATES SHULMAN has written four novels, a biography of Emma Goldman, and numerous stories and essays. Her fiction has been translated into more than ten languages. Since the late sixties she has been a political activist, feminist, and teacher. Much of the year she lives on an island off the coast of Maine.

JIM SHEPARD is the author of three novels, *Flights, Paper Doll*, and *Lights Out in the Reptile House*. His short fiction has appeared in *The Atlantic Monthly, Harper's, The New Yorker, Esquire*, and other magazines. He teaches at Williams College.

ELIZABETH TALLENT is the author of two collections of short stories, *In Constant Flight* and *Time with Children*, as well as a novel, *Museum Pieces*. She divides her time between Northern California and New Mexico.

DAVID UPDIKE is the author of *Out on the Marsh*, a collection of stories, and several children's picture books. A regular columnist for *Wigwag* magazine, he lives in Cambridge, Massachusetts.

WILLIAM WEGMAN's twenty-five-year career in photography, video, and painting is represented this year in a new monograph, published by Harry N. Abrams, ten one-person shows, and a retrospective that travels Europe before arriving in the United States next year.

Sources, Resources, and Further Reading

The following selected books have either been quoted in the Introduction or Afterword, or have provided significant groundwork and perspective for those essays. Moreover, these books are some of the more accessible and inviting works on their respective subjects.

Sources for quotations excerpted from the stories included in this anthology can be found on the Acknowledgments page.

ABBOTT, LEE K. "Once Upon a Time," in *Dreams of Distant Lives.* New York: G. P. Putnam's Sons, 1989.

ACKERLEY, J. R. *My Dog Tulip.* New York: Fleet, 1965. Reprinted, Poseidon Press, 1987.

———. *We Think the World of You.* Great Britain: Bodley Head Ltd., 1960. Reprinted, New York: Poseidon Press, 1988.

AISENBERG, NADYA, ed. *We Animals.* San Francisco: Sierra Club Books, 1989.

ARTHUR, ELIZABETH. *Binding Spell.* New York: Doubleday, 1988.

AUDEN, W. H. *The Collected Poems,* edited by Edward Mendelsohn. New York: Random House, 1976.

AVEDON, RICHARD. "Borrowed Dogs," in Sonnenberg, Ben, *Performance & Reality: Essays from Grand Street.* New Brunswick: Rutgers University Press, 1987.

BARSOTTI, CHARLES. *The Best of Charles Barsotti.* West Sussex: Rivette Publishing Ltd., 1989.

BECK, ALAN and AARON KATCHER. *Between Pets and People.* New York: G. P. Putnam, 1983.

BENTHAM, JEREMY. "Introduction to the Principles of Morals and Legislation," quoted in Serpell, James, *The Company of Animals.*

BERGER, JOHN. *About Looking.* New York: Pantheon, 1980.

CARAS, ROGER. *The Roger Caras Dog Book.* New York: Holt, Rinehart & Winston, 1980.

———. *Roger Caras' Treasury of Great Dog Stories.* New York: E. P. Dutton, 1987.

DAVIS, S. J. M., and F. R. VALLA. "Evidence for the Domestication of the Dog 12,000 Years Ago in the Natufian of Israel," quoted in Serpell, James, *The Company of Animals.*

DAY, CLARENCE. *This Simian World.* New York: Alfred A. Knopf, 1936.

FOX, MICHAEL W. *Between Animal and Man.* New York: Coward, McCann & Geoghegan, 1976.

———. *Understanding Your Dog.* New York: Coward, McCann & Geoghegan, 1972.

———. *The Dog: Its Domestication and Behavior.* New York: Garland STPM Press, 1978.

GOODMAN, JACK, ed. *The Fireside Book of Dog Stories.* New York: Simon & Schuster, 1943.

GRAY, CHARLES WRIGHT, ed. *"Dawgs!"* New York: Henry Holt & Company, 1925.

HOAGLAND, Edward. "Dogs and the Tug of Life" in *Red Wolves and Black Bears.* New York: Random House, 1976.

HEMPEL, AMY. "The Center," in *At the Gates of the Animal Kingdom.* New York: Alfred A. Knopf, 1990.

JÖNSSON, REIDAR. *My Life As a Dog.* Translated by Eivor Martinus. New York: Farrar, Straus & Giroux, 1990.

KATCHER, AARON H., and ALAN M. BECK, eds. *New Perspectives on our Lives with Animals.* Philadelphia: University of Pennsylvania Press, 1983.

KUNDERA, MILAN. *The Unbearable Lightness of Being.* Translated by Michael Henry Heim. New York: Harper & Row, 1984.

LORENZ, KONRAD. *Man Meets Dog.* New York: Penguin Books, 1954.

Sources, Resources, and Further Reading

MACCOBY, HYAM. *The Sacred Executioner*. London: Thames & Hudson, 1982.

MAETERLINCK, MAURICE. "On the Death of a Little Dog," from *The Double Garden*. Translated by Alexander Teixeira de Mattos. London: George Allen & Co. Ltd., 1904.

MORRIS, DESMOND. *Dogwatching*. New York: Crown Publishers, 1987.

RILKE, RAINER MARIA, letter to N. N., February 1912, in *The Sonnets to Orpheus*. Translated by Stephen Mitchell. New York: Simon & Schuster, 1985.

ROSENBLUM, ROBERT. *The Dog in Art from Rococco to Post-Modernism*. New York: Harry N. Abrams, 1988.

SERPELL, JAMES. *In The Company of Animals*. Oxford: Basil Blackwell, Inc., 1986.

SILVERMAN, RUTH. *The Dog Observed*. San Francisco: Chronicle Books, 1988. Revised reprint of *The Dog Book*, Alfred A. Knopf, 1984.

SINGER, PETER. *Animal Liberation*. Revised edition. New York: New York Review of Books, Inc., a division of Random House, 1990.

————, ed. *In Defense of Animals*. New York: Basil Blackwell, Inc., 1985.

STEPHENS, MARTIN L. *Alternatives to Current Uses of Animals in Research, Safety Testing, and Education: A Layman's Guide*. Washington: The Humane Society of the United States, 1986.

STRAND, MARK. "Dog Life" from *Mr. and Mrs. Baby*. New York: Alfred A. Knopf, 1985.

————, review of Silverman, Ruth, *The Dog Book. Vogue*, September 1984, p. 120.

THURBER, JAMES, interview with Harvey Breit, *New York Times Magazine*, December 4, 1940, p. 79.

TURNER, E. S. *All Heaven in a Rage*. New York: St. Martin's Press, 1965.

WEGMAN, WILLIAM. *Man's Best Friend*. New York: Harry N. Abrams, 1982.

————. *William Wegman: Paintings, Drawings, Photographs, Videotapes*. New York: Harry N. Abrams, 1990.

WOOLF, VIRGINIA. *Flush*. New York: Harcourt Brace Jovanovich, 1933.

Likewise, the following organizations have shared a considerable amount of printed materials dealing with various aspects of animal welfare. Each has specific fact sheets, booklets and newsletters dealing with issues relating to the human alliance with dogs. I have listed a few of those with which I am more familiar; this is, therefore, simply a starting point for more information. Readers should not overlook the availability of local resources. Animal shelters, veterinary clinics, local chapters of many national organizations, and hundreds of smaller, region-specific agencies are found in most areas of the country. (A comprehensive list that would locate organizations in a particular region can be found in a reliable guide that is published yearly, *Animal Organizations & Services*, compiled by Kathleen A. Reece. If your libraries do not carry this, suggest it to them, or order it from Animal Stories, 3004 Maple Ave., Manhattan Beach, CA 90266.)

ASPCA (The American Society for the Prevention of Cruelty to Animals)
441 East Ninety-second Street
New York, NY 10128

Fund For Animals
200 West Fifty-seventh Street
New York, NY 10019

HSUS (The Humane Society of the United States)
2100 L Street NW
Washington, DC 20037

The National Association for the Advancement of Humane Education
P.O. Box 362
East Haddam, CT 06423

PETA (People for the Ethical Treatment of Animals)
P.O. Box 42516
Washington, DC 20015

The Animals' Agenda
Animal Rights Network
P.O. Box 5234
Westport, CT 06881

Culture & Animals Foundation
3509 Eden Croft Drive
Raleigh, NC 27612

Michael J. Rosen is the editor of *Collecting Himself: James Thurber on Writing and Writers and Himself* (Harper & Row, 1989), and literary director of The Thurber House, the writers' center in the preserved boyhood home of James Thurber. His books include *A Drink at the Mirage* (Princeton University Contemporary Poetry Series) and a children's picture book of verses and illustrations, *Fifty Odd Jobs*. He is currently involved in a book he has conceived and edited called *No Place Like Home*, which will include twenty-six of the country's best-known authors and illustrators of children's books; the story will celebrate the home and benefit the homeless, and will be published in the fall of 1991. His fiction, articles and illustrations appear in *Gourmet, The New Yorker, The Atlantic, House and Garden, The New Criterion* and the *New York Times Book Review*. The recipient of NEA, Ingram Merrill, and Ohio Arts Council fellowships, he lives in Columbus, Ohio with his family and two retrievers, Paris and Madison.